'You know I have contacts abroad. In New York to be precise. These contacts of mine can offer the icon in circles where questions won't be asked. Very, very discreet art circles. Collectors who will pay mad prices to achieve a simple thing: to own something truly *unique*. And so crazy are they, they'll happily pay through the nose and then stash the thing away where no one at all can see it, not even their aunt. Look, you can sell a stolen Monet or even a Rembrandt if you can find one of these madmen, and he'll know that he can never in his whole lifetime admit to owning it. It's the ultimate expression of insensate greed. It's where the free market leads you if you travel all the way.'

'And you can set all this up?'

'I can.'

'And get it out of the country in the first place?'

'I can.'

'Bribing customs officials is a risky business.'

'Not a kopeck will change hands.'

'Stop being so damned allusive and tell me what you plan to do.'

About the Authors

Vitali Vitaliev, once a Soviet Investigative Journalist of the Year and once Moscow Journalist of the Year, was on the staff of the satirical journal *Krokodil*. He is the author of two volumes of journalism published in Britain and has provided his own highly individual picture of the British in a documentary for the BBC. He is now a columnist for *The European*.

Derek Kartun is a former journalist and industrialist whose five thrillers and two comic novels were published here and in the USA.

The Third Trinity

Vitali Vitaliev and Derek Kartun

CORONET BOOKS
Hodder and Stoughton

First published in Great Britain in 1993
by Hodder and Stoughton Ltd,
First published in paperback in 1994
by Hodder and Stoughton
a division of Hodder Headline PLC

10 9 8 7 6 5 4 3 2 1

All characters in this publication are fictitious and any resemblance to real persons, living or dead, is purely coincidental.

ISBN 0 340 59497 7

Printed and bound in Great Britain by
Cox & Wyman Ltd, Reading, Berkshire

Hodder and Stoughton Ltd
A Division of Hodder Headline PLC
47 Bedford Square
London WC1B 3DP

For Natasha and Gwen

1

The dog, which was a half-blind mongrel of furious temper, had been barking angrily for ten minutes or more. It always barked at anything that moved and sometimes it barked at the moon or the stars. The racket was beginning to irritate Father Vassili, who had just completed his evening prayers and was trying to concentrate on the task in hand. He sat on a stool drawn up to an ancient desk in the wooden hut which leant against the southern flank of the church as if it had landed there exhausted and could go no further. Along the wall opposite the desk there stood a bunk covered with an old army blanket. From its position on a table in the centre an oil lamp threw an uncertain light which failed to reach the corners of the room. There was a cuckoo clock hanging from a nail on a wall; a sink and shelves in one corner; an icon on the wall opposite with a candle flickering before it.

Before him on the desk lay a sheet of paper on which he had begun to write. The letter was intended for Blagochinny, bishop of the diocese, and Father Vassili, a man of modest education, was having trouble with it.

'Grant me the patience I no longer have, Holy Father,' he muttered to himself, his pen poised in mid-sentence. 'Forgive the beast outside; it, too, is old and past its best.'

The letter was headed 'Your Reverence'. Father Vassili had thought long and hard about writing it, since he had never known good to come from taking a problem upwards through the hierarchy, temporal or even spiritual. But his patience had been tried beyond endurance, and not only by the dog which continued to bark outside as if a life, or maybe a bone, were at stake.

> Your Reverence,
>
> I am writing to you on behalf of our little community here in Taman because I believe our precious Cathedral of the Dormition of the Mother of God is in danger from people who wish us ill. Yet here in Taman we are a small community, we mind our own business, do not meddle in politics or anything unwelcome to our Lord.

Father Vassili paused and considered what he had written. He had repeated himself already. The bishop did not need to be told twice that the Taman community was a small one. Composition was not easy. He scratched away at the sheet of paper.

> Since the time when the diocese was allocated a good sum of money for the cathedral's restoration, we have witnessed a number of discouraging events. I have to tell you, Holy Father, that the restoration team which arrived here a month ago on the recommendation of S. S. Marchenko, the Chairman of the Regional Committee for Religious Affairs, has been extremely inadequate . . .

Was 'inadequate' the right word? He should have used something stronger. No doubt the bishop would draw his own conclusions as to inadequacy. And now for the facts, as the dog continued to bark in the night.

> As you may know, my dear Father Blagochinny, the Chairman offered to supervise the restoration work in person. It may be an unkind and even unjustified suspicion on my part but I believe this may be because he has a plan to turn our little church into a museum.

This, no doubt, would be an attraction for the many tourists we have here on our Black Sea coast. But it would be a terrible blow to our faithful parishioners. And we find that whereas our parish is paying for the restoration team, we have no control over what they do. I have to tell you that these six young men from Moscow act in an unseemly and distressing manner.

They drink, they loiter in the town, they call out in a vulgar manner to our village girls, but do they pursue the much-needed restoration work? I fear not. And to my mind, their leader, one Baranov, is the worst culprit of all since he is clearly a man of some education who appears to have a certain knowledge of church architecture and decoration, and even of our holy icons.

These men demand to be paid in advance, but apart from dressing our church in scaffolding, they have done nothing. The man Baranov has demanded the key to the treasury on some excuse that he needs to check the church's foundations, but that I have refused and continue to keep the key safely under my robe. Then, only yesterday, I found traces of an attempted break-in. Someone had tried to force the door, but it is heavy and they were foiled.

The dog barked. Father Vassili peered at what he had written. Should he go further and complain to the archbishop about the way the local militia had sent him packing when he asked them to investigate the break-in? 'Church property?' the sergeant had said. 'Come on, little father, haven't you heard that the state washed its hands of religion long ago? We're busy doing other things.' And that had been that.

What am I to do, my dear Father Blagochinny? I am an old man. I cannot deal with these young men from Moscow who lack all respect. I fear our church will be looted. As you know, we have many fine icons and some silver. I fear for them. I fear for myself and our faithful here in Taman. What am I to do? I place myself in your ever-caring hands.

God be with you.

And he added a shaky signature. He would send the letter tomorrow. For now, he was concerned to stop the confounded dog out in the yard. With his brown robe buttoned closely at the neck he opened the door of the hut. Outside, the moonless southern sky was dotted with stars. There was a sharp wind blowing down from the steppe. The bulk of the cathedral, which was little more than a small country church, rose up behind him. The dog's kennel was on the far side of the yard. Muttering to himself, Father Vassili felt his way along the wall. Still the dog barked. A finger of yellow light from the window of the hut lay diagonally across the yard. Father Vassili headed for the point where the light fell on the far wall. The kennel lay a few paces beyond. As he reached the patch of light on the wall, he fancied he heard a noise behind him. There had been foxes in the area. Perhaps a fox had alerted the dog. Father Vassili stopped, and at that moment came the blow, followed by another as he sank slowly to the ground. The investigator from the militia was to say later that the first blow had been so powerful that the old man's skull had simply caved in, and so the second blow had been quite unnecessary. A hammer, he reckoned. Probably a six-kilo hammer.

And now the dog's barking had become a howl while its chain rattled furiously as the animal tried to free itself. It was only a matter of seconds before the six-kilo hammer crashed down on its skull and restored the silence of the night, disturbed only by the insistent squeak of crickets and the ebb and flow of the surf along the shore scarcely one hundred metres beyond the little church.

The Executive Committee of the Krasnodar Regional

Soviet of People's Deputies was housed in an impressive building on Krasnaya Street in the city of Krasnodar. The street, wide and tree-lined, was a fitting setting for this monumental home of the local bureaucracy. From it, tentacles of incompetence, self-interest and inertia stretched over the unfortunate Krasnodar region. Ideology held sway over reality. The past struggled with the present and confronted the future with sullen hostility. The solid pretensions of the building with its massive cornices and pilasters said it all.

The young man in the bomber jacket and Levis had alighted from a tram nearby and covered the short distance to the building on foot. At the door he presented his passport to the militiaman in blue uniform and peaked cap.

'Yes, comrade?'

'I have an appointment with comrade Marchenko. He's expecting me.'

The militiaman flicked the pages of the passport, checked the mug shot against the visitor's appearance and could find no fault. He motioned towards the door with his head.

'Second floor. You know the way?'

'Yes.'

Inside, the young man made his way up the marble stairs with their vivid red carpet. On the second floor he turned left into a long corridor. From behind identical doors he caught the sounds of typewriters, telephones and, occasionally, voices raised. Near the end of the corridor he stopped at a door on his left. The small brass plate fixed to the door read REGIONAL COUNCIL FOR RELIGIOUS AFFAIRS. CHAIRMAN S. S. MARCHENKO. The young man did not knock. Instead, he opened the door a short distance and poked his head round it.

'Do I disturb you, Stepan Stepanovitch?'

'People usually knock.'

'I knew you'd be glad to see me.'

'As I say, people usually knock.'

By now the young man was inside the room. He ignored the remark.

'I have things to tell you,' he said, advancing towards the large mahogany desk behind which Chairman Marchenko was sitting.

'As a matter of fact,' Chairman Marchenko said, 'I need to see you about this stupid killing in Taman. I have had the local militia in my hair all morning. What the hell is going on there?'

'Ah, that.'

'Is that all you can find to say?'

'The killing of the old man has nothing to do with me.' The young man's sharp features broke into a thin smile. He settled himself comfortably in a chair, pulled a pack of American cigarettes from his jacket and lit one. He allowed himself plenty of time to do so before adding, 'Nothing whatever. I haven't a clue.'

'I hope not, my dear Petya. Business is one thing, but murder is something else and I want no part of it.'

Peter Baranov allowed the smile to remain on his face for a while longer. Then he said: 'Looks as if the old man was killed by some drunkard from the village. I daresay a search through the toolboxes and garden sheds of Taman will throw up the weapon. I suggested as much to the thick-headed investigator who was pestering me and my men this morning.'

The chairman shook his head. There was a silence. Baranov blew smoke in the direction of Lenin's bust on a shelf against the wall. Better light from the chandelier would have revealed the heavy layer of dust on Lenin's head. The cleaners, Marchenko had had occasion to remark, were useless, impertinent and slovenly. It was only one of the many things which irritated and depressed him. The persistent clatter of typewriters from the neighbouring offices was another. These and a number of other things contributed to the Chairman's equivocal attitude to his job. Had he not been a loyal Party man for over thirty years, advancing the aims of the Party in a disciplined and principled fashion? So what had he done to deserve the unappetising post he now occupied? His had been a lifetime of devotion to the cause of socialist construction. And yet, when passably drunk he would reflect anxiously that there might be something in all this talk about God and Jesus after all. And if so, what about his immortal soul? When sober he recognised that he had no such organ and was prepared to give those who thought differently a hard time in the name of the advance to Communism. And that despite the fact that his wife and his ancient mother-in-law were both observed to cross themselves at moments of stress. The thing was a mystery and an aggravation . . . beyond him.

With or without her religious tendencies, his wife put more serious pressures on him. The latest was the absolute necessity for a new stove and total redecoration of the apartment. A neighbour had redecorated, so she too must redecorate. 'A shallow, envious woman,' Marchenko reflected as he moved papers around on his desk and delayed the moment when he had to plunge into yet another tedious report from Moscow. He had long ago ceased to esteem his wife in any way.

Now that he was nearing retirement, S. S. Marchenko wondered what he had to show for the years of devotion, man and boy, to the Party. All he had were the damned priests for ever buzzing round his head like flies, always after concessions, permits for this and that, tax adjustments, special dispensations . . . and always with their pathetic little envelopes stuffed with paper money. 'You will understand, Stepan Stepanovitch, a token of our esteem . . .' Or again, 'Please do not be offended, Stepan Stepanovitch, it is merely an expression of our gratitude in this difficult situation . . .' 'You are a true friend of our community . . . A man who understands . . . A man with an open mind.'

And there was the reverse side of this dubious coin: 'You will not be required to pay the nine hundred roubles on your church's assessment, Father Yakov. Here, do not ever say that we try to squeeze you to death. I have cut the assessment to four hundred, and you will also pay me four hundred for my own charitable purposes, thus saving you a hundred for yourself, my dear fellow. Simple!'

And why not? Weren't the big boys fitting out their dachas and trading up their cars on salaries which allowed of no such things? Times were hard, reflected Chairman Marchenko. They were getting harder. There was nagging at home, uncertainty everywhere, and Gorbachev and his perestroika were the very devil. 'You don't earn,' his wife said. 'You're a fool. Look at the others. They know how to look after themselves. My friends think you're stupid. Indeed, you *are* stupid.'

And so Stepan Stepanovitch Marchenko was an unhappy and irritable man, longing in moments of idle dreaming for what he termed 'the big one'; the coup, the little business deal which would be a big business deal; something which would free him at last from the constant hassle which led only to the pathetic little envelopes.

Now he said: 'The militia tell me the cathedral's treasury has been rifled.'

Baranov shrugged. 'I've had a look round.'

'And how did you get in?'

Again the smile and a shrug. 'I found the key.'

The chairman shook his head. 'I don't like the smell of this and it is perfectly clear to me that you are lying. This is thuggery, my dear fellow. I want nothing to do with it.'

'You will, Stepan Stepanovitch, when you hear what I have to tell about that treasury. Then, if you find the heat in the kitchen is too great for you, you can always get out and chew a crust outside. On the other hand, I need you and I fancy you need me.' Baranov inhaled deeply and let the smoke trickle out slowly through his nostrils. 'Incidentally, can one talk in here?'

'The security people are my friends. The room is clean.'

'One never knows. There was an occasion in Rostov . . .'

'Never mind Rostov. What was so interesting about the treasury? A few silver incense burners? Some grubby icons? Anything worth having disappeared from our churches years ago. By 1920 they'd been cleaned out.'

'What was so interesting about the treasury was that there was virtually nothing in it at all.'

'I don't understand.'

'With every respect to what was achieved in 1920, no one is going to tell me that that church owned absolutely nothing. I've worked on restoration in over a dozen churches and monasteries and every damn one of them had hidden away their little bits and pieces, and sometimes you'd come across something quite choice, as you know very well.'

'But if the treasury was empty . . .'

'Wait, I'm telling this story in my own way. So there was this musty cellar with the usual box of silverware and a few old books and papers on the ground – nothing else. I'm taking a close look at the silver but it won't yield much. "This," I said to myself, "is bloody nonsense. There has to be something the old fool was hiding. If not, what was the point of carrying that damn great key?" So I nosed around with my torch, and in a corner I came across this flagstone you could lift by a ring. Damned heavy it was too.'

The chairman had been toying with a carved wooden paperknife. Now he put it down and clasped his hands together on the desk.

'Like a cheapo melodrama, isn't it?' said Baranov. 'Anyway, I lift this stone manhole cover and there's a flight of steps leading down. So down I go, cursing that I haven't a more powerful torch. I can tell you, my heart was beating, I smelt treasure. I have a nose for it. From working in all those holy places.'

'Yes, yes, and what did you find?'

'Patience, Stepan Stepanovitch. Where was I? At the foot of the steps at last and in a deeper cellar, maybe four metres square.' He stubbed out his cigarette and took his time over lighting another.

'And?'

'And there was just one object in that hideaway. An icon leaning against a wall. But what an icon!' Baranov made a flamboyant gesture with his cigarette and the chairman noticed that his eyes were staring fixedly as if he could see the icon even now.

'What about this icon of yours?'

'Frankly, Stepan Stepanovitch, I do not know how to tell you, partly because I fear you won't believe me, and partly because this solitary icon in its hiding place in this ridiculous Cathedral of the Dormition which is nothing but a miserable country church with two blue domes – this icon has moved me deeply, I tell you. I am a cautious man, Stepan Stepanovitch, I do not jump to wild conclusions, particularly where art works are concerned. I've had my disappointments – late copies, fakes, misattributions – in the art-restoring business we come across the lot. So, you understand, I am being cautious here,'

'Yes, yes,' Marchenko said. He was tapping impatiently on the desk with the paper knife. 'So you're a cautious man. I understand that. Now kindly tell me what you are being so damn cautious *about*.'

'I can't tell you yet. I am not one for raising false expectations. In any case, I have no intention of making a fool of myself.'

'So what's the point of this rigmarole of yours?'

'Let's put it this way, Stepan Stepanovitch. This icon is just possibly of very great interest indeed. At all events, my friend, I must repeat that it has moved me deeply.'

'What's this suddenly, religious fervour? I know religion is back on the agenda in our country, but surely not you.'

'Not religious fervour: artistic fervour. I graduated with commendation from the Moscow Institute of Fine Arts. I know icons and their history, Stepan Stepanovitch. I am steeped in it and I love it. I am a cultured man, and I may – I repeat, I may – have made a discovery of major importance. I will put it no more strongly than that, though my instinct for such matters urges me to do so.'

'And so?'

'And so I am making tests, checking records, doing what is necessary to confirm my opinion.'

'And if this opinion of yours is confirmed?'

Peter Baranov stubbed out his cigarette, rose to his feet and started striding back and forth in front of Chairman Marchenko's desk. 'What then? Why, we shall have, you and I, what they tell me in the West is called serious money. Serious money! That's what then.'

The paperknife came to rest on the blotter. Marchenko grunted. 'I have to confess this sounds to me like romantic nonsense. What your friends in the West refer to as serious money is all very well. But it seems to me there's a hell of a road to travel before we get there. First of all, the damn thing has got to be what you say it is. Then it has to be disposed of, presumably illegally and in the West. Then payment has to be collected. And all that without trouble from the customs or anyone else. A tall order.'

'Of course it's a tall order,' Baranov said. He was still pacing back and forth, excited, impatient. 'Since when did real money fall into one's lap, just like that?'

'And me: what do you want with me? You certainly haven't come here merely to show how clever you are.'

'Patience, my friend. For the time being I must confirm my judgement. I called in at your lousy public library on the way here, looking for a certain learned tome on icons. Not there, of course. When I leave you I shall see what they have at the arts faculty of the university. If I'm lucky it will tell me what I need to know about a certain aspect of icon painting in the fifteenth and sixteenth centuries – basic stuff I knew and forgot years ago. Then I have some more work to do on the article itself, and by tomorrow I'll have news for you – possibly fantastic news.'

'Where is the thing now?'

'It's safe, back in Taman. I'll return there this afternoon, and you'll hear from me, tomorrow latest.'

He leant over the big disk, extended his hand. Marchenko took it and shook it limply.

'I don't like murder,' he said.

'Nor do I. You'll see, the militia will run someone in. Shame about the old priest; the dog too. But they'll run someone in.'

Peter Baranov strode to the door, threw a backward glance at Marchenko, Lenin's head poised on its shelf behind him, and let himself out of the office.

2

Like the Lubyanka, headquarters of the KGB three streets away, the weekly *Vperiod* was housed in the former offices of an insurance company, though a more modest one. But unlike the Lubyanka, which had swallowed the entire building and a great series of extensions willed by successive generations of secret policemen, *Vperiod* had only one floor to itself. This rabbit warren of cubicles and corridors had been much neglected over the years and apart from the editor-in-chief's office, there wasn't a carpet unscuffed or a panel intact in the entire place. But the editor-in-chief, one Georgi Galaktionovitch Chelidze, sat in a degree of comfort. He had heavy velvet curtains, a carpet from Dagestan, an ancient but rather grand desk in mahogany, and two standard lamps with tasselled shades on either side of an ottoman. On this his more important visitors were invited to sit. There they were offered mineral water from a cupboard above which there hung, over the years, portraits of successive leaders of the State.

Chelidze was a Georgian, and in the custom of his country was inclined to address members of his staff as genatsvale – a term of mild endearment which, with usage, had become quite meaningless. The thing had rebounded: he himself was known behind his back as Genatsvale. On the other hand, there was nothing especially endearing about the man.

He'd come up from his native Tbilisi twenty years back. How he had metamorphosed into an editor no one knew. The Party, it was said, had plucked him from the Komsomol office in Tbilisi and installed him as Party boss at the GUM department store in Red Square. The improbability of such a move was equalled a few years later. Following the unearthing of a substantial fraud in the buying office at GUM, Chelidze found himself heading the Party organisation at the Gorki Children's Film Studios. A further lurch in his career had propelled him into the editor-in-chief's chair at *Vperiod* at a time when his predecessor there had got himself into an obscure brand of trouble. The relevant Party department felt the need to install a sound man who would not kick over any traces. Ideology being all, Chelidze was deemed ideologically suitable.

At *Vperiod* he wrote no articles, edited nothing and offered no ideas of his own. But he funnelled the views of the ideological department of the Party into the editorial conferences with a certain steely charm and a weary lack of interest in the mechanisms of newspaper production. Glasnost, perestroika and their attendant political upheavals had passed him by, as they had passed by his mentors in the Party office. He was dimly aware of being an anachronism, and a certain passivity had overtaken Georgi Galaktionovitch Chelidze, as it had overtaken so many others in the nomenklatura. What would be would, he concluded, undoubtedly be. And now, since the office intercom had been out of order for some six weeks, he shouted to his secretary through the half-open door of his office: 'Vera, get Lyubimov in here, will you.'

There followed a familiar routine. Vera, known by all save her boss as Verochka, tottered out of the anteroom which housed her desk, her inordinately high heels clicking on the bare boards of the long corridor off which the reporters and sub-editors had their spartan offices. The clicking of Verochka's heels competed with the rattle of the Ericas on which the staff were pounding out their copy. At the far end she came to Slava Lyubimov's room, opened the door a fraction, shouted 'Lyubimov – he wants you,' and retreated back down the corridor. It was said on the one hand that such a degree of befuddled incompetence as

Verochka exhibited could only be tolerated on the basis that sexual favours of some kind were on offer to her boss. On the other hand, it was said that even such a dried-up little runt as Genatsvale could have done better. Verochka did not appeal to the staff of *Vperiod*.

Seated opposite his editor-in-chief, Lyubimov judged from the manner in which the other man was fussing with papers on his desk that the issue would be the Leningrad story. When the editor-in-chief was under instructions to curb the liberalising tendencies of his staff, his amiability would slap up against the rigorous stance which ideological purity demanded, and it would show.

'Ah, yes, Lyubimov genatsvale, I have to tell you that I have had representations. Rather firm representations, to tell you the truth. Something we at *Vperiod* cannot ignore, since it has to do with our duty to enlighten and guide our many readers.'

Lyubimov said nothing, seeing no reason why he should help in any way. He had suspected that his story from Leningrad would stir someone in the Central Committee to action and he was only mildly interested in what that action might be.

'Yes, your story on the mafia in Leningrad. That's it, Leningrad. And I have to tell you that they are not pleased at the Central Committee, not at all pleased with your Leningrad story.'

He paused, hoping Lyubimov would ask why. But he found himself staring at an expression of innocent surprise, tinged, he thought, with irony. He did not appreciate irony.

'It has been put to me, genatsvale, that your description of the lifestyle of these gangsters in Leningrad is too graphic, shall we say? All that boozing and stuffing, and the imported clothes, the Mercedes. Very graphic stuff and no doubt accurate, but negative in its implications.'

Lyubimov decided to venture a short distance into the conversation. 'As you know, I got a pretty close look at the

Leningrad set-up. How could a piece like that be anything but negative?'

'I'm afraid your report was considered to be negative in another sense. You see, it has been put to me that if we write about the high living of these criminals, our readers will conclude that that is the only way to live well and increasing numbers of our young people will resort to crime.'

'But it's the truth, you know.'

'I do not doubt it.' The pens were being shifted about again. 'But objectively speaking, such descriptions will generate envy and ultimately imitation, and so objectively their effect is negative. The conclusion will be: to eat well one must be a criminal.'

Lyubimov resisted the temptation to laugh. 'Are we not to report the doings of the mafia?'

'Surely, surely, but with a sense of ideological responsibility. And so it has been further suggested that you might turn your undoubted talents to other subject-matter. To things which demonstrate our regard for the interests of our readers, for the struggle for a better life, and so on.'

It was not the first time this had happened. Last year there had been the little upset about the factory director in Kiev who had been inventing output figures in his returns to the ministry in Moscow. The man appeared to think that the bonus payments thus earned could reasonably be diverted into his own pocket on the principle that whereas the ministry in its ignorance believed they should be paid to the workforce, the workers hadn't in fact produced the goods in question and therefore had no claim to the money. What Lyubimov had discovered when he started digging into the thing in the Party and Soviet offices in Kiev was that the factory director had long ago been rumbled and was perforce paying hush-money to local officials. He wrote the story and his editor-in-chief in a moment of ideological weakness let it into the paper. Then someone at the Central Committee had shouted abuse down the telephone. What about the black market? What about the criminal gangs? Why couldn't *Vperiod* devote its official allocation of paper to worthwhile matters of that kind? Why couldn't it serve the interests of the common people in a truly constructive way instead of trying to blacken the name of the Party? And so Lyubimov had been sent to Leningrad, and there he got into more hot water.

An irony, he reflected.

'I have a letter here,' Chelidze said. 'You'd best read it.'

He passed over two lined sheets which appeared to have been torn from an exercise book. They were filled with large, shaky writing. 'Dear Brothers in Christ, we earnestly seek your help . . .' Lyubimov read the thing to the end. It didn't promise much of a story. No doubt Chelidze didn't intend it to.

'Taman? A long way to go to investigate a bit of a rough-house in a church. Since when were we so interested in religion?'

'You know of the government's new line. We respect people's faith even though we know it flows from ignorance and superstition. Our paper owes a duty to the more backward elements in our population, though of course we must write with a critical bias. Sympathy tinged with criticism and instruction. And no sentimentality about holy faith and that kind of nonsense.'

'Are you serious about sending me all the way to the Black Sea to investigate the complaint of this *dvadtsatka*?'*

'Perfectly serious. It would demonstrate the broadness of our ideological position.'

'Not too broad for our friends at the Central Committee? In no time they'll be accusing me of being the mouthpiece of clerical fanatics – opium of the people and so forth.'

'A certain amount of objective reporting of church affairs

* The dvadtsatka, from dvadsat (twenty). The body of twenty parishioners who control the administration of their church affairs.

is deemed acceptable and we haven't run a church story this year.'

Lyubimov glanced back at the two sheets. The letter had been signed by a dozen members of the *dvadtsatka*, three of them with shaky crosses. It referred to bullies from Moscow desecrating the holy place, stealing relics and terrorising the village. It called them 'antichrists' and ended with the claim that their priest and his dog had been battered to death.

'Taman,' Lyubimov said. 'That wonderful tale of the blind boy and the mermaid girl.'

'What's that?'

'Taman. The setting of the third tale in Lermontov's *A Hero of Our Time*. It would be interesting to see it.'

'A very instructive trip for a man of literary tastes like you, genatsvale.'

'Lermontov actually prayed in this church during his military service in the Kuban.'

'You could work that into your story.'

'I think I am going to be hard put to it, Georgi Galaktionovitch, to make anything much of this, even with the murder thrown in. On the other hand, the weather could be pretty good down there. I'll kid myself it's just a literary pilgrimage and take a copy of *Hero* with me.'

'Vera will draw your expenses and get you an air ticket to Krasnodar. Get her to type out your assignment sheet and I'll sign it. You'll call on the committee for religious affairs first. Don't upset them. I don't want complaints about you filtering back to Moscow via channels. I'll call their chairman myself this afternoon.'

Later, as she handed Lyubimov his documents and air ticket for the following day, Verochka said: 'What is it this time, *Vperiod* Uncovers Mafia Fishermen at Black Sea Port?' Her voice conveyed sarcasm and distaste.

Lyubimov grinned. 'No, no, Verochka, we've had a very important lead on a truly sensational story.'

'What is it?'

'I'm not supposed to tell you.'

'Come on.'

'Promise not to tell your friends?'

'Promise.'

'Well, we've heard the KGB in the Crimea have trained man-eating sharks to oppose perestroika.'

'How do they do that?'

'Simple. Every time a supporter of the market economy goes swimming, these trained sharks sniff him out and eat him.'

Lyubimov ducked as a folder sailed past his head. 'I'll bring you a tangerine,' he shouted from halfway down the corridor.

As the TU154 climbed to its cruising altitude over the market gardens south of Moscow, Slava Lyubimov settled back in his seat, the daily papers and Lermontov's *A Hero of Our Time* on his lap, his knees rammed uncomfortably into the back of the seat ahead of him. He would re-read the Taman story as a kind of spiritual preparation for what would be part literary pilgrimage, part journalistic non-event. He opened the book and leafed through it until he came to the chapter headed Taman halfway through. He recalled the weird tale of smugglers but the first sentence struck him as an augury of some kind.

Taman is the worst little town of all the seacoast towns of Russia.

'That was in 1839,' he said to himself. 'It's probably even worse now.' Then he accepted a glass of tepid mineral water from the lumpy air hostess whose heart was clearly not in her job.

He was conscious that the dark-eyed girl in the next seat was eyeing his book. He had noticed her as they came aboard: a chiselled Armenian beauty, fine shoulders, small waist, long legs, something severe and overly serious about her. A challenge of some kind. You'd have to work hard to get a smile out of her, let alone anything more. It was the kind of task Lyubimov enjoyed. The girl would compete for his attention with Lermontov on the way down to Kharkov and on to Krasnodar, and would probably win. He closed the novel. Now would be a good time to start a conversation. Something trite about the weather or was she getting off at Kharkov or going on? No need to be clever about it.

'Can I lend you a paper?'

'Thanks. I left in a hurry this morning without a book.'

She liked the look of the tall young man with the mop of reddish hair and what she took to be smiling eyes. She had no urge to read.

'You're welcome to *Izvestia.* It has a fascinating story on pigmeat production. Fascinating because there doesn't seem to be any. It's that or maybe we could chat instead.'

'So let us talk.'

This would be heavy going. What did she mean by talk? An analysis of the political situation? Or the state of the economy, which was surely beyond discussion? Somehow, she looked like an academic. Or maybe a lawyer, a teacher?

'Tell me what you do?'

'I am an economist at a research institute in Yerevan and I am on my way to visit an aunt in Krasnodar. I was at a seminar in Moscow.'

'Interesting, your seminar?'

'Not at all.'

She liked the way he asked direct questions in the apparent certainty of getting answers, the way he would grin suddenly, the lines crinkling round the expressive eyes.

She asked, 'And what do you do?'

'I'm a journalist.'

'And is that interesting? I imagine so.'

'Interesting, yes. Also frustrating.'

'What's frustrating about it?'

'Editors. Also other persons whose idea of glasnost and perestroika is to permit a newspaper to reveal the date. As to the day of the week, they have their reservations.'

She did not smile. 'Are you a freelance?'

'No, I work for *Vperiod*. Sometimes we publish something useful. We do our best.'

'And you are on your way to Krasnodar to write something useful?'

'I'm on my way to Taman and there may not even be a story when I get there.'

He gave her an outline of what the old ladies of Taman had written. 'At all events,' he added, 'it will be an opportunity to see Lermontov's Taman. For me it's something of a pilgrimage.'

She nodded towards the book on his lap. 'I prefer his poetry.'

'Of course, but it's a wonderfully evocative novel.'

'The imagery is dated. And the coincidences are really preposterous.'

'They weren't preposterous when Lermontov wrote. Coincidence was a literary convention of the time, you know. We read it now for different virtues. And don't forget Chekhov said the Taman chapter was the best short story ever written.'

She shook her head. He thought she was rather a frightening young creature. Given to strong views on literature and no doubt on much else besides.

'My head has been full of Lermontov's poetry ever since school. We had a teacher who rated him with Pushkin.'

Lyubimov quoted, '*I have a bird of paradise/Upon a springing cypress tree . . .*'

'*She sits for hours while daylight flies,/And not a song by day sings she.*' The girl laughed delightedly. 'Those are the opening lines of "Hope", and I know the rest.' She paused for a moment, then she asked, 'And you, do you write poetry?'

'Not since the age of twenty.'

'Was it good – good young man's poetry?'

'No, terrible.'

He grinned and she noted again the good-natured lines which formed round his eyes.

'And a novel – surely you've written a novel? I thought all journalists were merely frustrated novelists.'

'That's a highly personal question, you know.'

'I'm sorry. I meant no offence.'

He laughed. 'In a drawer at home I have 220 pages of manuscript. It's been there for five years.'

'Have you shown it to anyone, to your colleagues?'

'To no one.'

'Why not?'

He paused and for a moment looked serious. 'I suppose I have no one to show it to – no one, that is, whose opinion would be . . . relevant, interesting.'

'I see,' she said. 'No wife with literary tastes?'

'No wife of any kind.'

'And this novel, when will it come out of its drawer?'

He laughed again. 'Probably never. You see, it is the classic first novel; all about childhood – stuff nobody really wants to read. A piece of self-indulgence to get a few things out of my system.'

'Is it about a happy childhood?'

'Yes, and that's difficult to do, you know. Misery makes better copy.'

Why was this girl, casually met on a plane, able to draw him out like this? He suddenly realised she was the first person to know his novel was about childhood. Perhaps it was easier to talk to a stranger. He'd often wondered wherein lay his own professional knack of getting people to talk, all kinds of people, saying all manner of things they'd never intended saying at all. And now this economist with dark, thoughtful eyes and fine legs was practising his own skill on him.

I think,' he said, 'I would prefer to talk about you. Tell me about economics in Yerevan.'

'There is nothing interesting to tell. Does your novel end sadly or with hope?' She had quietly, with charm, taken control of the conversation.

'As far as I can remember, both.'

Suddenly she said, 'I think I'm keeping you from your book.'

'No, no, I much prefer talking to you. Anyway, I've read *Hero* twice and this time I only planned to dip into it, maybe to re-read the chapter set in Taman, and I've plenty of time to do that.'

'That, too, was a young man's novel, wasn't it?'

He nodded. 'He was twenty-six when he wrote it and was shot through the heart in that ridiculous duel at twenty-seven. They said he was Pushkin's successor. I think he fought three duels, he was that sort of young man. Difficult, unpleasant on the whole. That, and a wonderful poet.'

'Very Russian, wouldn't you say?'

'I suppose so.'

'Russian arrogance, perhaps? We know something about that in Armenia.'

'I'm sure you do,' he said.

'I do not hold you personally responsible for all those misdeeds,' she said, and gave him a smile.

As they talked he idly riffled the pages of the book until he came to the chapter headed *Taman*. 'Look,' he said, 'how my chapter begins: "*Taman is the worst little town of all the seacoast towns of Russia.*" And it goes on: "*I almost died of hunger there and, moreover, an attempt was made to drown me.*" ' He turned to her, laughing. 'An augury for my little trip? What do you say?'

'I am not superstitious, I deal in figures. So I don't believe in auguries or signs or stuff like that. But be careful.'

He was still looking at her, somewhat intently now.

'What's your name?'

'My name's Raya – Raya Altunyan. And yours?'

He told her, and added. 'May I have your telephone number?'

'Why not?'

'And will you take mine?'

'Again why not?' She smiled again, searching in her bag for a pen.

'If ever you are in Yerevan on an assignment . . .'

'Or you are in Moscow at a seminar . . .'

They exchanged numbers. Who knows, he thought, Genatsvale may send me to Yerevan some day to interview a bishop as part of this new fashion for religious reporting. In which case I'd most certainly call her. Are there bishops in Yerevan?

The girl was thinking that behind those gentle eyes lay a lot of strength. Maybe, if she ever got back to Moscow . . .

They said goodbye in the concourse at Krasnodar airport. Lyubimov had not got beyond that first sentence:

Taman is the worst little town of all the seacoast towns of Russia.

What very beautiful legs the Armenian girl had as she walked away, turning briefly to wave and smile for the third time.

3

Peter Alexandrovitch Baranov has completed his third year at our Institute with distinction. He shows ability and determination in his studies, and his essays demonstrate a considerable insight in artistic matters. He has shown particular keenness in his field work, often leading our students' expeditions to ancient monasteries and churches where investigations and restoration projects are in progress. On the other hand, it has to be said that the student Baranov exhibits a certain individualism, and even a self-centredness, which has led to his self-exclusion from many of our class activities. This he must correct in future if his talents are to yield an appropriate result both for himself and for our joint artistic endeavours.

Thus the report of Baranov's professor some ten years earlier.

'It's rubbish, of course,' Petya Baranov had written to his father in Chelyabinsk. 'I'm as co-operative as the rest of them, though the prof is right about my good results. It's just that I find the others a bit on the stupid side, and if I'm to make my way in the world I can't waste my time on their political meetings and the Komsomol crap about self-criticism. I just get on with it, that's all.'

Money was tight. To his student's allowance of forty roubles a month his father was only able to add another thirty. You couldn't lead the good life or anything resembling it on seventy roubles. This was at the root of everything that transpired in the next ten adventurous years for Petya Baranov, art thief.

In the last term of his third year he had been in a group of Institute students making sketches at an abandoned church in the village of Kratovo, Moscow region. The place was derelict, no longer used even as a barn for the storage of fodder. The frescoes, dating back to the early nineteenth century, were of some quality but now damaged beyond repair by rainwater. The church's treasury was empty. The students had set up their easels among the gravestones surrounding the decaying pile and were making what they could of the onion domes, silhouetted against the cloudless summer sky.

'Why the hell should we be making lousy drawings of a ruin which wasn't even of any interest when they built it?' Baranov asked. 'I can render a dome or a collapsing bell tower with my eyes shut. There must be something more interesting to do in this godforsaken hole.' And he had wandered back to the wooden house of the elderly nurse on whom he had been billeted. The nurse was doing her rounds in a neighbouring village. Baranov found his way down to the cellar. Rummaging, he came across a pile of small icons. No doubt someone, sometime, had saved them from the church as it came down in the world. Baranov brought them out into the daylight. He judged two of them to be of interest; both early nineteenth-century, both pretty fair copies of earlier products of the Novgorod school. He particularly liked a sad Archangel Michael, robed in red and blue, with wings of delicate brown. He was to say later that it was the Archangel Michael who had made him what he was, had started him on his career, mapped out his destiny. He wore a medallion depicting the Archangel on a gold chain round his neck. 'My patron saint,' he would tell enquiring women. 'Best not tell him what we've just done.'

He slipped the two icons in his knapsack, returned the others to the cellar, and departed that evening with his fellow-students, having kissed the old nurse on both cheeks and promised to send her a card from the big city.

Petya Baranov made his first sale in the Serebryanny Bor on the outskirts of Moscow. He'd set up his easel and was making a desultory attempt at sketching a bend in the Moskva river, the icons in a bag at his feet. The spot had been chosen because he knew foreigners often made Sunday outings to the forest. The students sometimes managed to sell a sketch to someone who wanted to bring home a bit of Russian art but couldn't face the sulkiness of the young women staffing the city's art shops.

In the event it was a Dutch diplomat and his wife who became Baranov's first customers.

'You interested in Russian art?'

'Maybe.'

They were looking over his shoulder at the charcoal sketch. The conversation was in halting English.

'I don't mean what I do here. Just an exercise. I have more interesting things.'

'What do you mean?'

'Are you perhaps interested in genuine Russian icons?'

The woman seemed impressed. 'Do you know where we can get icons?'

'I suppose you know you cannot export genuine ones. The customs forbid it.'

'We know that. But – '

'But there are always possibilities. I am about to take a certain article out of my bag here. I will place it briefly on easel for you to see. Of course, if anyone comes, it returns into bag and you have seen nothing, right?'

'Of course, of course.' The woman was excited by her modest illicit adventure. The husband looked worried. Clearly, the lady ruled.

Baranov took out the Archangel Michael and placed him on the easel. It was certainly a beautiful thing.

'Mid-seventeenth-century, Novgorod school, exceptional quality,' he said. 'I am expert on our icons and I can say you find nothing like this in the city.'

'And the price?' The man had come back into the conversation.

'What good quoting you price if you can't take it out of our country?'

'My husband's a diplomat. Taking it out isn't a problem.'

'The price,' the man said.

'Three hundred dollars.'

'And you say it's seventeenth-century?'

'On my honour.'

Baranov gave them ten minutes of expert invention. 'You must treat it as investment,' he concluded. 'Either you like or you don't like, you believe me or you don't. You have no way to play safe, since both of us operate outside Soviet law. If you don't want, I put it away and someone will buy before this evening.'

Ten minutes later he had accepted two hundred dollars and had exchanged telephone numbers. The second icon fetched a hundred the following week. The Archangel had started him on his career.

Petya Baranov graduated with distinction from the Fine Arts Institute the following year and three weeks later he suffered his only piece of truly rotten luck. By then he had started to fence choice items lifted by a small gang of art thieves who specialised in break-ins at the apartments of leading officials – people liable to have marketable items of value. One Cherkassky had fallen through a skylight at a promising dacha and bleeding like a pig had offered no resistance to the militia. He had then been sufficiently roughed-up to give them more names than they'd dared hope for. Among the names was Peter Alexandrovitch Baranov, and in his room in the small hours the militia had found their man and a selection of items which did not belong to him.

Why the militia then handed the case to the KGB he didn't know; perhaps the importance of the dacha's owner had something to do with it. Whatever the reason, Baranov was to say subsequently that next to granting him a diploma with distinction it was the best thing the authorities had ever done for him.

In the office of one S. S. Marchenko at the KGB headquarters at the Lubyanka, the conversation had moved forward effortlessly and with a surprising degree of goodwill.

'This was not wise for a young man of education, a Komsomol member, too.'

Baranov shrugged and allowed himself a grin.

'It would be a shame to see a promising young man like you turned into a jailbird. In prison you'd learn more dirty tricks and you'd be lost.' Marchenko shook his head sadly at the prospect. 'What do you say to that?'

'I've been a fool. I didn't know the stuff was stolen. I just thought, you know, black market . . .' He shrugged again. 'These days there's more black than white. In any case, I only sell to crooks.'

'How do you make that out?' Marchenko asked.

'Simple. Foreigners who buy from me know they can't take the stuff out of the country without a shop receipt. So they must be smuggling these items out in diplomatic bags, or hidden somehow – I don't know. It's a criminal offence, of course, and that makes them crooks in my book. Someone said about the illicit art trade that you need two crooks and one of them is the victim.'

'And the other, I assume, is you?'

'I like to think I'm an intermediary, just oiling the wheels of commerce.' Baranov allowed himself a smile. His confidence was returning. Whatever the KGB man was, he was not valiant for truth and punishment.

'An interesting idea,' Marchenko said. 'Interesting, but not convincing.'

'I never expected you to be enthusiastic about it,' Baranov said. 'But all this is as old as civilisation itself, you know. The Romans used to fake Hellenic sculptures because everything Greek was fashionable at the time. And what about Michelangelo's Sleeping Cupid?'

'What about it?'

'One of the Medicis had the bright idea of burying it in acid soil for a bit to produce pitting and discoloration. Then, when it looked about one thousand five hundred years older than it was, he got a dealer in Rome to palm it off on Cardinal Riario for a neat two hundred ducats in gold.' Baranov smiled again. 'As I say, it's always gone on and always will, and people who are smart enough make a nice living out of the mugs, the crooks I say, who buy the stuff.'

Marchenko contemplated him for a moment, impressed by the very impertinence of the man. Then he said, 'And what am I to do with you, my young friend, answer me that?'

Again the smile. Was something being offered here, and if so, how was he to play it?

He ventured a first approach. 'Perhaps there's some way . . .'

'Perhaps, perhaps.' Marchenko opened a box on his desk and offered his prisoner a cigarette. There was a long silence. It was not the first time S. S. Marchenko had conducted this kind of conversation. He knew the value of a silence, a reassuring smile, a cigarette even.

'In the circles you must mix in – let's call it for our immediate purposes the underworld – in these circles, I say, you must meet many interesting persons who would be of interest to us here at the Committee for State Security. Persons who have negative social values.'

Leaning back in his chair, he looked at Baranov much as an indulgent uncle might look at a nephew who had unfortunately spilt his soup on the snow-white tablecloth.

'I suppose I do meet certain people in whom you would be interested.'

'Quite. And it would be a simple matter for you to meet me discreetly from time to time so that we might have a little chat, always on the understanding that we would do nothing here to endanger you in any way.'

'It would have to be discreet.'

'Absolutely. Also, you may consider it your patriotic duty, seeing that we are interested in foreigners who break our Soviet laws by smuggling art treasures out of our country.' He paused and allowed himself a broad smile. 'An educated citizen like you would naturally be concerned to defend the interests of your country.'

It was how his collaboration with Stepan Stepanovitch Marchenko had started. And when Marchenko had taken a spurious retirement from the KGB at the age of fifty-five to be appointed, despite his best endeavours to resist, to the religious affairs post in what he called the provincial shit-house of Krasnodar, the collaboration with Baranov had continued. Indeed, it had prospered. For by now money was changing hands between them, and under Marchenko's chairmanship the local committee found itself approving a sharply increased number of restorations, renovations and art surveys in the churches, monasteries and other monuments of the region.

'This place you put me in is disgusting,' Baranov was saying. 'The old cow keeps six cats and they all piss on the floor. Can't you smell it?'

Chairman Marchenko was sitting uncomfortably on the low bed, since Baranov was installed in the only chair in the room and showed no sign of yielding it to his guest. The stink was undeniable.

'It was all I could find. Taman isn't exactly a metropolis.'

He tried to settle more comfortably on the bed, but there was nothing on which to lean his back. He glanced up at the cobwebs on the ceiling and grunted. Then he lit a cigarette and left it hanging from his lower lip, the smoke curling up over his face.

'So it isn't a luxury hotel, granted. Now let's get on with

the matter at hand. If you pulled me down here – three hours in the car – it's because you must have a story worth telling.'

Baranov grinned. 'Would I inconvenience the chairman if I hadn't got news of absolutely major importance?'

'So show me the damned icon, for Christ's sake,' Marchenko said.

'First, a short lecture. Necessary I'm afraid, so that you will understand what you are seeing. And my lecture will be on the greatest of all painters of icons, the black monk, Andrei Roublev.' He paused dramatically, allowed a silence to develop.

'Even I know Roublev. That much we all know.'

'But what we do not all know, my friend, and what has only been surmised in the past is that the monk Roublev, back there in the fifteenth century, painted not two versions of his masterpiece, the Old Testament Trinity, but *three*!'

'Are you saying that what you've got is a genuine Roublev?'

'I am saying that, Stepan Stepanovitch, I am saying that, and I am adding that it will make us rich beyond our craziest dreams. *That* is what I am saying. A third version of Andrei Roublev's Old Testament Trinity.'

'Not a later copy?'

Baranov shook his head. 'I graduated with a commendation.'

'Not overpainted?'

'Never been touched. Exactly as Roublev painted it, with all the delicacy of drawing and the masterful handling of colour.'

'And its condition?'

'Could be better, but these things can be dealt with.'

'The size – what about the size?'

'About one metre fifty high. You'll see in a minute!'

'Difficult to transport discreetly.'

'Not for me. Or rather, not for us.'

'It would need to be authenticated.'

'*I* have authenticated it. Everything is there – the typical high foreheads and sunken eyes, the ivory highlights on the faces of the saints, the refined hands and feet – everything that says Andrei Roublev. But in any case, we can never show it to one of our Soviet experts.' Baranov smiled. 'State property, you know, the property of the Soviet people. And why do you think I tell you all this, my dear Stepan Stepanovitch, when I could just as readily look after the whole thing myself?'

'I was wondering why.'

'You will see.'

'The big one,' the chairman thought to himself. 'Perhaps this, at last, is the big one. An end to little envelopes. Some peace at home, at any rate for a while.' But Baranov was a risk-taker. Foolhardy. Greedy. Not at all to be trusted. But only a man like that, a man of truly insatiable appetite for money, would have the nerve to steal a Roublev icon – to organise a murder for it and now to embark on heaven knew what crazy adventures to turn it into cash. And why in God's name did Baranov need him, Stepan Stepanovitch Marchenko, to carry through this extraordinary coup?

Being a cautious man by nature, he reckoned more questions were called for.

'My understanding is that Roublev worked all his life in Moscow and in monasteries nearby.'

'Correct: Moscow, Vladimir, Radonezh.'

'Yet you think you've found one of his works down here by the Black Sea.'

'Also correct.'

'How do you account for that?'

'The Cossacks, my friend.'

'What about the Cossacks? Don't tell me they ever dealt in religious art.'

'A few facts. Fact one, this is the Kuban, a Cossack region, as you know. Fact two, the Cossacks started their wandering across the face of Russia in the fifteenth century, right?'

'If you say so.'

'Fact three, who were these early Cossacks? Bands withdrawing from mainstream society – young men fleeing from serfdom, criminals, deserters, and here we come to it, Old Believers who rejected the reformed Orthodox church. And this mixed bunch of misfits established a kind of wandering, militarised democracy of self-rule under their chieftain, the Ataman. They lived by hunting, fishing, murder and plundering – whatever served their needs. Sometimes the Tsars supported them against the Turks and Tartars, sometimes not. But always they were staunch supporters of the old faith with its ceremonies and – note this – its symbols. Which brings me to the question of icons.'

'An interesting lesson in history, but perhaps you can come to the point.'

'Peter the Great was an implacable supporter of the Orthodox church against the Old Believers, many of whom, as I say, fled to the Cossack bands, *taking their precious symbols, their icons with them.*' Baranov paused for effect. 'I see nothing extraordinary in finding a fifteenth-century icon in a distant Cossack region such as the Kuban. It just happens, miraculously, to be a Roublev, that's all.'

'And why would it be hidden away like that? You aren't suggesting the old man knew it was a Roublev?'

'Of course not. My guess is that it was stored away simply because it didn't fit into the iconostasis in that tiny church. If you bothered to go there sometime you'd see what I mean. The place is scarcely more than a chapel. The Roublev was too big to fit in line with the other icons and that's why it got left in the cellar. In my opinion what the old man was hiding wasn't the Roublev at all but his miserable collection of silver.'

The chairman said nothing. Baranov pulled a sheet of paper from his pocket.

'I found this. A letter the old man was writing. It's to the bishop, complaining about me. Found it on his desk.'

He handed the letter over. After reading it Marchenko handed it back.

'So?'

'So, my dear Stepan Stepanovitch, I offer you a partnership in this venture of mine, which is the disposal abroad of Roublev's third Trinity.'

'And what do you want from me, apart from refraining from denouncing you here and now to the authorities?'

'You surely won't do that. And what I want from you will become clear in time. But let's understand each other. I have no idea yet what the thing can bring in. And in any case we may run into trouble and end with nothing. So that I cannot put a figure on the value of your collaboration now. But when I know more about the possibilities we will talk about it and I shall play fair.'

'That is not satisfactory. You could walk away, disappear, and leave me with nothing. Also, you haven't spelt out what role I am to play.'

'You must trust me, Stepan Stepanovitch. You must trust me for the simple reason that you are in no position to do otherwise, to antagonise me.'

'That could be said of us in reverse order.'

'Precisely. And it is why I said just now that we need each other. But this business talk is boring. I now invite you to examine the most perfect example of post-Byzantine religious art that you are ever likely to set eyes on. Here, feast your gaze on Russia's precious heritage before it travels half across the world in the interests of that hateful proposition, personal gain.'

Baranov got up from his chair and crossed to the battered wardrobe opposite the bed. From it he took a large flat package wrapped in an old blanket.

'You'll soon see what I mean,' he said. Carefully, he unfolded the blanket and propped the icon against the wall. Then he stood back, head cocked to one side in yet another dramatic pose.

'There! The third Old Testament Trinity of Andrei Roublev. Millions staring you in the face.'

Marchenko on the bed grunted again, leaning forward to examine the icon through his cigarette smoke. Then he shook his head.

'And how do I know it's what you say it is? What about copies, forgeries, fakes?'

'I say it's a genuine Roublev.'

'Does that make it a genuine Roublev – pouf, just like that?'

'Four years at the Institute of Fine Arts. Graduated with honours, first class. My diploma subject: *The Identification of Fifteenth-century Icons of the Moscow, Suzdal and Novgorod Schools*. Is that good enough for you?'

'So how do you identify the thing as genuine? To me it looks anaemic.'

Baranov turned the icon to face the wall.

'First, the wood. Up to the sixteenth century painters on wooden panels used only local woods. Moscow region? Fir and ash. If this were oak, it would be the end of the story. But it's ash. So far so good. Next, how was the thing put together? See, the three panels running vertically have been reinforced with cross-pieces. That's unusual in the fifteenth century but Roublev did it; we find it in two other authenticated pieces of his. And see, there's been shrinkage on the cross-grain so that the planks are no longer firmly held by the frame moulding. That shows great age – unlikely in a nineteenth-century copy. The lateral joints have sprung, due to shrinkage – again a sign of authenticity.'

Baranov beckoned Marchenko to lean forward.

'Worm galleries,' he said. 'Look at them. *Anobium punctatum*, our little friend the woodworm. He never burrows straight. If the ageing of the wood had been faked, the worm galleries would necessarily be straight. It's the only way of faking them.'

He took a penknife from a pocket and carefully cut a

sliver of wood from the edge of the icon's frame. 'Look, the worm gallery disappears, doesn't follow the line of the cut. All good circumstantial evidence that we're on to the genuine article.'

He turned the icon round. The naked bulb hanging from the ceiling cast a harsh light on the painting. It showed three figures bending over a stone table on which stood a small chalice.

'What you have here,' Baranov said, 'is the traditional depiction of the Holy Trinity in the form of three angels representing God's visit to Abraham as the Old Testament tells it. A peaceful scene. Harmony. Intimacy and tenderness. All expressed with Roublev's incomparable technique. Such luminosity! Painted in bright pastels with Roublev's masterly overlay of washes and white highlights. No one has achieved such mastery before or since. I tell you, it can only be Roublev.'

Marchenko leaned back and grunted again.

'And what if some smart guy in the eighteenth century had simply copied your Roublev – what then?'

'Tell me,' Baranov said, 'if someone had copied Roublev with the aim of passing his work off, would he have made as exact a copy as he could?'

'I'd say so.'

'Would there be any point in hitting off Roublev's painting technique, his style and subject matter, and then failing to copy the *details* of the Trinity?'

'No point.'

'Well, look at this.'

Baranov fetched a large book from a shelf and opened it. 'I liberated this from the library today. It wasn't easy.' He grinned. 'See here, a reproduction of the Tretyakov Trinity. Now look at our version. See, the tower at the far left in the background has disappeared. And the position of the right-hand angel's feet is different. And the false perspective of the chair legs has shifted. Do you see it?'

'I see it.'

'And what does it tell you?'

Marchenko shrugged. 'It's different, that's all.'

'It isn't all. A copyist would never go to all that trouble and then make obvious changes. No, the artist himself would feel free to change details when doing another version of an existing work. Many artists did multiple versions of a favourite theme and invariably they made changes as the whim took them. And why not? Clearly, Roublev didn't bother with his tower, which added nothing to the composition. And no doubt we'd find other small changes if we took the trouble to make a close comparison.'

Baranov straightened up, crossed to the chair and sat down. He was clasping and unclasping his hands. 'I tell you – a genuine, a magnificent Roublev. A truly splendid work of art, here in this stinking room you put me in, cats and all, and not only that – a bloody fortune if we do what has to be done.'

'All right, all right. Try to calm down a little. This is not a symposium for art lovers. What I want to know is what modern testing techniques can do to your theories. After all, diploma or no diploma, all I've heard so far is your private opinion. How do I know the whole thing can't be exploded by science?'

'Very well, let's assume science does its worst. What do we have? They can date the wood. They can use infra-red photography to identify non-original retouching and overpainting. Electron emission radiography will reveal the joins in the wood and the worm galleries. And of course, any use of pigments such as white lead which were only developed much later are no problem at all.' He waved a hand. 'And that's just for a start. I won't confuse you with what they can do with an opaque microscope and polarised light, or gas-liquid chromatography, and – '

'All right, don't confuse me. So what next?'

'Just consider, what do we have here,' Baranov said. 'Not another second-rate artefact which fetches a few hundred dollars if we're lucky, which then has to be shared out with my associates. That's all child's play, and it's all behind us now. This, my friend, is the big time at last. Millions, bloody millions, and in hard currency, too. I tell you, we've arrived at last, and – '

'And let's have less of the histrionics and some practical detail. I admit the thing looks interesting, but how on earth do you move it from that old wardrobe to some place where it is worth something? Right now all it's worth is a long prison sentence and there isn't a kopeck to be had out of it.'

'Perfectly right. But what does perestroika teach us? Self reliance! Initiative! The exploitation of the free market! I am about to apply in practice what our betters have been preaching to us. I am about to allow the free market its head.'

'Please explain.'

'You know I have contacts abroad. In New York to be precise. These contacts of mine can offer the icon in circles where questions won't be asked. Very, very discreet art circles. Collectors who will pay mad prices to achieve a simple thing: to own something truly *unique*. And so crazy are they, they'll happily pay through the nose and then stash the thing away where no one at all can see it, not even their aunt. Look, you can sell a stolen Monet or even a Rembrandt if you can find one of these madmen, and he'll know that he can never in his whole lifetime admit to owning it. It's the ultimate expression of insensate greed. It's where the free market leads you if you travel all the way.'

'And you can set all this up?'

'I can.'

'And get it out of the country in the first place?'

'I can.'

'Bribing customs officials is a risky business.'

'Not a kopeck will change hands.'

'Stop being so damned allusive and tell me what you plan to do.'

'In the first place, there's luck. To achieve anything

you need a modicum of luck, and my luck is that in October an exhibition will travel to New York and the title of that exhibition, my friend, is Achievements of the Soviet Restorers' Art. Furthermore, a modest piece of mine is included in the show.'

'So?'

'So, a further achievement of Baranov will now be added and we have to get busy to persuade the organisers to have it included at the last minute. Fortunately, the team is headed by the Director of the Moscow Restorers, which is my outfit.'

'And you can persuade this man to make a change like this?'

'With your help I can do just that.'

'My help?'

'I want you to intervene through appropriate channels to say that the Krasnodar Region has a decent chance at last to be represented in a travelling show in the West, and that you insist, and so on and so forth.'

'Not easy.'

'I never said it was.'

'But in any case, how are you going to present this icon as an example of restoration without revealing in the first place what it is you have restored – a Roublev, no less?'

Baranov allowed a smile to spread slowly over his face. 'I am going to stand the art of restoration on its head.' he said.

'Please stop talking in riddles,' Marchenko said.

Like a character in a cheap melodrama Baranov flung out his arm, his finger pointing dramatically at the icon. The three angels, indifferent to the theatricals being played around them, gazed at each other with infinite compassion and serenity. The icon's musty odour reached Marchenko.

'You don't really appreciate it, do you, Stepan Stepanovitch?' Baranov said. 'You don't give a kopeck for our great Russian inheritance. To you it's a commodity, but to me it is a holy thing, an infinitely precious product of mankind's spirituality and his God-given skill.'

Marchenko had no idea whether all this was irony, hypocrisy or moral confusion. Perhaps Baranov genuinely loved this thing that he was about to sell.

'I will explain,' Baranov said. 'I will explain in terms which even you, my dear Stepan Stepanovitch, will understand. I will let you into some of the secrets of the restorer's art.'

'If you are going to explain, then get on with it. Your speeches I find tiring.'

Baranov smiled, approached the icon and shifted it to catch more of the light from the high window.

'You see the face of the angel on the left? What you could call a mediaeval face. You never saw a face like that in Krasnodar, my dear Stepan Stepanovitch. Such simplicity, such lack of guile, such holiness. Well, I shall repaint it.'

'Are you mad?'

'Not mad. Please bear with me. Now, the fold of the right-hand angel's blue cloak, there where it falls below the green garment, see? Well, I shall paint that out completely. And I'll do a bit of cleaning up all round while I'm about it. The haloes have faded so I'll brighten them up with a good cadmium yellow plus a little light cadmium red to warm it up. And the angels' wings need a bit of attention too.'

Baranov was enjoying the game of mystification, taking his time. 'And I think I'll make the whole thing pretty dirty at the edges while I'm about it.'

'Please explain and stop playing with me,' Marchenko said. 'Here you have what you tell me is a Roublev in acceptable condition and you propose to damage it in all kinds of ways. How then will you be able to place it on the market?'

Baranov laughed. 'What do we have? An Andrei Roublev so good, so perfect, that any knowledgeable art expert could identify it correctly almost at first glance. But what do we intend to *pretend* we have? An early nineteenth-century copy of a Roublev, pretty badly in need of restoration. So what must I do? I must make this genuine Roublev look like a copy, which is the precise opposite of what most art forgers do. They want the copy to look like an original. As I say, I have to turn things on their head. But, of course, there's more to it, and here you must follow me carefully. For we are presenting this, not as a straightforward nineteenth-century copy, but as a *restored* copy. Otherwise it wouldn't be in the exhibition, would it now?'

Marchenko nodded, his full attention engaged at last.

'So you see, this restored nineteenth-century copy of a fifteenth-century original has to be well enough done to fool knowledgeable people. We therefore go through three stages. First, we make it look like a later version by incorporating into it a number of the faults one can expect of a nineteenth-century copyist, including the use of styles, techniques and certain pigments which didn't exist in Roublev's day. So I shall repaint one, or maybe two of the faces because, just as there are no faces quite like these in the streets of your miserable city, so in the nineteenth century painters perceived the human face quite differently from the icon painters of the fifteenth, and anyone trained in these matters will know it at once. Then, I'll have a good deal of other repainting to do because the icon genuinely looks its age and has got to be made to look like a somewhat clumsy attempt to *copy* its age. Do you follow me?'

'I follow you.'

'I will work over the background using machine-ground pigment which yields a smaller particle size than the hand-ground pigments of the fifteenth century. Also, in the nineteenth century they used paints with unstable glazing mediums, especially in the browns and blacks. This produced typical cracks on drying, caused by a bitumen additive in the paint which in fact never dries out fully. The kind of cracks you find in the original tempera in which icons were painted in early times are quite different if you know what you are looking for, and they aren't concentrated in the dark areas either.' He paused for breath, seemingly happy to be showing off his knowledge. 'All this, my friend, will be known to the experts, who have to be fooled.'

'But when you've maltreated the thing in all these ways, how can it ever be restored?'

'Simple. I first apply a layer of common varnish, then I do what I have to do, and later all this muck will be removed together with the varnish and, presto, you have your Roublev intact, sublime, and worth millions.'

Marchenko sat in silence for a moment. Then he grunted and shook his head. 'There's a gaping hole in your argument.'

'And what's that, for God's sake?'

'You've turned the original into what I must assume is a fair imitation of a nineteenth-century copy. But what you haven't done if I follow you rightly is to *restore* it. How has it earned its place in your famous exhibition of the Soviet restorer's art?'

Baranov smiled. 'You are smart, but not smart enough. There are a number of answers to your question which I won't bore you with, but the chief of them is called *trateggio*.' He waited to be asked the meaning of the word as if forcing the question would afford him some kind of small triumph of will over the other.

'All right, what on earth is *trateggio*?'

'It's the technique used on the Crucifix by Cimabue after the floods of 1966 in Florence – the greatest achievement of the restorer's art in all history, the triumph of two Italians, Casazza and Baldini. And when I get out of this lousy country to live in the West, I'll head for Florence to shake those two gentlemen by the hand if they're still alive, in homage and professional respect. That, and pay a visit to the Institute of Electronics at Florence University, where they have all the equipment one could ever need to analyse and test works of art.'

'You're more likely to be on the run,' Marchenko said sourly.

Baranov paid no attention. 'You asked me what *trateggio* is. Well, briefly described it is a way of repairing an artwork which has lost completely part of its surface. The floods in Florence simply ripped whole areas of Cimabue's paint away, leaving blanks. And rather than repaint those areas in imitation of what the master had done, the restorers decided to fill in with hatched lines of carefully chosen colours which would blend perfectly with the surrounding paint areas without ever pretending to imitate what had gone before. In short, the crucifix looks like a wounded work of art, lovingly healed with patches of suitable colour – bandaged, if you will. That's *trateggio*!'

'And that's what you plan to do with your icon?'

'I will blank out some selected areas as if they'd been damaged at some stage, and apply *trateggio* in those areas in the style of Casazza and Baldini. And in the catalogue I will explain why I did not attempt to fake the areas which had been lost. I will assert that the icon, though a late copy, was so fine that I, a mere restorer, would not presume to paint in what was missing. Instead, I applied painterly bandages, just as they did with the Cimabue. Also,' Baranov added with a smile, 'the technique will help to obscure quite large areas of the Roublev, and that can only be good.'

Marchenko got to his feet. 'I only hope,' he said, 'that you know what you are doing.'

'I do,' Baranov said as he wrapped the icon once more in its blanket.

4

There was no way round the routine, which was precisely why the routine existed. Say the Donbas miners were on strike because safety regulations had not been enforced and there had been yet another pit disaster. A journalist would be sent by his paper in Moscow to do a story. Could he go straight to the miners and talk to them? He could not. Could he slip quietly into the mining village to discover what the widows were saying? Not at all. For he carried an assignment sheet, stamped and signed by his editor. And the sheet had to be signed, dated and stamped by the appropriate department of the District Committee down in the Donbas. After which, and only in co-operation with the local officials, could the reporter pursue the story. And while he was exercising his ingenuity to get away from his minders and get at the truth, the minders on their side exercised their own ingenuity to keep the reporter under control and stop him getting at any fact deemed unsuitable for publication. From this creative tension between the dark and the light a good reporter would distill his story, replacing hard factual writing where necessary with allusive hints and carefully crafted irony. And the readers had come to master this sign language. Slava Lyubimov now carried such an assignment sheet, and without the signature, stamp and 'time arrived' and 'time departed' from the appropriate official in Krasnodar there could be no onward journey to Taman and no investigation. In the present instance, the appropriate official was Stepan Stepanovitch Marchenko, Chairman of the Regional Council for Religious Affairs. It was therefore in his office that Lyubimov now found himself, seated on the far side of the big desk, his assignment sheet being fingered with distaste by the Chairman.

'I would have thought your paper had something better to do than send its reporters half across the country to write about some trivial bit of violence. How did you hear about it?'

'Some local supporters of the church in Taman wrote to us.'

'Do you always go rushing off like this when you get a letter?'

'My editor thought it might make a story.'

Marchenko grunted. 'It won't make any kind of story. Take my advice, young man, spend a day or two here in Krasnodar. I'll get you a permit to look over some of our new housing. Well worth seeing. I'll tell you what you need to know about this nonsense in Taman. Then you can get back to Moscow and save yourself hours of road travel to the coast.'

'Have they found the killer of the priest?'

'Certainly. The local militia discovered the murder weapon in a shed belonging to a local drunkard with a history of violence. As far as they are concerned the case is closed.'

'I think I should go to Taman.'

'Don't say I didn't warn you: there isn't anything there to write about.'

'I would like to talk to this team of restorers from Moscow.'

'I think they've left.'

'Are you sure?'

'I'm not sure. I could check and let you know.'

'When can I have transport to Taman?'

'I don't know that you can have transport. Down here in the provinces we're short of cars, petrol, everything.'

'So are we.'

'And what if I can't get you to Taman?'

'Then I suppose that will have to be my story. The

Regional Council unable or unwilling to allow *Vperiod* to report on the killing of a priest in Taman. It would make some kind of article, especially if I draw a parallel with the other famous mystery in Taman.'

'What other mystery?'

'The one Lermontov wrote about.'

'You are threatening me.'

'Not at all, Comrade, I am simply answering your question about what I would write if I cannot get to Taman. My editor would be very displeased with me if I came back with no story at all.'

Marchenko brought a heavy fist down on his desk. 'We do an honest job down here. We resist this pernicious drift back to religion, to obscurantism. We fight for the decencies and public order that our country knew not so long ago. And what we get is young journalists on the make trying to find muck where there's no muck, scandal where no scandal exists – out to make trouble in the idiotic belief that everything must be written about, every sore and pustule on the face of our society probed and examined. Bourgeois idiocy. What I call press hooliganism.'

Lyubimov decided that the urge to grin at this troglodyte in an ill-fitting suit should be suppressed. Instead, he leaned forward and nodded towards the document lying in front of Marchenko. 'Could we say tomorrow for the trip to Taman? Could we say early in the morning, perhaps, comrade chairman?'

'As a matter of fact,' Marchenko said suddenly, 'I had a call from your editor – what's his name, Chelidze? He says the people at the Central Committee are interested, though God alone knows why. So I imagine we'll have to get you down to Taman somehow.' He sighed, picked up a pen and scribbled on the line headed 'time of arrival' on Lyubimov's document. 'Be here at ten. I'll accompany you to Taman. We might as well both waste our time on this nonsense.'

Since getting Chelidze's call, Marchenko had been busy

wrestling with the telephone system. It had taken him an hour to get through to the local Soviet in Taman with an order to find Baranov and bring him to a telephone. A half-hour later Baranov was on the line.

'A journalist from *Vperiod* is on his way. They had a letter from the religious nuts in Taman about their priest. I'm told it includes some unkind remarks about the way your boys have been behaving.'

'Can't you head them off? After all, their man can't get here if you don't co-operate.'

'No good. It appears the whole thing comes from a sudden interest in religion at the Central Committee. As far as I can tell we've been caught up in some crazy ideological exercise.'

'You know what they say in the Ukraine, the old lady had no problems until she bought herself a pig.'

'I come from the Ukraine. And this is some pig.'

'So?'

'So I'll bring the journalist down myself and we'll keep an eye on him. It will also give us a chance to talk again.'

'We could get him drunk. I never met a journalist who didn't drink. It would cast doubt on anything he writes. "Man was drunk. Can't believe a word. Whole story's rubbish." '

'We'll see.'

'You wouldn't believe the trouble I have with the clergy around here,' Marchenko was saying. He and Slava Lyubimov were in the white Volga with its official 00 numberplate, travelling south along the foothills of the Great Caucasus range. 'What are they? Half-educated mystics, their heads full of crazy ideas and petty jealousy. "His stipend is greater than mine but he's got a smaller congregation." Or again, "Our roof's leaking, Stepan Stepanovitch, and we need five thousand roubles," when I know damn well they cut the holes themselves because they intend to take a rake-off. Scum, my dear Stanislav Petrovitch, nothing but scum from the past.'

Lyubimov did not answer; he had no desire to talk. The car was wheezing along the dusty road, passing farm trucks, carts, occasional decrepit jalopies. On both sides vineyards extended into the distance, the grapes hanging in heavy clusters, soon to be ready for the picking season. For a while they ran alongside a brownish, turbulent river, seen between the slender poplars lining the route. Soon the vines gave way to orchards and fields of wheat. Here and there women in headscarves worked in the fields.

'I'm afraid you won't find much to interest you in Taman,' Marchenko ventured. 'I've phoned ahead and told them to prepare us a decent dinner at the local stolovaya. The place is filthy but they make an effort for me and the food could be worse. I've checked since yesterday: the restorers are still there and their leader, one Baranov, will join us. A cultured fellow who knows a lot about churches.'

'The letter we got said he's an arrogant bully.'

'Nonsense! You'll meet him and judge for yourself.'

The white Volga raised its trail of dust through Abinsk and Krymsk, with their staring children and old men in caps. At Sennaya the Black Sea came into view and the car turned left onto the Taman road. The gentle winds from the south brought a tang of sea air to relieve the midday heat.

Lyubimov had built a picture of Taman in his mind, based on Lermontov's description, and he knew the place was about to disappoint him. Lermontov had said there was only one stone house in the village, the rest hovels of wood. Now he could see a few houses of stone, though most of the buildings were neatly constructed in wood. Ahead he caught his first sight of the grandly-named Cathedral of the Dormition of the Mother of God, with its modest bell tower and two onion domes, painted in china blue. Outside, two old women sat on a bench under the shade of an acacia. There were a couple of dogs sniffing their way back and forth across the open space in front of the portico. He would visit the little church later as Lermontov himself had visited it. Lermontov had prayed there. But he would be sniffing around after a story. Sniffing much like the dogs, he thought, and to no greater purpose.

The car coughed and sighed to a halt outside the offices of the local Soviet. The red flag of the Russian Federation with the blue stripe hung faded and slightly stained from a flag pole on the roof of the long single-storey building. If anything at all was happening in Taman it was not happening here.

'Let's meet the local bosses,' Marchenko said. They were out of the car, screwing up their eyes against the vivid sunlight.

'You do that,' Lyubimov said. 'I'm off to see my correspondent first.'

'Are you sure you don't want me to come with you?'

'Quite sure.'

'Let's meet for dinner at the stolovaya. It's across the way, a few steps along.'

'Very well.'

'At eight?'

'At eight.'

'The driver can take you wherever you're going.'

'No thanks, I'll find my way.'

Lyubimov made his way back to the church and the two women on their bench.

'Where can I find Ulitsa Cosmonavtov, Granny?'

What on earth had cosmonauts and suchlike national pretensions to do with this sundrenched backwater, obstinately clinging to its past?

'You from Krasnodar?'

'Moscow.'

'I have a nephew in Moscow. He drives a tram there. He was here last month. There's plenty of trouble in Moscow, he says. Here, we manage. But in Moscow . . .'

'That's right, Granny. And what about Ulitsa Cosmonavtov?'

'There's nothing to interest a young man there,' her companion said. 'Tourists usually visit our church, take a look at the sea and go away.' Her manner did not express any kind of approval of tourists and their habits. 'Maybe you have relatives living here?'

'Maybe.'

'Ulitsa Cosmonavtov runs behind the church. You can reach it down the lane.' She pointed to her left.

'Thanks, Granny.'

As he turned down the lane he caught sight of the driver walking towards the church. Hide-and-seek? Very well, if that was the game they wanted to play.

He flattened himself on the far side of the wall of an abandoned hut and waited for the driver to turn the corner and come down the lane. Soon, he passed the spot where Lyubimov was standing, hurrying his stride now that his quarry was no longer to be seen. At the intersection with Ulitsa Cosmonavtov Lyubimov saw him hesitate and make off to the left. The man was none too bright. He'd soon come to the conclusion that he'd have done better to turn right, then he'd be back, try the right turn, draw a blank there and be back along the lane in something like ten minutes or so. Lyubimov found a stone to sit on, out of sight of anyone coming back up the lane, and settled to await the driver's return. In just over eight minutes he heard the man tramping back up the lane. Then Lyubimov emerged from his hiding place and went in search of the home of Darya Petriayeva, residing at No. 7, Ulitsa Cosmonavtov, starosta of the governing elders of the church.

The small wooden house was newly painted and a bougainvillaea was in dazzling pink flower by the side of the door. Lyubimov's knock was answered by a trim little woman in carpet slippers.

'Yes?'

'I am from *Vperiod* in Moscow. You wrote to us?'

She stared at him for a long while before replying. Her hand was still on the handle of the door and there was no move to let him in.

'How do I know you are from the paper?'

He took his red press card and the letter from his pocket. 'Here, your letter. I am a journalist and we are interested in what you have to tell us. May I come in?'

She searched in a pocket for a pair of glasses, placed them on her nose, took the press card and letter and examined both. Then she peered at Lyubimov and seemed to make up her mind.

'Come in, young man. You are welcome.'

The room she took him into was spotless, most of it taken up by the big square bed with its white embroidered bedspread. On the bed lay a pyramid of cushions, their covers worked in lace. In a corner an oil lamp flickered before an icon, below it was a shelf with a towel hanging from a rail. A table with two chairs stood against a wall and in an easy chair sat a very old man in shirt and trousers, his knees covered by a rug. He was coughing quietly into a handkerchief.

'My husband,' Darya Petriayeva said. 'He is not well.'

The old man showed no interest in Lyubimov and did not respond to his greeting.

'A glass of tea?'

'No, thank you. Just a few minutes of your time.' She had motioned him to one of the chairs and now sat before him on the far side of the table.

'It is all in my letter. Our dvadsatka instructed me to write and so I wrote. We are victims here. These people are wicked. We have no protection from the authorities. We asked the people at our Soviet and they shrugged. Then the militia came, looking for the killer of our poor priest, and they say they found a weapon in the shed of Tolik Chernov and they took him away. But we have known Tolik ever since he was a boy.'

'Are you saying you think he is innocent?'

'Of course he's innocent. Certainly, he drinks too much, but he's as gentle as a child. He's always rescuing birds with broken wings or starving cats, and he's a good son to his parents. Everyone in the village knows he could never kill a priest, and certainly not the dog. He loves all animals, does Tolik, all animals.'

'So you believe someone put the weapon in his shed and then denounced him?'

She nodded.

'Who would that be?'

'We have no idea. But we believe something bad is going on here in Taman. Something wicked. And so we wrote to your paper.'

Lyubimov looked at the letter, lying before him on the table. 'You talk here of robbery at the church. Why did you say that?'

'There was valuable silver in the treasury. Holy things for our services. I know that because Father Vassili had shown us the church's treasure and told us he always kept the only key to the treasury on his person. He said to me once that at night he placed the key under his pillow.' She shook her head. 'A holy, devoted man, God rest his soul. And now we are told there was nothing in the treasury, nothing at all. But would such a church be entirely without treasure, despite what they took from us in the bad days? Of course not. No, it is clear that this gang of so-called restorers from Moscow are really thieves and nothing more.'

'And what do the militia say about that?'

'They ask for evidence. How do we know there was treasure? How can we prove it? Well, of course we can't prove anything. I said to them, "I have seen the silver many times with my own eyes." The captain of militia answered, "Perhaps your priest stole it." Hearing that, I confess I wept. There is no dealing with such people.'

She dabbed at her eyes with a handkerchief, sniffed and rose from the table.

'You shall have some tea.'

'Really, I – '

'I will make it.'

The old man in the corner was nodding slowly. Did he approve of tea or was he falling asleep?

Over the scalding glasses of tea Darya Petriayeva talked of her husband's bad health, talked of the problems of the church, talked of how things had perhaps been better in the old days when everyone knew their place and no one talked nonsense about democracy, which did not suit the Russian people, and everyone could buy the necessities of life. Politeness and the difficulty of drinking the scalding tea kept Lyubimov in his chair, never venturing a contrary opinion for fear of prolonging the monologue. But he noted one remark of Darya Petriayeva's.

'I wouldn't be surprised if they have stolen more than the silver. My cousin, who lives close by the church, says she couldn't sleep at all on the night of the killing – she always slept badly – and in the early hours she was looking out of her window and she saw someone – she doesn't know who it was – coming from the church, carrying something quite big. Only it wasn't a box, such as the silver would be in. It was flat, she says. Something like an icon. Only none of our icons is missing and Father Vassili never talked to me of valuable icons in the treasury. So perhaps my cousin made a mistake. She is elderly and doesn't see as well as she used to.'

He got away at last from the neat little house, the pious and talkative Darya Petriayeva and her silent, wheezing husband, plucking at the rug on his knees and nodding every so often. There still wasn't much of a story here. Accusations of theft which the militia were disinclined to pursue. Elderly ladies seeing dark figures with parcels from their bedroom windows. One Tolik Chernov who loved animals and who could never bring himself to kill a dog. A gang of bullies pretending to rescue Taman's famous church. And were they restoring it? Lyubimov made his way back along the lane to take a look at the restoration work. There was still an hour to the appointment for dinner.

The sun was hanging low now over the steppe, bathing the village in golden light and turning the china blue domes to purple. The breeze brought a salt tang in from the sea. The insistent chirp of the crickets was abating. A dog howled somewhere.

He reached the church and walked slowly round to the rear. The back of the building was encased in scaffolding. On the walkway at roof level three men were sitting, their legs dangling over the edge of the planks. They were smoking and a bottle stood between them. A game of cards was in progress. It was still light enough for Lyubimov to see that no work had been done on the peeling stucco and broken-down gutters. He watched for a few moments and then turned back to the main street and headed for the stolovaya and supper.

The meal was served in the side room of the stolovaya by a sullen village girl in a soiled apron stretched tight across her heavy breasts and thighs and emblazoned with traces of past meals. From the main room with its plastic tables on which squadrons of flies constantly landed only to take off in an endless quest for sustenance, the sounds of disputation, the clatter of crockery and occasional gusts of laughter reached them. The side room, as in all village stolovayas, was a modest improvement on all this, since it was reserved for important persons, including local dignitaries of various descriptions. There were curtains, wooden furniture, a carpet and a chandelier. The buffet boasted a modest display of cut glass bowls and decanters. The tablecloth was passably clean, the smell of cabbage water less pervasive.

With the cucumber salad a bottle of Kubanskaya vodka was mysteriously produced. The savage laws against public drinking had clearly not established themselves in the side rooms of Mother Russia.

The chairman of the Taman Soviet, with the vivid enamel badge of his rank pinned to his jacket, sat at the head of the table, proud to be entertaining distinguished persons from higher up the ladder. He was a colourful apparition: sharp brown suit, red shirt, yellow tie, all surmounted by an open, ruddy face topped with spiky jet-black hair. There were half a dozen pens and pencils poking above the top of his breast pocket, the true signs of his elevation from tractor driver to important person. There appeared to be no harm, no guile and little mental competence in the man.

Baranov sat, silent and watchful, on the chairman's right, with Marchenko opposite him. Lyubimov was seated on the fourth side of the table. Marchenko had filled the vodka glasses and now raised his own to eye-level.

'A toast to our distinguished guest from Moscow and to the success of his mission in Taman.'

Lyubimov's glass remained on the table.

'Come on, Slava, my friend, drink up.'

'Sorry,' Lyubimov said, 'but I've already told you my doctor has banned all alcohol. An ulcer. Alcohol is poison for me.'

'Just a little one. Don't tell me you can't take just one draught. And the quality's first-rate.'

'Sorry.'

The others drank and the chairman refilled their glasses and immediately downed his own drink. Soon Marchenko followed him but Lyubimov noticed that Baranov left his drink on the table. He was sipping mineral water.

The chairman of the local Soviet was acting the good-natured host, calling up food, chiding the waitress to get a move on and refilling their glasses.

The borscht was a deep ruby red flecked with yellow, with floating strands of cabbage, and tasted good. It made a pleasing counterpoint to the slightly sour tang of the moist black bread.

'Excellent,' Marchenko was saying. 'The best bread in

the Kuban is made down here.' His mouth was full as he spoke.

'An excessively greedy eater,' Lyubimov thought. 'It tells one something about the man. I daresay he's that way with money too.'

Meat and potatoes followed the borscht. Marchenko called toasts in rapid succession, still trying to get Lyubimov to drink, succeeding only in putting the chairman into a drunken stupor in which he first grinned idiotically at his guests, then tried to get a purchase on the waitress's ample behind, and ended with his face flat on the table, snoring quietly.

'So,' Baranov said, 'you've been looking round this wretched place?'

'That's right.'

'What did you find?'

'Not much.'

There was a silence. Marchenko appeared to be in a vodka-induced haze and was taking no interest in the conversation.

'Stepan Stepanovitch tells me you had a letter of complaint about me and my colleagues.'

'That is so.'

'Have you found any evidence down here?'

'Some. But I haven't finished my investigation.'

'I think you owe me rather more information than that, seeing that I may figure unfavourably in your article.'

'Well, I hear of bad behaviour on the part of your team. I also hear that the locals don't believe the militia have the right man. And I hear stories of figures emerging at night from the church with parcels. And of course, we all know the church's silver is missing from the treasury. But all that's only the outcome of an afternoon's work. You could say it isn't much to hang a story on, seeing that I have no corroboration of all these matters yet.'

Baranov smiled. 'And you believe the stories?'

'I didn't say that. I was merely answering your query about what I'd found so far.'

'But you intend to pursue all this?'

'It's my job,' Lyubimov said amiably. 'The paper has sent me a long way. I can hardly have dinner and report back that all's well in Taman.'

'This is where their fucking glasnost leads you,' Marchenko said suddenly. 'Would any of this have happened in the old days? Not on your life.' His sweeping gesture overturned a glass, and he dabbed at the pool of liquid on the tablecloth. 'In the old days – I'd call them the days of discipline and civic responsibility – newspapers had something better to do with their time and money. A journalist would come down here, discover our positive achievements and give us a choice piece of prose about how the Kuban is advancing to Communism. Stuff to inspire. But now? What will our friend the journalist from Moscow do? Why, he'll write that the militia in the Kuban have the wrong man; that the local church has been robbed; that I am not doing my duty. All lies, all destructive propaganda making for indiscipline among the masses. I've told him,' leaning confidentially towards Baranov, 'I've told the fellow what it is.' He brought a fist down on the table. 'Journalistic hooliganism! Free speech is a very fine thing, very fine. But they misuse it, my dear Petya. They turn freedom into licence. They destabilise.' He had difficulty with the word and repeated it carefully. 'De-stabil-ise, that's what glasnost leads to.' He winked knowingly. 'Brezhnev understood a thing or two. The old man knew how to handle us Russians.'

'You're a Ukrainian,' Baranov said coldly, trying to shut him up. But the vodka was full-strength and doing its work.

'I'm a party man above all,' Marchenko said. 'I may be a Ukrainian but I'm not a Jew.' He relapsed into silence.

'Let me give you a word of friendly advice,' Baranov said to Lyubimov. 'May I?'

'Please do.'

Baranov leaned forward. There was still a smile on his face. 'My advice to you is to drop all this. There isn't a story in it. You'll only upset the local people, the authorities, and things could end badly for you. I speak as a friend. I, too, am from Moscow, and I work all the time with these peasants. I tell you, it can only end badly if you go ferreting about when the militia and Stepan Stepanovitch's department have already made up their minds.' He paused, the smile fixed like a rictus on his face. 'That is my advice.'

'Thank you,' Lyubimov said. 'You have helped me to make up my mind.' He searched in his pocket, pulled out a rouble note and threw it on the table.

'What's that?'

'When I'm on an assignment I never accept hospitality. Like that, no one can say I have been influenced in what I write. Our two friends look pretty incapable, so perhaps you'd see they collect my contribution.' He rose from the table. 'And thank you for your advice.'

On the way out he bestowed a 'good night' and a cheerful grin on the waitress, who scowled back at him. He decided he was not among friendly people. It was beginning to smell like a story.

In the main room of the stolovaya he found the driver.

'Where am I sleeping tonight?'

'I'll take you there. Is Stepan Stepanovitch coming?'

'If you carry him.'

The driver shrugged. 'Come on.'

The room turned out to be a tolerably clean attic in a house on the edge of the village. It contained a narrow bed, a chair, a wardrobe, a strip of carpet and nothing more. Lyubimov was not sleepy. He settled in the chair to re-read the Taman chapter of Lermontov's novel. The hero, Pechorin, had been billeted in a hut on the edge of the village, overlooking the sea. There was a sea breeze in the tale and a sea breeze from the Black Sea now. Lermontov had described a southern moon, clothing itself in clouds, a rising mist, 'two little stars, like guiding beacons, sparkling in the dark blue vault.' Now the southern sky was a mass of stars, but Lermontov's moon was still in the heavens and there were even wispy clouds scudding across it from time to time. Pechorin had walked down the incline to the shore, where the drama had been played out. If this was a literary pilgrimage Lyubimov decided a walk to the shoreline was mandatory.

Pechorin had described it:

> The shore fell abruptly towards the sea, and below, with an incessant murmur, the dark blue waves splashed. The moon mildly surveyed the element, both restless and submissive to her, and by her light I could distinguish, far from the shore, two ships whose motionless black rigging was outlined, gossamer-like, against the pale horizon.

Lyubimov let himself out of the house and walked the short distance to the sea road. Things were different now. The road, deserted when Pechorin had stolen out for his tryst with the strange girl, now had houses along its landward side. No ships with black rigging rode at anchor beyond the small harbour. It was too dark to see what Pechorin had seen of the distant shore of the Crimea. But as literary pilgrimages went this one was promising. Lyubimov felt suitably moved, even excited.

He decided to walk along the beach, the surf only a few feet away, just as Pechorin had walked there and had overheard the conversation between the smugglers. He scrambled down the steep bank and regained a firm foothold on the strip of sand. There was just enough light from the moon for him to find his way, just as Pechorin, wrapped in his *beshmet*, his pistol in his belt, had found his way to near-disaster. Pechorin had hidden behind a rock to overhear the smugglers. When Lyubimov came to an outcrop of rocks he sat down, listened to the murmur of the surf and imagined himself into the famous scene, set by Lermontov 150 years before. Then he began to feel rather foolish, like an impressionable student with his head stuffed full of the works of the romantic poets. He got up, climbed back onto the road and slowly walked back towards the house.

The clouds had thickened and now the moon was obscured. He never saw the two figures emerging from the far side of the house – only heard the crunch of gravel a moment before he was seized from behind, an arm locked around his throat so that he found he could not utter a sound. A fist was driven viciously into his stomach, and though he was winded, the other man's grip on him made it impossible to double up. He gasped for breath, felt himself choking, his head seeming to burst. The fist was driven into his stomach again. Then the grip on his neck was released and he felt himself sinking to the ground. A thought flashed into his mind: now for the kicks to the head. Instinctively, as he fell, he buried his head between his folded arms. It would be the head or the crotch if they knew what they were doing. And what about the ribs? He decided he must protect his head at any cost. But there were no more blows. Their instructions must have been very specific: frighten him, don't ruin him.

'Don't meddle,' a voice said. 'Just don't meddle and you'll get out of Taman in one piece. We don't appreciate you shitbags from the Moscow newspapers. So don't meddle.'

He heard the sound of gravel again as the two figures disappeared. And as he lay gasping and tenderly holding his bruised stomach, an absurd thought installed itself in his mind. Was it not strange that the man who had told him not to meddle had a strong Ukrainian accent? Strange because Pechorin in Lermontov's tale had noticed that the sinister blind boy had a Ukrainian accent at one moment, and spoke perfect Russian the next.

No, it wasn't really strange at all. Just the kind of stupid idea one would get from trying to push romantic literary parallels too far.

After a few minutes he rose painfully to his feet, entered

the house, found mounting the stairs exceedingly unpleasant, and collapsed onto the bed without undressing. A good while later he managed, fitfully, to get some sleep. He felt a kind of gratitude to the man with the Ukrainian accent, who had neatly answered the question which had been bothering him. Was there or was there not a story in it?

Most probably there was.

5

The auctioneer was using his spectacles as a prop. They would travel back and forth to his nose without much regard for whether he needed to read the catalogue which lay open on the lectern before him. He liked to whip them off to wave at a bidder at the back of the room, then on again in order to peer over them at the row of young persons taking telephone bids over to his left. Above him, high on the wall, bids were flashing on the electronic display in six currencies. The black girl at the keyboard below the auctioneer's dais contemplated her fingers listlessly as she punched in the bids barely seconds after the auctioneer's fluting voice had uttered them.

'Lot 187. A Johann Winck. Late eighteenth. A charming thing. What am I started at, fifteen thousand dollars? Thank you, sir. Fifteen – twenty – twenty-five.'

The spectacles pointed here and there among the throng of spectators in rows before him. Others stood around the walls, some wandering in and out of the room. The Johann Winck – an effulgent burst of flowers in a crystal vase but badly in need of cleaning – was held up by two impassive youths. No serious bidders in the room even glanced at the picture. Their eyes were on the auctioneer's mobile and meaningful spectacles, which pointed now to the bank of telephones.

'I have thirty-five thousand dollars on the telephone. Forty on my right. Do you have forty-five, Heidi?'

Heidi, an emaciated blonde in a black shift, was uttering monosyllables into the phone and flicking a pencil from time to time in the direction of the auctioneer. Now Heidi did indeed have forty-five thousand dollars, then fifty-five, and soon seventy-five.

The bidding jerked forward, now in tens, to reach a hundred and fifty thousand dollars. The black girl's computer expressed the sum in dollars, yen, Deutschmarks, French and Swiss francs and pounds sterling. It was solid money in all six currencies.

'One hundred and fifty thousand dollars on the telephone,' the auctioneer was saying. 'Against you, sir, I'm afraid. No? One hundred and fifty against all in the room?'

The gavel held in his perfectly manicured hand came down with a small, definitive crack. The two youths removed the flowers in their vase to the space behind the dais, and Heidi whispered a word to her successful bidder far off in Zurich or Los Angeles. The electronic screen wiped itself. The auctioneer ran a hand through his blow-dry, replaced the spectacles where they belonged on his nose and peered through them at the catalogue.

'Lot 188. Olaf August Hermansen. My bid at fifteen thousand dollars . . .'

Out on Fifty-second Street a taxi drew up outside the auction house and the man who got out searched in a wallet for a ten-dollar bill.

'You going in there, mister?'

The driver had talked all the way from Columbus Circle without coaxing a word out of his passenger. The man nodded as he handed over the money.

'It true they sold that painting there for forty million?'

The passenger nodded.

'What asshole pays forty million bucks for a picture is what I wanta know.'

The passenger glanced back towards the cab. His voice was guttural, heavily accented. 'A Japanese asshole,' and he strode across the wide sidewalk towards the bronze and travertine marble portals of the auction house. He was a thick-set man, maybe in his mid-forties, maybe more, sallow skin, high cheekbones, a macho moustache carefully trimmed and greying at the edges, intelligent and mistrustful eyes under thick brows – a self-contained, possibly dangerous figure.

The security man at the door nodded to him and received nothing in reply. In the crowded auction room he moved quietly among the small groups of dealers, paying no attention to blow-dry and his ever-mobile spectacles.

'At forty-five thousand now. Against you at forty-five thousand. Against you, madam. Any more?'

A pause and the crack of the gavel.

The thick-set man, who was from Soviet Armenia, had moved by stages to the back of the room, nodding here and there and receiving acknowledgements in reply. He came abreast of a large man immaculate in dark grey mohair, gold at his wrists, a discreet tie – a heavy figure, bull-necked, with clean-shaven jowls and a completely bald head.

'Mr Kurtz, good morning to you.'

The big man nodded, his eyes still on the auctioneer.

'You in the market?'

'There's a picture I believe isn't quite what it seems. I may bid.'

'Ah.' A pause. The electronic display winked dollars, yen and other goodies at the assemblage. There was activity at the telephones.

'One hundred against you all now,' from blow-dry.

'This isn't your line, Grigoriev.' The big man still hadn't looked at his companion.

'Matter of fact,' the Armenian said, 'I looked in hoping to see you. I had interesting news.'

'From over there?'

'Over there, as you put it. Something rather extraordinary, I believe.'

'It is the extraordinary that interests me. You will know that.'

'Precisely. When can we talk, Mr Kurtz, sir?'

Ignoring the question, the big man pointed with a surprisingly delicate forefinger at a line in his catalogue.

'You see, my dear Grigoriev, "Antwerp Harbour at Sunset" by van der Meuwen. It may well be Antwerp but it is not a van der Meuwen.'

'Who, then?'

The question was again ignored.

'At forty thousand dollars I am interested. No more.'

The auctioneer had reached the lot, which he described as 'a most attractive little scene'. Bidding was sluggish. The big man, immobile at the back of the room, entered with a scarcely perceptible nod of his massive head at thirty thousand dollars. If it was something more desirable than a van der Meuwen no one else in the room seemed to know as much.

'Mr Kurtz, to you sir, at thirty thousand.'

The auctioneer consulted his catalogue as Kurtz and the Armenian made their way towards the door.

'We will go to my office if you wish after I have settled matters here.'

A half-hour later the two men sat opposite each other in pale pigskin easy chairs, a glass-topped coffee table between them. The Armenian sat four-square in his chair, workman's hands resting on his thighs, spread apart. He had been Genrikh Grigorian some forty years back in his native city of Yerevan, later calling himself Grigoriev in Moscow, where a Russian name carried advantages.

'Yes,' he was saying. 'I had a message from over there. You must understand what I have to say is – ' he searched for a suitable word ' – tentative? At this stage we cannot be talking business. We talk as friends, you understand, sir, as friends.'

Kurtz nodded. He was a man who spoke little, on the principle that he could have nothing to say himself that he did not know already, whereas other people's talk always had the possibility of profit buried somewhere within it. Silence, he found, led to people saying more than they had intended. And so he nodded and said nothing.

'This news I have – rather astonishing, you see. It concerns an icon. You, of course, have dealt in icons.'

A nod. 'I bought an item from you last year.'

'Quite. But this is altogether special. My man tells me he has been offered a Roublev, no less.'

Kurtz's expression did not change. 'Authenticated in Russia?'

Grigoriev shook his head. 'Completely unknown in Russia. A find – an astonishing find.'

'Where?'

'Later we will come to that. At this stage I want to put a question to you.'

'Put your question.'

Grigoriev stubbed out his cigarette, drew another from a pack and lit it, blowing a lungful of smoke to cloud the surface of the table.

'My position is this. If my friends have indeed located a genuine Roublev and if, as I am told, it is no less than another version – a *third* version, you understand – of his masterpiece, the Old Testament Trinity and if, as I am again told, it is in satisfactory condition and if I am able to deliver it to you, secretly, unknown and undamaged, what is that worth to you, Mr Kurtz?'

There was a long pause.

'Firstly,' Kurtz said at last, 'I would need authentication by my nominated expert.'

'Here?'

'Am I to make a commitment?'

'I would require that. You understand – there are heavy risks, very heavy risks. Also preliminary expenses – grasping people must be looked after.'

'In that case, authentication in Russia by my own expert before any money changes hands.'

'And this authentication, you will bear the cost?'

'If you can persuade me the project is soundly based,

I will bear the cost. But I will need persuading that it is a Roublev we are chasing and not a wild goose off the steppes.'

'Naturally, sir.'

'And I would need to be sure that what my man had authenticated in Russia was what was delivered here.'

'Of course. Your man will make his mark on the item.'

Another pause.

'So how much do you want?' Kurtz posed the question as if the answer were a matter of indifference to him.

'I was asking you for an offer,' Grigoriev said. 'Without obligation.'

'I don't deal in that way.'

'A dangerous enterprise, you understand, with high risks and heavy expenses back there.'

'So name a figure.'

'Also, my risk is that having bought over there I may fail through no fault of mine to deliver as required.'

'That is your problem. It would not interest me.'

'You realise that a third Trinity would be virtually priceless in the market. Like an undiscovered Vermeer. Every museum would have to bid.'

'Perhaps, but you know perfectly well your icon cannot find its way into the market. The Soviets would slap injunctions on us in our own courts at once. So it can only be worth what a private collector will pay for it. That is where my own risk comes in.'

'I estimate,' Grigoriev said, 'that a serious collector of icons would pay twenty million dollars. At least.'

Kurtz allowed another thin smile to crease his lips. 'You are talking nonsense. The buyer would not even be able to tell his friends. A Roublev out of Russia? A very hot potato.'

'Give me a price, Mr Kurtz.'

'If it is all you say it is, and subject always to quality and condition, let us say up to five million.'

Grigoriev laughed. 'You bargain hard, sir.'

'Show me the article and if it's worth more than five to me I will pay more than five.'

'It is not worth my time at less than ten.'

'It is not worth mine at more than seven.'

'I would be free to offer it elsewhere if your price is unsatisfactory.'

'And I would be free to refuse it if I do not like the look of it.'

'Between friends at this stage,' Grigoriev said.

'If you wish.' Kurtz lifted his bulk out of the armchair and slowly made his way across the room to a secretaire in a far corner. It had been fitted out as a drinks cabinet, the false spines of calf with their gilt lettering fronting not books but bottles of liquor.

'A vodka, since we may have something here to which we can drink?'

'Why not?'

'And you can tell me a little more, perhaps.'

Settled with vodkas and chasers of Perrier, the two faced each other across the table.

'I know of the monk Roublev, of course. I know of his Trinity in the Tretyakov gallery in Moscow and the second version in the cathedral at Zagorsk. I also know of the doubts about the attribution of this second version which surfaced throughout the nineteenth century.'

'Many clever copies of icons were made at that time but our best experts have pronounced the Zagorsk version an authentic Roublev,' Grigoriev said.

'The trouble with your best experts is that they have always refused to submit anything to modern scientific dating tests.'

'The bureaucracy doesn't want anything anywhere to be devalued. Nevertheless, I believe the Zagorsk version is authentic.'

'And this third Trinity? Why should that be authentic? Why not an eighteenth- or nineteenth-century fake? After all, it is a lot to swallow – the sudden emergence of a genuine

Roublev after what, almost six hundred years? And in good condition, you say?' Kurtz shrugged his massive shoulders and waved a hand in a dismissive gesture.

Grigoriev threw back the remains of his vodka, wiping his lips with the back of his hand.

'Your man will have to decide.'

'That will only be the first stage,' Kurtz said evenly. 'I will want a laboratory test when we get it back here.'

'Security would make that difficult.'

'I pay well for confidential reports. If the report is negative in this case, you will owe me the sum involved.'

'I understand.'

'Is the wood cracked?'

'I believe not.'

'And the size?'

'I am told about one metre or so tall.'

'Difficult to transport.'

'That's my problem, Mr Kurtz.'

Kurtz slowly inclined his head. 'That is indeed so.' He reached for the glasses, moved to the secretaire, filled them and returned to his seat.

'So what do we say?' Grigoriev asked. 'Do you have an expert ready to travel over there?'

'I do. It can be arranged in, say, a few days.'

'Let us drink to that.'

They lifted their glasses, the Armenian stretching forward to clink his glass against the other. 'To our little venture.'

Kurtz drew back slightly from the contact and drank without saying a word. Then, 'I will draw up a simple agreement and we will both sign it.'

'If you wish, though it cannot be a matter for the courts.'

'I will not need the support of the judicial system, my dear Grigoriev. It is sufficient that you are – what shall we say – vulnerable?'

Grigoriev got to his feet. 'The beauty of our business

relations,' he said evenly, 'lies in the fact that so are you, Mr Kurtz, sir, so are you.'

Back at Columbus Circle Grigoriev caught the D train. By the time the train had reached Sheepshead Bay on the elevated, he had achieved a profound scepticism about the Roublev. Was it genuine? Was it in marketable condition? Could it get past Soviet customs? Could Kurtz find a buyer and, if so, how could one be sure of payment? With the train clattering its way along Brighton Beach Avenue, showering sparks on the shoppers below, he fell to reflecting on the complexity of the project. Baranov, in his parochial and unsophisticated fashion, would be treating the whole thing as a simple transaction: finding a buyer, negotiating a price, ensuring delivery. 'A fool,' Grigoriev mused. 'A small-time thief who's stumbled onto a serious deal. When it comes to the moment of truth, the man could be a confounded nuisance.'

The train rattled to a halt at Brighton Beach and Grigoriev emerged into the afternoon heat and made his way down the iron steps to ground level and the elbowing mass of shoppers. Middle-aged, thick-set men and women in unsuitable clothes, with flash youths and their girls here and there, leaning against clapped-out cars or idling on street corners. The snatches of overheard talk were mainly Russian. In the window of the Rabinowitz Pharmacy showcards had been scrawled in cyrillic script. A discount store offered unbeatable bargains – closeouts, bankrupt stocks, fire sales. Madame Zita advertised her beauty salon in roman and cyrillic, without prejudice. The former summer haunt of the Brooklyn elite had been handed to the Russian immigrants. Someone had named it Little Odessa. Grigoriev felt comfortable here.

He walked the few paces to Fifth Street and headed down towards the ocean. The street was lined with apartment blocks dating back to the thirties, once elegant, now with peeling stucco and bricks in need of steam cleaning. Whoever had financed these developments had felt the need for a touch of class and had lavished it on the porticoes and on nothing else. Some were mock-Tudor, others faintly Egyptian or with Corinthian pilasters implying Roman splendour and maybe a touch of Roman decadence to give the realtors a pitch to the Jewish matrons who had been the modestly affluent first buyers.

Grigoriev turned in to No. 11, a five-storey building badly in need of renovation. He let himself into the ground floor apartment and made straight for the telephone.

'Lev, meet me at the Gastronom in half an hour. We'll eat something.'

'Is it important? You see, I – '

'I said half an hour.'

He rang off, went to the shower room, stripped and treated himself to a cold shower. As the water sluiced over his body, he picked up his thoughts. Refreshed, he dried himself, put on a change of clothes and made his way out of the apartment and down to the boardwalk. Baranov, he decided, was out of his class. If this was indeed an Andrei Roublev it was no project for a small-time art thief from Moscow and his gang of bullyboys.

The tide was out, revealing a great expanse of dull brown sand. Gulls swooped and screamed overhead, diving from time to time at the pools left by the tide. On the boardwalk groups of old men in sweat shirts and denims quarrelled in Russian. Sharp young Jews in bright colours sauntered aimlessly, killing time, waiting for a deal, a scam. The Gastronom Kharkov advertised french fries, knishes, franks and soda on its facade. A Russian pop song blared from a radio, enveloping in its sound a solemn foursome playing cards. There were no other customers. The place was filthy and smelt of fried onions and uncertain drains.

Grigoriev chose a table away from the card players and crooked a finger at the waitress who had absent-mindedly looked up from tending her fingernails. She took her time crossing the room.

'Turn that fucking sound down,' Grigoriev said in Russian. 'And bring me a Schlitz. I'll eat later.'

Without a word, the waitress moved behind the bar and the heavy metal sound was cut back. She returned to the table with the can of beer and a glass and banged them down in a weary gesture. She stood by the table while Grigoriev took a long draught of the beer. He put the glass back on the table and wiped the foam from his mouth with the back of his hand.

'You want something?'

'You know what I want.'

He shrugged and drank again.

'Leave me alone. Clear off.'

'You promised the money for Lida's summer camp. I did everything you wanted and you said you'd give me the money. The kid has to take the money this week.'

'Send her round. I'll give it to her.'

The waitress shook her head. 'You can be disgusting with me but I'm not having you interfering with the kid.'

'No visit, no money,' Grigoriev said. 'It's simple. Now fuck off and leave me alone. I'm expecting Lev.'

'I think you should keep your promise. You gave me a terrible time.'

He leaned back in his chair, looking at her. Then he got slowly to his feet, smiling, took a handful of her thick black hair, knotted it round his fist and tugged her head backwards. Her scream rose above the blare of the radio and the card players looked up from their game, looked down again quickly and were suddenly more absorbed than ever in the play.

'Send Lida and she gets the money. Don't send her – no money. And I should have beaten you maybe twice as hard. Now go tell the chef two shashliks and I'll have another beer.'

He released her hair and sat down again. The woman started to say something, thought better of it and walked away. Grigoriev was still smiling. The card players were bidding as if their lives depended on it.

The young man who walked in off the boardwalk was maybe twenty-five, twenty-six, a compact, heavily-muscled figure with a shock of black hair above a face which seemed to have been battered out of true so that the nose was askew and the mouth pulled slightly down to the left. The eyes, pale and blinking, lacked all expression.

He crossed the room, pulled a chair out and sat at Grigoriev's table.

'Bring Lev a beer,' Grigoriev called to the waitress. 'I've ordered food,' he told his companion.

'Thanks, but I've a date for later.'

'The food's ordered. Didn't I invite you to eat?'

'Sure, but you see – '

'Then you'll eat. Now what's the news?'

'They'll pay.'

'How much?'

'A thousand, like you said. I told them next time they get cute it'll double.'

'Did you have to make them see reason?'

The young man grinned, closing his dead eyes as he did so.

'We chatted, y'know. Told them a thing or two, like what happened to Petrovski down on Coney Island Avenue. That kinda impressed them. I didn't raise a finger.' He grinned again.

'And Szamueli?'

'That's for tonight. He'll be good as gold in the morning.'

'So where's the money?'

The young man fished a wad of notes out of his jeans and passed it across the table. 'A grand. It's all there.'

Grigoriev picked up the wad, counting the hundred-dollar bills slowly. Then he peeled one off and passed it back across the table.

'Buy yourself a piece of ass.'

6

'So you've got the story of the sharks who fight perestroika?' Verochka said.

'No, no, I couldn't get the story after all.'

'A long way to go for no story.'

She was smoothing her white chiffon blouse over a pair of breasts which Slava Lyubimov considered should have belonged to a nicer person.

'There was a perfectly good reason why I couldn't write the story of the sharks. You see, when I got to Taman I found they'd all been issued with Party cards and the local secretary had forbidden them to talk to the press. Bureaucracy, you see, my dear Verochka, always bureaucracy.'

He smiled sweetly at her.

Verochka shrugged. 'You won't be making stupid jokes in a minute. He wants to see you. I think he's hopping mad.'

'Of course he is. So would I be if I had the Party's Central Committee breathing down my neck. After all, it's an organisation with a bad case of halitosis.'

'He says for you to go in right away.'

'Without you, my dear Verochka, life in this office would be intolerable.'

She looked puzzled, never sure how to take Lyubimov's cheerful sarcasm. Or was it just conceivably his way of covering up some kind of obscure passion? She was a woman who held her own person in high regard and spent endless time before mirrors.

'Perhaps the most terrible creature in Moscow, and she

has to work in our office,' Lyubimov complained to Anatoli Panov, a shambling giant whose desk abutted his own in the cubicle at the end of the corridor. Panov was no writer – scarcely a journalist, more a dogged sniffer-out of obscure facts which those in the *apparat* were bent on suppressing. These he would serve up in fractured and limping prose, violently beaten out on a series of typewriters, none of which had been able to withstand for long the hammering they received from Panov. He would come stamping down the long corridor from an assignment, fall heavily into his chair, a frown on his Russian workman's face, and after pulling notebook and crumpled papers from his pockets, would attack the typewriter's keyboard as if the wretched and ill-constructed machine was in some way responsible for his difficulties with the art of composition. While he was labouring he would curse continuously under his breath, occasionally allowing an oath to burst forth and provoke Lyubimov to command him to shut up. There was no subtlety and no refinement of any kind in him. 'If ever you'd been unfortunate enough to be sent to interview Josef Stalin,' Lyubimov told him, 'you'd have asked Stalin as your first question why he had to be such a swine all the time.'

'First question and last,' Panov grunted. 'How do you spell glasnost; I've forgotten. As for Verochka, do you think I should take her to Sokolniki Park one Sunday and do terrible things to her behind a bush?'

Now, Lyubimov knocked unnecessarily hard on editor Chelidze's door and marched into the room.

'Ah, genatsvale,' Chelidze said, 'so you are back.'

'I'm back.'

'The people down in Krasnodar have been burning up the wires.'

'The people?'

'Stepan Marchenko, to be exact. I have to tell you he is furious. I also have to tell you I am not exactly pleased myself.'

'Verochka conveyed as much.'

'I am told you got drunk in Taman.'

'False.'

'I am also told you have suggested that the militia down there have arrested the wrong man for murder.'

'They have.'

'And that you insinuated all manner of things against the Moscow restoration team working on the church.'

'I did.'

'Anyway, Marchenko complained to the Central Committee Secretariat and demanded your recall. That's why I called you back.'

'Before I had time to complete my investigation and deliver you a splendid story. Ah well, a sad waste of money.'

Chelidze scratched his head and sighed. What, he wondered, was a man to do? First the Central Committee asks for more material on religious issues. Then, having found a story which at least promised not to bore the readers out of their skulls, one sends a competent reporter to cover it only to be insulted over the telephone from Krasnodar, and no doubt ticked off later by some placeman in the Central Committee who wanted peace and nothing but peace.

'So everyone down there has got it wrong, and you breeze in from Moscow and get at the truth in a flash.'

'Not a flash. I simply talked to the locals, nosed around a bit, formed an opinion of the chief restorer, and would have had a friendly chat with the militia if you hadn't called me back. As it is, I'm afraid you've killed the Taman end of the story but I'm interested to follow up one Peter Alexandrovitch Baranov, chief restorer, when he gets back to Moscow.'

Chelidze got up from his chair, walked round to the far side of the desk and patted Lyubimov on the shoulder.

'Impetuosity, genatsvale, such impetuosity. Not wise, not at all wise for a talented man who naturally wants his career to prosper. Take my advice, my dear fellow, stop chasing after the tricky ones, the stories which upset them over there.'

He nodded in the general direction of the Central Committee offices in Staraya Ploshchad. He still had a pudgy fist on Slava Lyubimov's shoulder.

'I know it would be useless to suggest you'd do best to go for the quiet life. But at least, try to steer away from issues which land us all in trouble. After all, if they lose patience with us over there, bang goes our paper allocation and we'll find ourselves talking to a handful of readers instead of our millions. Better to give the millions a piece of the cake than insist on a whole cake for a tiny handful, no?'

'As a matter of fact,' Lyubimov said, 'I don't actually think so. What I think is that all this licking of Central Committee arses will end badly. Times are changing, Georgi Galaktionovitch, things – people – aren't the same out there.' He nodded out towards the street.

'What do you mean, aren't the same?'

'Take the queues,' Lyubimov said.

'What about the queues? Everyone knows there are shortages now we have perestroika, whereas there were hardly any before we had perestroika.'

'I don't mean that. I mean the comparative length of the queues – that's the thing to keep your eye on. You only have to walk around the city to see that as the queues at McDonalds and the Lancome perfume shop get longer, the queue to see our revered Vladimir Ilyich Lenin gets shorter. Don't you think our citizens are trying to tell us something?'

'Never mind what they may be telling *us*,' Chelidze said. 'What I am telling *them* is that we need order instead of crime, work discipline rather than glasnost, and a decent sausage instead of Swiss experts on monetarism from the World Bank. In short, we need positive stories in our paper rather than your kind of muckraking journalism; stories to encourage our people to ever greater efforts.'

He looked at Lyubimov, shook his head and removed

his hand from his shoulder. 'Talent,' he said, returning to his chair, 'you have talent. What you lack, my friend, and what only comes with the hard knocks of experience, is a sense of proportion, a willingness to submit to the superior, collective wisdom of the Party.'

It was Slava Lyubimov's turn to shake his head. 'I'm afraid,' he said, 'that history is passing the Party by and the Party is too busy fussing over my stories to see it.'

'The Party,' Chelidze said darkly, 'will know how to defend itself. Meanwhile, what am I to do with you?'

'Accept the piece I'm going to write on a mysterious murder in Taman and the strange antics of a gang of Moscow restorers who don't seem to restore anything.'

'I absolutely forbid it. If you write it we shan't print it.'

'And how would you feel if I followed up this ruffian Baranov here in Moscow? You know – what is going on in the Restoration Works? Is anything being restored, and if not, why not?'

'Again, I forbid it.'

'I thought so. It was worth trying, though.' He got up to go. 'As to being drunk, your Marchenko was paralytic and so was the chairman of the Taman Soviet. Baranov was too smart to get drunk and so was I. But I knew they were bound to say I'd been drinking. It's what they always say.' He turned at the door. 'You know, Georgi Galaktionovitch, Lermontov got the atmosphere of Taman just about right. Great man.' And he left the room, closing the door quietly behind him.

As he passed Verochka's desk he blew her a kiss. And as he walked slowly down the long corridor, the clatter and chatter of editorial activity ringing in his ears, he decided that, Chelidze's diktat notwithstanding, he owed it to himself to take a closer look at Peter Baranov. Back in the cubicle Panov was chewing savagely on a pencil stub, a frown creasing his forehead, his great paws covering the keys of his Erica. Discarded and crumpled sheets of copy paper, each with a few words typed on it, littered the floor in a circle round the waste bin. Panov's aim was uncertain.

'Genatsvale has killed the Taman story,' Lyubimov said.

'Why?'

'They got at him from the Krasnodar Soviet. I'm not surprised. I wandered into some kind of cesspit down there.'

'And you're giving up?'

'I asked Genatsvale if I could follow up the story at this end.'

'And he forbade it?'

'He forbade it.'

Panov allowed the frown to dissolve into a grin. It made him look curiously dangerous, like a feral cat defending its supper.

'That will make two in one day.'

'What's the second one?'

Panov nodded towards the scattered notes on his desk. 'It'll be this business of the Olympic kids I've been working on. When I manage to get it down on paper, that is.'

'Trouble with the lead?' Lyubimov kicked some of Panov's discarded sheets away as he sat down.

Panov nodded and shrugged. 'You see, every time I think I've got the thing straight in my mind, one of them calls me to say a friend wants to tell me more, and I get another angle on the thing.'

'Well, what's your piece going to *say*?'

'That these kids are exploited, bullied, drugged with steroids and generally given hell in the name of Soviet sporting supremacy.'

'And you think Genatsvale will print that?'

'I'm trying to wrap it up a bit – make it palatable, you know – but the bloody facts keep obtruding themselves. There's this kid I found who won a gold in gymnastics. Her story's pretty hair-raising. Training till she dropped, pills, some lousy diet they invented, the lot. I reckon it's my lead. What do you say?'

'I say it'll make a great story which ends up on the spike.'

Panov nodded. 'Just what I think. That's why I say there will be two no-nos from Genatsvale. Hell, this kid had her health ruined for a lousy gold medal and food parcels for her family. I think I should try to write it and see what happens along the corridor. I might slip a few things past him.'

'You know what they said about Yegorov when he was editor of *Pravda*. Brilliant, they said, never wrong. He could always pick the best line in any article and strike it out. Well, Genatsvale may not be in that class, but he'll tear the balls out of your piece for sure.'

'So what'll you do about your Taman story,' Panov asked. 'A little freelance work?'

'Trouble is, I've got a couple of pieces to put together on the construction scandal in Ryazan. But this afternoon I think I'll take a ride on the Metro.'

It took Lyubimov nearly an hour that afternoon to reach the Moscow Central Restoration Works near the Kaluzhskaya Metro station on the southern outskirts of the city. It was, he decided, a dump, in need of extensive restoration itself. Rusting iron gates led to a courtyard with a long two-storeyed building of dirty red brick beyond. The yard was littered with pallets, broken masonry and statues in varying stages of disrepair. Lenin, Kalinin, Sverdlov . . . how well he knew them. Lenin, his arm outstretched, finger pointing to a rosy future in the gesture everyone understood, was there in some kind of weather-worn composition, only the famous finger had been broken off, revealing the top of the armature. Would there be a new finger or a new statue for the village that had sent Lenin back to Moscow? And where was Brezhnev, where Stalin? Melted down? Ground up for use as aggregate on some highway in the Urals? Was this sad place the Museum of Dashed Hopes of the USSR? Lyubimov wondered if it was a metaphor for something or other. In his mind a sour little piece was already taking shape – something that *Moscow News* might run on its back page and *Vperiod* never would. 'The Broken Finger' might make a title . . . nicely allusive, ironic . . .

There was a workman nearby, shifting planks of wood from one pile to another.

'Where will I find Peter Baranov?'

The man did not look up. 'Ask in the office.' He gestured towards the building, continued to shift his planks.

'Is Baranov in Moscow?'

'It's none of my business where people are. Ask in the office.'

'Thanks for your help,' Lyubimov said. 'Care for a fag?' He offered a packet and the workman took two.

'I've seen him around. Back from the south or wherever. They'll tell you in the office.'

'Is he here now?'

The man didn't look up. 'How the hell should I know?' The effect of the cigarettes had worn off. Lyubimov headed for the entrance to the building.

'Ask for Trofimich, the foreman,' the workman called after him, relenting.

Trofimich proved to be a middle-aged man in a soiled blue work-coat. Some spinal defect had bent him so far forward that his gaze seemed not to rise above Lyubimov's knees. He sat at an ancient desk in an office which boasted a metal filing cabinet, a framed photograph of President Gorbachev and nothing else.

'I am looking for Peter Baranov,' Lyubimov said.

'Official business?'

'Not exactly. We know each other.'

'He isn't here today.'

'Is he in town?'

'Yes, but he's working on a job in his studio at home. We don't expect him in this week.'

'Thanks, I'll contact him there.'

At the door Lyubimov made a show of hesitating and

turning round. 'I forgot, I've mislaid his address. Can you remind me?'

Trofimich took a notebook from a drawer and thumbed through it.

'He lives out at Zaveti Ilyicha.' He scribbled an address on a scrap of paper and handed it over.

'Thanks.' Lyubimov paused. 'I believe he just got back from the south?'

'He was on a job in Taman.'

'He told me before he went it was a cathedral. Not much of a place. But I suppose one stumbles on all kinds of forgotten treasures in places like that.'

'Usually not,' Trofimich said. 'Those country churches were all cleared out in the twenties. Anyway, it's against policy to take anything unless the stuff needs work. In that case we get a chit from the Religious Affairs Department of the local Soviet.'

'I must see what Peter found this time,' Lyubimov said. 'Is he working on something at home?'

Trofimich made an effort to raise his eyes to Lyubimov's face, bracing himself against the desk and leaning back in his chair. The effort cost him a grimace of pain. 'Perhaps,' he said. 'It's none of our business, young man, is it?'

'Quite so,' Lyubimov said. 'Anyway, thanks for the address. Maybe I'll drop out there to see him.'

7

Anton Kurtz's reputation in the New York art market was based on Old Master drawings, within which speciality he was further known as a world authority on the Dutch and North German Schools. He had appeared in New York late in 1949, a young man in a shabby suit and topcoat, carrying a small holdall and a portfolio. In the portfolio were some hundred or so drawings and etchings, among them Rembrandts, Boschs, Dürers, Hobbemas and Cuyps. In his pocket was the entry permit he had won from the US occupation forces in Frankfurt in return for services rendered in the flaccid and largely ineffectual programme of de-Nazification. To a tired and indifferent customs official on Ellis Island he had presented a document certifying that Anton Kurtz was authorised to remove from German territory the art objects as listed, being the property of the said Kurtz family, whose habitation and possessions were now under the control of the military forces of the USSR. The US customs officer had no interest in pursuing the matter further, stamped the document, since he did not know what else to do with it, and waved Anton Kurtz through.

Back in Germany, Kurtz had acted for two years as an interpreter at interrogations, with a sideline as a US undercover man in underground Nazi circles in the US zone of occupation. He would frequent bars in country towns on the instructions of his American handler, chatting up the locals and sniffing out members of the Waffen SS who had gone to ground. He would talk of escape routes and safe houses, putting himself forward as a former SS camp guard on the run. He did this with credibility, given that he spoke from experience: for twenty months, until the collapse of German resistance in the West, he had himself been a guard at Flossenburg, where he had screamed at, flogged and shot his quota of communists and Jews. He was nineteen at the time and a volunteer in Himmler's SS Death's Head camp guard battalions.

Two weeks before the first American patrols reached the camp, Anton Kurtz had slipped away. Having the run of the camp administration block, he had first taken the precaution of extracting his file from the personnel office and burning it. When he presented himself six months later at US headquarters in Frankfurt as the last survivor of a family of the small aristocracy in Silesia who had escaped from east to west across the Reich, he was put on the payroll by a harassed colonel who had long since despaired of tracing the antecedents of anyone eager to help in a thankless task.

Anton Kurtz was not an aristocrat and had never visited Silesia. His father had been a butcher in Trier and carried a prized four-digit Party card dating from the twenties. He had been local organiser of Ernst Rohm's SA brownshirts, and on the night of 9 November 1938, had put on his uniform, armed himself with a cleaver from his shop, and placed himself at the head of a gang of twenty or so similarly equipped men. Shouting anti-semitic slogans provided by the Propaganda Ministry, they had consulted their lists and descended on the Jewish homes and shops in the town. In the orgy of destruction which came to be known as Kristallnacht and lasted until dawn, Kurtz the butcher had smashed his way into the home of a Jewish lawyer named Hartzburg, driven the family into the street, and ransacked the house. In the lawyer's study he had come across a collection of drawings in a locked cabinet. Judging that a lock indicated value, he had helped himself to most of the collection, which he had wrapped in newspaper and carried outside where he joined others of the gang carrying pictures, clothing and items of cut glass and silver for presentation to their various wives waiting at home.

The Hartzburg family had been gassed in Mauthausen camp in 1944. Kurtz senior was crushed by a Russian tank outside Berlin in 1945. The collection of Old Master drawings, still wrapped in an edition of the *Merkür* of early November 1938, had stayed with Kurtz's widow until her son had come to collect it in 1948. The Hartzburg collection was to provide the basis on which Anton Kurtz, over the fruitful years in New York, had transformed himself into a respected judge of North European graphic art. His personal collection, destined for the Metropolitan Museum, was widely admired.

He sat in thought for a while after Grigoriev had left, then he picked up the phone and dialled a number.

'Gordon? Here is Kurtz. We should talk.'

'Certainly. When would you like?'

'It would be good if you could come to my office this afternoon. Is that possible?'

'Everything is possible if it is made worth my while.'

'It is business, and so worth your while.'

'Then I will be with you within the hour.'

Later, seated on the far side of the glass-topped coffee table, as Grigoriev had sat earlier to unveil his scheme, Victor Gordon waited, hands folded across his stomach, for whatever Kurtz had to say.

'It is a matter of authentication,' Kurtz said.

'Of what?'

'An icon. Something well within your expertise, my dear Gordon.'

'An icon of what origin?'

'A Russian icon.'

'Here?'

'No, there.' A pause. 'In the Soviet Union.' Another careful pause. 'I must add that its existence is so far unknown to the Soviet authorities.'

'Ah.'

Gordon, like Kurtz, was a listener rather than a talker.

'My source tells me that this is a quite extraordinary find. We are talking of substantial value, you understand.'

There was an impressive immobility about the man Gordon. The sallow, almost yellow skin was stretched tight over strong cheekbones, the eyes a liquid brown under heavy brows, a mane of greying hair left long at the sides and back. Women found him difficult to resist, responding to the enigmatic, silent personality. The long, tapering fingers were untwined now and brought together, fingertips united, below his chin. Victor Gordon had been born Viktor Gorokhov in Munich in 1950, only son of one Vladimir Gorokhov, a leading figure in the emigré NTS, Narodno-Trudovoy-Soyuz, the People's Labour League, centred in Berlin. On the morning of 12 October 1957, as Vladimir Gorokhov entered the lobby of his apartment building in a western suburb of Munich, a young man approached him, holding a thin metal tube before him. A moment later a small cloud of prussic acid vapour exploded from a glass ampoule in Gorokhov's face. He died the following day. His assassin reported back to Department 13 of the KGB's First Chief Directorate that the assignment had been successfully accomplished. The autopsy gave as cause of death 'heart failure', since prussic acid causes the blood vessels to contract as in an episode of cardiac arrest and then relax after death, thus obscuring the action of the poison. It was to be eight years before a KGB defector in Washington revealed the facts about Vladimir Gorokhov's death. The defector had been a member of the team sent by Moscow to dispose of Gorokhov, Lev Rebet and other leaders of NTS. Gorokhov's son, brought up in the United States by his mother and soon to be a US citizen, heard of his father's fate at the age of twelve.

These facts are necessary to an understanding of Victor Gordon's motivation in the matter at hand.

'Our little, er, venture, you see, must be carried through

without the participation in any form of the Soviet authorities,' Kurtz said. 'Thereby, of course, hangs some risk, but I fancy that risk is not great.' He looked carefully at the immobile figure on the far side of the coffee table. 'I take it you have no objections to acting in a manner which would not be in the interests of the Soviets?'

'You know something of my background,' Gordon said. 'You know what they did to my father, to my family. What have I in common with these people?'

'Also,' Kurtz said, 'the rewards in this venture of ours are fully commensurate with the risks.'

'And the article, what is the article?'

'It is a fifteenth-century icon of, I believe, inestimable value. A quite extraordinary find.'

Kurtz's verbal technique of revealing his story layer by layer, much as if he were peeling an onion, was perfectly suited to Gordon's own temperament. He was never hurried, never enthused, never seen to be animated in any way when it came to trading in art objects. His reputation as an expert on Russian religious art, and a trader of formidable subtlety and cunning in the objects of his expertise, was soundly based. Much like the great Bernard Berenson in the case of Italian Renaissance paintings, Gordon was a man whose artistic integrity had never been impeached but who would bend an authentication, gloss over the weakness in a provenance where very large numbers were at stake.

'And you wish that I examine this article, I take it, for a valuation?'

'I need your opinion on the simple matter of whether it is or is not genuine. The question of value does not arise in this instance, since it is unlikely to find its way onto the open market.'

'You say genuine. A genuine what?'

'An Andrei Roublev.'

'You are saying that there exists in the USSR a hitherto unknown Roublev?'

'That is my understanding.'

'You realise,' Gordon said, 'that that is a highly improbable thing.'

'Of course. Nevertheless, a man whom I know well has come to me with the information that a third version of Roublev's Old Testament Trinity has shown up and can be obtained. What I need is someone to go over there, examine the article and provide me with an opinion. You are the person best qualified to do it.'

'I have some questions.'

The fingertips were gently tapping against each other. There was no discernible expression on Gordon's face.

'Please.'

'First, where is the icon?'

'My understanding is that it will be available for inspection in Moscow.'

'In whose hands?'

'An associate of my contact. I believe these are serious people.'

'And you say the authorities there know nothing and are to know nothing?'

'Correct.'

'When is this inspection to be?'

'As soon as you can get over there. Next week, I hope.'

A pause. Then: 'What are you offering?'

'What is your fee?'

'It depends. If it proves not to be a Roublev I would expect five thousand dollars and my expenses. You will see no profit and so I would not wish to burden you with excessive expense.'

'And if it is indeed a Roublev?'

'Then, my dear Kurtz, I become very much more expensive, since we will be talking in millions when it is disposed of.'

'On the other hand,' Kurtz said pointedly, 'even if it is genuine I run great risks in getting it to market and may end up with heavy expenses and no profit. You will understand . . .'

'I understand perfectly and for that reason I will tie an important part of my reward to the successful sale of the item.'

'You are proposing a contingency arrangement?'

'Precisely. It is done to help you, my dear Kurtz, in the problematic early stage of the exercise.'

Kurtz inclined his massive head. 'On the other hand – and you will forgive the implications of what I say – you will find yourself in the invidious position of someone who has developed a vested interest in the icon being a genuine Roublev. Surely this might affect your judgement? Might it not tip you over into an affirmative position if the evidence proves to be, shall we say, inconclusive?'

There was still no expression on Gordon's face. 'I have my reputation to consider. I would not wish to have said yes and subsequently be found to be wrong by someone else you might show it to here.'

'Come, come,' Kurtz said, allowing a hint of impatience to creep into his voice. 'You know perfectly well that there can never be a public debate on the matter. The thing will be sold privately by me as a genuine Andrei Roublev icon and the intense privacy of the transaction would be the guarantee that your attribution can never be questioned. Certainly, my client would never want to have it pointed out to him that he had spent a considerable fortune on a fake.'

'Very well,' Gordon said, 'if you prefer I will quote you a straight fee, Roublev or not Roublev, of a quarter of a million dollars.' He replaced his hands in his lap. 'Plus expenses,' he added.

'You were always a difficult man to deal with,' Kurtz said. 'A hard man. Your proposal is impossible.'

'Then I offer the following: in the event it is genuine, fifty thousand dollars, with a further three hundred thousand when you have disposed of it.'

'You are trusting, my friend. It is not like you.'

'I am not. It is simply that I rely on your knowing that

you will have incurred my extreme displeasure if you should double-cross me, and I judge that is something you would not wish.'

'Threats?'

'Certainly not. Just a delicately phrased reference to the realities of our respective situations. After all – and if I may be frank for a moment beyond the limit of good manners – I shall be uniquely placed in the matter since I alone shall know this entire story, shall I not?'

'Not so. My contact here is necessarily informed on all these matters.' Kurtz had risen and moved over to the drinks cabinet behind Gordon's chair. 'I have to tell you that he and his associates are dangerous people, not to be trifled with.' He was moving bottles and glasses as he spoke. 'A martini, perhaps?'

'Thank you, no.' Gordon got to his feet, turned to face Kurtz. 'My fee is not negotiable. I am not an Arab. By all means call me when you have decided which of my propositions suits you best.'

'Both are too harsh. I may have to go elsewhere.'

'We both know,' Gordon said, 'that there is nowhere else to go in such a sensitive matter. Morton Ramsay? He would never resist telling his cronies, his women, even. Glucksman? What does he know of Roublev beyond what he may have seen in the Tretyakov. There is no one else on this side of the Atlantic. If there were, you would never have come to me. As you rightly say, in business I am a hard man. It is what life has taught me.'

He moved towards the door.

'Twenty thousand and a hundred on disposal,' Kurtz said. He had replaced the vermouth bottle and turned to face Gordon.

'You may not have heard distinctly. I said just now that I am not an Arab.'

'But even you must surely be willing to negotiate.'

'Not in such a case.'

There was a silence as Gordon moved towards the door.

'A gesture,' Kurtz said. 'Make me a gesture. I am not in the habit of accepting a price ultimatum.'

'I will make a gesture,' Gordon said. 'I will trust you to the extent of faxing my authentication, if authentication there be, from Moscow, and you will within the hour place ten thousand in my company's account by bank transfer. You will pay the balance of forty thousand within twenty-four hours of my return. And on completion of your deal I will accept a quarter of a million. I do this as a goodwill gesture.'

'Done,' Kurtz said.

Gordon took a diary from a breast pocket and leafed through it.

'I will make my visa application tomorrow and if all goes well I will fly to Moscow next Saturday. Before then I will notify you of my hotel and you will give me your instructions. Is that understood?'

'It is understood. I will inform my people.'

'One further thing,' Gordon said. 'You realise what you will get from me is an expert opinion. I assume there will be no apparatus at my disposal there to make a scientific judgement as to age and so forth. You are buying an opinion, and although I have every confidence in my knowledge in these matters, I am nonetheless fallible. I want that understood.'

'It is understood,' Kurtz said. 'Your fallibility is indeed one of my risks that I mentioned just now. I accept it.'

8

'Just touching base as usual,' Victor Gordon said, the telephone balanced between his chin and shoulder as he searched through an address book.

'Hi, Victor, welcome back to Moscow. How you keeping?'

'I am well, thank you. And you and yours?'

'Just fine, but we're driven crazy by the stream of top brass which keeps descending on us out of Washington followed by regiments of bankers and business school types all trying to make sense of the crazy economy here.'

'How do you see the future, Arthur?'

'Bleak, I guess. Gorbachev really needed to pull something off at the G7 meeting. You can imagine what will happen here if food runs short this winter.'

'And will it?'

'I guess it will.'

'And what will that mean for Gorbachev?'

'It'll mean the end of him. That is, if he lasts that long.'

'You think they're planning something?'

'Look, I'm a diplomat and this is a Moscow telephone, so please stop asking sensitive questions, Victor.'

'Sorry.'

'That's OK. Just look at it this way. A lot of jobs in the *apparat* are at risk. So are a lot of strongly-held ideas. If you keep those two simple facts at the back of your mind you won't find yourself being surprised, right?'

'Thanks, Arthur.'

'And what brings you to Moscow this time?' Arthur Ericson asked.

'I'm here to look at pictures. I keep an eye open for new talent. Nothing special in mind.'

'Will we see something of you?'

'Not this time, I'm afraid. I plan a couple of days of intensive nosing around. Some painters to visit in their studios, stuff like that. So as I say, I'm just touching base as usual and again as usual I shall call you each day until I leave. My usual little precaution '

'You at the Rossia?'

'Sure. This time room 1142.'

'So long.'

'Goodbye.'

Victor Gordon replaced the handset. While he had been talking to his friend Arthur Ericson at the American Embassy he had found the number he was looking for. Now he dialled it. The ringing tone sounded briefly.

'Yes?'

'I am from New York. You are expecting my call.'

Gordon was speaking in the halting Russian he had retained from his childhood. It had been an article of faith on his mother's part that the boy would retain some hold, however tenuous, on his roots. 'Who knows, one day . . .' she would say without ever finishing the sentence.

'You have my address?' It was Baranov.

'Yes.'

'Take a taxi and come to me this afternoon.'

'Very well.'

Gordon rang off, replaced the address book in his briefcase and descended to one of the vast hotel's many restaurants to pit his wits against the sulky bureaucracy of the catering staff. The aim: to eat lunch in less than one hour.

As ever, the staff triumphed and it was an hour and a half later that he made his way out to the sidewalk to negotiate with a taxi to take him to Zaveti Ilyicha. It took five minutes to reach agreement on a carton of Marlboros. The driver had demanded two cartons after making a show of refusing to travel that far at any price.

'You want to change dollars? I give the best rate.' They were bumping their way through the outer suburbs of Moscow at a terrifying speed.

'No, and please do not drive so fast. I am not in a hurry.'

'If I don't get a move on I'll be all day on this job. It won't pay me. I've got a living to earn, haven't I?'

'I dare say you have, but I have a life to live.'

The driver cut his speed by a fraction.

A pause.

'You interested in Dior nylons, genuine?'

'No.'

'I know a blonde, not seventeen, cute as hell, does it for a couple of Diors. If you're interested – '

'I am not interested.'

The driver lapsed into silence, discouraged. It was ten minutes before he tried conversation again.

'You from the United States?'

'Yes.'

'I plan to go there. Saving for it. I have a cousin there. In Pittsburgh. Name of Vasili Vasiliev. Drives a taxi. Makes a good living. You know anyone of that name in Pittsburgh?'

'I have never been in Pittsburgh.'

'Ever you go to Pittsburgh, you ask for Vasiliev. He'll see you right. Drives a '91 Chevy, a beauty.'

Gordon did not reply.

'How come you speak Russian?'

'I learned it as a child. I must ask you again not to drive so fast.'

They were racing through a countryside of birch forests and open fields. The driver lost a little speed.

'You visiting a relative in Zaveti Ilyicha? It's not the sort of place foreigners go to. A friend, maybe? Some nice people live out that way. The dachas are big, solid. Important people live in them.'

'Excuse me,' Gordon said, 'I prefer not to speak.'

'Please yourself,' the driver said. 'I was just being civil.' A pause. 'I offer forty roubles to the dollar for ten-dollar bills. You won't find better.' It was his last throw and Gordon did not speak again until the taxi had bumped its way over the railway line at Zaveti Ilyicha and come to a halt, seemingly worn out by its exertions, at the last house on the left on the winding road through a wood of firs and birches. Then he said, 'I shall be here for maybe half an hour. You will wait.'

'Can I come out back for a piss?'

'I doubt it. There are plenty of trees to piss against.'

The taxi driver grunted, said nothing, and Gordon climbed out and took a deep breath of country air with relief after the stale, tobacco-clogged stink inside the car.

Baranov had come to the door, drawn there by the clatter of the ancient taxi.

'Welcome. You are . . .?'

'From New York. My name is Victor Gordon.'

'Please come in. May I offer you something, a vodka perhaps?'

'No thank you. Let us proceed with what we have to do.'

'Surely, surely,' Baranov said. Then, 'I did not expect to be speaking Russian. I have some English.'

'The world is full of small surprises,' Gordon said as the front door was closed behind him and he was led through a sparsely furnished room to a door set in the far wall. The room contained a tall ceramic stove in one corner, a divan with tangled bedclothes still bearing the imprint of a body, and a square table and four chairs. A bookcase along the length of a wall was heavy with books. Newspapers and magazines littered the floor.

Baranov led the way through the further door, which gave into a larger, high-ceilinged room which served as a studio. There were canvases on stretchers in one corner, more magazines on the floor, another divan with cushions, and a stove. In the centre of the room stood an old-fashioned easel and next to it a stool and a table with painting paraphernalia. The easel was empty. The atmosphere was thick with the smell of turpentine.

Baranov moved to the far end of the room, lifted the icon which was wrapped in its ragged blanket, uncovered it and placed it carefully on the easel and stood back. The hard white light from the window bounced back at them, transmuted with infinite delicacy by the painting.

Nothing was said. Gordon placed himself first at a couple of metres distance, contemplating it in silence, his face expressionless. Then he approached and considered it close up, his head slightly inclined, his hands hanging loosely at his sides. He walked round to the back of the easel and examined the wood of the icon. Then he returned to contemplate it again from the front. His expression betrayed nothing. From the habit acquired over years he knew how to devalue a work of art by means of a resolutely undemonstrative manner. 'The slightest show of enthusiasm or even mild approval,' he would tell his staff, 'will cost you thousands. Act as if you were buying a can of beans. Your regular brand.'

Baranov could not stand the silence. 'So what do you think? A wonderful Andrei Roublev, no?'

'What I eventually think will be stated to my principals in New York,' Gordon said.

'Of course.'

Gordon produced a loupe from his pocket and examined areas of the icon. He appeared to be particularly interested in the faces of the saints, turning the easel slightly to allow the light from the window to strike the surface of the painting from varying angles. For Baranov there was no way of knowing whether this minute inspection satisfied him in any way. Still the silence was unbroken. Then Gordon said, 'I will need to satisfy my principals if they decide to proceed that what I am examining now is the same as what is ultimately delivered. For this purpose I propose to remove a small section from the back which will fit into place subsequently provided there is no substitution.'

He took a penknife from a pocket and carefully carved a star-shaped piece from one of the panels making up the wooden supports of the painting. Then he cut a tiny flake of paint from the edge of the painting itself, placing both scraps on a small sheet of tissue paper which he had produced. The tissue was then folded in a neat square and replaced in an inner pocket much in the manner of a diamond dealer with stones to carry from client to client. The whole inspection had taken close to thirty minutes.

'So?' Baranov asked again.

'I will report,' Gordon said.

'It *is* a magnificent Roublev, isn't it?'

'My report is to my principals, who are paying me, not to you.'

'I speak as an art lover,' Baranov said, seemingly desperate for some reaction, any reaction, from his visitor.

'I speak as an expert,' Gordon said. 'It leaves me no room for emotion, which can cloud one's judgement.' He offered his hand. 'Thank you for your time. You will no doubt hear further, one way or the other.' The handshake was brief and he turned, leading the way through the inner room and out to the front door. There he turned once more.

'My report will reach New York in a secure manner by tomorrow. So, as I say, you will hear from me. I am at the Rossia.' He nodded to Baranov, turned and crossed the short distance to the taxi. The driver brought the engine to life. 'We can go,' Gordon said. He did not look back to Baranov at the front door as the taxi bumped its way back along the country road in the direction of the city.

'You did your business, eh?' the taxi driver asked.

Gordon did not reply. They made the return journey in silence. He was reflecting on the fact that, beyond a peradventure, he had just examined a genuine Andrei

Roublev of the finest quality, that he had allowed himself to conclude a truly lousy deal with Kurtz back in New York, and that the deal had to be, could be, overturned. 'Anything less than a million and Kurtz will have robbed me,' he reflected. 'The money apart, it is a psychological ascendancy I cannot allow him, since it would give him a damaging head start every time we do business in the future.'

These thoughts occupied his mind until the taxi reached the centre of Moscow and turned into Razin Street, heading for the ungainly bulk of the Rossia. By that time he had developed in his mind what he considered to be a viable game plan.

'A genuine Roublev, for Christ's sake, and in fair condition,' he repeated to himself. 'Nothing less than a million.'

Later that evening he descended from his room to the lobby and waited his turn in line to reach the woman receptionist who interested him. He remembered her from a previous trip – a silent and resentful creature from somewhere beyond the Caucasus, or so he judged, with jet hair chopped short and a thick neck and bosom which promised heavy thighs and legs to match. His dealings with her over a matter of telephone charges had been full of stubborn hostility which had been ended, though not in any way transmuted into amiability, by a twenty-dollar bill.

'Good evening,' he now said, 'you may remember me from last April. You were helpful.'

The woman gazed steadily at him. 'I see many people. What do you want?'

'I wish to send a fax to New York.'

'Give me the text and it will be sent for you.'

'It is confidential and I wish to send it myself.'

'The regulations require that we send it for you. The rule is established by the Ministry of Communications – a security matter.'

As if the conversation were ended, she turned away to

exchange remarks with the woman next to her behind the counter. Gordon waited patiently. Then he said, 'This is an important matter for me – a delicate personal matter.'

'I am bound by the regulations. Do you wish to give me the text or not? There are people waiting behind you.' There was no expression on her face. An unhappy woman, Gordon decided, who had probably never sought or found pleasure in others. He leaned towards her across the counter, allowing himself the trace of a friendly smile.

'I would like to make a small bet with you. I will bet you fifty US dollars that you will not allow me to send my own fax.'

She turned again to answer a question from her colleague, making no sign that she had even heard Gordon's proposition. Then she turned back but did not look directly at him.

'I finish here at ten. I will wait for you at the door to the offices opposite the elevators on the first floor. Bring your text with you and be discreet.'

'You have won your bet,' Gordon said, 'and I will bring your prize with me.'

He stepped aside and she turned her hostile gaze on the next guest. Gordon heard what he took to be a Swiss voice raised in angry English as he walked away in search of something to eat. Later he found her at the appointed place and the hint of fear in her eyes was the first emotion of any kind she had displayed. He wondered what kind of small domestic tragedies, privations, or maybe banal varieties of greed led this stolid creature to accept bribes which of themselves could never transform her life save in the disastrous sense that they could lose her her job. No sentimentalist, Gordon allowed himself for a brief moment to picture an ancient, crippled mother at home or a backward child to care for, before returning to an explanation which fitted his own cast of mind more comfortably. 'Greed,' he said to himself, 'everyone has their price and this woman's appears to be fifty dollars.'

She led him through the door which gave onto a corridor, then through another into an office with a bank of old telex machines against one wall and a Japanese Nefax in a corner.

'Quickly, please, I will send it for you.'

'I will send it myself. I am familiar with the machine.' He took a sheet from his pocket, smoothed it out and fed it into the fax. He punched out Kurtz's number in New York and was surprised when it connected first time. The text went over the wire in what seemed an agonisingly long time. Then the transmission was completed and the confirmation of receipt was tapped out and delivered. He tore it off, pocketed it and turning to the woman, handed her two twenties and a ten. He was surprised when she stuffed them hastily into a pocket without checking them.

'Let us go quickly,' she said.

The message Gordon had sent read as follows:

> To: A. Kurtz – private and personal.
> I have carried out an inspection as agreed between us and will report in detail on my return. My report will be positive. Meanwhile I have the thought that our negotiation was not satisfactory, given the nature of the transaction and potential benefits thereof. For this reason I am revising my terms here and now. On receipt of this message you will make an immediate transfer to my bank account of one hundred thousand dollars, plus a further four hundred thousand on receipt of my detailed report on my return. On disposal of the item you will pay a further five hundred thousand dollars. This, in my more mature judgement, is an eminently fair and reasonable arrangement and is not, repeat not, negotiable.

The text was unsigned. Gordon considered it struck a note of finality with an overtone of menace which would signal clearly to Kurtz that the icon was genuine, that he, Victor Gordon, was to be more solidly embedded in the deal, and that if the tone of the fax was anything to go by he was not to be denied. 'In this matter,' Gordon reflected, 'he has no room for manoeuvre since I can readily break him with a simple telephone call, and he knows it.'

9

'We have a problem,' Anton Kurtz told Grigoriev on the telephone. 'I believe we may need the help of your associates over there.'

'I am at your service, Mr Kurtz, sir,' Grigoriev said.

'I have heard from the man I sent and I conclude the article we are interested in is authentic. At any rate, that appears to be his opinion if I am to judge by a fax I have here before me.'

'What then is the problem?'

'The individual himself is the problem. Not to put too fine a point on it, I am being blackmailed, Grigoriev. It is something I am not prepared to tolerate.'

'That, surely, will be your problem, Mr Kurtz, and not mine,' Grigoriev said. 'I take it the man wants more money.'

'An absurd sum which makes the entire deal impossible for me. He wants a fortune up front before I find my buyer. The risk is unacceptable.'

'So what do you want from me?' Grigoriev asked.

'You have friends over there who are prepared to take necessary measures?'

'Perhaps.'

'I think extreme measures are called for if this deal is to go through,' Kurtz said.

'You are saying, Mr Kurtz, sir, that this man is not to come back? Do I understand you, sir?'

'I am saying necessary measures.'

'There are risks.'

'I will make an appropriate financial gesture.'

'How much, Mr Kurtz?'

'An extra ten.'

'That is satisfactory. I take it the matter is urgent?'

'Of extreme urgency. I have already contacted my prospective purchaser and I have to fly to Tokyo on Monday. I have to know before then that my hands are freed.'

'I understand, sir,' Grigoriev said. 'I will keep you informed.'

His subsequent conversation with Moscow lasted five minutes and although nothing, overtly, was said, everything was understood.

Anton Kurtz had called the New York office of the Kobe–Yokohama Trust to check the whereabouts of their chairman, Sanjiro Ushida.

'Ushida san is in Tokyo,' he was told.

'Can he receive me on Tuesday of next week? Please fix me an appointment. Tell him I have a matter of interest to present.'

The reply had come later that day. Mr Ushida was pleased to invite Mr Kurtz to lunch at his home in Kamakura on Tuesday.

In Moscow Baranov called his most trusted associate, Gribenko, after his five-minute telephone conversation with New York.

'You will take the car and pick up one of the boys to help you. I will get this American to go to Novo-Alexandrovskaya Metro station by taxi. I'll find a pretext easily enough. I'll meet him there and take him to Kulakov Street where you'll grab him.'

'Do we lose him?'

'We lose him.'

'OK. And afterwards?'

'I have a plan for that.'

'What about the taxi driver? They'll trace him once

they start nosing around, and then they'll know where the American was taken.'

'Of course. So you'll have to lose him too, won't you?'

'I'll take the '48 and do it up close,' Gribenko said in his thick Ukrainian accent. He made it sound like routine.

'I don't want to hear the details. How will you find him?'

'Easy. While this guy was with you I made a note of the number of his taxi. I know how to work back from that.'

'You're not as big a fool as you look,' Baranov said. 'Anyway, get on with it.'

'I reckon I'm earning,' Gribenko said. 'And good money at that.'

'Yes, yes. Now get off the line.'

He turned to the phone again and dialled the Rossia. When he was through to room 1142 and heard Gordon's clipped 'Yes', he developed the story.

'I am very sorry to bother you again, Mr Gordon, but I have just had a call from my friends in New York. They have expressed an interest in another item that I have. Previously they said there was no market for it, but something seems to have changed and they're particularly keen for you to examine it for them. I shall be in the city within the next hour and would like to meet you near the flat of a friend who is holding the item.'

'I have no instructions on this,' Gordon said.

'I know. But a call just now gave me the name of a Mr Anton Kurtz who is the prospective purchaser. I am to tell you that he will make suitable arrangements when you return.'

'And does Kurtz say anything about the other matter?'

'I understand he will react to a proposal of yours by tomorrow.'

There was a silence.

'Give me the address.'

'I will be outside the Novo–Alexandrovskaya Metro station at ten this evening.'

'Very well. And please be on time.'

Exactly one hour later Gordon's taxi drew up at the rendezvous. Peter Baranov was standing under a street lamp and advanced to greet him as he got out of the vehicle.

'It is only a short walk from here,' he said. 'I have my car and I'll be glad to run you back to your hotel later. I suggest you get rid of your cab.'

Gordon paid off the taxi and they set out along Prospect Mira, soon turning left down Kulakov Street. 'Just a short way down here. My friend is a dealer who sometimes has interesting items from the provinces.'

'Is this an icon?' Gordon asked.

'It is.'

They walked for a few moments in silence. The half moon threw enough light to trace an outline of the apartment blocks on their right and low buildings on their side of the street. Gordon realised that they were on the edge of a residential area. The buildings on their left could be warehouses or factories. He stumbled twice on the uneven sidewalk, pitted with holes, Baranov walking beside him in the gutter. The distant hum of the city was punctuated from time to time by the clatter and roar of the traffic on Mira.

'It isn't far,' Baranov said.

'Why aren't we using your car?'

'It's parked at my friend's flat.'

The apartment blocks had given way to waste land. To their left, a long factory wall came to an end a few yards ahead of them. There was no street lighting.

Gordon stopped. 'Where the hell are you taking me?'

'My friend lives at the end of this street,' Baranov said.

'I'm going no further. This is some kind of plot.'

'I assure you, Mr Gordon,' Baranov said as Gordon turned on his heel and started back along the street, heading towards the lights of Prospect Mira. He had broken into a half run, but was stumbling on the broken paving stones. Baranov, protesting, was panting alongside him. And now there came the sound of pounding feet from behind them as Gribenko and his associate emerged from a break in the factory wall and ran to catch up. As the sound of his pursuers reached him, Gordon increased his pace, now thoroughly aroused to the danger. It was still some two hundred yards to the safety of Prospect Mira.

Baranov had fallen back, afraid that a stray shot from Gribenko's gun might find the wrong target. Gribenko was within a few feet of Gordon when he fired, the silencer's *phut* scarcely audible above the roar of the traffic out on the main road ahead. The heavy bullet hit Gordon in the shoulder, its impact sending him crashing to the ground. He was staggering to his feet as Gribenko's second shot, fired at point blank range from above, hit him in the neck.

He gasped, choking on the blood which flooded down his throat from a severed artery, sank back onto the pavement and lay still.

Gribenko fired again, unnecessarily, as the other man came abreast of them. He was carrying a sack.

'Right,' Baranov said. 'That nearly went wrong, but never mind. Let's get him wrapped up while I fetch the car. The bastard nearly got away with it.'

It was ten on the following morning and already there was a long line of yellow hearses outside the Reutov crematorium on the outskirts of the city. The day promised to be oppressively hot and the dull grey smoke from the crematorium chimney hovered above the stack, unwilling to disperse. The line of hearses bearing their loads of deceased Muscovites and crowds of grieving relatives stretched down the country road from the crematorium gates. On a gatepost a sign read DUE TO LACK OF URNS ASHES WILL BE GIVEN OUT IN POLYTHENE BAGS. Waiting time at the gates could run into hours but time would be made up inside: ten minutes were scheduled for each ritual of corpse disposal and whatever grieving the families and friends might cram into the available time.

A Rafik minibus with MOSCOW RESTORATION WORKS lettered on its sides drove past the waiting line of hearses, into the courtyard of the crematorium and on to a low building signposted WORKSHOP. Gribenko was driving, Baranov next to him. On the floor behind them a tarpaulin sack contained the last earthly remains of Viktor Gorokhov alias Victor Gordon, art dealer and victim, who had returned for good to the land of his fathers.

'In Soviet law,' Baranov was saying to Gribenko as he drew up before the workshop and killed the engine, 'if there is no body there can be no crime. Shortly, there will be no body. Leave it to me.'

'We could have buried him in the woods. Simpler,' Gribenko said.

'I don't take chances,' Baranov said.

He jumped down from the minibus, pushed open the door of the workshop and went inside.

The Reutov crematorium workshop had a single product-line in a variety of forms and materials: urns and caskets in marble, porcelain or earthenware, according to the financial resources of the client. The place was dimly lit, untidy, with the detritus of modelling and sculpture strewn about. No work of any kind appeared to be under way. A middle-aged man in black overalls came out of an inner room. He was directing a raw cough into a grubby handkerchief, staggering slightly as he came towards Baranov.

'I got your call. Nice to see you again. It's been a long time.'

'Ivan, my old friend, how are you keeping?'

The man coughed again. He was swaying slightly and his speech was slurred.

'Well enough, well enough. And what brings you here?'

'I need a favour and I'll do one in return.'

'Never refuse favours.' He repeated it twice. The alcohol was heavy on his breath and seemed to pervade the room. 'Remember the old days, eh?'

'I do,' Baranov said. 'Of course.'

The old days were when Ivan Kostenko had been a senior sculptor at the Restoration Works, much in demand for likenesses of a succession of Soviet heroes. His work graced the public squares of countless provincial towns and villages – here a Lenin pointing to the future, there a Kalinin, paternal, or a Maxim Gorki or Karl Marx himself. His likenesses of Marx were particularly admired but it was said that he could never hit Kalinin off to the satisfaction of his clients. All that, of course, had been in the past, before the vodka finally drained the skill out of his hands and his eye. Someone had found him a sinecure as foreman at the crematorium workshop where he allowed his workers to fashion their urns unhindered, always provided there were raw materials available. At present there were not.

'Come outside. Let's have a chat,' Baranov said.

Kostenko followed him out into the heat and dust of the courtyard. They stopped next to the minibus.

'I need help,' Baranov said, 'for two things. First I have a body to dispose of, and second I have a crate of vodka to dispose of as well, and you're the man to help me with both.'

'Bodies,' Kostenko said slowly, shaking his head, 'tricky things, bodies. Do you have a chit?'

'If I had a chit,' Baranov said, 'I wouldn't be bothering you, would I? I'd be down the road there in the line-up, waiting for my plastic bag. What I have is not a chit but a human problem. To put it bluntly, my dear Ivan, last night I ran a fellow down on the Yaroslavskoye Highway. Some sort of vagrant, blind drunk, staggering into the roadway just ahead of me. I had no chance to avoid him. I'd have gone straight to the militia only I'd had a few myself, you understand, and you know what that means.'

'The lock-up,' Kostenko said. 'Certainly the lock-up.' He seemed to find the idea amusing and sniggered to himself, repeating 'the lock-up.'

'Quite so,' Baranov said. 'So I picked the poor sod up, loaded him into the car, and what with one thing and another, here I am, asking you to do me a favour.' He paused. 'He was only a bum. Not likely to have anyone wondering where the hell he's got to.'

'A crate, you said?' Kostenko asked.

'A crate. And whatever you need for your mates over at the ovens. How much will it take?'

'They'll do it for fifty roubles. We had a thing like this some time back. It was fifty.' He wiped his nose on his sleeve and steadied himself against the side of the minibus. 'I could use a few roubles myself while we're about it. Plus the crate, of course.'

'Fifty for them and an extra twenty-five for you, right?' Baranov had taken a wad of notes out of his pocket. Waving them in front of Kostenko's nose, he dropped his voice: 'I am delivering the corpse of this unfortunate victim of a road accident in a tarpaulin bag, right?'

'Right.'

'The bag is securely closed, right?'

'Right.'

Dropping his voice a further tone: 'And it is not to be opened, right?'

'Right.'

'It goes into the oven with the corpse, you understand?'

'I understand,' Kostenko said, 'though it's a pity to waste a good bag. They're not easy to come by these days.'

'But it's how I want it,' Baranov said, 'and you must supervise the thing yourself.'

'Fine. Now just drive this unfortunate person over to the back of the crematorium and we'll do whatever is necessary to settle him once and for all.' Kostenko giggled again and started to cough. 'My lungs,' he said, 'not what they were. Christ, I could do with a drink.'

The transaction was then completed and later the minibus drove back in the direction of the Restoration Works at Kaluzhskaya. Baranov had not waited to collect a plastic bag with the ashes of Victor Gordon.

'You all set for the taxi driver this evening?' he asked as they drove through the city's suburbs.

Gribenko nodded. 'Alexei has a pal in the taxi office. He's tracing the registration number back to the driver and they'll give him the man's address. Then I'll pay him a visit.'

Grigoriev in Brighton Beach took the call from Moscow stark naked, perspiration dripping from his chin onto the matted hair of his chest. The mercury stood at 95 degrees, the humidity at 90 per cent and there was no breath of air coming in from the ocean. He threw himself into a chair, scratching at his crotch and wiping the sweat away from his brow with his forearm.

'That matter,' Baranov was saying. 'It's been dealt with.' There was a brief silence on the line. 'Definitely, you understand,' he added.

Grigoriev grunted. 'And what's the progress?'

'Progress is as planned. The show will be in the Lexington Gallery in New York on October 10 and the article will be included. It will – '

'I don't expect you to draw me a ground plan,' Grigoriev interrupted. 'All I wanted was confirmation of our instructions.'

'You have confirmation,' Baranov said.

Grigoriev hung up, heaved himself from the chair and made for the shower room, cursing the heat. Afterwards, he put on a robe, returned to the telephone and called Anton Kurtz in New York.

'Mr Kurtz, sir, I have spoken to my man over there and

he confirms the matter has been attended to as per your instructions.'

'I shall expect to see some kind of confirmation in the press.'

'No doubt, sir, no doubt.'

'I will then transfer the agreed sum to you.'

'Thank you, sir.' And Grigoriev hung up.

10

After the long flight westwards and a restless night, Anton Kurtz set off from the New Otani for Tokyo station, where he took the Yokosuka line, arriving at Kamakura an hour later. At Kamakura station Ushida's car stood surrounded by a wondering circle of admirers – a 3.5 litre 1938 Bentley drophead coupé with immaculate French bodywork, gleaming blackly in the midday sun, a diminutive Japanese chauffeur in full rig standing by its side, his café-au-lait uniform blending nicely with his sallow complexion. He saluted Kurtz as if he were a commander-in-chief, opened the door of the car and bowed from the waist as Kurtz climbed in. Moments later they were riding with infinite smoothness and dignity through the tree-lined streets of Kamakura, past shrines set in immaculate gardens, groves of bamboo and rows of neat houses, with the mighty Amitabha Buddha glimpsed from time to time in the distance. Away from the horrors of Tokyo, this was where the Ushidas of Japan had their houses and dreamed of market share. The Bentley had cost half a million dollars at a sale in California.

Sanjiro Ushida himself stood at the door to greet his guest – a sign of special respect for an old business associate, underlined by the presence of his wife and daughter making up a tiny delegation of welcome immediately behind him. There was bowing in plenty, expressions of mutual respect and a touch of giggling by the ladies, who were not noticeably westernised. This effect was underlined at lunch, which was taken Japanese-style on mats, with the ladies serving but not partaking.

'Mizuwari?' Ushida poured the mix of whisky and water into his guest's glass and raised his own in turn for the compliment to be returned. The meal would be slow, formal and tedious. On the other hand, it was a necessary overture to the play which was to follow.

It was not within the norms of Japanese good manners for Ushida san to be the first to touch on the purpose of Kurtz's visit. On the other hand, it would not be regarded as polite for Kurtz himself to approach the subject with anything that could be construed as haste. Both men knew their meeting was, ultimately, about buying and selling, and both knew that to get from the niceties of traditional hospitality to the hard bargaining of a business transaction – art or no art – was a kind of quantum leap in social intercourse which required the greatest delicacy of touch. For this reason, nothing was said about the purpose of the visit during the meal. Warm tokkyu sake was drunk as each repeatedly served the other, tea appeared, then, at last, steaming towels. And meanwhile, Ushida had talked of art.

'You see, my dear Mr Kurtz, my interest in early Christian art from the West dates back to my days as a young man when I first began to collect very modestly. It was at that time, you see, that I began to realise that there were fascinating parallels between the art of the icon in its finest manifestations in the fourteenth and fifteenth centuries, and our own art of the woodblock print at its most fine in the work of the Ukioye School.'

'You would have in mind such masterpieces as Moronobu's dancers, and of course much of Hokusai.' Kurtz took care to speak with suitable modesty and with a tentative tinge to his voice, as if, a mere Westerner, he were unsure of his standing in the matter. In fact, he disliked Japanese art and had he been so minded could have held forth with eloquence on the manner in which the feudal character of Japanese society had led to ossification and every kind of artistic rigidity.

'The parallel I have in mind,' Ushida said after listening

politely to Kurtz's rejoinder, nodding and smiling as he simultaneously slurped his noodles as a sign of appreciation of the cooking, 'the parallel is, I believe, to be found firstly in the idealisation of life expressed both in early Christian art and in ours. It was an astonishing contrast – the brutality and barbarity of life at that time compared with the sensitivity, the delicacy of the art. An escape, you see. There as here. Also, as the tradition decayed, as all traditions do, authority destroyed creativity in old Russia as it did in Japan.'

He was enjoying his noodles. His remarks were punctuated with sounds indicating as much. The sake glasses were filled and refilled. Kurtz, on the floor with his legs painfully crossed beneath him, was conscious of a developing backache which he knew would outlast the trip.

'I have found a most interesting thing,' Ushida was saying in the manner of a man accustomed to deciding himself whether what he had to say would interest the other party. 'As you will know, my dear Mr Kurtz, the Russian Orthodox Church held the Council of the Hundred Chapters during the sixteenth century to lay down all manner of rules and regulations governing religious observance and so forth. And at the Council they also laid down rules for the painting of icons and even for the personal behaviour of icon painters. Rules, mark you, as if art can bow to rules made by priestly bureaucrats and still be art. Needless to say, the rules killed the art of the icon and reduced it to mere copying, to the work of the technically skilled but creatively barren artisan. And what I find interesting is that Stalin and his art commissars did exactly the same thing between the wars, thus killing a later secular upsurge of Russian creativity. History, you see, repeating itself. Is it not interesting?'

'Exceedingly,' Kurtz said. 'A most perceptive insight.' More sake. His back would soon be in some kind of seizure.

'I will show you some of my collection,' Ushida said as

they finally rose from their mats and the ladies bowed and retreated to some nether area of the house.

In the adjoining room, vast by Japanese domestic standards, icons of various sizes were displayed on stands – a kind of private iconostasis such as any Russian church would have abjured God himself to possess.

'As you know,' Ushida was saying, 'I have specialised in the Novgorod School, not because I regard it as superior to the Moscow School – indeed, Moscow is finer, more pure and spiritual – but because the works of the Moscow School are so very difficult to come by in the market.' He stopped before a broken fragment depicting the head and shoulders of a saint in austere colours. 'This you will remember – my one unquestioned example of the work of Theophanes the Greek.'

Kurtz nodded. 'Indeed,' he said, 'a masterpiece.' He did not ask how Ushida san had acquired such a treasure.

As they progressed slowly round the room, a moment came when Ushida deemed it suitable to ask, 'And you have something to offer me, Mr Kurtz?'

'I have.'

'Then let us sit a while and have a cognac.'

Over vintage cognac served in over-sized balloons, Kurtz developed what he liked to call his game plan. The principle would be misdirection: the putting forward of a proposition which was quite other than the one in which he wanted the buyer to interest himself. Attacking the matter, as the French would say, on the bias.

'You know the Doubting Thomas from St Sophia in Novgorod?' Kurtz asked. 'It is now in the Novgorod Museum.'

'Of course. I saw it a few years ago. Brilliant technique, but lacking in spirituality.'

'But certainly a typical masterpiece of the School.'

'No doubt.'

'I am aware of a small icon which will shortly come onto the market and which the experts agree is from the same hand. The size is some twenty inches by sixteen.'

'And the provenance?'

'A family heirloom, apparently. Taken out of Russia in the emigration of the twenties and kept in a bank vault somewhere in Paris all these years. With a death in the family the thing has come to light and has been offered to me.'

'And the price?'

'They are talking a million dollars.'

Kurtz had chosen the sum with care. It should be high enough to make his trip credible and his host's hospitality appropriate. On the other hand, the family heirloom did not exist and the sum had to be low enough to signal to Ushida that the item was unlikely to add much lustre to his collection. 'There should always be bait,' Kurtz would reflect. 'And there should always be a certain reluctance to sell what you are actually there to sell.' He was therefore undismayed when Ushida, in a fine example of polite Japanese circumlocution, declined the offer of a Novgorod icon.

'A most interesting offer,' Ushida said. 'It would give me the greatest pleasure to own such an item, and I am naturally flattered that you should come so far to make me the offer. It is something which I must think about.'

When something was to be thought about, Kurtz knew perfectly well, it was also to be allowed to die subsequently of neglect.

'Perhaps,' Ushida said, 'you have something else for me? It is some time since I had the pleasure of buying from you.'

'As a matter of fact, I do have something else but the whole affair is really preposterous – preposterously difficult, and therefore absurdly expensive. I did not think . . .' He allowed his voice to trail off and his shoulders to rise in a gesture which said that only under extreme provocation would he bring himself to discuss the matter at all.

'Tell me, my dear Mr Kurtz, as an old friend. It may be that I would have an interest. I am always attracted to what is difficult.'

They both drank, sensing in their separate ways that this was some kind of moment of truth.

'The problem here,' Kurtz said slowly, gazing into his glass as if that was where he'd find the problem's solution, 'the problem, I say, is that the work in question is literally priceless.'

'There is a price,' Ushida ventured, 'for everything in this life.'

Kurtz allowed a thin smile onto his face, held it briefly and removed it. 'I did not intend to raise this matter with you at all,' he said, 'because I did not think you would be interested in such a heavy investment. You have always been a shrewd judge of an item, with an equally shrewd sense of value. This, frankly, requires in the buyer the mentality of a . . . a Croesus, shall we say? A gambler? I don't know.'

'But tell me, Mr Kurtz,' Ushida said gently, as if any eagerness on his part would somehow blow the whole thing into thin air, 'tell me what is this extraordinary object that you speak of?'

'I have at my disposal a newly-discovered version of Andrei Roublev's Old Testament Trinity.'

He allowed the bald statement to stand alone while he took a long sip of his brandy. He did not intend to break the silence.

Finally, Ushida asked. 'You say a version. Are you suggesting it is by Roublev himself?'

Kurtz nodded his great head silently several times, as if the matter were beyond mere words.

'And this is on offer . . . officially?'

'Not officially.'

'A private deal, if I understand you?'

Again the solemn nodding of the head. And Kurtz proceeded to talk about the Roublev icon, the circumstances of its discovery and the modalities of its intended disposal, for some fifteen minutes. Ushida sat motionless, his brandy glass untouched before him. And as he approached the end of his presentation, Kurtz knew that he had his man.

'I see a difficulty at once,' Ushida said, seeking to soften the price before it had even been hinted at. 'I could, of course, be extremely interested in this icon. I regard Roublev as greater even than Theophanes, and his extreme delicacy is more to my taste than the Greek's severity of form. However, I am currently developing a substantial joint venture with the Russians. Four of their naval vessels are due for repair in a shipyard at Vladivostok in which I hold a 40 per cent interest, and I am negotiating right now for further concessions which can be of benefit to my shipping line. The problem, of course, is that one is not altogether certain who in Moscow one should be dealing with nowadays, but that is a separate matter. No, my concern is that if it became known there that I had acquired this icon which had left the USSR . . . unofficially, as it were, then that could jeopardise these ventures I am speaking of.'

Kurtz said nothing, as prudence and an overdeveloped acquisitive instinct struggled for ascendancy in the Japanese tycoon's breast. He did not believe that prudence would win the day.

'It is a risk I could contemplate with equanimity,' Ushida continued, 'were it not for another consideration. You see, I must have reassurance as to the genuineness of this icon. Believe me, it is not that I doubt your word for one moment, but even you, my dear Mr Kurtz, could perhaps be misled by a clever copy. And the only way I see to obtain reassurance is for the Russian experts to pronounce the icon as authentic. That is one point. And if it is to be spirited away, then the sound of their discomfiture must be audible to me here in Japan. In other words, I would need the reassurance which can come only from the sounds of anguish emanating from the Russian authorities.'

Kurtz deemed it prudent to limit himself to one word. 'Difficult,' he said.

'Undoubtedly difficult, but, I am afraid, necessary. For is it not the only guarantee that I have that what I am buying is what is claimed for it?'

'I do not know that such a thing can be arranged,' Kurtz said.

'Then I fear I would have to miss the splendid opportunity you have kindly placed before me.'

'I must consult those involved,' Kurtz said. 'As I say, it is difficult.'

'And the price, my dear Mr Kurtz? What, pray, is the price?'

'The price is thirty-five million dollars.'

Ushida's face betrayed no reaction. Then he said, 'And you tell me Victor Gordon has authenticated it?'

'That is right.'

'I think, perhaps, it would be wise for me to speak to Gordon.'

'It can be arranged.' Kurtz had expected the suggestion.

'The price is high,' Ushida said.

'The risks are great and so are my expenses. It seems to me a very fair price for what is, after all, priceless.'

'My attitude to the price is not that of an investor who must keep his purchase cheap in order to get an adequate return on his investment. I know as well as anyone that art is not in fact a sound investment, contrary to what the dealers will tell you. I have seen the American academic study which demonstrates that major art works viewed over the space of three centuries up to the 1960s brought a real mean compound rate of interest of only 0.55 per cent per annum, whereas an investment in good quality government securities would have returned 2.5 per cent. So that my approach to price is not that of an investor, but that of a collector, and in this case a collector who will not be able to display his purchase. And it is as a collector that I offer you twenty million dollars on the understanding that I may return the article to you if in my opinion it is not a genuine Roublev or not in the condition one would expect.'

Ushida's twenty million being precisely what Kurtz had expected of him, indeed had intended him to offer, the rest would be, as it were, a gilding of the lily.

'I fear twenty million is far too low.'

Ushida smiled. 'And is not thirty-five far too high?'

'Perhaps,' Kurtz said, 'we could meet at, say, thirty, which is my best price.'

'But you realise that I cannot display this piece. I cannot show it to my friends. I cannot catalogue it in my collection in readiness for my legacy to the Kyoto Museum.'

'In two years Japanese law will protect you and the Russians will no longer have any claim,' Kurtz said.

'No legal claim, certainly, but I fear my substantial business interests there, the joint ventures of my companies, would be gravely endangered. No, my Andrei Roublev would have to remain a very expensive secret.'

With infinite Japanese delicacy the two edged towards each other and settled towards sundown for twenty-eight million dollars, sealed with a handshake and a certain amount of bowing as Kurtz was ushered back to the Bentley. As he was driven through the fragrant evening with its gentle breeze from the sea he wondered how an outburst from the Russians could be engineered. 'I must hear them,' Ushida san had insisted at the end. 'Victor Gordon is a great expert, but . . . but. So how can we be sure you have sold me an unknown work by the incomparable Andrei Roublev unless the Russians deafen us with their protests?'

It was, conceded Kurtz, a point.

11

'Hey, you, would you mind stepping off my corn.'

Major Ponomarev muttered an apology and shifted as best he could. The owner of the corn reeked of tobacco and cheap Troinoi eau-de-cologne. Ponomarev reckoned he'd been drinking the stuff. The veins on his nose looked like a map of the Metro itself.

'Intellectuals!' a woman with an avoska string bag announced to no one in particular. 'He wears a hat and that gives him the right to stamp on other people's toes.'

Ponomarev made a mental note to resist next time Marina thrust a hat at him on his way out. The weather was stifling and no hat was called for. But Marina was a thoroughgoing Muscovite, obsessed with colds, draughts, pneumonia, cold ears . . . Ponomarev might be a major in the Moscow militia, but to his wife he was the baby she'd never had. And now these uncultured people in the centre-bound train from Medvedkovo were taking the piss. He wished he'd been wearing his uniform.

At Ploshchad Nogina he escaped from the carriage, his hat still in place, made his way to the escalators and up to the street. Five minutes later he was outside the Rossia. He had to admit that he felt some affection for the absurd building. He'd done a five-year stint there, first as a simple militiaman, then as chief of the Rossia militia station. When they'd built it in a fit of gigantism it was the largest hotel in the world. For all he knew, it still was. And at that size it needed its own police force. Partly to manhandle the drunken Swedes and Finns, but mainly to keep the whores out. Not fit work for a serious man, determined to make his way in the Moscow militia. But now he had his extra pip and a squad to run at the Petrovka headquarters. And he didn't mind an occasional trip back to his old haunt on Razin Street.

He flashed his red militia card at the doorman and made his way across the lobby to the bank of elevators. The manager could wait. A chat with the floor lady and a look round the American's room would be more interesting.

Colonel Yegorov, his boss, had handed him the brief before he'd had time to sit at his desk.

'We've had the Americans on. Seems one of their nationals has disappeared from the Rossia. Fact: he checked in four days ago, that would be Saturday. Fact: he has the strange habit of calling his embassy every day while he's in Moscow.' Colonel Yegorov allowed himself an expressive grin. 'Now why would anyone want to do a thing like that? As if a foreigner wasn't perfectly safe in our law-abiding city! Anyway, yesterday he failed to call, and again today, and the hotel claims he hasn't slept there either night, which is our fact No. 3.' The colonel shrugged. 'I can't work up much enthusiasm for the case, but foreigners . . . you know. Maybe he's holed up with a woman somewhere.' He dropped a scrap of paper on Ponomarev's desk. 'That's the name; Victor Gordon, room 1142. Be a good chap, get over there and see what you can make of it. I had to promise the Americans they'd get a report.'

In the elevator he pressed the button marked 11, removed his hat and unzipped his windcheater. He must find a way of saying no to Marina without upsetting her. If it wasn't hats it was warm underwear. Or she'd buy him ever longer scarves. No doubt the woman with the string bag had a point.

He reached the desk on the eleventh floor as the floor lady hurried up from a corridor.

'Alexander Ivanovitch, what law have I broken?'

Ponomarev grinned. 'I don't know, but we'll soon find out.'

'How are you, then? We haven't seen you here for years.'

'Fine, fine, Anna. I'm here on business.'

'There are no corpses on this floor.'

'Not corpses; an American, room 1142.'

'Haven't seen him since he went out the day before yesterday. The under-manager said there was to be an investigation.' The floor lady shrugged, as if to underline that it was no business of hers. Americans were free to disappear from their rooms, no questions asked. It wasn't at all like the old days.

'What time did he leave his room on Sunday?'

'About eight-thirty. I have a good memory, Alexander Ivanovitch.'

'If you have such a good memory please be more specific.'

'I don't keep glancing at my wristwatch. I have work to do.'

'Was it before eight-thirty or perhaps after eight-thirty?'

'How should I know? I'd been on since six and my friend Natalia brought me a glass of morning tea at eight-fifteen. That's when I look at my watch. Then about fifteen minutes later, and it's only a guess, this American comes down the corridor from the direction of 1142, passes my desk and waits there by the elevators.'

'And did he say anything as he went past?'

'He passed by as though I wasn't even there. The foreigners usually like to show off their two words of Russian. *Dobroye utra*, they'll say, and that about leaves them exhausted. But this American looked as if he had bigger things to worry about. Never glanced at me, as I say. One thing, though, I remember his jacket. Must have been pure mohair. Beautiful, I never saw such a jacket. The colour of honey.'

Ponomarev was not interested in jackets.

'And when did you see him again?'

'He returned late in the afternoon that day and that's

the last I remember of him until the next day, which would be the day before yesterday.'

'But he could have been back here and out again during the day?'

'Certainly he could. It's not like the old days when I had to glue my bottom to this chair and make a note of all the comings and goings for them.' She loaded 'them' with deep significance.

'So we come to the next day, Monday,' Ponomarev said.

'Well, I never saw him at all until I was going off duty at eight in the evening. He came past again.'

'Did he say anything?'

'Looked straight through me.'

'And what else can you tell me about this American?' Ponomarev asked.

'I? Why, nothing.'

'And what about women?'

'I come on at six. There were no women on this floor. If they sneak out, I see them.'

Ponomarev allowed himself a sardonic wink. 'Come on, Anna, you know the hotel is overrun with whores.'

A shrug.

'Do you mean to tell me there were no women on this floor?'

'Better ask Vera Ivanovna. She's on nights.'

'I will, I will. Meanwhile you can show me the American's room.'

Anna took her master keys from a drawer in her desk and marched down the corridor ahead of the militia, stopping outside 1142. Keys rattled and the door swung open. Ponomarev walked in. 'You can go back to your post, Anna. I'll call if I need you.'

There was nothing noteworthy about the room's appearance. The bed had been made up. The bathroom had been cleaned and fresh towels laid out. A faint aroma of Virginias clung to the curtains and furniture. Ponomarev went through drawers and cupboards according to the rule book, assembling what he found in a neat pile on the bed. He made a cursory inspection of the underside of the mattress, climbed a chair to look on top of the heavy wardrobe, poked about in a desultory fashion behind the radiator and even lifted the toilet lid.

'Nice gear,' he thought. 'Very nice gear. Silk shirts. Monogrammed too. Never saw that before.'

There was a briefcase on the writing table. Inside were some papers, a pocket calculator and a notebook. Ponomarev placed it on the bed. Then he let himself out of the room and marched back to Anna's desk.

'I'll be back. I want nothing touched in there.'

'Why would I touch anything?'

Down in the hotel manager's office, Ponomarev pulled a cigarette from a crumpled pack and thrust it into his mouth.

'Now, this American we're all so interested in. You have his passport?'

The manager pulled a folder towards him on his desk and opened it. 'Here, comrade investigator, passport and our registration form.'

Ponomarev pocketed them.

'Phone calls?'

The manager pushed two chits from the switchboard across the desk. 'One to the United States, two local. You have the US number there, but the locals aren't traceable.'

'So tell me what you know of this American's movements.'

'I've talked to the reception staff. One of the girls remembers that he came down to the lobby around nine in the morning on Sunday.'

'He left his floor at eight-thirty,' Ponomarev said.

'Breakfast. He must have gone to one of our restaurants for breakfast.'

'Ah, carry on.'

'At the desk he asked how he could get a taxi. They just

told him to go outside and find one. They know a foreigner will be picked up by a taxi tout and offered a fancy deal; a Marlboro pack for there and back anywhere in Moscow. I imagine it's what happened to the American.'

'I'll talk to the lads outside,' Ponomarev said. 'And what about Monday?'

'It seems no one remembers seeing him about, though one of the girls thinks it was some time in the evening that he deposited his key at the front desk. Only she can't be sure.'

Ponomarev was dragging on his cigarette as if trying to get up a head of steam. 'Yes, yes, comrade manager, and what about the whores?'

The manager was new. No one had told him that Major Ponomarev had spent five years in a battle of wits with the whores of the Rossia.

'We don't allow the girls into the Rossia. Not at all, comrade investigator. Strictly forbidden. Moral turpitude. Disgraceful.'

Ponomarev allowed a smile to spread carefully across his face. 'Everyone knows – the militia knows, *I* know, the KGB knows, Intourist knows, and above all, our esteemed foreign guests know – that the girls swarm into this place every evening at nine like a flock of homing pigeons in miniskirts. Perhaps, comrade manager, you are the only one in your innocence who doesn't know.'

'I deny it categorically.'

'For the time being my dossier is headed FOREIGN NATIONAL, DISAPPEARANCE OF. It is not headed VICE INVESTIGATION, HOTEL ROSSIA. So we'd better talk man to man.'

'Who can control it?' the manager said unhappily. 'I am aware of the directives. I respect the directives. Moral turpitude. All that. But what can you do – lock the street doors? Then how would our guests get in and out?'

'And how would you earn yourself a little extra for the

wife and kids?' Ponomarev winked and shook his head from side to side.

'I – '

'Never mind. We are men of the world here, and so I will now go outside to talk to the lads.'

There was the usual group of drivers outside the hotel and what they were arguing about was the dollar rate.

'I'm getting thirty-five to the dollar.'

'If you know where to go you can get thirty-seven roubles for a green.'

'And where the hell is that?'

'Don't listen to him. He always has to know best.'

The talk died away as Ponomarev appeared. A couple of the drivers sloped off towards their beaten-up taxis. A squat man in a black leather jacket grinned at Ponomarev.

'So the major comes slumming, eh?'

'Yura, a little chat,' Ponomarev said.

He led the other man over to the stone parapet. The river moved sluggishly below. On the far bank the stacks of the power station belched thick grey smoke into the sky.

'Now what have I done?'

'Probably a good deal but it isn't why I'm here.'

'You know me, I help when I can.'

'So do I.'

They had scratched each other's backs for most of Ponomarev's five-year stint at the Rossia. Yura kept order among the drivers, rationed out the jobs, negotiated prices with the foreigners. He'd been a driver once, but now he lived from the rake-off paid by the group of a dozen drivers whose pitch he controlled. He was slightly honest, slightly not. A useful man.

'Were you here on Sunday?'

Yura nodded, accepted a cigarette and a light. Then he hawked and spat over the parapet.

'I'm interested in an American from the hotel.'

'Not many Americans this time of year.'

'That's why I thought you might remember him.'

'What time on Sunday?'

'Maybe around nine in the morning, or maybe later. His passport says he's fifty-two. His floor lady says he was wearing a very fine jacket, colour of honey. We know he took a cab but we don't know where he was heading.'

'I remember him. Shortish, greying hair, dark complexion. Colour of the jacket was more like shit, but never mind. And it was more like three in the afternoon.'

'So who took him?'

'He waved a pack and I handed him to Gena. It was his turn. The man said he wanted the car for the rest of the afternoon. He spoke Russian.'

'Where's Gena?'

'Haven't seen him since then. He's working out of another taxi park.'

'Which one?'

Yura squinted at Ponomarev, dragged on his cigarette and grinned again. 'I am not a police informer, major.'

'It will take me all of fifteen minutes back at headquarters to find your friend Gena. Why not save me the trouble and store up a little credit?'

'The lads don't like this kind of thing. It's even tricky to be seen talking to you.'

'You can say you're in trouble over a complaint we've had from a foreigner who was ripped off by your lot.'

'No. 2 Taxi Park over by the Bolshoi Kamenni bridge, and I never said a word.'

'And what about Monday?'

'I was off Monday. The boys had to fend for themselves. Anyway,' Yura added, 'you know they won't talk to you, and if they do it'll be lies.'

'Thanks,' Ponomarev said. 'See you around.'

The controller at Taxi Park No. 2 was an elderly man. He seemed to have lost an eye. He peered one-sidedly at Ponomarev's ID card, squinted up to make sure that the man holding the card was the same as the one whose mug shot he had just examined, said nothing.

'I'm looking for a driver who's said to be working out of this park.'

'What name?'

'He's known as Gena.'

'What's he wanted for?'

'Routine enquiry.'

'Like hell it is. What's he been up to?'

'Never mind what he's been up to, Dad, where can I find him?'

'Haven't seen him since Monday.' The controller made his way back to his hut.

'Is that surprising?'

'Not really. He's a guy with what you might call other interests.'

'Where can I find him?'

The controller ignored the question, regained the hut and heaved himself onto a tall stool inside. Then he scrabbled among dog-eared cards in a box, found what he was looking for and made a note on a scrap of paper.

'There, his address.'

'Thanks, Dad. What do you know of this Gena?'

'What do I know? I know he has a gold watch. A foreign watch. He didn't buy that with roubles. I know he often has a crate of vodka in the boot. Seen it myself. I know he can get you anything – stuff that isn't in the shops. That's what I know about him.'

The address was a block on Prospect Vernadskovo. The place was run-down, stinking of boiled cabbage, dry rot and piss. The flat was on the fourth floor and the elevator was out of order. Ponomarev arrived panting a little, irritated with the whole project, wanting his lunch. He had better things to do than go slumming after taxi drivers. A routine enquiry: he should have handed it to one of the juniors in the department. The place was disgusting. A stream of filthy language floated down from the floor above, answered by hysterical shrieking. 'Cultured people,' Ponomarev said to himself.

Automatically, he gave the door a shove before banging on it. He was surprised when it swung inwards. He walked slowly into the apartment.

'Anyone here?'

He looked round the room. There were empty bottles stacked in a corner, a TV and video, a pile of old magazines on a sofa, gaudy porcelain figurines in a row on a shelf. On a table, the remains of a meal, laid for one, a half-filled wine bottle next to the empty glass. There was still food on a plate; a congealed mess which Ponomarev reckoned had once been sausage and gravy. An interrupted meal.

He went through to the bathroom. The door was shut. He turned the handle and pushed it inwards, and the thought struck him that much of his life now consisted of pushing doors open in the expectation of enlightenment.

A single bulb hanging from the ceiling was still burning. The bath was to his right. A tap was dripping. The smell in the room was foul and Ponomarev recognised it. He looked reluctantly into the bath. It was nearly full of water, a film of grey scum on the surface. In the water, half submerged, was a youngish man, fully clothed. The face was ashen, a thin line of scum round the cheekbone. In the centre of the forehead, a small black hole, a thin trickle of congealed blood tracing a brownish line down to the ear. The eyes stared glassily at the ceiling. The dead mouth had fallen open in a rictus.

'No more driving for you, my friend,' Ponomarev murmured to himself. 'Here am I, minding my own business, full of goodwill towards all citizens, and do I find a missing American? Do I hell. I find a dead taxi driver. So where on earth do we go for our missing American now?'

He allowed himself a brief moment to consider his question before providing the reply. 'The forensics and the rest of the gang can take over here. I'm off in search of Gena's taxi.'

Always in the presence of death, particularly violent death, a feeling of sadness would well up, with an admixture of disgust, nausea even, according to the circumstances of the case. Now he had to enter into closer communion with the dead man than he fancied, hardened as he was to so many aspects of human beastliness. He pulled up the sleeve of his jacket, unbuttoned the cuff of his shirt and rolled it back. Gingerly, he immersed his hand in the cold water, feeling along the thigh of the corpse until he encountered the hard shape that he sought. Slipping his hand into the pocket of the jeans he felt the outline of a bunch of keys and carefully eased them out, to emerge dripping from the bath. As he did so, the pressure of his hand caused the corpse to roll slightly towards him, the staring eyes engaging his own gaze in a kind of supplication. Or so he fancied.

'Poor devil,' he said to himself. 'Taxi driver, small-time black marketeer, and now dead meat in a bathful of dirty water because he picked the wrong fare.' And the feeling of sadness that he knew on such occasions seemed to reach him with an added poignancy.

He washed his hands at the sink, shook the water from the keys and dried them off on a dirty towel which hung from a rail. Then he left the bathroom, closing the door carefully behind him, this time without touching the handle, and made his way down to the street. The beaten-up taxi with its yellow disc stood by the kerb across the way and he crossed to it, opened the driver's door and eased himself into the seat. In the glove rack he found a clipboard holding a sheet of ruled paper on which Gena appeared to have jotted city destinations and times. One of the scribbled notes was difficult to decipher. The time was written in as 'Sun – 2.50'. Ponomarev made out the letters Zav . . . They meant nothing to him. The word that followed appeared to start with the letter I, and it was only back at his desk later that some bright lad announced that it had to be Zaveti Ilyicha. 'I know it because my granny lives in the next village down the line. The guy's fare must have been taken there.'

'Thanks, Sherlock Holmes,' Ponomarev said. 'I'd be lost without you, wouldn't I?'

'It's only because of my granny living down there,' the bright lad said, grinning sheepishly but immensely pleased with himself.

'Well, now you can be really useful and a credit to your granny. You can call forensic and the fingerprint people and tell them to involve themselves in all this. Then you can go over to the apartment and find out what a dead taxi driver in a bathful of water looks like.'

12

The Moscow train's loudspeaker system crackled uncertainly into life: 'Zaveti Ilyicha station.' As Lyubimov stepped out onto the platform, the soft country air enveloped him. Forty minutes out on the railway line from the Yaroslavski station was this other world of silver birch trees, well-tended plots and dachas. Outside the station a miniature market had come mysteriously and rapidly into existence and would melt away once the few arrivals had disappeared about their business. Old country women in white kerchiefs offered cherries and strawberries in thick glass tumblers at a rouble a glass. A couple of young men in sharp jeans and bomber jackets offered T-shirts, toilet paper, dubious cartons of American cigarettes. An old woman fingered her entire stock – five or six packets of herbs. A small boy shouted something about hazelnuts, a paper bag on the dusty road at his feet.

The village had been renamed Zaveti Ilyicha – Lenin's Bequests – in 1924, the year of Lenin's death. Before that it had been Mamontovka, named in honour of Mamontov, industrialist and patron of the arts, whose grand establishment lay nearby. How long would it cling now to Lenin's name before another rechristening? Maybe one of the hard-faced young men peddling odds and ends in the village market was destined to be a future Mamontov and would have his village renamed after him. Were not the aspiring tycoons of Russia's future selling T-shirts in the country's street markets right now, honing their commercial skills for the advent of capitalism?

Lyubimov found an old man sitting on a low wall, read

to him from his note of Baranov's address, and was directed across the railway track and onto a road which wound its way haphazardly through a wood of birch, fir and poplar. Here and there on either side of the road stood the dachas – country houses masquerading as log cabins in a kind of compromise between the rural simplicities of the past and the sparse luxuries which the factory directors, the middle-ranking military and the successful literary and artistic achievers of Stalin's Russia could offer themselves back in the thirties. Nowadays, the grandchildren of Stalin's elite found the closets at the bottom of the garden had their disadvantages which were barely offset by the birdsong and scent of blossom. And so, most of the dachas were let out to tenants who commuted into the city to work. By kind and wholly unofficial agreement of the landlords, many of these tenants could be registered as residents of Zaveti Ilyicha, and thus of Moscow itself; their unofficial presence becoming official by virtue of an internal passport carrying an official stamp.

Round a bend in the road Lyubimov came to the house he was looking for, a structure much like the others, save that an extension had been built onto its side, clearly at a later date. A large window pierced the extension's wall, thus meeting some painter's need for a studio with a northern light and, Lyubimov reflected, affording Baranov the space in which he was said to be working. It was only as he approached the house that Lyubimov addressed his mind at last to why he was here. To talk to Baranov? But what would he ask and what kind of reply could conceivably tell him anything worth hearing? To take a look at the house, and maybe the studio itself? But what would Baranov allow him to see that could be worth looking at? Maybe just to feel out the setup, to get an intuitive grasp of . . . of what? He didn't know. But he could already discern the outlines of a piece in which this dacha and its contents might well figure, a piece which dealt with he knew not what and which Chelidze would never publish.

He crossed the grass verge to the front door and the impact of the heavy iron knocker reverberated through the house. Shortly there was the sound of steps on flagstones and then a moment of silence. Lyubimov had noticed the spy-hole set at head-height in the door. No doubt he was being inspected from within. After a pause came the sound of bolts drawn back, then a rattle as the door was pulled inwards on a short chain, opening a crack through which it was impossible to see inside.

'Yes?'

The voice was harsh, hostile. It did not belong to Baranov.

'I called to see Peter Baranov.'

'Who are you?'

'A friend.'

'He has many friends. Your name?'

The accent was Ukrainian.

'My name is Lyubimov.'

'Peter Alexandrovitch isn't here.'

'I was told he was working at home.'

'He's out.'

'When do you expect him back?'

'I've no idea.'

Then the door was slammed shut and Lyubimov heard the bolts being thrust home and the footsteps retreat heavily on the flagstones. It rated a paragraph of local colour in the piece that Chelidze would never publish, the more so as he had recognised the grating Ukrainian voice. He had last heard it come out of the dusk at him as he gasped for breath near the seashore town in Taman. 'Just don't meddle and you'll get out of Taman in one piece,' was what the voice had told him then.

'Let's try for another paragraph,' he told himself as he turned away from the house and stepped back into the road. There was another house opposite and one further back on the same side. But Baranov's house appeared to be the last in the row. Beyond it the woods continued in a wild state until another bend in the road closed off the view. Lyubimov walked on for fifty metres or so before turning into the woods on his left, picking his way through the trees, stepping onto a thick, springy carpet of pine needles. He would skirt Baranov's property, aiming to approach it from the side with the large window. Perhaps something significant was to be seen, perhaps not. Maybe Baranov himself would show his face. Maybe, even, he would get a glimpse of the inside of the house. Maybe he was a bloody fool.

He skirted the house, keeping well out of sight, judging the distance, treading carefully. When he reckoned that he had returned to a point beyond the property, he turned left towards the road and soon saw that he had judged the thing nicely. The house suddenly appeared between the trees slightly to his left. A clearing had been made behind it and no doubt it had once served as a garden. Maybe vegetables had been grown in neat rows; possibly a few flowers for the house in summertime, when the family would move out here from Moscow and their friends would visit for the day to have a lunch of cold borscht, pancakes and strawberries in the shade of a tree. Now the garden was overgrown, abandoned, fast being reclaimed by the forest. The area was littered with household rubbish. Someone had dumped a load of rusty iron there – maybe the remains of some discarded agricultural machinery? There were packing cases and logs piled against the wooden privy. Lyubimov reckoned none of this afforded cover for anyone approaching the house. If he was going to get close enough to take a look through the window he would have to make a dash over open ground like someone escaping across a frontier. He stood uncertainly, half concealed by one of the trees edging the clearing. A scampering squirrel on a branch above his head made him start. He told himself he was behaving like a romantic fool again, just as he had on his walk in Lermontov's footsteps in Taman. No doubt it would end in painful farce just as the walk had done.

He was on the point of deciding that discretion should prevail when a sudden resounding *crack* next to his right ear made him duck instinctively. It was followed by the sound of a window slamming shut. A jagged piece of rock had ricocheted off the trunk of the tree next to him and fallen into the carpet of pine needles to his right. He was being warned off in the simplest possible manner. It gave him his second paragraph. The third would say that he'd judged the place too dangerous to investigate further and what, pray, would an official picture restorer be doing holed up with a Ukrainian thug who either rammed his fist into your gut or hurled rocks at you from the window of a barricaded house in the forest?

The fourth paragraph would let it be understood that the cautious author had made his way back to the road and thence to the railway station and so to the safer anonymity of the Moscow streets. And none of it, he concluded, would Chelidze publish.

But as he walked slowly back along the road through the trees he saw a car coming towards him. As it approached, the driver slowed and the car came to a halt as it drew level.

'Don't I know you?' the man next to the driver called out to him. 'Aren't you the journalist who did a story last year on my office?'

Lyubimov walked over. 'You're Major Ponomarev,' he said. 'I covered the Filatov case with you.'

'And what are you doing in Zaveti Ilyicha?'

Lyubimov grinned. 'And you, major?'

'A routine enquiry,' Ponomarev said. 'I've answered your question, now you answer mine.'

'As a matter of fact, I'd be happy to have a chat,' Lyubimov said.

Ponomarev turned to his driver. 'Pull over. We'll be a few minutes here.' He got out of the car, shook Lyubimov by the hand and led him to a fallen tree by the roadside. 'We'll sit here for a bit and you'll tell me whatever enters your head, right? I remember you well now: a lad who gets around, hears things, knows what two and two add up to. So tell me about Zaveti Ilyicha and those of its citizens who are known to you.'

The fourth paragraph would have to change. Indeed, it could make a lead to the story.

13

The hotel in Pushkinskaya Street attached to the Ministry of the Interior possesses on its ground floor a modest restaurant, known to its habitués as the Militseiski. The place is frequented by Ministry officials and occasionally by officers of the Specially Serious Crimes Squad – the Specials – from the nearby Petrovka. So relaxed and inconspicuous is it that quite a few Muscovites who have nothing to do with officialdom know the place and are allowed to use it unchallenged. And it is worth using, not only for its outstanding food, but for the unusual amiability of the staff and the cleanliness of the table linen. It was at this oasis in Moscow's gastronomic desert that Major Ponomarev and Slava Lyubimov occupied a corner table, before them a zakuski (hors d'oeuvre) of salmon, red caviar and meat salad. It was one-thirty on the day following their chance meeting in the woods and a half hour before vodka could legally be served.

'I am not in the habit of co-operating this closely with the press,' Ponomarev said between mouthfuls of salad.

'I don't think there is any danger of my publishing anything to embarrass you,' Lyubimov said. 'My editor will see to that.'

'I'd have thought it would make a good newspaper story.'

'It would, but although we are supposed to be living in enlightened times, my editor still calls the Central Committee to ask permission to blow his nose, and he thinks this one will upset them.'

'Let us exchange confidences,' Ponomarev said.

The waitress was clearing the remains of the zakuski and soon returned with a chicken Kiev flanked by potatoes, currently in short supply.

'The food is good here,' Ponomarev added, 'and although I shouldn't tell you this, it's one of the few restaurants that isn't bugged.'

'I know,' Lyubimov said simply, and Ponomarev raised an eyebrow and allowed himself to grin. He did not ask how Lyubimov knew.

They ate in silence for a while, carefully extruding the hot spicy sauce as they cut into the chicken thighs.

'Excellent,' Ponomarev said. 'My wife makes better, but for a restaurant, excellent.' Lyubimov nodded, his mouth full. Then Ponomarev looked up from his plate. 'What do you make of all this?' he asked.

'As I told you when we had our chat in the woods yesterday,' Lyubimov said, 'I believe the man Baranov took something from the cellar of the cathedral in Taman. Then I was told at the Restoration Works last week that he was working on an icon at home. To me it smells of a classic case, theft from a provincial church, probably regularised by one Marchenko, the boss of religious activity in Krasnodar. You'll probably find what he's stolen will either be sold on the black market here or to the regional museum in Krasnodar. Either way, our friend Baranov and his gang are crooks.'

'So what we have here, according to you, is a simple case of theft, right?'

'You're the policeman, major, so you're the one to say.'

'I have to tell you, young man, that there is a very simple rule of detective work and it is this: if you find a dead body riddled with bullet holes on the railway tracks, you do not concern yourself with the fact that the dead person had been crossing the line at an undesignated place, thus committing an offence. You keep your mind focused on the murder. Well, here I am investigating a disappearance – probably a murder – plus another certain killing. So I am not to be diverted into enquiring about the alleged theft of an icon by a small-time thief whom our records reveal to have done something of the kind before.'

'Quite,' Lyubimov said, for want of something better to put forward. 'On the other hand, might not the two be connected?'

'Of course they might,' Ponomarev said, 'and that's why I've obtained a search warrant to take a closer look at what the man Baranov is up to.'

'I hope they don't throw rocks at you, major.'

'You see,' Ponomarev continued, 'I am told this American was a distinguished art expert. It could be argued that he had come to Baranov's place to examine this icon, returned to Moscow, went about his business, and then disappeared. The disappearance may or may not be connected with his visit to Baranov, of course, and I suspect I'll have a good deal of work to do before such a connection can be established. But meanwhile we'll have to see what Baranov has to say for himself.'

'I would be grateful,' Lyubimov said, 'if you'd allow me to stay in touch with you. Since my visit to Taman, where I was roughed up a bit, I've developed a kind of fondness for this story and I hope there may come a point where I can write it up and maybe place it with an editor who is less terrified than friend Chelidze at *Vperiod*.'

Ponomarev wiped his mouth on his napkin and waved to the waitress for the bill. Then he looked quizzically at Slava Lyubimov.

'I can't pretend I've ever been that fond of the press,' he said. 'On the other hand, you made a nice job of the Filatov case. Only two errors of fact and you covered the Specials in glory. You might even come in useful on this one. In fact, I've an idea on that score.'

'What do you want me to do?'

'Well, there's one thing you can do this afternoon. I have my authorisation to take a look at Baranov's place, but of course I'll need my witness. Usually a neighbour gets hauled in. But if you like, you can act as witness. Be at Petrovka at four and we'll drive to Zaveti Ilyicha.'

He took the bill from the waitress.

'Tell the chef his chicken Kiev was up to standard, Lena.'

The waitress smiled and nodded.

As they parted outside on the pavement, Ponomarev said, 'I'll see you at four.' Then he turned and marched off in the direction of the Petrovka.

Slava Lyubimov walked over to Tverskaya Street, heading towards the Red House, headquarters of the Moscow City Soviet. With time to spare before an appointment with a contact in the planning department, he wandered on to Pushkin Square and stopped to listen to the crowds arguing over what they read in *Moscow News*, posted up on boards along a wall.

'When Gorbachev goes to the West and asks for credits, know what they do? They fart in his face, the lot of them.'

'It's time that clown got the sack. He's led us into nothing but trouble. You'll see, the Party will get rid of him somehow.'

'To hell with the Party. I'm an Afghanets – two years out there. Left half my right foot in the fucking place. But we fought them, upheld the honour of the army, and what does that bastard do? Sacks fifteen divisions overnight, throws my mates out of a job. The Yanks must be pissing themselves laughing. So I say, give the army a chance to run the show. I say Yazov's a good man.'

'My wife's sick,' an elderly man was saying to anyone who cared to listen, 'and d'you think I can buy aspirin? The hell I can. The pharmacy says aspirins are no problem, it's the bottles. Seems they've no bottles, so they can't deliver aspirin. Bloody madhouse we live in.'

'I'll tell you why.' It was a gaunt woman with a pinched, unhappy face. 'The Jews,' she said. 'Pamyat is right. They remind us, over half Lenin's Politburo who made this damned revolution were Jews, and now what are the Jews up to? They're scuttling, aren't they? Leaving the country in the mess they made of it.'

'Don't know about that,' someone said. 'All I know, things were better under Brezhnev.'

'You're all talking rubbish,' a young man in a T-shirt and shorts was saying.

Lyubimov drifted away and headed back towards the Red House. Outside a shop selling glassware and trinkets a line of would-be customers was marshalled behind barriers by a couple of bored militiamen. What were they queuing for? A bit of cut glass? An ashtray? Was an ashtray preferable to cash in the bank? Evidently so. An ashtray was an ashtray, whereas a rouble wasn't necessarily anything like the original rouble a month later. Lyubimov was half inclined to look inside to see what it was exactly that people would line up for in their patient, orderly fashion. Then he glanced at his watch, saw the time of his appointment at the Red House was imminent and headed across the street to meet his contact and ask about the failure of the City Council to issue certificates for the formation of certain co-operatives, thus breaking the law of the land. Chelidze had some kind of grudge against the Moscow leadership. He might publish something on the subject. It would leave time to reach Petrovka by four.

As they got out of the police car outside the dacha, Ponomarev said, 'Remember, you are an official witness and as such you do nothing in there but watch to see *I* don't break the law.'

There was a long silence after he had banged the heavy knocker against the door. He knocked again. Soon, footsteps echoed on the tiled floor within, bolts were drawn back and the door opened. Baranov had prepared a smile, which disappeared from his face when he caught sight of Lyubimov. Ponomarev held up his police identity card for Baranov to see.

'Moscow militia, Major Ponomarev of the Specially

Serious Crimes Squad. This is my witness, Stanislav Petrovitch Lyubimov. I have a warrant to search these premises on suspicion of a crime having been committed.'

'No crime has been committed here, major,' Baranov replied. He had managed to restore the smile. Then, looking past Ponomarev: 'I remember you, Lyubimov. Surely it's irregular to use a journalist who is nosing after a story as an official witness?'

'You are welcome to call in as many of your neighbours as you like,' Ponomarev said, 'but you are not at liberty to exclude my witness. Shall we add to the numbers?'

'Not necessary.' Baranov stepped aside, holding the door open. 'Come in and look around. I have nothing to hide, major.'

'Nice to see you again,' Lyubimov said to Baranov as he stepped into the house. 'I was wandering around this way yesterday and someone threw a rock at me from one of your windows.'

'Surely not,' Baranov said. 'It isn't the kind of thing I'd dream of.'

'Maybe not, but that tame thug of yours, the Ukrainian, wouldn't think twice about it.'

'No idea who you're talking about. There are no Ukrainians here.'

Ponomarev was wandering round the room without touching anything. Then he nodded towards the divan. 'Let's have that out into the middle with the cover off, please.'

Without a word Baranov complied, pulling the heavy piece of furniture clear of the wall. Ponomarev grunted, moved over to the stove and glanced behind it. Then he examined the long bookcase, removed some volumes at random, glancing into the spaces left. He replaced the books on top of the shelves.

'What exactly are you looking for?' Baranov asked. 'Maybe I could help you if I knew what all this is about.'

Ponomarev ignored the question, nodded towards the door in the side wall. 'Let's have a look through there.'

Baranov crossed over and opened the door. 'It's a studio. I do a certain amount of work at home. After you, major.'

They went through the door, Lyubimov bringing up the rear. In the centre of the room, facing away from them and towards the high window, stood the easel, the stool and table with painting equipment next to it. Ponomarev started to walk slowly round the studio, lifting pillows from the divan and replacing them, picking up magazines at random, even lifting the corner of a worn rug as if he expected a trapdoor beneath. Clearly, Lyubimov thought, the major hadn't the faintest idea what he was looking for and hadn't even a decent technique for making the search appear purposeful. Baranov stood aside, perfectly relaxed, a half-surprised, half-amused expression on his face.

'You work here?' Ponomarev said, as if he were expected to make polite conversation.

'I work here,' Baranov parroted him.

'And this thing here?' Ponomarev had walked round to the front of the icon on the easel and stood surveying it dubiously. 'What's this, then?'

'An icon,' Baranov said.

'I see that.'

'Then what else can I tell you, major?'

'Whose is it, for a start.'

'I suppose the legal owners must be the Krasnodar Regional Executive Committee, but I'm no lawyer, just a picture restorer.'

'And what is it doing here?'

'I am restoring it, working at home by agreement with my boss at the Moscow Restoration Works.' He allowed a pause, then added: 'I often do that. The place is a dump.'

Lyubimov had moved round to look at the icon, which presented very much the aspect of a work-in-progress. It had been overpainted in many areas and it was only with difficulty that one could see beneath the layers of paint and varnish what appeared to be a version of the famous Roublev masterpiece.

'Tell me about this icon of yours,' Ponomarev said. 'Tell me where it comes from and where it's going.'

'For that,' Baranov said smoothly, 'I'm afraid I must refer you to the owners in Krasnodar and to the Moscow Restoration Works. I am merely the restorer, you understand, and naturally I have no personal standing in the origins and ultimate destination of the piece.'

'How do I know it is legitimately in your possession?'

Baranov took a paper from his pocket and handed it to Ponomarev.

'Somehow, I thought you might ask me that, major, so I have my authorisation handy.' He passed the paper over. Ponomarev glanced at it and handed it back. Then he turned away and continued his listless examination of the room.

'Anyone else here?' he asked.

'No one else. I live alone.'

'What about yesterday, was anyone here then?'

'No.'

'I understand you work with a team. Where are they?'

'No doubt you'll be able to contact them through the office,' Baranov said. He allowed himself the trace of a further smile.

'And the day before? Not an American, by any chance?'

'I'm afraid I don't know any Americans, here or anywhere else.'

'If an American art expert had been in this area, would there be anyone else round about who might have reason to be his contact?'

No, Baranov said, after a moment apparently deep in thought, he would gladly help the major in his task, whatever that might be, but no, he couldn't think of anyone in the immediate vicinity who was interested in works of art, though the major might care to try the Beliayevs, four houses down on the opposite side. They'd been known to sell modest artworks from time to time, had sometimes sought his opinion. But it was very inferior inherited stuff, unlikely to interest a foreigner, though you never knew, did you? And would they have a drink, now that their little search had been concluded, presumably to the major's satisfaction? No? Very well, on duty and so forth. And certainly, he'd be available if needed.

On their way back to town, Ponomarev said, 'What did you think of that?'

'Well, you said earlier he had a record of some kind, and I know he employs this Ukrainian roughneck to do his dirty work for him. Also that his gang stole silver and very probably the icon down in Taman. So surely we have to assume he was lying?'

Ponomarev said nothing for a while as the car moved fast towards Moscow. Then, 'I am investigating a disappearance, possibly a second murder, and I seem to have stumbled into a case of small-time theft of church property.'

'It looks as if the theft has been regularised somehow by our friend Marchenko in Krasnodar.'

'God preserve me,' Ponomarev said, 'from getting involved in that sort of provincial mess. I repeat: I am interested solely in a murder, possibly two.'

'There's one other thing,' Lyubimov said.

Ponomarev turned to look at him.

'Yes?'

'You said two murders, but in fact it's three. You see, the priest at the church from which the stuff was stolen was bludgeoned to death with a hammer.' He paused. 'Four, if you count his dog.'

That evening in New York Anton Kurtz telephoned Grigoriev in Brighton Beach. Betraying none of his own misgivings, he conveyed Ushida's condition: the Russians must protest loud and long at the loss of the icon.

'Very difficult, Mr Kurtz,' Grigoriev said.

'I dare say. On the other hand, it is a condition laid down by my client, and therefore by me. I have a sale sewn up, subject to that condition.'

'I will see what can be done. I will call my man over there.'

'Very well. And please do not come back to me with arguments.'

It was at that point that Grigoriev came reluctantly to the conclusion that he would perhaps need to pay a last visit to Moscow himself. He hadn't seen the place for six years and there was no reason in these days of perestroika why they shouldn't let him in. Weren't the dissidents and refugees and victims going back in droves nowadays – in and out in a manner unthinkable a few years ago? He wouldn't go near Yerevan; the Armenian authorities no doubt still had their records. But Moscow? Why not, if that was called for? And seemingly it was.

14

At eight next morning the phone rang in the apartment near the Kolkhosnaya Metro station where Slava Lyubimov had a room. His landlady, a cheerful soul who worked in the *parterre* cloakroom at the Bolshoi Theatre, with all that that implied for Lyubimov's ability to lay his hands on tickets for the ballet, called out from the living room, 'Slava, a lady for you.' As he came in to take the call, she added, 'A nice voice, this one,' and bestowed a smile on him. She regarded her lodger as an excellent catch for some suitable girl.

'Lyubimov here,' he said into the mouthpiece.

'You may not remember me; I am Raya. We met on the flight to Krasnodar and we said whoever reached the other's city first would call.' There was a pause. This was somewhat forward for a respectable Soviet girl. 'As I'm in Moscow again, I fulfilled my side of our bargain.'

'This is splendid,' Lyubimov said. 'When do we meet?'

'I'm here on an economic delegation in connection with the treaty they're signing next week, so I haven't much spare time. But since we had a deal . . .' She allowed her voice to trail off, waiting modestly to be persuaded.

'Surely you have *some* time,' Lyubimov said. 'What about dinner tonight? I know a place.'

'Official dinner, I'm afraid.'

'Then afterwards?'

'We're dining at the Intourist Hotel in Tverskaya Street. If you came by, say at ten-thirty, perhaps we could say hello and have a chat, and then you can play the journalist and try to find out what the delegation is all about.'

'And you won't tell me.'

She laughed and he liked the sound. Then he said, 'Ten-thirty is fine. I'll be there, and we can compete again on Lermontov's poetry.'

'*A solitary sail that rises/white in the blue mist on the foam . . .*' She had the quotation ready for him.

There was a pause as Lyubimov struggled to recall the rest of the stanza. 'Is it something about a far land?'

'*What is it in far lands it prizes?/What does it leave behind at home?*' Then she laughed again.

'You looked it up in order to catch me out.'

'No, it's one I learned at school and it's never left me. I can even tell you he wrote it in 1832, so there.'

'I shall spend most of today swotting up on his poetry and tonight I'll outclass you.'

She laughed. 'I must go; my rather dreary colleagues can't be denied. We'll meet at ten-thirty.' And she rang off.

'A nice girl?' his landlady asked.

'No, not a nice girl, a wonderful girl. This is my truly lucky day.' And he seized his landlady round the waist and planted a kiss on her left cheek.

Later at the weekly editorial conference in Chelidze's office, he was not so sure it was all that lucky.

They discussed assignments and story ideas. It was a discussion which lacked thrust and purpose, since most of the stories the staff were interested in were also stories which for one reason or another, and all of them in essence political, Chelidze had no intention of allowing into the paper. The eight members of the staff who attended these weekly charades had long since given up trying to turn the journal into something any sensible citizen would want to read. For them it was a case of salvaging what they could of their professional self-respect by trying to smuggle a few subversive items into each issue. Then, back home, they could face their various spouses with some dignity.

'What crap again this week!' Panov's girlfriend would announce, skimming through an issue and throwing the thing down in disgust. 'I don't know why you bother.'

She was a spirited and frequently angry little thing who worked as an illustrator on an obscure magazine and though Panov could lift her up in one hand without flexing a muscle – and sometimes did – she was well aware that she terrified him and it had never occurred to her that the huge disparity in their sizes had any bearing on the matter.

Now Chelidze was glancing through a sheaf of papers lying in front of him. Then he looked up at Lyubimov.

'I have an assignment for you, genatsvale, which will at last be something entirely to your taste. You like football, right?'

Lyubimov nodded.

'You follow Moscow Dynamo right?'

'Right.'

'And, you are an admirer of Mikhail Lermontov and his story about Taman.'

'That's right, but – '

'But nothing. You'll see that I am able to offer you an assignment which, strangely enough, combines two of the subjects closest to your heart. I want you to be in Naro-Fominsk tomorrow. It's the base of the Taman Tank Division and tomorrow they have a football match. Their team, which I'm told are the army champions, are playing Moscow Dynamo's second team. A friendly match to inaugurate their new stadium. It starts at two and you can do us a nice piece on the stadium, the civic role of our army lads, stuff like that. And maybe a paragraph on the game itself. And nothing sarcastic about Afghanistan, please.'

There was a murmur round the room and someone laughed briefly.

'A splendid way of spending a Saturday afternoon,' Lyubimov said, without sarcasm.

'Everything's been fixed with the adjutant's office at Naro-Fominsk,' Chelidze said. 'Vera has the details.'

Then the discussion turned to matters directly political.

'We've the signing of the treaty with the republics on

Tuesday,' Gennady Ivanov said. 'I'll be covering that with Nadia at the Kremlin. We might need someone to get some street reactions.'

Ivanov was the paper's political analyst, a man with good contacts and a sensitive nose for the workings of the wildly unstable political scene. Now he said, 'I can't put my finger on it, but something is undoubtedly going on.'

'What does that mean?' Chelidze asked.

'I get different vibes in the President's office and the Central Committee.'

'What vibes, as you call them, and what differences?'

'Well, at the Kremlin, they're all optimism about the treaty and pleased with themselves like a lot of kids who've won a football match, since football seems to be on our agenda. But over in Staraya Ploshchad the noise is quite different. My contacts are telling me that the big boys in the Central Committee still hate the treaty and someone heard Pavlov say in his usual mumbling fashion that nothing was really settled and we'd all have to see what happened, wouldn't we? That, from the Prime Minister, has its significance.'

'Over at the Moscow Soviet,' Lyubimov put in, 'I was told Luzhkov is going around declaring that the old guard will simply never stomach Gorbachev's treaty and they're likely to try something on.'

'Being deputy mayor of Moscow, and an indifferent one at that,' Chelidze said, 'does not provide Luzhkov with insights which are denied to the rest of us. In any case, if there were any substance in all this Gorbachev wouldn't be on vacation down at Cape Sarich. He'd be back here defending his precious treaty.'

'It's just that there's an atmosphere building up,' Nadia Krasina, the paper's political commentator, said.

'And this journal is not going to add to it,' Chelidze snapped.

And on that note the meeting broke up. As they retreated

down the corridor Lyubimov told Panov, 'We might as well be on *Pravda* and get a decent salary.'

Later he called Major Ponomarev's number at the Specials. The major was out, was there a message? 'Just tell him,' Lyubimov said, 'that Slava Lyubimov will be out of town tomorrow – just in case he needs me.'

They met soon after ten-thirty that evening in the tatty and depressing lobby of the Intourist Hotel. She was wearing a silk dress in midnight blue which hugged her figure and Lyubimov thought he had never seen anything quite as exciting as this Armenian beauty with the rather solemn manner and the fine legs. He asked her about her delegation.

'We're negotiating some of the detail on economic relations after the new treaty comes into force,' she said. 'It isn't very newsworthy stuff, and in any case I'm not free to tell you about it.'

'I never thought I was chasing a story,' Lyubimov said. 'I thought I was meeting a friend for a chat.'

'Good, then you can tell me about yourself,' she said. 'I am interested to know how one becomes a journalist, also *why* you became a journalist.'

There was a touch of the social scientist about her, Lyubimov thought. Was she at all interested in him, or was she merely interested in the *genus* journalist, of which he was a convenient example?

Then she blushed. 'I am very rude, shooting questions at you in this way. They call me the interrogator in my family – a terrible commentary on my lack of manners. But you see, I am always so curious about people. It is my defect of character.'

'Your family has failed to understand a very important principle,' Lyubimov said. 'It's that people love to be asked questions. Look, I can't remember when anyone asked me about my wretched novel, as you did on the way down to Krasnodar, only to follow up now with your charming catechism on the way one staggers or drifts into journalism. It's . . . gratifying.'

'Well then, tell me.'

She had a way of looking directly into his eyes. It was, he thought, a shade frightening.

'Please start at the beginning,' she said now. 'With your parents. Like that, I will understand what comes later.'

'My father, Pyotr Nikolayevitch, worked as an engineer at the ZIL factory here in Moscow. A quiet man, undistinguished, I'd say, but very kind and patient. And a lover of books. My mother seemed to spend most of her time rushing back and forth along the long, dark corridor which ran the length of our dreadful communal apartment. Fifteen neighbours shared the kitchen and the toilet. The din was indescribable. My mother was a saint, but a saint who could shout louder than the fifteen neighbours.'

'What did your father make in his factory?'

'ZIL limousines for our masters, trucks, and sometimes refrigerators. He worked now on this production line, now on that. But I particularly remember the fridges because we had an enormous ZIL at home. No room for it in the kitchen, so it stood like some polar monster with indigestion in a corner of our room. The damn thing rumbled, grunted and whirred and sometimes it stopped working altogether. I suppose I have more vivid memories of the fridge than anything else in my childhood. Its size frightened me and the disgusting noises it made frightened me even more. I was convinced a Baba Yaga or maybe a polar bear was hiding behind it, belching and making those indecent noises.'

She laughed. 'Did you put your fridge into your novel?'

'Of course. But I'm telling you about it now because I've always believed it was responsible for my ambition to write. It massaged my imagination at an impressionable age, you see. There's nothing like delicious fear, even unpleasant fear, to stimulate a child to invent, to decorate a drab sort of life with colourful fancies. So you could say I became a writer because my father worked at ZIL and got a reject fridge on the cheap. And you must understand that to be classed a reject at the ZIL plant the thing had to be positively useless. All the genuine rejects were shipped out to the public. As to my father, he had learned English as a youngster, loved the English novelists and had a precious collection of tattered English books. He encouraged me to work at my English and to read whatever he had. I owe him a lot.'

'And he had Lermontov?'

'He had a beautiful edition of *Hero* in tooled red leather, and *The Demon*. Also, two collections of his poetry. My father was a cultured man who worked at a lathe all his life.'

'And all that led you towards a writing career?'

'Yes. I managed somehow to beat my way into the Thorez Institute of Foreign Languages despite the lathe in my background and there I started contributing to the ridiculous little house journal we had. Eventually they made me the editor. The ink had entered my bloodstream and I was lost. After I left I started bombarding journals with stories, *feuilletons*, anything I could think of. I remember, it took me sixteen months before something was accepted. After that, I found a job at *Soviet Literature* as a translator, contributing occasional pieces of my own. Then I met a fellow called Panov who wrote for *Vperiod* – I hope you'll meet him before you leave Moscow – and he put in a word for me and I landed the job I'm in now. And that,' he concluded, 'is how I became a journalist. As to the "why", the answer must be the fridge in our room.'

'I think,' she said, 'you should take your fridge out of your novel and put it into a story for children. The Refrigerator Which Had Indigestion. It would have incredibly delicious things to eat inside it, too; hence the indigestion.'

They both laughed.

'Now you must tell me about yourself and how you became an economist,' Lyubimov said.

'There's nothing very unusual about me,' she said. 'My father was born in Syria and his parents found themselves there because the Turks had deported close to two million Armenians to Syria and Mesopotamia during the First World War. The Turks also went to the trouble of killing 600,000 of them in 1915, but my grandparents were lucky and survived. My father found his way back to Armenia after the Second World War, and there he married my mother who is a Russian. Her name is Larissa and she is very beautiful.'

'And your father?'

'A typical Armenian, which means to say that he is a typical victim. We Armenians are all professional victims, and as victims we have learned all kinds of skills designed to give ourselves moral support, self respect and a way to live in a dangerous world. Perhaps that is what has made us into traders with a sharp eye for value and equity, much like the Jews, I suppose. Maybe it led me into economics and the comforting thought that two and two make four in a very uncertain world.'

'And what was your father's work?'

'My father, the typical victim, trained as an architect. But with his so-called foreign background the Soviet *apparat* would never trust him, and so he has had to work for most of his life as a construction worker. But like your own father, the cultured lathe operator, my father also was a cultured man, but with brick dust under his fingernails. A parallel, is it not?'

'It is. Perhaps there's something of the victim about both of us.'

She smiled. 'On the other hand, you mustn't forget that I come from a paradise on earth, according to the poets. You know what Byron had to say when they told him about the Armenian paradise – "I went seeking it, God knows where, and did I find it? Now and then, for a minute or two." I suppose we all hope for a minute or two of paradise on earth.'

She looked at her watch. 'It's very late and I can hardly keep my eyes open. So now I must get some sleep so that tomorrow I get the output figures for textiles right first time.'

Could they meet tomorrow, perhaps, when he got back from Naro-Fominsk? No, the delegation would be working all day and late into the evening. There were protocols to be readied for the Monday, and it meant a weekend of solid work. But she'd call him again, she said, and perhaps they could fix something before she was due to leave Moscow in midweek.

When they parted at the door of the hotel he held her outstretched hand rather longer than seemed natural, leant slightly towards her as if he would chance an embrace of some kind, then seemed to think a rebuff was likely and merely said goodnight. There was a trace of a smile on her normally rather solemn face, as if to say that had he ventured he might well have succeeded in some modest progression, say by way of a chaste kiss on the cheek. We Russians, he said to himself as he crossed Tverskaya Street, heading for the Metro on the corner of Okhotniy Ryad, we Russians are still full of crazy inhibitions with women. Depardieu or Sylvester Stallone would have swept her up in his arms and whisked her off to some place where one could make immediate and passionate love to an Armenian beauty in town to discuss what deliveries of textiles and citrus fruit Yerevan would make to Moscow next year.

Next day in Naro-Fominsk there was nothing but aggravation. The place proved to be pretty exactly Lyubimov's idea of a garrison town – six-storey blocks of military flats laid out in neat rows; something slightly grander which appeared to be an officers' club; a vast parade ground with, in a far corner, an ancient T37 on a plinth, its long-nosed gun pointing at the Taman Guards Division's administration block. At the gates of the headquarters he offered his passport, press card and assignment sheet to the sergeant on duty in the guardhouse, who peered at the documentation as if it had been drawn up in Urdu, reached for the phone and put the whole thing to what was presumably the adjutant's office. Then he listened to what was being said at the other end of the line, answered yes several times, asked what he should say to the visitor, and hung up.

'There's no football match today,' he announced to Lyubimov.

'Yes, there is,' Lyubimov said. 'It's even been in the newspapers – a friendly against Moscow Dynamo 2 to launch your new stadium. I passed the stadium on the way over from the station. It looks as if it's ready as far as I can see.'

'The stadium's ready but there's no match today,' the sergeant said. There was no expression on his face.

'So what's happened to the fixture? Has it been cancelled?'

'I'm only authorised to tell you there's no match.' The sergeant allowed himself a shrug. 'I suppose,' he added, 'they've cancelled it for some reason.'

'Can you think what reason?' Lyubimov asked. 'I could at least write about that.' He opened a pack and offered a cigarette. The sergeant took one and slipped it into the breast pocket of his tunic. 'For later. I'm on duty, see.'

'Sure.'

The sergeant was inclined to gossip. 'I reckon it's cancelled because something's on the move, though I don't know what. Leave's been cancelled too.'

'Tough.'

'I'll say. My sister's getting married today. I was due to go to Moscow for the weekend. The bastards cancelled my leave. Wouldn't listen. Anyone would think there's a war on.'

In the middle distance Lyubimov could hear the metallic roar of tank engines revving up, starting and stopping. There seemed to be plenty of activity in the vast courtyard beyond the guardhouse. A platoon was being drilled. A staff car speeded towards them, racing through the gate which a soldier closed behind it. Lyubimov caught sight of pips, shoulder flashes within.

'Manoeuvres,' he suggested to the sergeant while something else began to grow at the back of his mind.

'Looks like it, only we've been told nothing. Usually, they work up to manoeuvres for bloody weeks. All I know, tank crews were paraded at dawn and got an earful from their commanders.' The sergeant shrugged again. 'Christ knows what they were on about. None of my business, right?'

'Right.' Lyubimov gave a grin. 'So what happened to the Dynamo team, then?'

'The poor sods turned up a couple of hours ago in a coach and simply got turned back. Told the whole thing was cancelled. Something about orders from on high. I can tell you, they were thoroughly pissed off. There was a lot of yelling and cursing before they shoved off.'

'Well,' Lyubimov said, 'thanks for the chat. Good luck.'

As he waited for a train back to the city he reflected that the Naro-Fominsk base reminded him of nothing so much as an army getting ready to go into action.

But where was the war? On Saturday, 17 August 1991, there was not, as far as he knew, a war requiring the presence of one of the three centrally controlled crack divisions of the Soviet army. In the distance, carried across the still summer haze, he could hear the tank engines, nothing but a hoarse murmur now in the distance.

15

In the sultry August weather, with the fumes from the power stations hanging in a grey pall over the city, the population of Moscow floods onto the streets on Sundays, filling the Arbat, streaming up to the Kremlin and down onto Red Square and taking the Metro out to the vast street markets at Izmailovo. Heavy clouds were piling up on the horizon but it was still walking and queuing weather – queuing for McDonalds or for Baskin Robbins ice cream, or tea in the Georgia House in the Arbat; queuing for the museums, queuing wherever a case could be made for it. Marina had wanted to go out to Gorki Park and sighed like any policeman's wife when Ponomarev announced that three days on, the intractable case of the vanishing American had produced the usual backlog in the office.

'Sorry,' he said, 'I know how you feel, but if you'd married a bureaucrat things might have been different.'

'I'd have had more money, more social life, a better apartment and imported lingerie. On the other hand, I'd have had a bureaucrat in my bed every night, and that hardly bears thinking about. It's going to rain so be sure to take your waterproof and umbrella.'

Ponomarev bent to kiss her, said he'd be back for supper, and managed to get out of the apartment without the umbrella. In the office he buried himself in work which, he reflected, was purely bureaucratic, trying to push to the back of his mind the messy case of the American and his taxi driver; trying because all his experience told him that it would not – by its nature, could not – offer any joy.

'It has an international dimension, and that means sooner

or later there will be interference from on high, and that in turn will mean police methods will have to give way to political expediency. And the journalist has quite rightly pointed out that there's a significant provincial angle to the case, and from the Kuban, of all regions. What does it spell in capital letters? It spells CORRUPTION for sure. Someone paying someone else to trip me up.'

He pushed aside the pile of papers on his desk and held his head in his hands. He stayed like that for ten minutes, deep in thought and making no sense of what he had in the way of facts.

'Do I take a trip to Krasnodar, or even to Taman?' he asked himself. He doubted they'd sanction the expense of the journey anyway. Yesterday, he'd called the Krasnodar Regional Council and Stepan Stepanovitch Marchenko wasn't in his office, it being a Saturday. A call to his home elicited no reply. No doubt he was in some dacha for the weekend. Marchenko would have to wait until tomorrow. And what if he did go down south? What could he hope to discover when he got there? That an icon had been stolen – a fact that would no doubt be hotly denied by Marchenko? And even so, what had that to do with the vanishing American? Nothing, really, unless it could be proved that the icon was so valuable that . . . He sighed, straightened up and pulled the papers back towards him and started turning them over listlessly, his mind elsewhere. Then he picked up the phone and dialled the Moscow Interpol bureau. Would they please pass an enquiry to Interpol in Washington concerning a certain Victor Gordon? He gave what details he had, including the fact that Victor Gordon had disappeared. He'd like to know exactly what kind of vanishing American he was dealing with – full description, anything from the US police and so forth. Dental records? No, not yet. There was no body, indeed there was nothing yet to say the man was dead. A kidnapping? More likely. 'That's the lot?' the Interpol duty officer asked.

'One more thing. There's a reference to an Anton Kurtz in Gordon's papers that interests me because it appears next to flight details for his Moscow trip. You could ask Washington to check on Anton Kurtz, probably in New York and probably in the art or antique business. It's all I've got, I'm afraid.'

'No problem,' the duty officer said.

'Another thing,' Ponomarev said. 'A year or two back there was a nice little racket going in Fabergé eggs. They were disappearing from national collections here and turning up in odd places like Texas and Venezuela. My office was involved in the case and we came to know about a set-up in New York called the International Foundation for Art Research. It's run by a group of formidable young women who keep records of all reported art thefts around the world. And what interests me right now is that they have a very handy register of names of individuals who have been accused, convicted, or even just mentioned in any court proceedings about stolen art. I'm interested, of course, in anything touching on Russian art – icons in particular. Would you please ask Washington to be sure to have these ladies contacted and quizzed before replying to my query. The impression I had was that they knew more about such matters than the New York police authorities or the FBI.'

'I've got it down.'

'Many thanks.'

'Know what?' the Interpol duty officer said. 'This is the first enquiry we've had for weeks which wasn't about a stolen Merc in Germany. Makes a change.'

'We don't get much into car theft here at the Specials,' Ponomarev said. He felt himself in a mood for some professional gossip. Anything to get away from the mess on his desk. 'You'd have to knock off a whole fleet of 'em to interest us.'

'Oh, they do,' the duty officer said, 'and then they smuggle them over here one at a time and sell them for dollars.'

‘How does the thing work?’

‘Well, the first thing to understand is that under current conditions the effectiveness of our border controls, for which we used to be famous, is nothing but a myth. So if I am part of the great army of European car thieves and I’ve stolen a Merc in, say, Frankfurt, what do I do? First I drive it, as a tourist, you understand, to Poland – maybe to somewhere like Katowice where I have a pal in the vehicle registration office who can’t get by on his salary, given the inflation. This friend of mine kindly supplies a certificate showing the car was inherited from my old dad, or maybe was a part-payment for services rendered to some Western finance outfit. Armed now with my precious certificate, I make for our border. My certificate, mark you, is made out in Roman script and in impeccable Polish, though the Soviet regulations insist on Cyrillic and Russian. At the border, the poor devil on duty peers solemnly at the document, understands not a blind word of it, asks if there’s a Russian version and gets a couple of hundred roubles in lieu, as it were. After being treated to a verbal translation and a slap on the back he waves the stolen Merc through, and if you stand for five minutes on Kalinina on a busy day you’re likely to see it being driven fast by some young man in an Italian suit.’

‘Interesting,’ Ponomarev said, ‘and what kind of progress are we making against these people?’

‘Progress? No progress. But it keeps this office busy, doesn’t it?’ The duty officer laughed sardonically. ‘I’ll fax your query and let you know when we get something back.’

‘We could use a Merc or a Volvo here,’ Ponomarev said. ‘Let me know if they ever capture one.’

Then he called Marina, told her he was fed up with work and would cut it short after lunch. He arranged where to meet her in Gorki Park at three if the rain kept off.

* * *

The downpour started at nine and was to continue intermittently for two days, playing a role of truly historic significance which no one could have foretold. But at nine, as the first heavy drops began to fall out of a leaden sky, sending the crowds scurrying for shelter in the centre of Moscow, the rain was welcomed as a relief from the sultry heat and the heavy pollution over the city. Raya darted out of a taxi and into the bar off the Arbat where she had arranged to meet Slava Lyubimov. The place was lit by occasional candles and a solitary sixty-watt pink bulb behind the bar. Through the gloom she caught sight of him. They waved to each other and she crossed the room, pushing between the closely packed tables. A pirated Pink Floyd tape, volume high, was battling against all conversation and winning.

Lyubimov introduced Anatoli Panov, the giant, and his girlfriend Nina.

'We're eating shashliks, which are good here. Will you have one with a Pepsi?'

Raya nodded and leant towards Lyubimov so that he could hear her above the din from the sound equipment: 'After a very hard day all I can tell you is that no one can figure out how an independent Armenia is to pay for her oil imports. But it's not for publication.'

'Are you at it again tomorrow?'

'At eight.'

Lyubimov had been telling the strange story of the Saturday football match out at Naro-Fominsk that never took place, shouting to be heard above Pink Floyd. Panov lumbered over to the bar and persuaded the youth in charge to turn down the volume. Back at the table, he turned to the diminutive Nina, perched on a stool, blonde head cocked slightly to one side like a brilliantly plumed exotic bird. Her small body was entirely enveloped in a vivid purple shift.

'Tell them, Nina, what you told me,' Panov said.

Nina adopted what she took to be a conspiratorial

manner, leaning forward across the table, her mass of blonde hair falling over her eyes.

'You know my sister, the stupid bitch, works for Frolov at *Pravda*. I think old Frolov fancies her in between pretending to edit his lousy rag. At all events, she gets her bottom pinched from time to time but as it's accompanied by quite decent food parcels, she puts up with it.' She grinned through the strands of hair. 'Anyway, she called me this afternoon to say Frolov has been acting odd lately. You know, hinting at God knows what, rushing off to meetings at the Central Committee, kicking her out of the office when certain phone calls came through. No way, in short, that he usually treats his secretary.'

'Jumpy, you see,' Panov said.

'Who's telling this story?' Nina demanded. 'Anyway, like I say, she calls me after lunch today and it appears Frolov told her not to come in to the office tomorrow morning but stay at home and be sure to tune in early to the news on the radio. She asked what news and the old fool looked mysterious and said it was going to be important news and she'd be safer at home than out on the streets. Then he said: "We'll be making history," and shut up.' Nina tossed her hair back and took a sip of her drink, well pleased with herself.

'Did Frolov mention any actual time for history to be made?'

'No, he just said it would be tomorrow morning.'

'It looks,' Panov said, 'as if we'd all better have our radios on.'

'What do you think it means?' Raya asked.

'All those tank engines revving up,' Lyubimov said, half to himself.

'What's that?'

'Look, when they wanted to get rid of Khrushchev they waited until he was on vacation, then called a quick meeting of the Central Committee and simply voted him out. But since Gorbachev persuaded the Party to change the voting procedure, it can't be done that way any more. So maybe this is the 1991 version of our time-honoured way of changing our leaders by means of a coup, a palace revolution while the boss is on holiday.'

'You said tank engines,' Nina said.

'That's right. Tanks on the streets instead of a lot of Party hacks raising their hands for the vote. It's not impossible.'

'There would be a blood bath,' Panov said. 'The country's changed. I can't think they'd be such bloody fools.'

'Maybe some of these bright lads at the top haven't noticed the change.'

'Men,' Nina said, wriggling on her stool and screwing up her exquisite little face into a grimace of disapproval, 'men *are*, generally speaking, bloody fools. So what are we all acting surprised about?'

When they parted close to midnight Slava Lyubimov seized Raya by the shoulders and was surprised when she offered her mouth to him a moment before he had summoned up the courage to do anything but kiss her, traditionally, on either cheek. Afterwards she gave one of her rare smiles, dimly seen in the dark of the street.

'I hope you'll call me tomorrow morning – if you can tear yourself away from the radio.'

He laughed. 'I've just lost interest in all that nonsense.'

It was already raining heavily as he made his way to the Metro.

On the line to Krasnodar that evening, Baranov explained to Marchenko that New York was fucking about, had gone crazy, was demanding the impossible.

'It's easy for those jerks to sit in comfort in the West and demand this and that,' he said. 'But how the hell do we get the authorities here to make a fuss about an item that they don't even know exists, for Christ's sake?'

Marchenko grunted. 'This is your project, Petya. You're

the smartass who had everything sewn up. Don't come to me for solutions to crazy problems.'

'Look, the thing isn't even recognisable any more. I've given it the treatment I described to you, and I have to say it's a brilliant success. No expert is going to be able to recognise it for what it actually is, and so no one is going to make a fuss when it leaves the country.'

'Perhaps you'll have to restore it to its original condition,' Marchenko said.

'And then what? How do we reveal the thing and still get it out of the country? And by the way, is this conversation secure?'

'It's secure,' Marchenko said. 'As to getting the thing out, I repeat, this is your scheme.'

There was a silence. Then Baranov said: 'I've done positively beautiful work on it. Masterly work. It offends me deeply to have to undo that. And it would still leave us with the problem of getting the thing out.'

'The borders no longer present much of a problem,' Marchenko said. 'I am told the border with Poland in particular bears examination. And that's the only suggestion I can make.'

'I'll think about it,' Baranov said reluctantly. 'I'll think about it.'

16

From six-thirty onwards on the following morning – Monday, 19 August – all Soviet radio and television stations started broadcasting bulletins issued by a new body calling itself the Emergency Committee. The bulletins were flanked by solemn music, as if a great personage had recently died. President Gorbachev, according to the Emergency Committee, was ill in his villa at Cape Sarich and unable to continue to perform his functions. Government of the state would be assured by the Committee, headed by Vice-President Yanaev, until such time as President Gorbachev could resume his duties. Citizens were urged to remain calm. It was also announced that only an approved list of journals would be allowed to continue publication.

'A standard, guaranteed 100 per cent proof coup,' Nina told Panov over coffee at the kitchen table. 'What did I tell you?'

'Obviously,' Panov said, 'Gorbachev is no more ill now than Khrushchev was when they played the same little game and replaced him with Brezhnev.' He shook his head. 'The way we Russians are governed!'

'What do you know about Yanaev? He strikes me as utterly useless.'

'He drinks like a fish,' Panov said. 'He's said to get through hardly any work because he's too busy slipping loose women in and out of his office and wiping up afterwards.'

'Don't be vulgar,' Nina said.

At midday the writers of *Vperiod* met in Editor Chelidze's office.

‘In the new situation created by the President’s illness I propose that we get out a special edition of the paper,’ Chelidze announced. He seemed to be quietly pleased with himself, as if a weight had been lifted from his shoulders. He was having some difficulty in repressing a smile.

‘What will this special edition say?’ Gennady Ivanov asked.

‘Naturally, it will rally support for the new leadership.’

At that there was uproar, with Panov shouting through the din that he proposed the immediate removal of Editor Chelidze.

Finally, Ivanov managed to make himself heard. ‘Even an idiot can see the thing’s illegal. Where’s the evidence that Gorbachev is ill? Where are the doctors’ reports? Why haven’t they convened the Supreme Soviet? Why have they banned dozens of newspapers? And isn’t it significant that they haven’t banned ours? No doubt,’ he said, pointing dramatically at Chelidze, ‘they thought Georgi Galaktionovitch could deliver *Vperiod* for this gang. In fact, he can’t.’

‘We haven’t seen half of it,’ Slava Lyubimov said. ‘I’d expect the tanks of the Taman Division to be on their way to the city right now. What is it, some eighty kilometres to Naro-Fominsk? You can expect them on the streets this afternoon. And why would they need tanks if the thing’s constitutional?’

‘Order,’ Chelidze bleated, ‘order must be kept.’ His words were drowned in a howl of objections.

Panov brought a fist crashing down on Chelidze’s desk. ‘Instead of getting out a new edition defending this miserable crew, we should be out on the streets, the lot of us.’

‘I propose,’ Ivanov announced, ‘that we convene a meeting of the staff collective for six this evening with one item on the agenda: the future leadership of the journal.’

‘That would be unconstitutional,’ Chelidze shouted, trying to assert himself above the hubbub in the room.

‘No more unconstitutional than what Vice-President

Yanaev and his mob are trying to do,' Lyubimov said. 'If matters are to be settled by means of coups, let's have a coup here.'

Then the meeting broke up.

Lyubimov set out on foot for the Moscow City Council in Tverskaya Street. Outside the red brick building a small crowd had gathered, staring at a dozen paratroopers posted at the entrance – pasty-faced youths from deep in the countryside who appeared not to understand why they were deployed in the heart of Moscow. Lyubimov marched past them and up the steps inside, expecting to be stopped at any moment. They just stared. In the lobby, on the stairs and on the landings groups of city councillors were arguing, sometimes shouting at each other, passing leaflets from hand to hand. Lyubimov nodded to several officials whom he knew and made his way to the Deputy Mayor's office. The door was shut. A paratrooper stood guard, an automatic rifle slung across his chest. As Lyubimov approached, the door opened and he heard the tail-end of an angry exchange. Then he recognised General Myrikov, head of the Moscow Chief Directorate of Internal Affairs. Suddenly confronted by Lyubimov, the General appeared astonished to be interviewed on the hoof and his surprise seemed to stop him making a quick escape.

'What is the attitude of the Moscow police, General?'

'We will naturally enforce order on the streets,' the General snapped.

He had no idea whether he was talking to a journalist or a member of the City Council.

'Under what regulations?'

'Under the state of emergency announced this morning.'

'Do I take it you support the Emergency Committee?'

At that point the General's suspicions seemed to crystallise in his mind and he nodded towards the paratrooper. Lyubimov felt the muzzle of the rifle poking him in the ribs as the General marched past, signalling to his bodyguard to follow him.

'I got two replies and a poke in the ribs from an automatic when I asked a few civil questions in the City Council,' Lyubimov was to write later. 'But later on I found that not all our police took the same view. Indeed, quite a number of traffic police officers were to guide the military convoys in the wrong direction, creating some splendid traffic snarl-ups on the ring roads.'

Deputy Mayor Luzhkov appeared at the door of his office. He recognised Lyubimov.

'I see your rag is one of the favoured few allowed to publish?'

'It won't last,' Lyubimov said. 'Our collective meets this afternoon and I can promise the line will change.'

'Good.'

'Where is the mayor?'

'He's on vacation. We've sent for him. Meanwhile, I am in charge.'

'Can you tell me what General Myrikov had to say?'

'He told me the police will support the military, who are already in the suburbs, and that police cells are being readied for those who break the curfew tonight. He asked for my co-operation.'

'Did he get it?'

'No.'

'What else can you tell me?'

'At ten this morning I had a call from General Kalinin. He told me he had just been appointed commandant of the city.'

'And what did you say?'

'I told him Moscow has a City Council and has no need of a commandant.'

'Is what you've told me confidential?'

'No.' And Luzkhov retreated to his office, closing the door behind him.

On the way down the stairs Lyubimov met a reporter

from *Pravda* whom he knew from press conferences.

'I see *Pravda* supports that bunch of incompetents and drunkards,' he said amiably.

'Don't blame me,' the other man said. 'Frolov is prancing around our office like a dog with two cocks. If you ask me, the thing's a farce. I've just come from the press conference given by our new masters. Yanaev twitched, Pugo grinned, and I understand Premier Pavlov is at home drunk. So whatever happens, don't blame me.'

And the *Pravda* man wandered off in search of a story his editor would publish.

Lyubimov made for Petrovka Street where confusion appeared to reign around the police headquarters. Waving his press card and shouting Major Ponomarev's name, he managed to get past the guards on the gate. Discipline and regulations, it appeared, were beginning to crumble from below. He found Ponomarev in his office.

'What position are the police taking up, Major?'

'I suppose it depends which policeman you happen to meet,' Ponomarev said.

'General Myrikov says you'll support the Emergency Committee.'

'The General is entitled to his opinion.'

'I shall be writing that it looks as if feelings among the police are mixed. What do you say to that?'

'We're told it's becoming a free country, my friend,' Ponomarev answered. 'Who am I to contradict you?' He was grinning.

'And do you have any more news on the missing American?'

'We've been in meetings on and off since yesterday, so I'm afraid crime as such has simply had to wait.'

'And what will you be doing instead?' Lyubimov asked.

'It's none of your business, of course, but you can write that you heard somewhere that the Specials have been given the assignment of arresting a number of distinguished people, and that includes Deputies.'

'Who have immunity from arrest?'

'Who have immunity.'

'And when will that start, Major?'

'Say you understand the Specials are waiting for orders from the Emergency Committee. And now, off with you; they should never have let you in here in the first place.'

Discipline, Lyubimov reflected as he made his way out of the building, was breaking down at middle levels too.

At six there was uproar again at *Vperiod*. Most of the staff had crowded into Chelidze's room, with an overflow on Verochka's territory outside. Verochka herself was heard shouting, 'This is subversion, mob rule! Scum! Get out of my office!'

No one moved.

'We appreciate you deeply,' Lyubimov told her solemnly, 'but we think you are talking drivel, so please be quiet.'

Chelidze managed, briefly, to make himself heard above the cries of 'Resign!' and 'Let's elect a new editor!'

'This is unseemly and undemocratic,' he shouted. 'At least let matters be handled in an orderly fashion. I am only carrying out the instructions of the Central Committee, but everything can be discussed.'

'So much the worse for the Central Committee,' someone shouted.

'I am the editor of this paper,' Chelidze said unwisely.

There were cries of, 'Not for long.'

'This move was necessary. The country is falling apart. The treaty will be the last straw.'

'Who says so?'

'You're all creating chaos on behalf of Gorbachev while the country has rejected him.'

'Since when has the country been clamouring for Yanaev and the KGB instead?'

Finally, Ivanov made himself heard as a hush fell on the crowd of jostling men and women.

'I propose a motion: The staff of *Vperiod* reject the leadership of Editor Chelidze and propose a ballot to elect a new editor.'

A sea of hands went up.

'Carried,' Ivanov said. 'We reconvene in half an hour. Anyone can be nominated by two people. Nominations to come to me meanwhile and we'll take a vote. Let's have a little democracy around here.'

Lyubimov made his way through the crowd to Ivanov. 'Will you stand?' he asked.

'If there's a general feeling that way.'

'OK, I nominate you.'

'I second,' Panov said.

There was a murmur of approval from those around them.

'You realise,' Ivanov said, 'that the Party will instruct the Ministry to cut off our paper supplies if we go through with this. We may be committing collective suicide.'

'There's a flaw in that reasoning,' someone said.

'And what's that?'

'If we do nothing, the Emergency Committee wins, and as far as I am concerned, that's disaster anyway. On the other hand, if we stand up to them we have a chance of defeating this gang, in which case *finis* to the Party telling us when we can and when we can't wipe our noses.'

'That's roughly my position,' Ivanov said, 'but I wanted to be sure we knew what we were doing.'

'A tape's coming off the machine which says tanks and personnel carriers of the Taman division have reached the inner ring road,' someone announced.

Chelidze was sitting at his desk, his head in his hands, saying nothing. 'I'm sorry, Georgi Galaktionovitch,' one of the writers said to him, 'it's nothing personal, you understand. It's just that history has passed you and your friends by.'

'I am a patriot and a Leninist,' Chelidze announced. 'I believe the Union must be held together, as Lenin taught us. And I believe the Party is everything that's best in the

Union. That has been my life and mob rule on the streets or here in the office will not change it.'

Verochka had pushed her way through the crowd. 'I haven't seen an egg for three weeks,' she announced. 'My mother queued three hours yesterday for a kilo of lousy sausages, and we haven't eaten meat this week or last. Every time the people on the floor above empty their bath, the bathwater comes up in our bath-tub, and you can come and see the scum it leaves whenever you've got the time. Can I get a plumber to fix it? Can I hell. And now Gorbachev says the republics can do as they please – break away, send their produce wherever they fancy, make sure I don't even get a bit of cheese when I want it because it used to come from Lithuania and now they're selling it to Finland for dollars. You're crazy, the lot of you. As far as I'm concerned, Gorbachev's illness can prove fatal. Then maybe the price of tomatoes will come down.'

'The voice of the people,' someone muttered, 'and not so daft either.'

'Verochka thinks a couple of drunkards and the KGB will fill the shops with goodies. The only thing the KGB ever managed to fill was the camps.'

'We Russians,' Nadia said, 'why is it the only way we know of conducting our political life is to wait until the top man is on holiday and then to organise a coup to get rid of him? We simply don't know how to make democracy work.' She turned to Verochka: 'Do you really think this pathetic bunch can make a decent sausage between them and deliver it to your local shop?'

'I only know things are worse under Gorbachev than they were before,' Verochka said.

'Look, I was at their lousy press conference,' Nadia answered. 'You should have seen them! It would settle the sausage problem once and for all. I asked myself what kind of system throws up a bunch like that. Pugo, who masterminded the killings in Lithuania; Kryuchkov, who stood behind the suppression in Hungary in 1956; Yanaev who everyone knows is only interested in vodka and women; and the rest of these nonentities. Know what they've done since this morning? Ordered a cut in the price of children's clothes, which makes no sense, and brought the tanks onto the streets of Moscow, presumably to mow us down if we think the price cut isn't big enough.' She sighed. 'Verochka, you should really grow up before it's too late.'

When the vote was taken shortly afterwards, the entire staff, with the exception of Verochka, elected Gennady Ivanov as editor.

Chelidze had tears in his eyes. 'Genatsvale,' he said, 'haven't I been a good leader? Haven't I tried to run the paper on principled lines? Have I not defended our positions often when a different view was taken at the Central Committee? This illegal move against me will rebound against you when I make my report. It will mean death for our paper, death.' He stopped, and no one cared to say anything. 'My conscience is clear. I stand by my belief in the future of Communism. You are opening our country to Capitalism, profiteering, usury and crime. You are all profoundly mistaken, and I predict it will end in tears. Now I ask you to leave my office. I have a report to write on these shameful events.'

As they left, Panov said to Lyubimov, 'A decent man, really. Decent but blind as a bat. I'm sorry for him.'

'Not me,' Lyubimov said. 'He and his cronies have damn nearly destroyed us all. It's what too much ideology does to you. The facts of life don't fit the idea, so much the worse for the facts. Ignore them. Then shoot a few people to tidy things up. Time-servers like Chelidze stood behind a lot of shooting in their day.'

The staff stood around in the corridors for a while, shaken by what they had done. Then someone told a Stalin joke as a way of easing the tension. What did Stalin say after seeing *Othello*? 'This fellow Iago . . . not a bad organiser.' Then they began to disperse about their business. Lyubimov went to his room and tried to contact Raya on the telephone, but the system was misbehaving and he got nowhere.

17

From early morning on the following day, Tuesday, the summer rainstorms swept the city, forming rivers of dirty water in the gutters and driving all but the most politically determined off the streets. By early afternoon, Slava Lyubimov had found Raya. They met near Red Square, both wrapped in plastic against the driving rain, running for the nearest Metro station. 'We'll head for the White House,' Lyubimov panted. 'It looks as if that's where the action will be. I understand they failed to arrest Boris Yeltsin at his home. He's at the White House now with most of the Russian deputies, so I expect the leaders of the coup will order the army to go after them there.'

They reached the Metro and boarded a train which was packed with people, most of them young.

'Will the army act?' Raya asked.

'We get unconfirmed stories of rows between the generals. It's said the Emergency Committee has an Alpha group of 15,000 men ready to attack the White House at dawn tomorrow. A contact of mine called me to say the man to watch is Deputy Defence Minister Achalov – an ambitious brute, as far as I can gather.'

When the train stopped at the Barricadnaya station the passengers flooded out onto the already packed platform.

'A suitably named place to alight,' Lyubimov said.

The crowd was heading for the escalators. They carried waterproofs, umbrellas, sheets of plastic. Here and there furled banners could be seen. The atmosphere was one of nervous jollity. It could have been a crowd heading for a football match.

As they walked down Krasnopresnenskyi Val, heading towards the river, the crowds thickened. Roughly-lettered banners could be seen here and there: BORIS YELTSIN. 'NO' TO THE PUTSCHISTS. DEMOCRACY. INDEPENDENT RUSSIA. The distant metallic growl of tank engines reached them from the direction of Prospect Kalinina. They passed the stark red brick mass of the new American Embassy, never commissioned after the CIA discovered that the Soviet builders had buried listening devices all over the construction. It stood now, empty, a grotesque monument to the cold war. As they followed the curve in the road, heading down towards the embankment, the ungainly bulk of the Russian Parliament, the White House, came into view on their right. Then they came abreast of the first barricades – abandoned ironwork, carts, planks, branches of trees, piled high across the approach to the rear of the building. Young men sat defiantly on the lower reaches of the barricades. Two soldiers with Kalashnikovs leaned against a low wall, rainwater dripping from the barrels of their weapons. From the front of the building, facing the river, the roar of the crowd could be heard.

'Let's go down there,' Lyubimov said. 'My press card might be useful.'

But the crowd in front of the building was solid and they found themselves wedged immovably in the roadway as Boris Yeltsin appeared on the steps, flanked by members of the Russian parliament. A microphone was set up and the crowd fell silent as he warned that an attack was expected during the night. 'I stay here to fight to the end,' he declared, as the crowd burst into applause and cheers, and Yeltsin waved with both arms.

'A great guy,' Lyubimov said.

'When all this is over and if he's still there,' Raya said, 'I would be very careful if I were a Russian.' She had not clapped and shouted like those around her.

'But he's a necessary symbol around which the people can rally. The proof is that the others tried to arrest him.'

'In the early days,' Raya said, 'Stalin must have looked good too.'

'You Armenians,' Lyubimov said, 'you don't trust us. I can understand it, but Yeltsin has been right all along.' He tried to keep the irritation out of his voice.

'Why should I trust an ex-Party demagogue just because he's opposed to a KGB plot?'

'Pretty cynical, that.'

'All of us in the Soviet Union – Russians, Armenians, Georgians, whatever – we're all mesmerised by the leader idea. The great man who will do our thinking for us. All I'm saying is, watch out: if Yeltsin wins this time he'll fall for the great man nonsense himself. I'm surprised you don't see it.'

Major Ponomarev was having difficulties that day with his Marina. 'Some of us,' he told her, 'have decided we have to stand up to be counted in this thing. We've a meeting this evening in town to decide what to do.'

'And what about your career? I'm frightened for you,' Marina said.

'You're always frightened. If it isn't the weather it's the gangs on the streets, or what my boss might say. Try to calm yourself. I know what I'm doing.'

'You are not to go,' Marina said. 'There are plenty of others to put their careers on the line if they want to.'

'I'm going. This gang make me sick.'

'I forbid it. I beg you not to go.'

'Don't I always do what you say in the end?' Ponomarev told her.

'Usually.'

'Well, this time I can't. For some reason which isn't clear to me, I feel the need to live in a civilised country, and what's happening is a throwback to our barbarous past.' He gathered up his cap and raincoat, stepped across the room and pecked her on the cheek.

'Be careful,' she said. 'Don't do more than you need to do. Where will you be?'

'We're meeting down on the embankment and maybe we'll see what they're up to at the White House. But I'll be careful.'

As he reached the door he turned and tried a grin, but she shook her head and sighed. Then he was gone.

That afternoon, Peter Baranov in Zaveti Ilyicha called Stepan Stepanovitch Marchenko in Krasnodar.

'Down here,' Marchenko told him, 'we support the Emergency Committee. The thing's being fought out in the local Soviet and we've got the militia out on the streets to keep order. The army is with us. The population doesn't give a damn. They're mostly queuing for milk anyway.'

'You're all crazy,' Baranov told him.

'Since when have you been a Gorbachev fan?'

'Wake up,' Baranov said. 'Isn't perestroika the best thing that ever happened to people like us? Do you want to go back to the days when they could lift you off the street and ship you out to Siberia on a charge of hooliganism if they couldn't make anything else stick? Don't you see this craze for democracy and the free market was made for folks like us?'

'I am a loyal citizen and I tell you the free market is a disaster. It will end in riots.'

'Maybe, but meanwhile it's no disaster – it's an opportunity. There's a Bulgarian proverb, you know, which tells us to seize opportunity by the beard since it's bald behind. Remember that, Stepan Stepanovitch, and hang on to the beard.'

The conversation dragged on for a while.

'What about our project, then?' Marchenko asked.

'There's a development,' Baranov told him. 'I had a call from over there. My contact is coming over. He'll be here on Thursday.'

'Is that good?'

'I don't know until I see him.'
'Keep me in touch,' Marchenko said, and rang off.

That night, in the underpass carrying the Garden Ring Road under Kalinin Prospect, the cause of democracy in the Soviet Union gained its three martyrs, two young men crushed beneath tank tracks and a third killed by a ricocheting bullet fired by an armoured personnel carrier. All three fatalities arose from the panic of the troops, caught in their vehicles between barricades in the underpass. It was a moment of historical significance, the meaning of which became clear on the following Saturday when vast numbers of Muscovites flooded into Manezh Square to pay their last respects to the three. But that night the local commanders drew back from further bloodshed. The tanks were ordered to switch off their engines, batten down their hatches and await help. They could have fired and battered their way out of the trap but did not attempt the manoeuvre. The army had no stomach for killing the citizens of Moscow.

At the Russian parliament building, when the news of the tragedy in the underpass was received, the belief was that the long-awaited attack on the building and its defenders would start at any time. But the attack never came. Instead, army commanders and politicians involved in the coup spent their time arguing. Their historic opportunity passed them by.

Next morning at the White House the crowds manning the barricades heard a voice over the loudspeaker system: 'Comrades, there is good news. Esteemed defenders, I have to tell you that Pavlov has had a heart attack. I have to tell you he has resigned.' Pavlov was the prime minister, a member of the Emergency Committee. It was the first public crack in the facade of solidarity among the organisers of the coup.

At two that afternoon news came in of massive tank movements on Leningradsky Prospect in the north of the city. Tank columns were moving out of Moscow. There were other tank columns heading out towards Vnukovo airport. And soon a convoy of black government limousines was seen heading for the airport, weaving in and out of the column of tanks. The leaders of the coup were on their way to see President Gorbachev down in the Crimea. To beg forgiveness? To negotiate?

The question remained unanswered because Gorbachev refused to talk to them.

The coup had collapsed.

At *Vperiod* that afternoon the senior writers assembled in the editor's office.

'Where's Chelidze?' someone asked.

'No one seems to understand the legal position,' Ivanov said. 'I'm trying to get his salary and pension sorted out, but meanwhile we have a paper to produce so let's get on with it.'

'Is the Central Committee bothering you yet?' Panov asked.

'An extremely irritable person called this morning and demanded to know what the hell we thought we were up to. I was summoned to appear and explain myself.'

'What did you say?'

'I said that when I had time I would come round for the purpose of handing in my Party card, but beyond that I had nothing to say.'

'And what did the irritable person say?'

'He said that this would end badly for me, for the paper, for the lot of you, and that unprincipled behaviour was not to be tolerated. I said that given the coup and all that, the Central Committee was not well placed to talk of principles. After which, this person snorted down the telephone and rang off.' Ivanov grinned. 'Now let's see what we have to lead page one.'

'I'm told at the mayor's office that they'll be sending a heavy crane round later to lift the statue of Dzerzhinski off its plinth,' Lyubimov said. 'The crowd's been tugging at it for hours but old Felix won't budge. We should get a photographer round there. It will make a nice shot – Dzerzhinski flat on his face in the foreground with his beloved Lubyanka behind him with insulting slogans painted on the walls.'

18

On the following day Grigoriev arrived in Moscow from New York. Two squat, dark-skinned men in ill-fitting dark suits met him at the airport. Hugs and kisses were exchanged, Armenian-style, and Grigoriev was led to the car park where they found a grey 1990 Mercedes 240 with a young man in a sweat shirt at the wheel. The back of his shirt proclaimed the slogan UNIVERSITY OF CALIFORNIA. He, too, was from Armenia. He did not bother to look round at the new arrival as the others climbed in the back of the car. He drove them expertly and at high speed out of the airport and onto the highway, heading for the city.

One of the men addressed Grigoriev in Armenian. 'So you've had enough of the West?'

'Not at all. I told you on the phone, I'm here on business. I fly out again next week. There may be work for you to do.'

'So we gathered. What sort of work?'

'There's time to explain. Where do I stay?'

'With me,' the other said. 'The boys will be round this evening. We've laid on a little party. You know, to celebrate your return. They'll be glad to see you after – what – five years?'

'Six.'

'And how's business in the West?'

'No problems.'

They drove in silence for a while and soon straggling houses announced the outskirts of Moscow.

'Where's your place?' Grigoriev asked.

'Tushino.'

'Isn't it dodgy for you to be back here?' the other man asked.

'What do you mean, dodgy?'

'You know, after what happened with the Avakyans.'

'That was in Yerevan, right?'

'Right.'

'And this is Moscow, OK?'

'Sure, but a murder rap . . .'

'I don't want to hear old stories, understood? So you'll keep your mouth shut from now on, is that clear?'

'You haven't changed, Grigoriev,' his companion said with a nervous laugh.

'I don't like gossip and I don't like people asking nosey questions. You'd better tell your people tonight that I'm not here to hold a fucking press conference but to do some business which may involve them and may not. It will be for me to decide.'

'I have to tell you – no offence, of course – that things have changed a bit since you went away. You know, the lads are feeling their oats, have a point of view, like, after operating here in Moscow for a few years. They've gained, like, self-confidence, and they're liable to speak their minds, that's all.' He paused, and getting no reply, added: 'I thought I'd warn you, you know. As I say, no offence or disrespect.'

'We'll see,' Grigoriev said. 'I haven't come back to Moscow to have arguments or to fart about on the kind of cheap operations we had six years ago.'

Nothing more was said until the car came to a halt in the courtyard of a group of apartment blocks and the Armenians led the way to an apartment on the fourth floor of one of the buildings. In contrast to the shabby, run-down stairway and corridors, the inside of the apartment was comfortable. There were fine rugs on the floors and the walls were hung with tapestries. There was plenty of cut glass on the highly polished sideboard. Large open-fronted bookcases were filled with porcelain and more glass. In the living room low divans were piled with cushions embroidered with brightly coloured silk thread.

'This is a bit better than the hovel you were in when I left,' Grigoriev said.

'We've not done badly these last few years.'

'Currency?'

'That and other things.' They laughed. 'Make yourself at home. A drink?'

'Why not?'

Ararat cognac was served, with quarters of tomato and gherkins on a dish. Soon, others came and were introduced. It became clear that they deferred to the older of the men who had been at the airport. They addressed him as Razmik. Grigoriev sat smoking, saying nothing, listening. Of the seven presently installed with drinks, he knew Razmik and two others from the old days.

The man known as Razmik called for silence and the conversation died away. 'I'm happy to welcome our friend back from the United States,' he announced. 'He will be staying with us for a few days and may have a little business for our group.' He turned to Grigoriev beside him on the divan. 'Will you say something?'

Grigoriev looked round at the men in the room. They were mostly young, in their twenties. All had the black hair, heavy moustaches, sallow complexions and stocky build typical of Armenians from the south. They lounged on chairs or the divan, legs apart and extended with a kind of assertive insolence.

'I have some business here in Moscow,' Grigoriev said. 'Those of you like Razmik who know me from the past will know that I am a businesslike person who does not tolerate argument, gossip or interference. If I need help, I lay down my terms and whoever wishes to help may do so on those terms. If there is risky work to be done I explain the risks, and those who are yellow can keep away. In the present instance there may be work to do and that work may carry risks.' He paused, blew smoke through his nostrils and looked round the room. 'I pay well,' he added.

'Roubles?' someone asked.

'Dollars.'

'What are we talking about here?' a young man asked. 'Are you putting out contracts or setting up an international deal, or what?'

Grigoriev turned slowly to the man who had spoken. 'Obviously,' he said quietly, 'you weren't listening to what I said.'

'We all heard what you said, only it wasn't clear.'

'Then let me make it clear. I repeat: I do not tolerate argument, gossip or interference. I now add that I do not answer questions until I am ready to do so.'

'Are these American customs?'

'Maybe.'

'We're not used to them.'

'More's the pity.' He turned to Razmik. 'What do you know about the icon trade?'

'We've done a few deals.'

'Through Berlin?'

Razmik nodded. 'We had a black dacha too last year.'

'I don't know the slang. Please explain.'

'It's a route out of the country for icons, usually smaller ones. We've two black diplomats who'll get the stuff out in their personal baggage. Then there's guys at the other end in Africa who'll pick up the merchandise and move it on to wherever it's going.'

'Which embassies?'

'Never mind which embassies until we know what we're talking about here.'

Grigoriev hawked and spat into a handkerchief, examining thoughtfully what he had produced before folding the handkerchief back into his pocket.

'And Berlin?' he asked. 'What about Berlin?'

'There's a bunch of yids from Odessa installed there. You know the form: the emigration to Israel of the early eighties, only they go missing from the transit station in Vienna, buy themselves some useful passports, end up in West Berlin. Simple. They know the trade, have the clients, you understand. There's a well-established run for icons and jewellery across the frontier. And they wet their pants for Fabergé. One of the lads gets the merchandise to Berlin, calls a certain antique shop in the Wedding suburb, checks the password and gets out there in a cab. The fence checks the icon, and if it's OK he pays cash. Sometimes they get a novodel and fall for it, but generally you can't fool them.'

'Novodel?'

'It's what we call a fake. The trade's highly specialised, has its own vocabulary.'

'And the prices?'

'They vary. A Mamka, eighteenth-century or earlier, in good condition, can fetch a decent sum, according to size.'

'What the hell's a Mamka and what do you call a decent price?'

'A Mamka is what we call an icon of the Mother of God. A Nikolka is a St Nicholas, and so on. As to price, it's what they can get in the market. No fixed prices.' He paused. 'Leads to trouble sometimes. You can imagine.'

'I read about Kamkin,' Grigoriev said. 'Fished him out of some lake near Berlin, didn't they?'

'Right. Roughed him up pretty bad before pitching the bastard in. A matter of broken faith. A greedy swine.'

'Eyeballs missing,' someone said. 'Testicles missing too, and it wasn't the fish that got 'em.'

'It's a temptation,' someone said. 'When you're buying at a thousand and selling at maybe ten or twenty thousand, it stands to reason, people fall out over margins like that.'

'So what you're telling me,' Grigoriev said, 'is that you ship the stuff out and what you get is what the yids in Berlin think they can get away with giving you?'

Razmik nodded. The men in the room said nothing.

'The whole thing's fucking stupid, isn't it?' Grigoriev said.

'Where's all the risk? Here. Where's the real profit? There. I never heard such rubbish.'

'That's right,' someone said.

'It's not our main thing, anyway,' Razmik said. There was an apologetic tinge to his voice. 'Sometimes we come across some merchandise and we do a deal, that's all. In the main, we're into other stuff.'

'Let us speculate for a moment,' Grigoriev said. 'Just speculation, mind. I find my way to an icon here in Moscow. Quite a useful item, nothing spectacular, but worth taking a bit of trouble over. And I want to get it out to the West – not to the Berlin mob, because I don't work for other people's profit. That's something I've learned in the States, and no doubt you'll learn it yourselves some day. But like I say, here's this item I want to get out. My question is, can you help, and if so, how?'

The men were nodding. Razmik said, 'Sure, we can help if it's worth our while.'

'I may need to look after some opposition.'

'No problem,' a heavily-built youth said from his position stretched out on the floor.

'How many can you muster?'

'On a confidential job, say up to six.'

'And do you have a safe house?'

'Sure.'

'Out of the city?'

'To the north. Nicely tucked away – no problem.'

Grigoriev nodded, then he said, 'And your route out of the country?'

'That's to talk about if we do a deal,' Razmik said.

'It's to talk about now. I don't want a half-assed plan which collapses because they changed the unit at the frontier and no one told you.'

'We can do a frontier operation into Poland,' Razmik said. 'Also, we have another way out.'

'What is it?'

'One of the lads has a brother who's a merchant seaman

sailing out of Archangel on the timber trade. He's done a couple of jobs for us.' He paused. 'We have to look after one of the officers as well. Costs a bit.'

'And this brother,' Grigoriev said, 'when's he next in port?' There was a flicker of interest in his eyes.

One of the men spoke up. 'Matter of fact, he docked yesterday. His ship does a six-day turn around.'

'He could take a parcel?'

The man nodded.

'Where does he sail to?' Grigoriev asked.

'He's on a run to North America.' The man was about to continue when Razmik cut him short. 'Details later,' he said, 'if we make a deal.'

'Right, we'll talk again,' Grigoriev said. 'When do we eat?'

'Masha will bring in food soon. Meanwhile, cognac.' A fresh bottle was produced. Glasses were filled.

'To the venture, whatever the hell it is,' someone declared.

Later, Baranov arrived at the apartment from Zaveti Ilyicha. The group had been dismissed, leaving Grigoriev and Razmik.

'Shall I disappear?' Razmik asked as the doorbell rang.

'Yes.'

Grigoriev and Baranov embraced – Baranov effusive and talkative, Grigoriev cool and wary. They sat over tea and sweetmeats.

'You had no need to come back,' Baranov said. 'I can handle it.'

'Perhaps so. On the other hand, much is at stake and it was agreed with my principals in New York that I should take over control of the affair here.'

'Take over?' Baranov said. 'There's no question of anyone taking over, my friend.'

'Then there can be no deal,' Grigoriev said. There was no expression in his eyes – nothing to indicate the degree of insistence behind the proposition. 'Under the new rules, laid down by the ultimate purchaser, we have the delicate task of revealing the icon and then snatching it from under the noses of the Soviet authorities. We do not have the confidence that you can be relied on to carry through such an operation on your own.' He looked impassively at Baranov. 'That is why I am here.'

'Unacceptable,' Baranov said. There was an aggressive ring to his voice, betraying his lack of confidence. Grigoriev sensed the sign, said nothing.

'I found the thing. I ran all the risks, took difficult steps to bring it to Moscow, devised the whole scheme, including how to get it to the West, and I have no intention of giving up control. In any case, I'd have difficulties with my people. They'd never stand for it.'

'If you can't control your people that's another reason why the venture should be handed over. Where's the icon?'

'It's hidden.'

'I imagine so, but I asked where it is.'

'It's hidden,' Baranov repeated, 'from you and anyone else who tries to muscle in on this deal. You get your share at the far end and I get mine here. Simple.'

Grigoriev did not answer for a while. When he spoke his tone had mellowed. 'Let's not fall out over this, Petya. There's room for both of us in the deal. It's just that we want to be sure, you understand, that the thing goes smoothly. So let us talk about it, what do you say?'

'There's not much to talk about,' Baranov said.

'Well, there's the little problem of the protests we have to get from the Soviet authorities, isn't there?'

'It's crazy,' Baranov said. 'How the hell does anyone expect us to do that? We're asked to hand the damn thing over, then somehow steal it back. Ridiculous!'

'Necessary,' Grigoriev replied. 'No official row, no deal. In short, it's what I've come over here to confirm and, if necessary, organise. So how do we do it?'

'I've given it some thought and I have a method.'
'What's that?'
'Frankly, it's none of your damn business. I repeat, you're the American end of the venture and I'm the Russian end, and that's that.'
Baranov reached for a cigarette and Grigoriev noticed that his hand was not steady as he lit it.
'Let's not fall out,' Grigoriev said again. 'Maybe I can help. At least you owe me some reassurance. My customer has already invested in a trip to Japan and I've paid to come here, so that there's a community of interest you can't escape. So how do you plan the thing?'
'I'll tell you this much,' Baranov said. 'I'd arranged to disguise it and smuggle it out as part of the travelling exhibition of the Soviet Restorers' Art. That much you know already. Now, of course, that can't be done. So I plan to let news of the find leak out – and I know how to do that – and then, after the icon's been officially authenticated at the Moscow Restoration Centre, my men will lift it. What I do next is strictly my business, but rest assured it'll turn up in the West. As to the official indignation, you'll hear that, all right.'
'I would like to see the icon,' Grigoriev said. 'Our friend Victor Gordon is no longer with us, according to your message, so how do we know what he authenticated is what we're actually getting?'
'He took some samples from the picture and the backing. We took them off him, of course, and I'll see you get them.'
'My principals expect a message from me confirming its existence in good order,' Grigoriev replied, 'so I repeat, I'd like to know when and where I can see it.'
'There's no point in your seeing it, since you won't be able to tell the difference between a genuine Roublev and a cheap modern copy. Here.' Baranov took an envelope from his pocket, opened it and produced two Polaroid prints. 'Look at these and give me your expert opinion.'

Grigoriev took the prints and glanced at them. Then he tore them carefully in two and dropped the pieces on the floor in front of Baranov's chair. 'I think we are misunderstanding each other, so let me spell things out for you. Firstly, I do not tolerate impertinence from a small-time thief, particularly if he's a Russian. Second, there's serious money at stake here and I and my principals are not to be denied. Then again, your memory is failing you, since you don't appear to remember that my friends and I, here in Moscow, were in the habit of getting our own way in such matters. Well, I have to tell you that my friends are still here and they aren't the kind to tangle with. And so I repeat, I wish to see this icon of yours.' His voice was scarcely above a whisper when he added. 'Where shall I come, say tomorrow at midday?'

'Don't get upset,' Baranov said, essaying a laugh and failing with it. 'We'd be crazy to fall out over this. Sure you can see it. It's in my studio out at Zaveti Ilyicha. I'd disguised it somewhat and the disguise is almost all removed; you'll see what I mean. I intend to return it to the workshop tomorrow anyway as part of my plan to meet your need for an official row.'

'What is your plan?'

'Maybe I'll tell you something about it tomorrow, maybe not.'

He had taken a scrap of paper from his pocket and scribbled instructions on it. 'That's where I am at Zaveti Ilyicha. And I trust you won't take offence if I point out that I, too, have friends who know how to look after themselves.'

He got up and extended a hand. 'I'll see you tomorrow at midday, my old friend. And let us not fall out, eh?'

Back at the dacha, Baranov worked into the small hours cleaning off the remaining overpainting from the icon. Close to 4 a.m. he threw himself on the divan in the studio, removed his shoes and managed to sleep fitfully for a couple of hours. As the dawn light flooded into the room through the ceiling-high window, he arose, made himself black coffee and went to the telephone in the neighbouring room. His call was to Gribenko.

'I want you and as many of the lads as you can muster to be here by eleven,' he told him. 'We may have a spot of trouble on our hands.'

'Do we bring the ironmongery?' Gribenko asked.

'You do.'

'What's it all about?'

'You'll learn when you get here. And don't be late.'

Shortly after midday the Mercedes came to a halt outside Baranov's dacha in Zaveti Ilyicha. Grigoriev and Razmik got out, leaving two Armenians and the driver to stand in the road. All were wearing bomber jackets despite the heat, their weapons carried in shoulder holsters.

Grigoriev's instructions, issued in the car as it headed out from Moscow, had been brief: 'If he's on his own, we lift the icon.'

'Do we lose him?' Razmik asked.

'Use your head,' Grigoriev answered. 'If we lose him, we have the militia on our tail. Whereas, if we give him a beating, just to signal him to leave us alone, he won't go calling for the law, will he now, seeing that he doesn't need the militia poking into his affairs either. So which of you usually does the enforcing?'

'Zaven here,' Razmik said. He nodded in the direction of the muscle-bound youth who had lain on the floor in the apartment.

The youth called Zaven, sitting next to the driver, turned and grinned. 'No problem,' he said.

Razmik asked: 'What if his people are with him?'

'I want no shoot-out,' Grigoriev said. 'We only do him if I give the signal. If the thing smells like an ambush, no signal. And I want discipline, understood?'

They nodded.

'Do you want a gun?' Razmik asked him. 'I've a Tokarev 716 in the car.'

'If I wanted to do the shooting myself, I wouldn't be paying for your young friends here to come along. And if I thought an ambush were likely, I'd have more than the five of us along, wouldn't I?'

They had completed the journey in silence, and now Grigoriev and Razmik advanced to the door of the dacha. Razmik's jacket hung open on his shoulders, his right arm held diagonally across his body, loose, palm inwards, the fingers extended. The three men in the roadway had positioned themselves in a line facing the house. The young man called Zaven was leaning back against the car. Something resembling a smile hovered on his good-looking face. 'I keep him like you'd keep a fighting dog,' Razmik had told Grigoriev. 'Like a fighting dog, I have to let him loose regularly. I think the psychiatrists call scum like him psychopaths. I've known him to do some disgusting things, but it's what he likes, the way you or I might like women.'

The knocker resounded through the house and almost at once came the sound of footsteps, bolts being drawn, and a key turning in the lock. Then the door was slowly pulled open by someone standing out of sight.

'Tell your people out there that there's five of us around the place, all armed, two of us with Kalashes, and we're prepared to do as much shooting as necessary. Now one of you can come inside, but with his hands up.'

The voice, quiet and rasping, had a strong Ukrainian accent. It came from behind the door.

'Where's Peter Alexandrovitch?' Grigoriev called from the doorway. He and Razmik did not move.

'He's inside. Which of you is Grigoriev?'

'I am.'

'You can come in, but put your hands up.'

Grigoriev nodded to Razmik. 'Stay outside and tell your lads to hold back. Don't let your mad dog loose, understand?' He raised both hands to shoulder height and advanced into the house. 'I am not armed,' he announced. 'I am not used to this uncivilised behaviour and I now propose to lower my arms.' As he did so, the front door was pushed shut behind him, revealing Gribenko, a Kalashnikov slung across his chest.

The studio door opened and Baranov came into the room. 'I am sorry about this reception committee,' he said, 'but when someone turns up to see me with a private army I naturally take some simple precautions.' He nodded towards Gribenko. 'OK, take it easy. We're not going to have any trouble.' To Grigoriev he said, 'Come into the studio, I'll show you what you want to see.'

Grigoriev advanced, shaking his head. 'I shall not forget your hospitality, Petya,' he said. 'I am not accustomed to being told to put my hands up, and so I have to tell you that you will come to regret your lack of civilised standards.'

'I'm afraid you are out of touch with what has been happening in our country,' Baranov said. 'Some criminologist said in a report recently that Moscow is now as violent as Detroit, with gang warfare a commonplace. What you are witnessing here is an example of how one has to look after one's security nowadays, nothing more. It isn't personal.'

They moved into the studio. The easel carrying the icon stood in the centre of the room. 'Let me give you these,' Baranov said. He handed the folded tissue paper to Grigoriev in which Victor Gordon had placed the scraps taken from the icon. The two men spent some minutes checking the flake of paint and sliver of wood against the places on the icon from which they had been taken. Then Grigoriev looked at the icon itself.

'And this is what is said to be worth all those millions?'

'That's right. A priceless Andrei Roublev. The find of the century. Absolutely beautiful.'

Grigoriev shrugged. 'And are we going to co-operate in this venture, or are we going to fight?'

'I've been thinking since we met last night,' Baranov replied. 'It seems stupid to fight each other, with our private armies in confrontation. I suggest we call the bullies off and settle this in a civilised fashion. Come and sit down, have a cognac and we'll talk.'

They went into the next room and Baranov nodded to Gribenko to disappear. Installed with glasses and cigarettes, he turned to Grigoriev. 'I'm sorry my man told you to put your hands up, but with your fellows lined up out there . . .' He gestured with his glass in the direction of the window.

Grigoriev ignored the remark. 'Who else knows about the icon?'

'Marchenko, of course.'

'Can we rely on him to keep his trap shut?'

'Certainly. If we go down the tubes, so does he.'

'Who else then?'

'The people at the Restoration Works know I have it but don't know what it is. As far as they are concerned, it's a straightforward restoration job, approved by Krasnodar, and the icon is to be returned there for the museum. They're people who don't look at the work of art; they look at the chit which comes with it. That is their reality. Bureaucrats.'

'Anyone else?'

'There is someone else,' Baranov said, 'a bloody nuisance by the name of Lyubimov, a hack at *Vperiod*, pure as driven snow and therefore a troublemaker. He's cottoned on to the fact that I lifted the icon out of the church in Taman, though he doesn't know its value. What surprises me a bit is that *Vperiod* haven't published anything on his trip down south. If they do, it could be awkward, seeing that the old priest in charge of the church got himself totalled with a blow on the head.'

'And this Lyubimov, what do you plan to do about him?'

'Well, I had a bit of an idea only this morning. We could give him the story, complete with the fact that it's a Roublev. It would be a neat way of interesting the authorities, which is what you need.'

Grigoriev sat in silence for a moment, then he drained his glass and looked hard at Baranov.

'It seems to me,' he said slowly, 'that it's just as well I came over. Isn't it obvious that this Lyubimov, far from being used, has to be eliminated? If what you say is true, he's the one risk we run. Christ almighty, a journalist sniffing around for a story, knowing there's been a murder down in Taman, and of course a couple more here in Moscow, and you think *you* can use *him*! It's the stupidest bloody idea I ever heard.'

'More killing,' Baranov said. 'Not a good idea. It's all right for you, sitting in New York issuing contracts at a distance, then flying in here and ordering more, but I live here, man. I have to live with the consequences.' He shook his head. 'No more killing, thank you.'

'I have to ask you,' Grigoriev said, 'are we co-operating or are we not?'

'Sure.'

'Then I say this journalist has to be taken out, and if your people won't do it, mine will.'

'There's a problem,' Baranov said.

'It looks as if there's more than one fucking problem,' Grigoriev answered.

'The problem is quite simply that Lyubimov is in touch – I might say close touch – with the Specials who are in charge of the Victor Gordon enquiry. He turned up here as a witness for a Major Ponomarev. If Lyubimov's to go it has to be an accident – copper-bottomed, with no foul-up.'

'That,' Grigoriev said, 'is not a problem. My people can handle it. Also, it needs to be done before we let the authorities loose on the icon story. Otherwise, as soon as the news is published that a Roublev has turned up and then disappeared, your journalist will be round to the procurator's office like a shot, urging them to reopen the investigation of the priest's death, Gordon's disappearance, the lot. They'll run you in, put you in a cell smelling of piss, question you for days on end, offer you phoney deals – you know the form. You have to be a prick not to see it.'

'So how do we do it?' Baranov asked lamely.

'I'll talk to my people and let you know,' Grigoriev said.

19

There was nothing in the Interpol report on Victor Gordon himself that Major Ponomarev found particularly illuminating. The brace of wives, the Manhattan duplex, Connecticut farm, and gallery on East 52nd Street were, for all Ponomarev knew, standard for successful New York art dealers. Gordon's monographs on early Christian art and his two-volume survey entitled *The Icon in Russia* confirmed what Ponomarev already assumed about the purpose of his man's trips to the Soviet Union. None of this, he felt, carried matters forward. Under CONTACTS on the second page of the fax from Washington, however, there were paragraphs which Ponomarev underlined carefully, using a ruler and a red ballpoint.

> Subject is known to have had business dealings over a period of twelve years with Anton Kurtz, art dealer, 1102 Park Avenue, New York. Informant states that Gordon acts from time to time as valuer/expert on Kurtz's behalf, and they are also known to have bought and sold items together. On two occasions – 1987 and 1989 – the Art Fraud Squad of the NY City Police Department, together with insurance interests, investigated thefts of art objects from Gordon's premises. The view is expressed in insurance circles and by the International Foundation for Art Research, NY, that the insurers were on those occasions victims of a well-known scam in which a dealer (in the event, Gordon) holds goods on consignment from a principal (Kurtz) who then arranges theft of the goods, thereby claiming insurance. In neither case were the

goods recovered. Suspicion fell on associates of Genrikh Grigoriev (see below). No arrests were made.

The Interpol report then went on to delve a little more deeply into the doings of Anton Kurtz and his contacts:

> Kurtz is known to have dealings with one Genrikh Grigoriev of 11 Fifth Street, Brighton Beach, NY, of no settled occupation but known to be a figure of importance in organised crime in the Brighton Beach/Coney Island area. Grigoriev is involved, according to local police sources, in protection rackets, prostitution and other criminal activities. Subject came to the USA from the USSR on 14 March 1985, and despite a number of court appearances since that date has no convictions recorded against him and has not been the subject of expulsion proceedings. Relevant FBI files have not been available for scrutiny in this instance. Subject Grigoriev, according to immigration records, was born in Yerevan, USSR, on 8 December 1944. Present enquiries at US Immigration Department indicate that subject left the USA via JFK airport on 22 August last, destination Moscow, USSR. Subject is in possession of a return ticket bearing an open return date.
>
> Subject is unmarried in the USA and without known dependants.

The Interpol report went on to describe certain of the alleged misdeeds of Genrikh Grigoriev, for none of which had the NY Attorney General's department managed to put together a case which proved water-tight in court.

'Found me a decent Mercedes yet?' Ponomarev asked the man at Interpol when he called to thank him.

'Got the dollars?'

'Don't talk nonsense, man. I haven't even got the roubles.'

'Was the report any use?'

'Could be. Anyway, thanks.'

Then Ponomarev called the militia headquarters in Yerevan and asked what they knew about one Genrikh Grigoriev, born 8 December 1944, and presently an emigrant in the USA. 'Probably known on your patch as Grigoryan,' Ponomarev told his contact in Yerevan.

'We're very busy down here,' a disobliging voice replied, 'considering that we're getting ready to blow the place to pieces for political reasons.'

'So are we up here in Moscow,' Ponomarev said cheerfully.

'Christ knows when our archive people can get around to this sort of query. As a matter of fact, and no offence meant to you personally, Major, we couldn't give a fart for your problems in Moscow, seeing that we have *real* problems down here in Armenia.'

'I'm sorry to hear it,' Ponomarev said, 'and I personally regret the many punitive expeditions we Russians have sent down to you over the centuries, and if it were up to me, there'd be an end to them.'

The irony was lost on the man at the other end. 'If there's one single reason why we should put ourselves out over a query from Moscow, I'm damned if I can think of it.'

'Nor can I, nor can I,' Ponomarev replied, 'but it would be nice if you could do it merely as a favour between professionals. And I'll do the same for you some day.'

There was a silence.

'Fuck you,' the militiaman in Yerevan said, and rang off.

Ponomarev had the impression that he'd probably get some kind of reply to his query.

He called a friend in the Moscow CID.

'Alyosha, you have mysterious links with the Moscow Armenians, right?'

'Who told you that?'

'Never mind. I'm interested in one Genrikh Grigoriev who has form maybe six years back in Yerevan. He's been in the USA since then, and back in our country since 29 August. Flew into Moscow, probably under his own name, though I can't be sure. I suspect he's still here.'

'And what do you want from me?'

'Just find him for me, that's all.'

Ponomarev explained his call to the Yerevan militia. 'I'll pass on what they have to tell me, if I ever hear from them again.'

'I'll see what I can do,' his friend said, 'but my writ doesn't run outside the city.'

'Let's try the city for a start.'

Surprisingly, Yerevan called back the same afternoon.

'Your Grigoriev. It turns out our people are interested in having a friendly exchange of views with him. Where is he?'

'He may be in Moscow. We're looking for him.'

'He has plenty of form. Matter of fact, there's a warrant out. Murder, first degree. Seems he was executioner for a gang who ran protection here in the city. Our warrant is for the killing of a shopkeeper who refused to pay up. Your Grigoriev barricaded him in his shop and set fire to the place. Man was fried. We have witnesses who'll actually go into court now that Grigoriev's not around. That and a previous case of aggravated assault. The file says he had a nasty habit of cutting off the ears of people who had displeased him. And it's written here that he has brutal and disgusting sexual habits, not specified. I'm putting all this on fax for you, plus the names of his associates, some of whom we think have shifted to Moscow over the years. They may lead you to Grigoriev.'

'Photos?'

'We've a mug shot, not good enough to go over the wire. I'll post it.'

'Thanks,' Ponomarev said. 'We'll keep our ears to the ground and let you know if we find him.' Then he called his friend Alyosha in the CID and brought him up to date.

'I started out,' Baranov said, 'believing that it was yet another copy of the Roublev Old Testament Trinity. God knows, I've seen enough of them.'

'Haven't we all,' Trofimich said, leaning back on his wooden chair to get a view of Baranov's face. As ever, his back was giving him hell, making him irritable and disinclined to chat.

'Certainly, it was a brilliant copy – probably late eighteenth-century, I reckon. Then I began to have second thoughts. I suppose it was the faces which really bothered me. No one since the fifteenth century had faces quite like that, or at any rate *painted* faces in that way. It was the spirituality; I couldn't get round the spirituality of the thing. I sat staring at it for hours and slowly the impossible became possible. It had to be a genuine Roublev.'

'And that would make me Tsar of all the Russias,' Trofimich said sourly. He had slumped forward again, staring at the desk beneath his nose, not bothering to strain upwards to look at Baranov. With no second chair in the bare room, Baranov was standing in front of the desk. He had placed the icon, wrapped in its blanket, leaning against a wall.

'And if it isn't a Roublev,' he said, 'I am the Tsarina. Anyway, I did a bit of cleaning, took a good look at the painting itself and the support, and what I now put to you is that we should call in Abramov. Maybe he'll turn out to be Rasputin,' he added.

'You can call in who you like as long as you don't claim I was the one who thought he'd discovered a lost Roublev. I suggest you lock the damn thing up meanwhile. Nowadays they steal the sugar out of your tea.'

'I'll call Abramov at the University and get him down here,' Baranov said. 'What's more, I'll lay my reputation on the line from the start. "We've a genuine Andrei Roublev here at the Restoration Works," I'll tell him. "Would you care to be the expert who identifies it?" That,' Baranov added, 'will have him here within the hour.'

'And what if it does turn out to be a genuine Roublev?' Trofimich asked.

'It seems to me that since we were the first to identify it we should be given the honour of doing the restoration work. It could use some further cleaning and the support is in pretty poor shape.'

As Baranov lifted the icon and made to go, Trofimich had second thoughts. On the one hand. he had no desire to have experts, professors, bureaucrats from the University's Art History Department and maybe from the ministry, crawling all over the Restoration Works, finding fault and making life a misery. Nor did he relish being told he and his staff were talking rot and the icon was a copy and a poor one at that. On the other hand, was there not glory to be derived from having discovered and identified such a treasure – if it *was* a treasure? Where did the balance between trouble and glory lie? He leant back on his chair until he could get Baranov's head into his line of vision.

'If outside experts are to be called in, it is my responsibility to call them. Leave Professor Abramov to me.'

'Then don't you want to *see* the damn thing?' Baranov asked.

'You're the expert,' Trofimich said. 'If my resident expert tells me I have a Roublev, I must accept what he says until such time as he's proved an idiot, at which point I will have to see what is to be done with him.' He slumped forward again. 'Take the thing away and lock it up. I'll call Professor Abramov myself.'

Later on the telephone Professor Abramov was sarcastic.

'Where was your alleged Roublev found?'

'In a church in Taman on the Black Sea.'

'A Roublev on the Black Sea? Are you sure it wasn't in Tadjikistan?'

'Our expert says he's certain it's a Roublev.'

'And what do you say?'

'I leave such judgements to the specialist staff.'

The Professor sighed. 'Look, man, we have people bringing in rubbish here at the University all day long. They all think they've stumbled on a treasure of some kind – Theophanes, Roublev, whoever. And of course, they never have.' He sighed again. 'I suppose you'd better send it over and we'll have a look at it.'

'I'm sorry, Professor, but I am not free to let it leave our jurisdiction. We have signed for it officially, you understand, and we're responsible to the authorities in Krasnodar, whose property it remains.'

'I am not asking you to send it to Washington. This is Moscow University. We are responsible people. We will not steal your damned Roublev. We will even sign a piece of paper for you if that is what you need. But we're too busy to come out on a wild-goose chase.'

Christ, this self-important personage was beginning to annoy. And the back was giving exceptional hell this morning. Furthermore, rules were rules, and signatures were signatures. Trofimich was in no mood to give way.

'I am sorry, Professor, but I must ask you to come to us, or send a competent person. I am guided by the regulations.'

The Professor was heard to sigh into the telephone again. During the conversation he had been thinking. What if the icon were indeed a Roublev and he had refused to have anything to do with it? What then? He had no way of knowing that his thoughts were running parallel to the earlier thoughts of Trofimich. Many years of experience had taught him that to take the initiative in anything was indeed dangerous – formerly a danger to one's life, but nowadays still a danger to one's career. On the other hand, not to act could also be regarded in higher quarters as an example of initiative, since it implied that a choice had been made between action and no action. The trick lay in correctly judging in any situation which of the two risks was the greater.

The Professor decided that to have refused to look at what later was identified as a genuine Andrei Roublev constituted too great a risk to run. Better to lose an afternoon examining what would certainly turn out to be a fake of some kind.

'I will be with you this afternoon at three,' he said.

'I have an expert coming to authenticate it today,' Baranov told Grigoriev on the phone.

'When do you plan to lift it?' Grigoriev asked.

'Assuming the expert agrees it's a genuine Roublev, I must give him time to tell his associates at the University and, no doubt, the Ministry of Culture. Let's assume he'll be as excited as hell, unable to keep it to himself, and off to impart the good news tomorrow morning. Then they'll want to grab the icon for themselves – you know, do all the tests, the restoration, learned monographs and all that. So I expect they'll be sending for it the day after.'

'Would you have to let it go?'

'Probably. The fools who run this place will try to hang on to it for the glory, but they'll collapse under the weight of all that top brass.'

'So that you'll have to lift it tomorrow night latest?'

'Yes,' Baranov said. 'I'll be seeing my people this evening.'

'Do you have somewhere to take it?'

'Yes.'

'And then?'

'And then I move it on.'

There was a silence.

'We must talk about that,' Grigoriev said at last. He was speaking very quietly. 'You will please come to my place this evening, say at seven. I shall be waiting for you.' And he rang off before Baranov had a chance to reply.

Soon after three Professor Abramov arrived, accompanied by a colleague introduced as Dr Stanislav Zimin. The

Professor proved to be a very large man with a beard that he had perhaps modelled on that of Karl Marx. Dr Zimin was elderly, bald, sallow in complexion and highly nervous in manner. They left their car and driver in the yard of the Restoration Works and found their way to Trofimich's desolate office.

'Now where is this alleged Roublev of yours?' the Professor demanded irritably.

'Please follow me to the studio,' Trofimich said, pulling himself with difficulty out of his chair and leading the way out into the corridor and up a flight of iron stairs.

In the studio, which ran the length of the building and contained paintings and icons in various stages of restoration, Peter Baranov was introduced.

'So you are the young man who knows all about Andrei Roublev and discovers his work in the Kuban, eh?'

'I was lucky, Professor.'

'We don't know yet whether you were lucky or foolish, do we, young man?'

'I think I was lucky.'

The icon was on a stand facing a window, a cloth draped over it. Baranov approached and withdrew the cloth with a flourish. 'There is my luck, gentlemen.'

Professor Abramov and Dr Zimin approached the icon as if they were dealing with an animal which might prove dangerous and capable of biting them. For a long while neither said anything as they examined it from all angles, had it off the stand to inspect the back, demanded a magnifying glass with which they inspected different areas of the painting, grunted and exchanged comments beneath their breath. Baranov and Trofimich stood by in silence, Baranov with a slight smile on his face, confident of his judgement, waiting for a positive verdict as if no other were conceivable.

'And where exactly did you find this object?' Professor Abramov asked at last. He had turned away from the icon and was facing Peter Baranov. Dr Zimin was still examining an area which Baranov had cleaned. He was muttering to himself, sometimes shaking his head, hopping from foot to foot as if the floor were hot. From time to time a loud 'Hah!' escaped from him.

'I found it in a concealed room at the Cathedral in Taman,' Baranov said. 'The room had obviously been undisturbed for years, perhaps for centuries. The priest clearly had no idea of the icon's importance.'

'Does this priest of yours know that it has been removed for restoration?'

'There was a tragedy,' Baranov said. 'The priest died.'

'And the authorities down there, what about them?'

'As I understand it, the icon will go to the museum in Krasnodar when we've restored it.'

'And documentation, what have you got in the way of authorisation?'

Trofimich appeared to emerge from a reverie at the mention of documents. 'I have the authorisation of the Chairman of the Regional Council for Religious Affairs in the Kuban to carry out whatever restoration work we consider necessary. My authorisation states that the icon is, according to law, the property of the Regional Council and is to be returned into the care of the chairman for transfer to the Fine Arts department of the museum in Krasnodar.'

A little breathless after this, Trofimich reached for a chair and sat down heavily. In front of the icon Dr Zimin was heard exclaiming and grunting. He had taken a notebook from his pocket and was making notes as he continued to scrutinise the icon inch by inch. Suddenly he proclaimed, 'Ash?' and relapsed into silence.

'I had checked the wood,' Baranov told Professor Abramov. 'Ash, presumably from the Moscow region.'

'Support fitted with crosspieces,' from Dr Zimin. And again, 'Unusual but possible in the case of Roublev.'

'What equipment have you got here?' the Professor asked. 'Infra-red, radiography, advanced microscopes?'

From his chair, Trofimich shook his head. 'Since when

would they grant us that kind of money?' He allowed himself a sardonic laugh. 'We haven't even got decent lighting.'

'It will have to come to us for proper analysis,' the Professor said.

Dr Zimin was showing signs of growing agitation, beckoning to the Professor like a dog trying to draw its master's attention to a ball which required to be thrown.

'What is it, Zimin?'

'What you have here,' Dr Zimin was muttering, 'is the genuine thing. Beyond a doubt a genuine Roublev – a version of his Old Testament Trinity in remarkable condition. Some fascinating variants on the Tretyakov version. Astonishing!' He kept shaking his head, still hopping from foot to foot.

'Just as I told you,' Baranov said. There was a fixed smile on his face which signalled, 'We did not need Karl Marx and his faithful hound to tell us what we already knew.'

The Professor stood back and gave the icon a long, searching look. Then he issued his pronunciamento.

'Speaking as an art historian and from a purely artistic and aesthetic perspective,' he declared, tugging solemnly at his beard, 'I would hazard a very high probability that what we have here is a work by the black monk, Andrei Roublev. A late work, I might add, and certainly a slight variant on his Old Testament Trinity. That, as I say, is my present judgement from an art historical point of view. On the other hand, speaking as a scientist I have to say that this contention is not proven and needs to be subjected to scientific analysis in the usual manner. That we will need to do at our laboratories at the University, and until we have a positive outcome from those tests we cannot say with certainty that it is in fact a Roublev. I therefore propose to take it back with me to my department for analysis.' There was another tug at the beard and a further 'Hah!' from Zimin.

'Impossible,' Trofimich said.

'Why impossible?'

'I am not authorised to release it.'

'Good heavens, man, I speak for the University. Do you think we'll spill coffee on it?'

'It can't leave here without proper authorisation from Krasnodar.'

'Then get authorisation, man, and get it fast.'

'Not so easy,' Trofimich said, pleased to have become the key to the entire transaction.

'Can't you use the damn telephone?'

'Certainly, but I'll need a document and that will take time. You realise – signatures and so forth, and then the post. These things aren't done overnight.'

'Then do it as fast as these procedures of yours permit. I shall call you tomorrow to see what progress you're making. And meanwhile, lock it up and keep your mouths shut, all of you. You may have a national treasure there on that stand.'

Beckoning the highly excited Dr Zimin, the Professor shook hands, gave his beard a valedictory tug and descended the iron stairs to the ground floor, whence he and his companion hurried out to their car, talking and gesticulating to each other.

'Lock it in the storeroom,' Trofimich told Peter Baranov, 'and don't talk about it to the others.'

'Of course not,' Baranov said.

'Get the keys from my office and be sure you return them right away.'

20

'If I am not out of there in forty minutes,' Baranov told Gribenko, 'come and get me and bring Mitya with you. The flat is in this corner block, fourth floor left. You kick the door in and come in fast with the safety catches off, right?'

'Do we shoot?'

'If you have to. My guess is it won't be necessary, though they won't be happy about the door.'

Mitya in the back of the car asked, 'What's the layout inside?'

'You turn right inside the front door and it's maybe three metres to the living room. There's a divan against the right-hand wall and a couple of chairs facing it to the left. I'll try to be on the divan, so watch out to your left, but I can't be sure.'

'And how many will be there?'

'No idea. I'd expect Grigoriev, Razmik and the woman, maybe one or at most two more. I can't see them putting on a bigger show than that.'

Gribenko grunted. 'Forty minutes?'

'Yes,' Baranov said as he got out of the car. Then he made his way to the entrance to the block and took the lift up to the fourth floor. His ring was answered almost at once.

'Come in,' Razmik said. 'He's waiting for you.'

But he turned left in the corridor and led Baranov into the tiny kitchen. At the square table sat Grigoriev. Razmik took a chair to his left and signalled Baranov to sit on the other side of the table.

'I do not much appreciate being summoned like this,'

Baranov said. 'It was difficult for me to free myself this evening.'

From the living room down the corridor he could hear voices, with music from a radio behind them. There were shouts of laughter.

'Tell them to shut up,' Grigoriev said. 'I am not interested in drawing the neighbours' attention to the place.'

Razmik went out and the sound subsided as he returned and sat.

Grigoriev looked at Baranov and said nothing. He had a can of beer before him and a glass. Razmik had the same. Neither offered Baranov a drink. The small kitchen was oppressively hot, airless. Baranov felt his shirt sticking to his back, a trickle of sweat on his brow. The long silence was getting on his nerves. Still the others said nothing.

'You didn't get me here just to look at me,' he tried, grinning.

Grigoriev took a swig of beer, leaving a thin line of froth on his moustache. He replaced his glass on the table almost delicately, continuing to hold it in his powerful hand. Baranov noticed the thick fingers, the line of black hair along the back of the hand. It struck him that it looked like the hand of a killer.

'Well,' he said, 'the experts came and were duly impressed. They want to take the icon away for scientific tests.'

'When?'

'There's paperwork first, as usual. Probably they'll want to fetch it the day after tomorrow.'

The hand continued to caress the half-full tumbler of beer. The other hand came up and wiped away the froth on the moustache, then came to rest on the table. Razmik was leaning back in his chair, smoking, saying nothing. Baranov felt the muscles of his diaphragm contract, a slight nausea developing in his stomach. He knew the signs, had experienced them at break-ins. He was aware that fear was causing his lower lip to tremble when he spoke, to make his voice unsteady, as if it were being forced from his throat. And still Grigoriev was saying nothing, nursing the tumbler, staring at Baranov, facing him across the small table.

When he spoke it was scarcely above a whisper. 'My people will go in to lift it.'

'*Your* people?' Baranov's voice came out husky and uncertain.

'You heard me correctly.'

'I never agreed to that. The operation is mine.' Saying it cost Baranov an enormous effort. The sweat was pouring down the back of his neck, soaking his shirt. He was aware that his lip was trembling but was unable to control it.

'What did you say?' in the same whisper.

'I – I said the operation's mine. That's the deal.'

Grigoriev leaned slowly across the table, extended a hand and gripped the front of Baranov's shirt. Then the other hand which grasped the tumbler of beer came up and the beer was dashed in Baranov's face.

'People do not speak to me like that,' Grigoriev said, still gripping the shirt, forcing Baranov to lean forward over the table. 'You are not treating me with respect and that is unacceptable. You are a miserable little Russian thief with no class and no brains, and if you do not behave yourself one of my people will shoot you between the eyes.' He loosened his hold and sat back. There was no expression on his face and his eyes seemed distant, uninterested. 'Is that understood?'

'There's no need to get rough,' Baranov said, wiping beer from his face. 'These things can be negotiated between friends.'

'There are no friends here,' Grigoriev said. 'This is business and people do not cross me in business. I have come back to this filthy country to rescue a business deal you were fucking up and it will now be done my way. Is that understood?'

'But I don't know what the deal between us is any more.'

'The deal is what I decide it to be when we have the icon out of the country.'

'What are you doing, screwing me out of my share?'

'I am taking the deal over. If you do as you're told you'll get a share. That share will be decided by me. If you don't, you're out, and maybe you'll be out in one piece, maybe not, but I warn you that Razmik here has resources.' Grigoriev slowly took a pack of cigarettes from a pocket and took his time over lighting one. He repeated 'resources' as he blew a cloud of smoke towards Baranov. 'Also, we will be looking after the journalist. I shall have some men on his tail. Now, you will tell us exactly where the icon is stored at the Restoration Works.'

He pulled a sheet of paper and a pencil from a pocket and threw them on the table.

'Draw me a plan, and it had better be accurate.'

Baranov's mind was racing. A plan which led Grigoriev's mob to the icon would lose the whole venture for him. The thought made him sick with frustration. On the other hand, attempt to mislead them, to delay matters, and they'd be after him. It would be a typical gangland killing, especially painful and public in order to discourage anyone else who might have moments of defiance. He took up the pencil and slowly started to draw a plan of the upper floor at the Restoration Works. He plotted in the storeroom and found himself indicating accurately the spot where the icon had been placed.

'Mark in the light switches,' Grigoriev said. Then, 'Where do they keep the keys?'

'They're locked in a safe in Trofimich's office on the ground floor, but he takes the safe keys home with him.'

'What about the door to the storeroom? Describe it.'

'It's a metal door with heavy hinges. You'd have trouble breaking it down.'

'And how did you expect to get in there?'

'A crowbar. A couple of strong men could do it.'

'Now tell me about getting into the works themselves. Any nightwatchmen?'

'There's an old fellow lives in the gatehouse on his own. He'd hear anyone trying to break through the big gates to the yard.'

'So how would you get round that one?'

Baranov had regained some of his poise and now his mind was functioning again. Could he abort Grigoriev's attack on the Restoration Works? Suggest a way into the place which wouldn't work? If so, it would have to look like bad luck and not bad advice. But how? Tentatively, a plan began to form in his mind. Concentrate – he must try to concentrate despite the menace in the room, the dispassionate eyes fixed on him, the violence scarcely held in check.

He decided to play it straight.

'I wouldn't recommend trying the main gate. Breaking it open would be noisy, and given its height and the wire on top, climbing over is dodgy. But there are windows along the wall to the right of the gate. They're about three metres above ground level, so you'd need a ladder to reach one of them. The glass isn't reinforced, so getting in isn't a problem. It's probably your best plan.'

'Is it a main road or what?'

'A side road, unlit. And there are empty warehouses on the other side.'

He glanced at his watch. He must get out of here before Gribenko and his men came hammering at the door. To judge by the sounds from the living room, they hadn't a chance anyway. Thirty minutes had passed. Ten to go. He got up.

'There, I've given you all the help I can. When do you plan the action?'

'The time is none of your business.' Grigoriev and Razmik got to their feet. 'Listen,' Grigoriev said, 'I don't like you and I don't trust you. I make that perfectly clear. However, I am prepared to reward you for your co-operation. By the same token, if you try to double-cross me, if anything you've told me turns out to be a lie, I'll have you killed, my Russian friend, and in a most painful way. We have a lad out there who enjoys doing it, and you know what these enthusiasts can be like when they're let loose.' Grigoriev had again taken hold of Baranov's shirt, pulling him close, face to face. 'He has a special dislike for intellectuals like you. An inferiority complex he can't get out of his system, you understand. Christ, he'll make you suffer. So we have the truth, eh?'

'You have the truth, I swear it.'

Grigoriev released him. 'Now get out.'

Downstairs, in the car, Baranov told Gribenko, 'The fucking bastards. They think they're double-crossing us, but they overlooked one thing.'

'What's that?'

'Never mind what it is. I want all of you available tonight. We'll meet at your place at ten.'

'Guns?'

'Guns. And see there are wire cutters and a crowbar in the van, and let's have a short ladder on the roof.'

The man called Mitya said from the back of the car, 'We don't know what the hell all this is about.'

'You don't need to know. You just need to do as I say and not go blabbing to your woman or your mother-in-law, right?'

'Right.'

'Tell me,' Baranov said to Gribenko, 'if you were doing a job at a place like the Restoration Works, what would be your best time in the night?'

'Certainly not before two in the morning; not later than three-thirty. It's when people are dead to the world.'

'Would you risk it between midnight and one?'

'Never. People are still coming home.'

'Good. We'll do it between twelve and one.'

'It's crazy,' Gribenko said. 'Asking for trouble.'

'It's because it's crazy that we'll be doing it that way. Now let's get out of here.'

21

'If we look back over the stories Genatsvale turned down in recent months,' Gennady Ivanov said, 'we'll probably find enough good stuff to fill several editions of the paper.'

He was chairing the editorial committee, which had been widened to include several new faces, among them Panov, who had draped his huge frame over an inadequate chair.

'What have we got?'

'Well,' Panov said, stirring on the protesting chair, 'I have this story of the kids in training for the Olympics – you know, steroids, neglected education, harsh training, all that. It's a bloody scandal. I could give you a nice little series on it. I've got great sources . . . quotes, the lot.'

'Let's try it,' Ivanov said. 'What else?'

'Slava Lyubimov's story from Taman,' Panov said. 'Murder, theft, corruption, the desecration of a church – it's got everything.'

Lyubimov nodded. 'It also has the special virtue that the Central Committee would positively hate it. And it now has a Moscow angle and I've the right contact in the militia.'

'I would remind you,' Ivanov said, 'that as of this week the Central Committee no longer exists, since the Party has been wound up by Yeltsin and his friends.'

'Sorry, I haven't got used to it yet.'

'And this story of yours – mafia?'

'Maybe that and a bit more,' Lyubimov said. 'It even includes a disappearing American, a dead taxi driver and what is probably a major art theft.'

'Let's do it,' Ivanov said. 'Can we have something for the next edition?'

Lyubimov nodded.

'What else?'

'There's a letter from a reader which I rather like, which could be dressed up as a lead,' Nadia said. 'This woman is furious about the banning of the Communist Party. Her thesis is that you can't wipe out seventy years of a noble ideal and the allegiance of millions of honest citizens simply by issuing a decree and putting strips of sticking plaster across the doors at Staraya Ploshchad. Also, what do you achieve by pulling down statues? And since Peter the Great did some horrible things, why not pull his statues down too? It's rather eloquent, really, and I think we should run it and let the readers answer back.'

'Anyone against?' Ivanov asked.

Several were. The meaning of democracy was debated. The freedom of the press was held up to the light and examined. Why, someone asked, extend to the Communist Party the kind of consideration it had never extended to anyone else? But if one now had democracy, someone countered, why not?

'We are learning,' Nadia said. 'It's painful, but we're slowly learning not to win arguments by shooting each other.'

They decided to publish the letter.

On his way out of the editorial meeting, Slava Lyubimov stopped by Verochka's desk. She was filing her nails and made a point of not looking up. 'My dear Verochka,' he said, 'things around here have changed. I know you were distressed that we'd wasted precious cash on my trip to Taman. Well, we're to run the story after all. Aren't you pleased?'

The point was lost on her. Looking up from her nails, she said, 'When my mother and I can afford a decent cut of meat again, I'll interest myself in your concerns about who did and who didn't kill a priest down on the Black Sea. And if the price of fresh tomatoes comes down, I'll even read what you write about missing icons, or whatever it is. Meanwhile, I'm not interested.'

Lyubimov found he had no ready reply and tramped off down the gloomy corridor to his cubicle.

'I can see why we never got the mass of the population onto the streets to defend Gorbachev and Yeltsin last week,' he said to Panov. 'Someone – I think it was Brecht – said something to the effect that morality and suchlike comes only after the belly has been filled. It was a point.'

'Not that much of a point,' Panov said. 'Our bellies were reasonably full for years and we never got around to morality. Meanwhile, I'm damned if I can get a decent lead onto this story.'

'Keep trying,' Lyubimov said. 'I'm expecting Raya. We promised each other a walk in the park, then it's back on the job for both of us.'

'When does she leave Moscow?'

'She doesn't know. It seems her delegation is bogged down because neither they nor the people they're negotiating with can get sanction from their principals to proceed to the next stage. It's the story of our lives.'

Panov was searching through his untidy notes and shaking his head. 'Almighty God, why did I ever sink into this impossible profession? Nina is right. She says I'm entirely without talent and should be driving a tractor.'

Lyubimov found Raya chatting to Verochka in the entrance lobby. Verochka was holding forth on the growing crime rate.

'Let's go,' Lyubimov said. 'Fresh air and ice cream.' They left the building and walked the short distance to the Metro arm in arm. On the platform for trains to the October station a few travellers were waiting. They walked a short distance down the platform and stood side by side near the edge. A sallow young man in T-shirt and frayed jeans who had followed them down on the escalator moved slowly towards the place where they were waiting for the train and took up a position leaning against the wall behind them. Neither of them had noticed him. They were talking animatedly as the roar of the approaching train reached them.

'Fruit-flavour!' Raya said. 'How can a real man eat *pink* ice cream?'

'I'm sorry,' Slava Lyubimov was saying. 'I have no false pride about such things. I am not at all macho. I like fruit-flavour ice cream and that is what I plan to have this afternoon.'

'Ugh! Give me chocolate.'

The front of the train had emerged from the tunnel and the noise drowned Lyubimov's reply. She turned towards him, her back to the track. Suddenly, she grabbed his arm with surprising strength and pulled him violently towards her. As she did so he felt a body thrust against his other shoulder. The front of the train had reached them and was past amid a screech of brakes. The sallow young man, who had plunged towards them from behind as the train approached, managed to regain his balance on the edge of the platform. Then he ran for the escalators and disappeared from view before Lyubimov had time to realise what had happened.

'I saw his face as he came at you,' Raya said. 'He was going to push you onto the track – kill you; I saw it in his eyes. Horrible!' She was trembling, still clutching Lyubimov's arm.

'You saved my life, then,' he answered. 'We'll find a specially large chocolate ice cream.'

'How can you make jokes at a time like this? We should go after him.' Her anxiety had made her angry.

'With a start like that there's no hope of catching up. What did he look like?'

'A southerner. Just a scruffy youth in jeans.'

'Would you know him again?'

'Anywhere.'

'A junkie?'

'There was nothing doped about those eyes. I'd say a killer. But why you?'

They had allowed the train to leave without them. No one else appeared to have seen the incident. Raya was trembling, still clinging to Lyubimov's arm. She kept saying: 'Horrible, horrible!'

'It seems,' Lyubimov said, 'that the Taman story is even better copy than I thought. That's the second time they've expressed their annoyance with me.'

'What about the militia? You must report what happened.'

'I shall see my friend the major, but I don't expect he or anyone else is likely to get very far.'

'Right away.'

'No – right now it's the park and chocolate ice cream.'

Another train had arrived. They boarded it and got off at the October station. Then up into the blazing heat of the late August day, and so into Gorki Park, Raya still holding tightly to his arm, both walking in step, saying nothing.

'What are you thinking?' she asked at last. 'You look puzzled.'

'Not puzzled – just trying to remember . . .' He paused. 'Ah, I have it: the last stanza goes like this: "*And say I died and for the Tsar,/And say what fools the doctors are;/And that I shook you by the hand,/And spoke about my native land.*" Lermontov at his finest. It's what I'd have gasped out to you if that train had hit me.' He laughed and squeezed her hand.

'If that train had hit you you wouldn't have had time to quote Lermontov or anyone else, and I'm still too upset to compete. But I know the poem – the last words of an officer dying on the battlefield in Dagestan.'

They had reached a booth serving ice cream and now, bearing cones, they headed towards one of the lakes.

'We'll take a boat,' Lyubimov announced, 'and eat our ices on the water.'

'You are an interesting person,' Raya told him later as they sat facing each other in the boat, each trailing a hand in the water. 'You've just escaped a nasty death by purest chance because I happened to turn round at that very moment, and all you want to do is eat pink ice cream and go boating. You aren't even indignant about it.'

Lyubimov laughed. 'My father used to say I was too phlegmatic and it would take an unusually spirited woman or a major disaster to wake me up.' He looked steadily into Raya's eyes and his expression was suddenly serious. 'I haven't yet encountered the disaster which could wake me up, but as to the spirited woman . . .'

'Yes?'

'Yes, I've found her.' He leaned forward in the boat and took one of her hands in his. 'I have to tell you that I'm falling heavily and rapidly in love with you, and there is nothing at all phlegmatic about that.'

She left her hand in his and he felt a slight pressure of her fingers. She smiled and threw her head back. Looking at the sinuous line of her neck, olive skinned, he thought he had never seen anything more beautiful in his life.

'I like what you have just said, I like it very much,' she said. 'It is always nice, isn't it, when you find that another person, quite independently, is reaching a similar conclusion to your own.'

'It is only fear of capsizing this absurd and badly built boat which stops me moving to your end and kissing you,' Lyubimov said.

'Don't do that. If we fell in I'd have to change into my formal dress. I'm travelling light.' As she spoke she brought her other hand forward to clasp his. 'I would be devastated,' she said, 'if anything were to happen to you. Please promise me to be careful.'

'I am always careful.'

'I don't believe it. In your quiet way you are a typical macho Russian. I must impart a little of our Armenian softness, our sinuous deviousness – the ways of an oppressed minority which has learned how to survive.'

When they landed from the boat he seized her round the waist, drew her towards him and kissed her on the mouth. She clung to him, panting a little.

'I have to go back to Yerevan, to my job and my family,

and you are complicating my life!' She laughed, delighted, and offered her mouth again.

'We Russians are the master race – the bosses,' he said. 'You will do as I say and stay on a bit longer in Moscow. We still have a lot of talking, kissing, laughing to do.'

'And our poetry contest isn't over,' Raya said. 'I shall yet out-quote you, you know.'

He was suddenly serious. 'We must make love. It is absolutely impossible for me to let you go away without making love to you.' He was looking into her eyes, thinking it was the one moment in his life he would never forget. 'What do you say to that?'

She smiled up at him. 'Maybe, maybe. We should talk about it. And now we must both get on with other things. I am expected back by my delegation, and you must see your major.'

'Tonight,' he said, 'you are not available for work.'

'Who said so?'

'I said so, and here's the reason.' He took two tickets out of his pocket. 'The Bolshoi. *The Queen of Spades.*'

'Oh!' Her eyes sparkled. 'How on earth . . . ?'

'I told you about my landlady who works in the cloakroom there. Well, she came up with these this morning.'

'And you kept the secret until now!'

'First the little disturbance in the Metro drove it out of my mind, then *you* drove it out still further, so I've only just remembered. What do you say?'

'I say if my delegation wants to work through the evening on a project which looks less and less likely to come to life, they'll have to do it without me. What time?'

'Ten to seven at the theatre. Best seats in the *parterre*. And when Hermann dies in the last act you're allowed to cry because Tchaikovsky cried as he composed it.'

'I've never seen it.'

'Nor have I, but I've an old recording I'm fond of. It's wonderfully lyrical music. Of course, all the critics attacked it after the first performance, which proves how good it is. You'll see.'

They walked arm in arm to the October Metro, took a train and parted at the Kiev interchange.

At the militia headquarters in the Petrovka, Lyubimov found things had more or less returned to normal. He was subjected to the usual puzzled scrutiny by the blank-faced guard at the entrance and finally found himself in Major Ponomarev's untidy office.

'Stirring times,' the major said. 'Much like the stirring of a bowl of kasha; no one knows what the damn thing will taste like when it's cooked.' He shrugged, like a man who, having seen it all, wanted no further part of it. 'That,' he added, 'is not on the record. So tell me what brings you here.'

'Well, for a start I was the target of a murder attempt an hour or two back and I thought I ought to mention it to someone.'

Ponomarev raised his eyebrows. 'Would you care to elaborate?'

Lyubimov told him of the youth in the Metro.

'A southerner?'

'It's what my friend says. I didn't really see him myself.'

'An Armenian, perhaps?'

'Perhaps. At all events, I don't think he was Baranov's Ukrainian who attacked me down in Taman.'

'And that's what you came to tell me – an official complaint of assault in the Metro, assailant unknown?'

'I know that should go to the local militia, major. I'm just mentioning it to you because it seems to me it must be connected with the Baranov affair and the missing American. Also, I thought you might like to know that as a result of recent events we have a new editor at *Vperiod* and we'll be running as much of this story as I can piece together. So I'm here to ask whether the Specials have anything more to tell me.'

'We haven't,' Ponomarev said, 'but it might suit me for you to publish something. Keep in touch.'

'I will.'

'And there's another thing. Do you have any contacts among the Armenian community in Moscow?'

Lyubimov reflected for a moment. 'I have one.'

'And does this person have contacts in the Armenian underworld?'

'He's a barman. The bar is Armenian, paying protection money as usual, and I'd have thought it was the Armenian mafia that's on to them.'

Ponomarev told him about Grigoriev. 'A man like that coming back to Moscow, it's bound to be a talking point in the Armenian underworld. Just see what your barman knows and call me, right?'

'Sure.'

As Lyubimov reached the door, Ponomarev added: 'As to the attack on you, don't try to get smart with these people. They're likely to try it again, so don't wander about on your own at night. Remember, the most dangerous moment is coming home to your apartment after dark. A gunman can wait in the lobby with a silencer on his gun, shoot you and walk away with no one the wiser. We get a lot of killings done like that – neat, no fuss, very little mess. It's best to stay home.'

'Thanks for the advice,' Lyubimov said and made his way out.

22

It was not common practice for the militia to work with journalists, but then Major Ponomarev was clearly no common militiaman. Slava Lyubimov had developed the cosy feeling that he was gradually gaining some mastery over the disjointed facts, suppositions and puzzles which made up the Taman story with its promised Moscow extension. The facts seemed to be falling into place.

Taman provided a fine lead to the tale: a murderer who bludgeons an old priest to death and then kills his dog; the faithful who believe the wrong man has been arrested; then the theft of – what? – from the cellar beneath the cathedral; and an attack on your correspondent himself. All that from what the great Lermontov had described as the worst seacoast town in all Russia.

A good start. Then a disappearing American and a dead taxi driver here in Moscow; a dubious picture restorer who consorts with bully-boys; and now an Armenian mafioso back from America . . . for what?

Good copy, all of it. And the more cultured type of reader would appreciate the link with the great poet. There would be neatly chosen quotations from *A Hero of Our Time*. And the *apparatchik* Marchenko in Krasnodar, a symbolic figure from the past, would be woven into the tale.

A post-coup story, Slava Lyubimov told himself. Unpublishable only last week. Perhaps there was a future for journalism in Russia after all.

He took a bus to the Boulevard Ring Road, alighted at Pokrovskiye Vorota and walked east along the Ring Road, glancing behind him, Ponomarev's warning in his mind. It was five-thirty and the rush hour had filled the broad thoroughfare with traffic, weaving its way around deadly potholes amid choking fumes from the broken-down exhaust systems, the poison hanging in dim clouds in the windless August air. Some two hundred yards along the Ring, Lyubimov turned into a lane which ran south between houses which had been residences of rich merchants of the nineteenth-century city and now housed obscure offices and workshops within their peeling and cracking masonry. Some had been shored up with wooden stays. Others were encased in scaffolding. Some had simply collapsed, exhausted, and had been left there to die. Ahead of him a sign in red neon announced YEREVAN BAR. It protruded above a narrow doorway flanked by windows glazed in dark yellow glass. There were lights within.

Lyubimov knew the barman at the Yerevan Bar as Khatchik, though he doubted that that was his name. A giant of a man in a dirty sweatshirt and torn jeans but with plenty of gold about his person – signet rings, an imported watch, a necklet. Between Lyubimov and the man calling himself Khatchik it was a case of a favour done, a favour owed – currently to Lyubimov, who had considerately left Khatchik's name out of a story on one of the rackets in the Moscow liquor trade. The Armenians had found a way of intercepting liquor deliveries to Moscow restaurants, cutting the liquor with tap water and thereby creating new bottles for enforced sale to the establishments enjoying their protection. Khatchik had been a middleman in one of these operations. Lyubimov had stumbled on the story, and seeing Khatchik as a future source, had left his name out of a piece which had led to a couple of arrests.

Now, he decided, it was time for Khatchik to return the compliment.

The bar was empty, ill-lit, smelling of liquor and dry-rot. The Beach Boys wailed in their plaintive manner from a loudspeaker. There were empty glasses amid puddles of wine and beer on the tables. Behind the bar Khatchik polished glasses with a dirty rag.

'My friend the journalist!'

He reached for a bottle of brandy and two glasses. 'You'll drink.' It was an order.

'A small one,' Lyubimov said.

'You'll drink properly!' Khatchik's voice echoed round the empty room in a kind of muffled roar. The glasses were filled and one was pushed across the bar to Lyubimov.

'What the hell are you doing in here?'

'I came to see you.'

'Cheers!' Khatchik declaimed. 'Drink up.' He poured half the brandy down his throat, extended an enormous hand and crushed Lyubimov's fingers in his grasp.

'So what bit of dirt are you chasing after this time?'

'No dirt. I'm just after a small favour and you're the man who can provide it.' Lyubimov drank and replaced his glass on the bar top.'I need help,' he said.

'Between friends?'

'Precisely. Completely off the record.'

Khatchik grunted, then he shook his enormous head. 'It's what they all say.'

'I mean it.'

'I could pick you up in one hand and throw you through that window,' Khatchik said amiably. 'You know that, don't you?'

'I know that.'

'Good.' He let out a bellow of a laugh, seeming to find the idea hugely to his taste. 'Right through the fucking window and into the lane outside. With one hand.'

'That's right,' Lyubimov said. 'Probably all you'd need is a couple of fingers.'

'That's good,' with a roar of laughter. 'A couple of fingers!'

The man is simple, Lyubimov reflected. Like some great animal which doesn't know its own strength. Maybe a bear.

'You're a cunning old dog,' he told Khatchik. 'No one can put anything across you, so I'm not trying. I just need a bit of harmless info – nothing that could cause you any aggravation, right?'

'Cause me aggravation and through the window you'd go, eh?'

'That's right – through the window.'

'So what is this goddamn bit of info you have to have?'

'I'm doing a big piece on the Armenian mafia in Moscow.'

'Never heard of them,' Khatchik said primly.

'Of course not. You're the last person . . .'

'The very last.' Khatchik brought his index finger down onto his thumb. 'Don't forget the window.' And he let out another bellow.

'I certainly shan't.'

The glasses had been refilled and Khatchik stood, arms akimbo, waiting for a reply to his question about info.

'I've heard on the grapevine, you understand, that one of the Tsars is back in Moscow.'

'Tsar? What Tsar? I thought Stalin was dead.' Khatchik grinned, pleased with his little joke.

'A famous leader of the Armenians in Moscow,' Lyubimov said. 'I heard on the street that he's back from the States. It gives a nice angle to my story.'

'And what is the name of this person?' Khatchik asked, opening his eyes wide.

'His name's Grigoriev.'

There was a silence, and while it lasted Lyubimov noticed that Khatchik glanced towards the street door. Then he looked down at Lyubimov.

'Never heard of the fellow. Not the sort of thing I'd know, anyway, is it? I serve at the bar, keep my nose clean, stay out of the newspapers, eh? Why should I know your Grigoriev, tell me that?'

'You must hear things in here,' Lyubimov said. 'We both know what sort of clientele you have.'

'The best.' Khatchik was grinning again. 'No riff-raff, no doubtful characters, right?'

'Come on,' Lyubimov said. 'You forget the story I did last year.'

'What story? Never heard of it.' Another grin. Khatchik's jewellery glinted as he downed his drink.

'I was hoping you'd help,' Lyubimov said. 'As I said, strictly off the record.'

'Strictly off the record your man's back in town on a job, and I tell you that because for my money he's a bastard and I'd drink anytime to his falling under a truck. Let him fuck the Americans and leave us alone.'

'Had trouble with him?'

'It goes way back,' Khatchik said. 'Back before he left on his travels, and it's none of your damn business.'

'What's this job he's on?' Lyubimov asked.

'He doesn't confide in me, does he now?'

'Even so . . .'

'As far as I can make out it's something to do with art theft. I mind my own business in here but a man can't help overhearing snatches, like, from time to time. A bunch of them were in the other day, and like I say, it could be art theft if my ears didn't fool me.'

'And where's he hanging out?'

'No idea.'

Khatchik leant his great frame over the bar, bringing his face close to Lyubimov's. 'It's all I'm going to tell you, my friend, and now I politely suggest you piss off before anyone comes in here wondering who the hell you are. And if my name gets linked with anything you're writing, why, I'll kill you.' He was smiling broadly. 'That is, if they don't get to me first.'

'Thanks,' Lyubimov said. 'I'm off, through the door, not the window.'

Another great bellow of laughter accompanied his exit into the lane and the oppressive heat of the city, the laughter mixing strangely with the Beach Boys wailing about lost love.

It took him twenty minutes to find a public telephone prepared to accept his coins. Getting past the switchboard at Specials headquarters proved equally troublesome. When he reached Major Ponomarev he told him what he knew and where he had picked it up.

'A bit thin,' Ponomarev said ungraciously, 'but thanks anyway. Were you followed?'

'I don't think so.'

'Remind me to explain how to be *sure* you weren't followed.'

'I will.'

Major Ponomarev called his friend Alyosha at the CID and repeated what Lyubimov had told him.

'That will be the Armenian gang,' his friend said. 'They work that part of town. The barman of the Yerevan bar is a mate of the leader, known as Razmik, and makes the monthly payment to keep his nose clean with us. He complains to the local militia, drops them something from time to time, and is recorded as a victim and not a criminal. In fact, he provides cover for these people, and for all we know he shares in their loot.'

'This Razmik of yours – can you locate him?'

'We know where he lives, up in Tushino somewhere, but I won't risk my men's lives in a raid unless we have evidence which will make the charge stick when it gets to the procurator's office. And the evidence has to be made of diamonds to withstand what the procurator is likely to do to it.'

'What remains a mystery,' Ponomarev said, 'is why the protection racket hasn't been designated a serious crime and given to us.'

'You'd do no better. We aren't fools here.'

'So what are you saying, that this Razmik is untouchable?'

'You'd have to catch him with a smoking gun in his hand and a dozen dead citizens at his feet to make a case stick against him. And then the court might accept a plea of provocation.'

Ponomarev was silent for a moment, thinking. Then, 'Do you have any bright men to spare? And a car,' he added.

'I've got bright men all right, but no one to spare. I'm about 60 per cent below strength here. As to cars, I even have to use the Metro myself. We've only a dozen cars in the entire division and they're all over ten years old. But perhaps you were joking.'

'I wasn't. I'd like some surveillance done on this Razmik and his mob. I've a hunch we shall be seeing some action any time now.'

'Afraid you'll have to do it yourself.'

'My problem is cars too, and what happens when we do manage one? A Mercedes on their side, an ancient Zhiguli with clapped-out suspension on ours. We might as well stay at home with a good book.'

'My sentiments exactly.'

'I'll come back to you,' Ponomarev said. 'You've cheered me up no end.' And he rang off, sighing.

In the outer office he beckoned a sergeant from his desk. 'I want you to go down to what they laughingly call the transport department and capture me a car, preferably one that is still in running order and has a full tank.'

'Difficult,' the sergeant said.

'Correct. Nevertheless, you'll do it or you'll be in deep trouble, my friend. Then choose a couple of your best men, maybe Andreyev and Gromov. It's a surveillance, starting just as soon as you can get things together this evening.'

He told him what he needed to know about the Armenians and how to get the address from his friend in the CID. 'What I want,' he said, 'is to find out about a job they appear to be mounting, including the movements of one Grigoriev.'

He described what he knew of Grigoriev.

'Ideally, we'd like to detach Grigoriev from the mob, spend a happy hour questioning him here, and then ship him off to Yerevan where our colleagues also have a few questions to ask about a murder six years ago. See your men are armed and warn them the assignment is dangerous. They're not to get into an argument with a whole bunch of villains, understood?'

'Understood.'

'The car will be difficult,' the sergeant repeated. 'The motor pool's nothing but a puddle these days.'

'I don't want to know. If you have trouble, tell them downstairs I'll have them up on charges if they supply a wreck.'

He returned unhappily to his office, expecting very little from the exercise. 'We need a coup,' he muttered to himself. 'Not the one those jokers tried last week, but some kind of coup. I don't ask for much; a regular supply of decent sausage and transport for the militia. Then both Marina and I would be a bit more relaxed with each other.'

23

At precisely 6.50 that evening Raya and Slava Lyubimov met on the steps of the Bolshoi Theatre and together ran the gauntlet of the thirty or so ticket touts crowded shoulder to shoulder around the main doors.

'You see,' Lyubimov told her, 'that's how our brilliant command economy works. They keep the seat prices dirt cheap – ten roubles on average – because culture, as we know, is for the masses. Then, by fair and foul means dozens of touts manage to get hold of tickets every night, probably paying a premium but still getting them at give-away prices. Then they offer them at maybe a dozen times their official value or even more.'

'And people will pay that much?'

'Sure, if the official price is so stupidly low. Look, I buy, say, ten tickets at 15 roubles and offer them at $100 each, hard currency only.'

'You're joking.'

'Not at all. Americans will pay me that much. It's cheaper, I'm told, than the opera in New York. Anyway, say I only sell three, that's $300, which I'll convert back into roubles if I want to at the black rate, giving me at least 1,500 roubles. Net profit: 1,350 roubles, if I throw seven unsold tickets away, which I do if I'm a tout. Result: ordinary folk can't get seats, the black market gets rich, and you'll see when we get inside, there will be plenty of empty seats corresponding to all those torn tickets which will litter the road outside. Marxist economics!'

'Not quite. It's the economics of Utopia – of ideas about human nature which have been thought up in the study and not on the street. That, and what scarcity will do to make people just a bit worse.'

'There were little old ladies touting out there,' Lyubimov said.

'I saw them. We're all capable of it, I suppose.'

They found their seats and sat gazing into each other's eyes as they waited for the house lights to go down. And as the orchestra struck up the opening bars of Tchaikovsky's overture, Lyubimov took her hand into his and decided this was nothing short of bliss.

Just before 10 p.m. an unmarked Zhiguli with two plainclothes men parked across the way from an apartment block in Tushinskaya Street in the Tushino district in the northwest of the city. The driver killed the engine and they both lit up. The driver, Andreyev, pulled a bottle of mineral water from a plastic bag and offered it to his companion. They both drank.

'Can't we park somewhere a bit less visible?' his companion asked. 'Sitting here we've surveillance written all over us.'

'It's the only spot to see the entrance to the courtyard, isn't it?'

The other man nodded and said nothing. The evening air was stale, heavy with the city's pollution. The day's heat was unabated.

'To hell with these open-ended assignments,' Andreyev said. 'Who are we waiting for? We don't know. What do we do if this unknown individual comes out? We don't know that either. What if six of the bastards come out together? We beat it because we're out-armed and this car is due for the knacker's yard. Ponomarev is off his head.'

His companion sighed. Across the way residents emerged from the courtyard from time to time in ones and twos. The two militiamen had a rough description of the Armenians and had had confusing orders about what to do when they saw them.

'How the hell should I know what you should do?' the sergeant had asked, exasperated. 'Ask the major.'

But Major Ponomarev, equally upset by the heat and the department's pathetic transport resources, was scarcely more lucid.

'You can tell an Armenian criminal when you see one, can't you?' he'd snapped at Andreyev and Gromov, standing awkwardly before his desk. 'Well, then, use your heads and let's see a bit of initiative. I chose you two because you're less dim than some of your colleagues, so prove me right for a change.'

'What do we do, then, if we identify one of them?'

'If he makes off on foot, you mount a foot surveillance, don't you? If he gets in a car, you follow, hoping your jalopy doesn't fall apart on the way.'

'And if they come out in a bunch, like?'

'Be damn careful.'

It was no kind of reply and the two men had said nothing. The major was not his usual self.

At 10.42 a man who looked in the dim street lighting like a possible Armenian emerged from the courtyard, looked around, spotted the car across the way, crossed over and sauntered a short way down the street. Then he returned, eyed the car and its police number plate while trying to look as if he was just taking a breath of night air, and made his way back to the courtyard.

'We're rumbled,' Andreyev said. 'Shit!'

'Bound to happen, wasn't it?'

'So what do we do?'

'We stay here. We aren't breaking any laws.'

They took another drink and both got out of the car to stretch.

At 11.04 Gromov was out of the car, relieving himself against a wall, when the man appeared briefly at the entrance to the courtyard, looked across at them and disappeared again. When his companion was back in the car, Andreyev said, 'If they're planning a job tonight our being here won't put them off one bit. You'll see, they'll all troop out, bold as brass, and march off to wherever their cars are parked. Wouldn't be surprised if they wave to us.'

'Whoever rules the streets of Moscow these days, it isn't us,' Gromov said.

Across the city in a yard behind warehouses in the Nagatino district Gribenko and three others were climbing into the van. It was 12.10 as they set out, heading westwards for the Restoration Works some two miles away. The streets were deserted and the van was driven at speed along the Proletarskyi Prospect, turning right onto the Kashirskoye highway then onto secondary roads leading to the Restoration Works in its side street close to the Kaluzhskaya Metro.

'Where's Petya?' one of the men asked. 'Or is he keeping his nose clean tonight?'

'He'll meet us there,' Gribenko said.

'Isn't this a bit early to be doing a break-in?'

'It is.'

'So?'

'So it's what he decided and he must have his reasons.'

They relapsed into silence, tense, much like infantry before an action.

Gribenko stopped the van in the lane bordering the Restoration Works. As he switched off the headlights a figure came towards them out of the shadows.

'Petya?'

'It's me,' Baranov said. 'Keep your voice down. Are the boys with you?'

'Yes.'

Baranov climbed into the van, the men moving up to make room for him.

'Here's what we do. You'll see there are windows along this wall which can be reached with the ladder. I take it it's on the roof?'

'It is,' one of the men said.

'I want one of you to open up a window. There are no bars, so you can break a pane and deal with the closure by shoving a hand through. Then he's to climb in and I'll follow.' He designated the man closest to him.

'The rest of you stay out here to look after our rear. I'm not expecting trouble but if the militia stumble on us you're to remove the ladder and make some sort of disturbance and even get yourselves run in without letting on that your mates are inside. Is that clear?'

'It's clear,' Gribenko said. 'And what happens to you inside?'

'We'll find our own way out later. Remember, I know the layout of the place. However, I don't expect a scenario like that. Instead, we'll be inside maybe ten minutes or so – time for me to find the keys and get what I'm looking for – then we'll be out with the package. But we'll take the tools with us just in case the keys are missing.'

'I've got the tools here in a bag,' someone said.

'Sure this package of yours will go through the window?' Gribenko asked.

'Smart question,' Baranov said. 'Do you think I'd be so stupid as to set all this up without thinking of a thing like that?'

'And what about alarms, watchmen, stuff like that?'

'No alarms, and the watchman will be in his place, fast asleep, on the far side of the building. Any more questions?'

'What's the drop from the window inside?'

'About a metre. No problem.'

'Can we use our torches?'

'When I say so.'

There was a pause. The inside of the van was stifling, the air heavy with sweat and stale tobacco.

'Any more questions?'

There were none.

'Shine me a torch,' Baranov said. By the yellow finger of light he checked his watch. 'Twelve-thirty. Let's go.'

Silently they climbed out of the van and lowered the lightweight ladder from the roof rack. One of the men heaved his bag of tools onto his shoulder. Almost opposite the van Baranov selected a window and propped up the ladder beneath it.

'You all carrying your guns?' Baranov asked.

'We're all armed; automatics,' Gribenko assured him.

The man with the tools climbed to the top of the ladder. He had a hammer with a cloth wrapped round the head and was swinging it at the window. The crash of glass echoed down the narrow lane, soon followed by the squeal of rusted hinges as the window was forced open. The man on the ladder was young and agile. In a few moments he was through the window and standing on the floor of the workshop within. He was followed by Baranov. Gribenko returned to the van and installed himself in the driving seat. One of his companions stood at the foot of the ladder and the other walked the fifty yards to the corner of the lane, placing himself so that he could see cars approaching at the intersection.

It was 12.38 as he took up his position leaning against the red brick wall of the works and wishing he'd not left his fags in the van.

At ten minutes past midnight Andreyev at the wheel of the Zhiguli had dug a fist into his companion's arm, waking him from the sleep he'd fallen into a few minutes earlier.

'Here they are, the bastards. So what do we do?'

A group of men had emerged from the courtyard, striding purposefully left to turn the corner of the building. There were five of them, and as they strode past the car one of them did what Gromov had predicted: he made a mock bow, followed by a jaunty wave of the hand. It was the man who had twice been out to check on them.

Andreyev offered a short prayer as he turned the ignition key. The car spluttered into sluggish life. Someone had remembered to check the battery after all. As the troop of men disappeared round the corner, Andreyev eased the car forward until its bonnet protruded into the intersecting street. He saw the men enter a drive-in beneath an archway.

'They'll have their cars in there,' Gromov said. 'So do we block them?'

'Is that what you call being careful? Didn't the major say be careful if they're in a gang? And if that isn't a gang, complete with bulging hip pockets and no doubt with Kalashes in the boot of the car, then I've never seen an Armenian gangster.'

'So?'

'So my idea of how to avoid a shoot-out in which we'd be massacred in, say, fifteen seconds, is *not* to block their exit.'

'But still – '

'There's no but still, my friend. I remind you: forty-six militiamen have been killed in Moscow so far this year. Do you want to volunteer as number forty-seven or shall I?'

The other nodded and said nothing. Andreyev was carefully heading the car round the corner in the direction of the spot where the men had disappeared. He was within a few yards when he caught the sound of a car engine and almost at once a large Mercedes, followed by another, shot across their path, turned right and was out of sight in a few moments, heading south.

'And that,' he said, 'is bloody well that, and we can go home to bed.'

They set off in the direction of the Petrovka, swapping ideas on how best to present the night's events. Meanwhile, the two Mercedes containing Grigoriev, Razmik and his men were driving fast towards the Restoration Works some six miles to the southwest. Seated in the rear of the second car, Grigoriev nursed a Soviet-made Walther pistol on his lap, working the safety catch and weighing the weapon carefully in his hand. Razmik sat next to him.

'What are the automatics?' Grigoriev asked.

'We've got Czech Skorpions. Very light, retractable wire butt for stashing away, and accurate enough for our purposes. The boys are comfortable with them.'

'In my day it was Kalashes.'

'Too many breakdowns,' Razmik said. 'Lousy workmanship. These Czech jobs are beautifully made.'

'I repeat what I said back in the apartment,' Grigoriev said. 'I want a totally disciplined operation. With luck we'll be there before Baranov. In which case we lift out the icon and beat it. But if they've been fools enough to risk an early raid themselves and we run into them, we do whatever has to be done, and that includes force.'

'Right,' Razmik said. He was tired of being ordered about.

'I don't mind who gets hurt on the other side,' Grigoriev said.

'Including Baranov?'

'Yes.'

Razmik paused before asking, 'Do you want someone to look after him?'

'It would not displease me in the slightest but I'd prefer to take him alive and deal with him later.'

'Right.'

'And there's another thing you'd all better pay attention to. Our object tonight is not to have a party but to lay our hands on an icon – a piece of wood a metre or so in length and covered in paint. Only the paint makes it worth its weight in gold, right? Now, maybe when we get there someone will be carrying this bit of wood, and just maybe you'll have to shoot them. But if one of you lets fly at the icon, I will personally blow his brains out afterwards. Is that clear?'

There was silence and a couple of the men nodded.

'You will keep your eyes skinned, right, and you will not spray bullets all over the district. Discipline,' Grigoriev said, 'there will be discipline.'

The cars were approaching the Selepichinskyi Bridge over

the Moskva, still heading south. The river gleamed dully in the reflected light from the street lamps. There was no traffic. They sat in silence.

As they reached the bridge taking them over the main railway line to Minsk the driver said, 'We're cutting through the back doubles here, otherwise we'd be passing the militia barracks on the Minsk road. They've been known to put up road blocks there.'

The two cars regained the main road just short of the intersection with Lenin Prospect, stretching dead straight, endlessly, down southwestwards towards Kiev and Budapest. There was no traffic at all on the highway and they crossed at speed. Then they were back on side roads, passing a small park with its ornamental lake, apartment blocks to their left. The lead car had dropped its speed and soon ahead of them their headlights picked out the dirty red brick wall of the Restoration Works.

'The windows Baranov told us about are on the far side,' Razmik told Grigoriev. The cars were approaching the intersection where Gribenko's man was standing, bored and relaxed, not believing for one moment that the militia might stumble on them in the dark. Since when did the Moscow militia mount night patrols in godforsaken corners like this? But now he picked out the headlights of a car – no, two cars – approaching from his right: the first sign of life since taking up his position against the wall. He stiffened, dropped his right hand to the revolver in his hip pocket and realised his heart-beat had accelerated. Judging by the pattern of the headlights these were not militia cars at all. No doubt they'd drive past.

But the two cars, now nose to tail, were slowing down to a crawl, and one after the other the headlights were dimmed. The man against the wall felt something like fear take a grip on him as he pulled his gun out and eased the safety catch off with his thumb. He started walking slowly towards the corner sideways like a crab, so as to keep the cars in sight. He had formed a plan in his mind. Clearly the cars were interested in the works. Maybe they'd turn left into the lane, maybe not. But either way, Gribenko and the others must be signalled. After all, it was what he'd been posted as lookout to do. When he reached the corner, a few feet away, he'd turn and run for the van – a matter of half a minute or less.

Now he could tell from the edge of the pavement before him that he'd come to the end of the wall. He turned quickly on his heel, and as he did so a thin beam of light from the leading car swept quickly across the wall, alighted on his back and stayed there. He was already running when the first bullet hit him in the lower spine, flinging him to the ground as two more shots were fired, one of them reaching him below the ribcage. The phut from the silenced gun did not reach Gribenko and his companion at the van. Nor did they see the dimmed headlights.

A man leapt from the leading car and ran to the figure on the ground. The wounded man was moaning softly. The second bullet had smashed through an artery and blood was already pumping out into a dark pool on the pavement. The man from the car bent over as if to help him in some way, pressed his silenced pistol to the nape of the neck and pulled the trigger. The head was jolted violently forward against the ground by the force of the bullet.

The man returned to the car, poked his head in and said, 'OK, what next?'

At the moment when Gribenko's man was being shot to death, Baranov was unlocking the door to the first floor storeroom where he had placed the icon. His story to Grigoriev that Trofimich took the keys home with him was untrue: the keys were kept in Trofimich's office desk in a drawer which was locked but had yielded in five seconds to a chisel and mallet.

The man with Baranov held a torch, beam shining down to the floor, while the icon in its blanket was picked up. Then they left the storeroom. Baranov locked it behind him and they made for the broken window. In a senseless fit of bravado which he recognised as untypical of him, Baranov tossed the keys into a toilet bowl as he passed. At the window they called softly to the man at the foot of the ladder. The icon was handed down and they prepared to follow.

Baranov's companion had reached the ground and was turning towards the van when the hoarse rattle of the Czech Skorpions tore the night apart. One of the Mercedes, lights extinguished, had covered the short distance to the van in seconds and stopped within a few feet of its tail. Gribenko was still at the wheel of the van and his companion was carrying the icon towards the van's front door. The hail of bullets, carefully aimed, tore into him and he was sent crashing onto the pavement, the icon in its blanket falling from his grasp. The man who had come down the ladder had time to draw his revolver, but he was caught in the same hail of bullets, fired at chest height, and died a moment after hitting the ground, his heart drilled by a round from the Skorpion. One of Razmik's men had raced round to the front of the van, spraying bullets into the driving cabin. Two shots lodged in Gribenko's head, another in his neck, and he slumped forward over the steering column and did not move.

The level of fire had been too low to reach Baranov, still midway down the ladder. He turned and clambered back through the window. Grigoriev had come up from the second Mercedes.

'Two of you come with me. I'm going in after him. I think I'd like to take him alive. Is that understood?'

Razmik nodded and all three went up the ladder and climbed through the window.

'We've very little time,' Grigoriev said. 'Someone must have heard that racket and might even have called the militia. We'll never be able to see this bastard in here so we'll have to hear him.'

Inside the workshop they stood motionless. After a few seconds a faint metallic sound reached them from their left.

'We move fast,' Razmik said. 'Use your torches. If you can't take him alive, you take him dead.'

Panic had seized Baranov as he leapt back inside and hesitated for a second before making a fatal decision. The stairs down to the yard lay to his right. He would have had no difficulty in finding his way out to hide there among the masses of junk. But already he was having trouble controlling his bowels and he found his legs had weakened beneath him so that he could scarcely make them obey him. His mind refused to work rationally. He realised that he was soiling himself and he found he was unable to detach his thoughts from the shameful fact. As he heard footsteps on the ladder beyond the window some strength returned at last to his legs and he darted forward – to his left and away from the stairs to the yard. His route took him across the long workshop and into a corridor with a number of smaller rooms leading off it. As he felt his way along a wall he grasped at last that there was no way out. Already he could hear the sound of his pursuers climbing in through the window. He stopped, feeling disgust at the stench rising from him, a wave of misery engulfing him. Then he advanced on the balls of his feet into a small storeroom which he knew contained carboys of acid and drums of paint and thinners. It was as he reached the door that his foot sent a loose bolt sliding across the floor to come to rest against the metal door of the storeroom. It was the sound that Grigoriev and the others had heard.

Baranov pulled the heavy metal door closed behind him, thanking fate that its hinges had been oiled. Then he climbed behind a pile of drums and sank to the ground. His revolver was in his hand. The sound of his heartbeats seemed to him to echo across the room. He found that he was weeping with frustration. A great wave of misery gripped him as he realised it could only be a matter of minutes before they found him. He had no doubt that they would shoot him there on the ground in his filth, but, dear God, let it be quick – in the head. The tears poured down his cheeks and he found he was unable to hold his gun steady.

He could hear them tramping along the short corridor, throwing open the doors of the storerooms. His door was flung open and a beam of light from a torch fingered its way rapidly across the drums and carboys of acid, missing him. Then the searcher moved on.

'Baranov! Come out with your hands up and you won't be harmed.'

He recognised Razmik's voice from somewhere in the corridor. 'We give you ten seconds. Then we shoot.'

They did not know yet where he was. But it could only be a matter of time. Should he risk coming out? If Grigoriev had decided to kill him they'd shoot him as he emerged from the room. But if he stayed here, hoping to shoot first if one of them searched the room, he had no chance of living beyond his first shot.

Delay? If he could delay matters, surely someone would arrive outside, attracted by the shoot-out down in the lane? His mind was beginning to function again. Yet he felt his whole being was disintegrating – as if what had happened to his bowels was a symptom of a total collapse of intellect and personality. He found he was unable to move, and when he tried to cry out no sound would come from his parched throat. He felt a wave of nausea assailing him. This was terror – engulfing and destroying him.

'Time is up.' It was Razmik again. 'We're coming to get you.'

The sound reached him of doors kicked open, objects thrown about in the next storeroom. A couple of shots echoed through the empty workshop. Someone had fired at a shadow. Then a figure appeared inside his room. A torch was shone and this time it revealed the toe of his shoe, protruding from behind the drums of paint.

'Don't shoot, I'm coming out.'

Baranov managed to get the words out, scarcely above a whisper. But the man, startled by the croaking voice, fired a fusillade at random towards the spot where Baranov was hidden. Bullets pierced the drums and a round smashed into a carboy of hydrochloric acid. The acid flooded out across the floor, and as the firing stopped it was followed by an agonised scream from Peter Baranov as acid splashed his hand and soaked his jeans, burning at once into the flesh of his leg.

'Stop shooting.' It was Grigoriev's voice. 'If you're still alive, come out. We don't want to harm you.'

Baranov's screams were echoing through the place. He had struggled to his feet, caught in the light from the torch as Grigoriev appeared at the door.

'Acid! I'm burned by the acid!' Baranov was shrieking. 'For pity's sake, get some water. For pity's sake!'

'We have no water, Petya,' Grigoriev said quietly. 'You will have to come with us just as you are.' His voice was calm, even caring. Then he added, scarcely raising his voice, 'Shut up, you snivelling little Russian swine!' He turned to the others. 'Get him out of here.' Then he turned and walked away.

Baranov was dragged from the room, out to the window and the ladder. He was sobbing, begging them for water to wash the acid away. On the ladder he stumbled and one of the men drove a fist into his back. He lost his footing and plunged six feet to the pavement. He lay moaning as others dragged him to his feet and hustled him into the back of the leading car.

He heard Grigoriev's voice. 'Now, out of here, fast. You know where to go. And be careful with that package.'

The cars were reversed in the narrow lane and driven back to the intersection, leaving mayhem behind them.

24

By inconvenient chance it was the day after the shoot-out at the Restoration Works that Major Ponomarev was summoned into the presence of one of the deputy ministers for foreign affairs. He had been on the point of setting out to meet his friend from the CID at the works when the call had come through: the deputy minister required a personal account of the progress of the search for the missing American, Victor Gordon. Would the officer in charge of the case present himself at 10 a.m.?

At ten, therefore, Ponomarev found himself standing before the deputy minister, who sat at a desk piled with papers and telephones of various colours. The man looked harassed and as untidy as his desk. He did not invite Ponomarev to sit.

'This enquiry, Major, where are you?'

'Not very far.' Ponomarev was not in communicative mood. He felt he should be treated to the courtesy of a chair.

'How far?'

'We are in touch with Interpol, who tell us the American was of dubious reputation. We are making the usual enquiries here in Moscow, so far without success. We have some leads which are not specially promising. And that is about all at present.'

'The Americans are pressing us,' the deputy minister said. 'It seems this American has leverage at the Embassy. I need results, Major.'

'I understand that, Minister. We do our best and could no doubt do better if we had the necessary resources.'

The deputy minister veered away from the question of resources. 'What can I tell the Embassy then?'

'I suggest you say something to the effect that no effort is being spared.' Ponomarev saw no reason to give this man the form of words he should be devising for himself.

The deputy minister scratched his head. Then he shook it. 'You are not helpful, Major.'

'I do my best. When I have an outcome I will see that you are the first to hear of it.'

'Do you think this American is alive?'

'Either he disappeared on purpose or he was coerced,' Ponomarev said. 'On purpose seems to me unlikely. Coercion? That would mean one of two things: murder or kidnapping, presumably for a ransom. If the former, there's no body so far. If the latter, we would surely have had a ransom demand by now. So that unless we are dealing with a highly eccentric situation, murder seems to me the likeliest answer. The man was probably here to buy icons or some similar art works illicitly. He has, as I say, a bad reputation back in America, so that his contacts here are likely to have been dubious, even dangerous. We are pursuing that line of enquiry.'

The deputy minister looked unhappy. 'And that is the most cheerful thing you can tell me?'

'Yes.'

'Very well. Please keep me informed.'

And Ponomarev made his escape, wondering how long this man would hang on to his telephones and untidy office in the present uncertain state of the Soviet administration.

It was close to midday before he was able to join his colleague from the CID at the Restoration Works. The forensic people were still busy inside the building and in the lane where the massacre had taken place. The bodies had gone to the morgue. Police photographers were at work and Trofimich was being interviewed for the third time.

'A gangland killing,' the man from the CID told

Ponomarev. 'We know this bunch: art thieves on a fairly small scale.'

'And I have a pretty good idea who did it,' Ponomarev said. He recounted what Andreyev and Gromov had described of their vigil in Tushinskaya Street the night before. 'The Armenians,' he said. 'You might care to send a squad to pick them up.'

'We have good tyre marks and plenty of bullets and cartridge cases. If we can get at their car and maybe pick up some of their weapons, who knows – we might even mount a useful case against them.'

'Don't forget my interest in the man Grigoriev,' Ponomarev reminded him.

Trofimich had been making a major fuss about the Roublev icon.

'Priceless!' he kept telling the militia. 'Absolutely priceless! We identified it as a lost Andrei Roublev and Professor Abramov confirmed it here only yesterday.'

'Which of your staff knew about it?'

'Only my senior restorer, Peter Alexandrovitch Baranov. No one else.'

'And where is this Baranov now?'

'I've no idea. I called his place out at Zaveti Ilyicha twice this morning. There was no reply.'

'Would you suspect him of stealing this icon?'

Trofimich shrugged. 'That, or he told a friend who then stole it. No one else knew about it save the people from the University.'

'And who did *you* tell?'

'No one – I told absolutely no one.' Trofimich saw endless trouble ahead – more questioning, enquiries of one sort and another, trouble with Krasnodar and no doubt with the Ministry. 'Terrible!' he kept saying. 'A terrible thing! Priceless!' The militia officer moved on to talk to the rest of the staff.

To reach the Metro from his apartment block, Slava Lyubimov had to cover a distance of two hundred metres along a narrow street bordered on either side by old houses standing behind narrow front gardens and separated from the pavement by low walls. At eight in the morning, when he set out, this street was deserted save for a small child walking a dog on the far pavement. Remembering the advice he had been getting about taking care, he had looked both ways as he emerged from the apartment building and had glanced behind him as he turned into the quiet street. The main road was busy with the morning rush-hour traffic, but the street led nowhere of value to those going to work and the traffic passed it by. As he turned into it, Lyubimov noticed a large foreign car parked a few yards from the corner. The driver and his companion were staring ahead, immobile, as if waiting for someone. Lyubimov had the uncomfortable feeling that the men and their car did not belong there.

'Paranoia,' he told himself as he turned the corner. Even so, an instinct made him cross the road so that any traffic coming from behind him would be on the far side of the road. He told himself he must remember to get the major to explain how to be sure one was not being followed.

He set off down the narrow street, walking faster than usual, as if there were good reason to get to the far end as soon as possible. He heard the sound of a car approaching from behind and turned for a moment. It was the foreign car, driving fast towards him. There was nothing in the situation to warn him of danger, yet he knew instinctively that the danger was there. The car was gathering speed as it came, still on the far side of the road. When it was still fifty metres from him, Lyubimov glanced to his left, saw that he was alongside a low wall. Now the car was travelling at speed and had moved over to the wrong side of the road, the side on which he was walking. And suddenly he realised that it was coming at him, would mount the pavement and attempt to run him down. As it came abreast and mounted the low kerb with a screech of tyres, he leapt for the wall. He caught a glimpse of the driver's face, expressionless, the eyes concentrated on him. There was the sound of metal against brickwork as the car's front wing scraped the wall, barely missing his legs. Then the car veered back onto the roadway and was driven fast down the rest of the street and out into the main thoroughfare beyond.

Lyubimov found his heart beating furiously as he climbed down onto the pavement and realised his legs were unsteady as he continued walking.

'I saw that,' the child with the dog said as Lyubimov came level with him. 'Why did that car go up on the pavement like that?'

'Bad driving,' Lyubimov said.

'It nearly hit you.'

'That's right.'

'Were you frightened?'

'I was terrified.' And he hurried on towards the Metro, where he took a train for the Kaluzhskaya station.

The gate of the Restoration Works was open and he walked in unchallenged. At the far side of the yard he saw Ponomarev with other militia officers and he made towards them.

'You have a nose for the trouble spots, eh?' Ponomarev called out to him.

'What trouble, Major?'

Ponomarev turned to his friend from the CID. 'This young man is what they call an investigative journalist, which is another way of saying he keeps poking his nose into police matters. On the other hand, I have to admit he has his uses.'

'Thanks, Major,' Lyubimov said. 'What's going on here?'

'Not much: your friend Baranov has disappeared, there were the four corpses of his friends outside in the road until we took them away, and I understand a valuable icon has been stolen.'

'What can you tell me about the icon, Major?'

'It's said to be a genuine Andrei Roublev.'

'Who says so?'

'A Professor Abramov from the Fine Arts Department of the University. I'll be talking to him later.'

'And the dead men?'

'The man Baranov's gang. It looks as if they were breaking in to steal this icon when they were overtaken by some rivals. There was a little difference of opinion and shots were fired in anger, it seems. That's all I know at present.'

'Do you have an idea of who might have done the shooting?'

'Some idea, yes, but I don't discuss ideas with the press.'

'Thanks,' Lyubimov said, and made for Trofimich's office. He spent ten minutes there, shooting questions at a dazed Trofimich who kept repeating, 'Priceless'. Then he took a look at the bloodstained pavement outside and the bullet-riddled van, asked a morose militiaman standing guard what he knew and found he knew nothing, and finally made up his mind where to go next. He regained the Metro and took a train running north into town, changed twice and alighted eventually at the University station. Then he walked the short distance to the vast University complex.

Encouraged by the excitable Dr Zimin, Professor Abramov had persuaded himself that the icon was indeed a newly-discovered version of Andrei Roublev's great masterpiece, the Old Testament Trinity. During a restless night in which intense professional excitement had kept him awake he had come to believe that the scientific tests which caution dictated were little more than a formality. His eyes had told him this was a Roublev. His eye for this sort of thing was famous and had never let him down. And the faithful Zimin had insisted on it. The Professor congratulated himself on his wisdom in casting doubt aside on the previous day and travelling out to see the icon.

And so what next? He would contain his excitement as best he could until that crippled fool at the works had got hold of his bits of paper. Then he would bring the icon to his lab, do the tests, see the minister and make recommendations for its future care and housing. Clearly, the thing was far too important to be sent back to some ill-kept, unsupervised museum in Krasnodar. This was an artefact of the highest museum quality, fit only for a major Moscow institution. He would put that to the minister, with whom he was on terms, and after careful restoration the wonderful object would be found an appropriate home. All this had been buzzing through the professor's head since the previous day and his excitement was still preventing him from turning to other matters when he was informed that a journalist from *Vperiod* was asking to see him about an icon.

The professor's first instinct was to send the journalist packing. How had the story reached the press so fast? And what would be the consequences of having it in the public prints before everything had been done tidily and in due form – an official, scientifically backed authentication, and a decision as to the icon's future home?

On the other hand, if he refused to see him, the man would no doubt go over to the Restoration Works and pick up a garbled version of the facts. He decided an interview would be less troublesome than no interview, and so Lyubimov found himself facing the forbidding Marxist beard in the professor's room some minutes later. The professor had called in Dr Zimin, who took up a position behind the professorial chair like an academic version of a security man, alert for any type of terror attack.

'I wondered,' Slava Lyubimov said by way of opening, 'whether you had yet heard of last night's events at the Restoration Works?'

'What events? We've heard of no events.'

Dr Zimin was shaking his head in silent agreement.

'I believe there was an icon there which you had identified as an Andrei Roublev.'

'I cannot comment on that. More tests are needed.'

'I'm afraid that will be difficult,' Lyubimov said.

'Why difficult?'

'The icon has disappeared. It was stolen last night.'

The sudden silence in the room was finally ended by something resembling a screech from Dr Zimin. Professor Abramov's beard appeared to bristle in disbelief.

At last an anguished, 'What!' emerged from within the beard.

'I'm afraid it's true. A gang broke in and took it, some time during the night. Then it looks as if they were overtaken by a rival mob and four were shot. The police are there now.'

'But the icon – priceless, a historic find – what of the icon?'

Lyubimov shrugged. 'Gone! That's all I know.' He felt genuinely sorry for these two enthusiasts, denied the artistic find of their lives. 'Were you both certain it was a Roublev?'

'I stake my reputation on it,' Dr Zimin cried, before the professor could get a word past his beard. 'A wonderful example of the master's finest period, and in very acceptable condition. A miracle that it survived unharmed.'

The professor was nodding.

'Does the ministry know about this find?'

'Not yet.'

'Will you be reporting it?'

'Of course. I shall see the minister as soon as he can receive me.'

'Do you share your colleague's enthusiasm for the icon?' Lyubimov asked.

'I do.'

'Thank you, gentlemen,' Lyubimov said as he made his way out. The story was coming together nicely. It was time to get back to the office to get something down onto paper.

On the way back in the Metro he toyed pleasurably with the problem of the lead to his story. Perhaps the apocalyptic mode would suit?

The greatest artistic find – and the greatest artistic disaster – in 500 years of our country's history, typical of the turbulent times we are living through . . .

Or would the sardonic catch the reader's attention? *Your correspondent saw Professor Abramov's beard shake with horror when he told him that . . .*

Or should he tell the story in the historic/consecutive mode, starting where the events had started, in Taman, and moving up with the icon to Moscow? *Down on the Black Sea a poor priest and his dog savagely murdered, while in Moscow a taxi driver is found dead in his bath, an American art dealer vanishes, and four members of a gang of art thieves are shot to death in a street massacre – all this because a priceless icon has been found and then stolen . . .*

It made, he reflected, good copy. Editor Chelidze would have hated it.

25

The high politics of the previous week had left the administration of what was rapidly ceasing to be the Soviet Union in increasing disarray. Whole ministries were disintegrating as new organisms of the Russian Federation struggled to be born. Boris Yeltsin, making policy on the hoof, had cut a swathe through the Soviet establishment and no one knew who had responsibility for what and how long they might hang onto it. It was less a question of the ship of state having no rudder than that there was a fist-fight proceeding on the bridge and confusion in the engine room. So Professor Abramov found himself in some difficulty. Should he go to his friend the Minister of Culture of the USSR? Or had power already slipped from that individual's hands? If so, to whom, for God's sake?

Abramov decided to try the minister, called him, and between old friends was accorded an immediate interview. In the minister's office the story of the Roublev icon had poured out of the distraught professor, who could barely maintain coherence, and had difficulty in not bursting into tears.

'A disaster, Sergei Petrovitch,' he kept repeating. 'What is happening to our society? The gangs rule the streets. A disaster!'

The minister, who had been a Gorbachev man against his better judgement and was trying hard to become a Yeltsin man despite his distaste for that ambitious politician and everything he seemed to stand for, had other and more pressing matters on his mind. Among them, uncertainty as to the continued existence of his ministry. He did not need the hysterics of professors of fine art. Even less did he need a scandal in which the intelligentsia, united behind a new and troublesome cause, would screech in the public prints that the state did not know how to look after its priceless treasures and why wasn't the minister called to account?

He tried to calm his friend down. 'Unfortunate,' he said. 'But no doubt the militia will see to it.'

'We must make a public statement,' Abramov cried. 'It might flush these people out.'

'Up to the militia,' the minister countered.

'But they'll want to keep the thing quiet. If they announce it and then fail to recover the icon they'll be in deep trouble.'

'Very true.'

'So we must go public ourselves.'

The minister was thinking fast. It was a talent for extreme caution which had carried him into government and kept him precariously there through the turbulence of recent times. Caution and an impressive immobility were perhaps the only attributes he fully understood. And caution, in the instance, imposed silence. He would go further: it imposed vigorous suppression. He explained his thesis to the unfortunate Abramov.

'Look at it this way. A fine icon has been discovered. But it has also disappeared. What will be said if we reveal that fact? That we do not know how to look after our art treasures. That we should even have uncovered it ourselves years ago. That the art authorities are incompetent, the militia is incompetent, that even you, my dear Abramov, should never have left it in the hands of these fools at the Restoration Works once you realised what it was. In short, that you too, and by extension your entire faculty, were incompetent. And who benefits from all that? Only those who seek to destabilise us. The enemies of our society.' He lowered his voice, following the instinct of a lifetime. 'These new political forces – I do not need to name them – always looking for sticks to beat us with.' He shook his head solemnly. 'This matter must remain strictly secret. I will see that the militia are told as much.'

Behind his beard, Abramov's face was a picture of misery. 'But I have to tell you, Sergei Petrovitch, that that is already impossible. A journalist from *Vperiod* is about to publish the whole thing.'

'No problem,' the minister said soothingly. 'I will call them myself and tell them not to.'

They shook hands and Professor Abramov made his way out to the street and back to his office, reflecting that his friend's confidence in his ability to muzzle the press was perhaps, in these new and troublesome times, somewhat misplaced.

The minister had checked with his secretariat on the name and political reliability of the editor of *Vperiod*, and was surprised to find on getting his call that Georgi Galaktionovitch Chelidze had been replaced by one Gennadi Ivanov. He made a mental note to bawl the secretariat out later. Put through to Ivanov, he decided to approach the matter jovially.

'This business of an alleged Roublev icon,' he said. 'I am informed that it has disappeared.'

'So I understand,' Ivanov said.

'Of course,' the minister went on, 'it may not be a Roublev at all. I have seen Professor Abramov, who is certainly not prepared to swear to it being anything of the kind, since no scientific tests had been carried out. You realise that?'

'Yes, Minister. But the professor has already told our reporter that he's convinced it is a genuine Roublev.'

'Your reporter has clearly misunderstood him, my friend.'

'He is a very reliable man.'

'Anyway, I am calling to warn you not to publish this nonsense. No doubt some icon or other has disappeared, but it would not serve the public interest for you to claim it is an important part of our national heritage. Such irresponsibility,' the minister said pompously, 'can only be counter-productive. I repeat: you will not publish the story.'

'I am sorry, Minister,' Ivanov said, 'but we have decided to run it in our next issue as a matter of wide public interest.'

The minister's experience of the press had never extended to any kind of refusal to do anything. For a moment he did not know what to say or in what tone to say it. Then he decided that he had been reasonable for long enough.

'You will damn well do as I tell you,' he shouted down the wire. 'I am the minister and I order you not to publish this dubious and damaging story. Is that understood?'

'I understand it very well,' Ivanov said quietly. 'Nevertheless, in the new situation in our country I'm afraid we at *Vperiod* do not feel obliged to be the poodles of the government. Those days are over.'

'I will have measures taken against your paper,' the minister shouted.

'I think it is only fair to tell you, Minister, that your demand for suppression and your threat against the paper will naturally be incorporated in the story, since we recognise your right to have your view expressed alongside ours. I shall put the whole thing to our editorial board, and if they agree with me that is what will be done.'

The click told him that the Minister of Culture had slammed down the receiver.

'New times,' Ivanov exclaimed, telling the editorial board later. 'I find it hard to get used to it myself. I think the minister finds it impossible. And he's by no means the worst of them.'

'If anyone's looking for a headline,' Lyubimov said, 'I offer EIGHT DEATHS FOR AN ICON. That includes the vanishing American, and I could make it a total of nine since I've a hunch the restorer, one Peter Alexandrovitch Baranov, is unlikely to reappear.'

Someone said, 'I make it seven without your Baranov.'
'The dog,' Lyubimov replied. 'You've forgotten the dog.'

26

After the shoot-out the two Mercs had rapidly gained the Garden Ring road, travelling anti-clockwise round the Moscow suburbs and turning northwards onto Mira Prospect. Soon they passed the dim outline of the cosmonaut monument on their left, soaring bravely into the night sky as if the rocket at its tip were able to take off into space. The giant worker and his girlfriend from the collective farm atop their plinth at the entrance to the Exhibition of Economic Achievements was the last statement of Soviet optimism offered by the capital as the cars headed out towards the open country. Soon they had crossed the motorway ringing the city and buildings gave way to forest. The cars' beams were reflected off the silver trunks of the birches, ghostly in the pitch black of the night. They were on the Yaroslavl Highway, running due north for 1,500 miles to Archangel and the sea.

In the second car Baranov sat slumped between two of the Armenians. From time to time he mopped with a handkerchief at a gash in his scalp which oozed damply. The smell of his blood renewed the nausea which had attacked him in waves. The two men were silent.

Half way to Pushkino and some ten miles out from the city limits the leading car slowed and signalled a right turn. The second car slowed in response. Both drove onto a track which carved a way through the trees.

In the first car Grigoriev said to Razmik, 'How far?'

'Maybe a kilometre, not more.'

'Isolated?'

'Completely. It's an abandoned woodman's cottage.

There's a few of them dotted about but nothing nearby. We've had it for a couple of years – never been disturbed.'

'Do people live out here?'

'There's gypsies here and there, minding their own business, and a few illegals from the south with no papers. No one with any interest in causing trouble.'

The car had slowed to a halt. Ahead the track petered out. They could make out the dim outline of a single-storey dwelling huddled among the trees to their left.

'That's it,' Razmik said. 'The safe house.'

The men alighted with a couple of storm lamps which threw a yellow glare forward towards the house. Someone unlocked a heavy padlock securing a bar across the door and all trooped inside. Baranov was hustled forward.

'There's a room at the back where he can go,' Razmik said.

'Take him in there and one of you stay with him,' Grigoriev said.

He and the others entered the main room and one of the lamps was placed on a wooden table. There was no other furniture in the room, but against a wall a pile of dirty mattresses and blankets emitted a stench of human sweat to mingle with the other odours which pervaded the house – dominant among them a smell of rotting flesh.

'Field animals get in and can't get out again,' Razmik explained. 'They starve to death and stink the place out, but it doesn't pretend to be a palace anyway.'

The men had crowded into the room and someone was loosening the bars on a boarded-up window.

'Stop that,' Grigoriev said. 'We don't want lights showing outside.'

'It's quite safe out here,' someone replied.

'I said stop it.'

The men stopped and crowded round Grigoriev and Razmik.

'What do we do with him?' Razmik gestured with his head towards the back room.

'I will deal with him,' Grigoriev said. 'The rest of you wait here. And you will not open those shutters.'

In the back room Baranov was lying on a rusted iron bedstead which had neither mattress nor bedclothes. Blisters were forming on his thighs and hands where the acid had burned him and there was no relief from the pain. One of the Armenians had placed the storm lamp on the floor and was standing over it, his shadow thrown, grotesquely magnified, onto a wall.

'Get out,' Grigoriev told him.

The man left as Grigoriev turned to Baranov, who sat up on the bed's iron frame and started dabbing again at the wound on his head. For a moment neither of them spoke. Then Grigoriev said in his quiet, almost inaudible voice, 'This, Peter Alexandrovitch, is the moment of truth for you.'

Baranov stared up at Grigoriev, said nothing. His lip was trembling and he felt he would burst into tears if he risked any kind of answer.

'It is very simple,' Grigoriev was saying. 'You will tell me exactly how you planned to get the icon out of the country, and you will tell it truthfully. If you refuse, we will make you talk, and if I come to the conclusion you are lying we will make you suffer in the most expert ways. Is that clear?'

With a supreme effort, Baranov steadied his voice. 'I truly have nothing to tell you. I had no plan beyond getting it out as part of the exhibition. When that didn't work, I simply reckoned I'd get it to the frontier and buy my way over. Marchenko says the Polish frontier's best, and that's all I know.'

'You are lying.' It was a mere whisper.

'I swear on my mother's head it's the truth. What good would it do me to lie to you now?'

'I don't know – maybe you're fool enough to think you can still get something out of lying to me. At all events, you're expendable, and so we will test whether you are lying or not.'

'What do you mean?' The tears were welling up and the waves of nausea had seized him again.

'My friends out there have a man who enjoys sorting out the truth from the lies. I am told he is truly terrible when he gets going. He'll come in shortly and later you can tell me what you think of his methods – if you can still speak, that is.'

'No, no, I beg you. I'll do anything. I can't stand pain. You can have whatever you want. Why should I lie to you when I'm at your mercy? It doesn't make any sense – no sense at all.' The words came tumbling out, scarcely coherent, mingled with sobs.

Grigoriev looked down at Baranov. 'I think,' he said, 'you should still be tested since I am not impressed by your devotion to your mother. A good beating would be a more reliable way of arriving at the truth. That has been my experience.'

'This violence against me – it makes no sense. I've never harmed you. It's only a business dispute. So take the damned icon and leave me alone.'

'You are offering me something you do not possess,' Grigoriev said. 'It doesn't impress me. As to violence, I use force when I am crossed and you have crossed me and my associates. I do not tolerate it.'

He paused and it seemed to Baranov that an idea had come to him. Then he said, 'I will make a deal with you, and if you do what I say I may make things easier for you.'

'What deal?'

'You will tell my associates that the icon is a nineteenth-century copy of a Roublev, worth about $10,000 in the West, where they know nothing, but only a couple of thousand roubles here. And you will persuade them that you are telling the truth. Do you understand that?'

'Yes.'

'Of course, as soon as I leave this room you will hit on a plan to double-cross me by throwing yourself on the mercy of these people, telling them it's a genuine Roublev and all they have to do is kill me and you'll lead them to great riches, right?'

'No, no, I swear . . .'

'If you do that they'll shoot me, all right, but then they'll shoot you, my friend, and try to sell the icon to the Berlin Jews. You see, they are fools who have never heard of Roublev and only think in small sums – what the Americans call quick bucks. And when someone presents them with a problem their solution is to destroy that person as a way of clearing their minds. So that I think you will not be so unwise as to double-cross me. Like that you have at least a small chance of survival, right?'

'I swear I won't double-cross you.'

Grigoriev contemplated him for a moment, then he seized the lamp from the floor and opened the door. Baranov caught the sound of voices from the front room. 'If you do it right,' Grigoriev said, 'you might even survive to steal some more icons.' Then he walked out of the room, slamming the door behind him.

Back with the others, Grigoriev announced his plans. 'We will take the better of the two cars and travel north to Archangel to your brother.' He nodded in the direction of the man Zaven whose brother was a seaman. 'At Zagorsk you will call him to check that he can take the package. I shall want you and a driver to come with me in the car. The others can return to Moscow in the second car: I shan't need you.' He had loosened a money belt he was wearing and started to extract $100 bills. 'I will now pay what I owe.'

'We haven't made a bargain yet,' Razmik said. 'What are you offering?'

'I am offering $2,000 and a further $200 for expenses.' He was counting out the money. 'And I'll pay the brother another $1,000 on safe delivery on the other side.'

'Bloody useless,' someone said.

'The options are simple,' Grigoriev said. 'You can shoot me and bury me out here among the trees and take the icon.

But how would you be better off? Would you get more from the yids in Berlin for a nineteenth-century copy of an early icon, which is what this is? The hell you would.'

'Then why is it worth more to you?'

'Because I have no middlemen to look after and in any case I've a mug back in New York who believes what I tell him, and what I'll tell him doesn't contain the words nineteenth-century.'

'We've only got your word,' one of the men said. They were crowding round Grigoriev in the eerie yellow light of the storm lamp, Razmik standing a little apart. 'How do we know it isn't worth far more?'

'You don't because you're a bunch of ignorant roughnecks, that's why.'

'We could ask the guy in there. If he was after it he'll have an idea what the hell it is.'

'Ask him,' Grigoriev said.

'I'll go,' Razmik said. Nodding to one of the men, he added, 'You can come with me.'

Grigoriev made to join them.

'No pressure,' Razmik said. 'We prefer to see him alone.'

Grigoriev shrugged. 'As you please.'

They left the room and the others stood round in awkward silence. Five minutes later they returned.

Razmik announced: 'He says it's a nineteenth-century copy of a thing by Andrei Roublev – a Trinity of some kind. He says it's a very good copy – good enough to fool foreigners who don't know about these things, and it'll fetch a useful sum in the West. I asked how much and he says Grigoriev here told him ten thousand. So I suppose we're getting the truth.'

The men looked at each other. Grigoriev was expressionless in the dim light.

'Make it $3,000,' Razmik said. 'There's been aggravation and while you're safe over there, we'll have the militia on our tails over the shooting. It's worth three.'

'I do not bargain,' Grigoriev said. 'Two, or you can make off with the icon and try to do better with the Jews.'

'Two and a half,' one of the men said.

Grigoriev was putting the banknotes away in his belt.

'All right,' Razmik said. 'We'll settle for two plus the expenses and the payment on delivery, and you can use the car for the run to Archangel if you buy the gas on the way.'

'Done.'

'And what do we do about the guy next door?'

'My advice is to lose him. It's up to you, but I'd say he knows too much for his own good.'

'We'll deal with it,' Razmik said. He smiled and slapped Grigoriev on the back. 'So I suppose you'll be off now.'

'Yes.'

'What about your gear back at my place?'

'I'll pick it up when I get back from Archangel. Then I'll fly out of this shitty country for the last time.'

They left the house and were approaching the car, followed by the driver and the man who was to travel with Grigoriev. Suddenly, Razmik waved the other two back and fell a little behind Grigoriev, who had his hand on the handle of the front passenger door of the Merc. He could not see Razmik reach inside his bomber jacket and bring out his gun. The phut of the silenced revolver scarcely disturbed the stillness of the forest night. The bullet, carefully aimed, smashed through Grigoriev's spinal cord at the base of his neck and he collapsed against the side of the car and slid to the ground without a sound. Razmik glanced down at him as he replaced the gun in its shoulder holster and prodded him with the toe of his shoe, absently, as if to test for life or death. The others had crowded round, looking down at the corpse of Genrikh Grigoriev in the pale yellow light from the lamp, sprawled in a grotesque huddle against a gleaming body panel of the Mercedes.

Razmik turned to the others. 'He lied. The guy back

there knows about icons. He says it's a genuine Roublev and it's worth a fortune. We will now discuss what we do.'

27

An enterprising radio reporter who had a contact in the Moscow CID managed to get a newsflash of the killing at the Restoration Works onto an early bulletin. Ponomarev, enough of an old-fashioned Soviet policeman to hate all unauthorised publicity, cursed as the bare facts, distortions and all, crackled at him out of his radio as he struggled with various aspects of the bureaucracy. He had reached his office early, after three hours of sleep, and his first call had been to his friend at the Moscow CID.

'Can you put a watch on the Tushino address?'

'We can.'

'I suggest you pull in anyone who tries to approach the place, but without alerting whoever's inside. I suspect they'll keep away for the time being, but you never know.'

'Agreed.'

'Do you have any other Armenian addresses of interest?'

'I have one,' his friend Alyosha said. 'Guy calling himself Zaven Levonyan. He's got form – that's how we know him, mug shot and all. A little Armenian thief trying to make it in the gangs.'

'Can you send over anything you have on him? We may be able to make use of it.'

'Sure, I'll send a man over with his dossier.'

'I'll get a tap onto the phone at the Tushino address,' Ponomarev said. 'It may produce something.'

But the Communication Security department at the KGB proved troublesome.

'What do you mean, you can't put a tap on this number without authorisation from higher up? Since when were you people reluctant to tap the telephones of honest citizens, let alone the mafia?'

He brought a fist down on his desk as a voice in his ear muttered about signatures and the rule of law, finally promising action some time later that day if the relevant chit were forthcoming.

'Look, man,' Ponomarev said, controlling his voice with difficulty, and surprised to find himself talking sharply to the KGB, 'I have to have the tap on *now*. We are talking about multiple murder, theft and heaven knows what else. If I don't get immediate action we'll go to the minister himself and put the blame squarely on you and your damned rule of law. You'll have your signature later today when I can get hold of it. Meanwhile, I want action.'

Grudging noises which signified agreement were made at the other end of the line and Ponomarev hung up.

Then he called *Vperiod* and asked for Slava Lyubimov. 'You can help,' he told him when he came on the line.

'What can I do, Major?'

'This contact of yours at the Yerevan Bar – I'd like to squeeze a bit more out of him.'

'I don't know that there's much in there,' Lyubimov said.

'We can try one of two ways. Either you go back and weave a tale of some kind, or we pull him in and scare the wits out of him in the usual way.'

'It may sound sentimental,' Lyubimov said, 'but I promised I'd keep him out of things. So let me see what I can do.'

'Right, but please do it fast. You can guess what I need – any hint of where this bunch may be hiding out.'

'I'll get back to you as soon as I have something,' Lyubimov said. Then he made for the door, announcing to Verochka as he passed that he was off on a life or death mission and he'd buy her orchids if he survived.

It was close to 11 a.m. when he pushed open the door of the Yerevan Bar, to be met by a cacophony of Russian heavy metal on the loudspeakers. An old man sat at a far table, contemplating an empty glass and nodding solemnly to himself. The place stank of stale alcohol, dry rot and vomit.

'You again!' Khatchik roared above the din. 'In through the door, out through the window, eh?'

'I hope not.'

The giant poured two small glasses of vodka and planted himself opposite Lyubimov, who sat on a bar stool.

'What brings you back – more inquisitions?'

Lyubimov grinned. 'Let's say you could be even more helpful if you'd care to.'

The assault of the music did not let up. The old man at the far table appeared to be dozing through it. The giant behind the bar threw back his vodka, slamming the empty glass down on the bar and wiping a hand across his mouth.

'Why should I care to?' he asked.

'Two reasons, maybe. One, you don't like this fellow Grigoriev; two, it's all credit if you ever get into trouble with the militia or whoever.'

The significance of the propositions appeared to be filtering slowly through to Khatchik's brain. 'Depends,' he said, 'on how much I have to tell you.'

'Not that much.' Lyubimov swallowed his drink, giving his man time to adjust to the idea of stooling for dubious advantages.

'I don't know much,' Khatchik said. 'No one confides in me. I just serve drinks, throw out the drunks and mind my own business, don't I?'

'That's right.'

'And pick up troublesome journalists in one hand and throw them through the window, eh?'

He roared at his joke and Lyubimov thought it expedient to laugh with him.

Heavy metal stopped abruptly. The tape appeared to have wound to its end. After the noise, the silence seemed somehow oppressive. Using it, Lyubimov dropped his voice to what he took to be a confidential mode. 'This gang Grigoriev's working with – it looks as if they killed a lot of people last night.'

'Heard it on the radio,' Khatchik said. 'These things happen.'

'Things were pretty quiet among the Armenians, according to my information, until this madman came in from the United States.'

'They're not bad boys,' Khatchik said. 'A bit unruly – out to make a living if they can – but they don't usually shoot, what was it, four, five people in one night. Excessive, that, and it can only end badly for them.'

'That's right. I'm doing this piece on it and I need a bit more info.'

'So what do you want to know?'

'I want to know where they hide out when the heat is on.'

'How the hell would I know that?'

'You hear things. All barmen hear things. And you Armenians, you're a clannish lot, you hang together, know each other, run your little emigré circles here in alien Moscow, right?'

'Maybe.'

'Well then,' Lyubimov said, sensing Khatchik's reluctance was more style than substance, 'well then, you must know something of the kind I'm after.'

Khatchik made a show of gathering up their glasses. Then he moved to the back of the bar and fiddled with the sound equipment so that an Armenian folk song droned out of the speakers, engulfing the place in a kind of dismal complaint.

He turned back to Lyubimov. 'This shit Grigoriev,' he said, 'I wouldn't go to the firing squad for him, but it's a near thing. I had a buddy who got on the wrong side of him, that would be a few years back, you know, and this madman shops him to the militia, like that. But first he gives him a terrible beating. Did it with a length of wood with a couple of nails in it. Made a right mess of my pal's face. A shocking sight it was. But the worst was, this swine seemed to enjoy doing it. Said as much. And then he shops him.' Khatchik grunted, recalling the event. 'We Armenians, you know, we're a clan, like you said. But we don't like you Russians and we like your damn militia even less. And one thing we don't do is squeal to them.'

'Sure,' Lyubimov said. 'On the other hand, I did you a favour.'

'And I told you the man Grigoriev was back in town.'

'Thanks to my favour your kids still have their Dad at home. How are they?'

'They're fine and they're none of your damn business.'

Lyubimov ignored it, pursuing his line of attack. 'You Armenians, you're strong family men, right? I kept you out of jail to look after your family, and now, when I want a bit of info to top up my story, you turn your back on me.' He shook his head. 'A plank with nails in it, you said?'

'Am I talking to the press or am I talking to the cops?' Khatchik asked.

'You know damn well I'm the press.' A pause. 'His face, you said. He smashed up your pal's face? Nasty?' Another pause. The giant was struggling clumsily with his emotions, his fears. He looked across at the old man at the table with the empty wine glass. His head had fallen forward on the wet table-top. He was snoring.

All right, Armenians didn't squeal to the cops, but a friendly journalist who had done a favour? It wouldn't be his fault if the journalist let something slip to a friend in the militia, would it now? And there was the shit Grigoriev, and certainly a favour to take into account. He was confused and not a little drunk.

'I know they have a place somewhere off the Yaroslavl Highway,' he said. 'This side of Pushkino. Now get going. If you write it and they've seen you in here they'll have my balls off.'

'Thanks,' Lyubimov said. 'But tell me what happened to your friend.'

'Oh, him? A bit impetuous, like. Later on he got ten for murder. He's still inside. A very decent guy,' Khatchik added. 'I miss him.'

Out in the heat and fumes of the city Lyubimov reflected that he hadn't been in the least sentimental after all, since his next task was to call the major and tell him where to start looking for Grigoriev and his friends. He made his way back to the *Vperiod* office and after calling Ponomarev, settled at the ancient typewriter to compose the first of his pieces on the fate of Roublev's third Old Testament Trinity and the trail of destruction surrounding that supremely spiritual work of art:

This strange and violent story starts in Taman – the Taman which Lermontov called the worst little town of all the seacoast towns of Russia . . .

28

They emptied Grigoriev's pockets and money belt before dragging his body into the forest.

'No point in trying to bury him,' someone said. 'The wild dogs will have him up within hours, so we might as well make things easier for them.' They covered his body with fallen leaves and returned to the house as Razmik counted out close to five thousand dollars. 'I'll hold it,' he said. 'We'll see about a share-out later.' They had brought Baranov out of the back room and one of the men dabbed at his scalp wound with a handkerchief soaked in water from a flask.

'Grigoriev told me that if I tried to co-operate with you, you'd take the icon and shoot me,' Baranov said. 'As you see, I read the situation differently. What we have is an icon worth untold millions and you need me to renew the contact in the West, get the icon out and into the hands of the buyer, and collect the cash. Without my help you'll get peanuts and whoever you sell it to will make a fortune. So it stands to reason it's worth your while taking a chance on me.'

'So what do we have to do?' Razmik asked. The others stood around, watching.

'For a start, let's see what was in his pockets.'

The contents of Grigoriev's pockets were laid out on the table: passport, notebook, Diners and American Express Gold cards and little else. Baranov seized the notebook, went through it carefully, taking his time.

'Well?' someone asked.

'I am looking for a name and telephone number – the name of his principal for this deal. He must have it with him, and there's no reason why he should have disguised it in some way.' He looked up at the others. 'There's nothing here. It must be back at the apartment. Someone will have to fetch his stuff.'

'Risky,' Razmik said. 'The militia may be round there already.'

'Can you call the apartment?'

Razmik turned to one of the men. 'You'll have to get to a public phone. Call Masha and tell her to take his things, all of them, and meet you somewhere. Take the car.'

'Where shall I meet her?'

'A busy spot, so that you can be sure neither of you is tailed. Say the intersection of Mira and the Garden Ring. You'd best leave it till midday, when there'll be plenty of people and traffic. Tell her to take the Metro and watch her rear: she knows what to do. And she's to bring food and drink. You'll tell her that and nothing more – no mention of where we're heading. I don't want her blabbing to the other women, understand?'

The man nodded.

Razmik turned to Baranov. 'You're sure you know what you're doing?'

Baranov's self-possession had been slowly seeping back, and with it a note of authority had found its way back into his voice. These Armenians would be easy. They knew nothing of icons and even less of the international art market. In his contempt for the Armenians and growing confidence in his own abilities, he could smell success at last. They had the icon, they had dealt with Grigoriev, there would soon be a howl of indignation from the university and the government. All it took now was steady nerves, and Baranov's nerves were steadying as he recovered from the horrors of the night. He reflected, too, that he no longer needed to take account of Marchenko down in Krasnodar.

'I know precisely what I'm doing,' he told Razmik, 'but I'm not fool enough to imagine I can carry this through without your help. For instance, what was to be your route out of the country?'

'Tell us first what yours was,' Razmik said.

'The Polish frontier crossing at Bobrovnik.'

'You have a contact there?'

'Yes,' Baranov lied.

Razmik told him of the brother sailing out of Archangel. Baranov pretended to weigh up the relative merits of the two routes. 'Your idea has its advantages,' he conceded, 'since it gets the icon direct to the USA. But I had planned to go with it myself, which is simple enough via Poland. Would this seaman get me aboard?'

'He's done it before,' the brother spoke up. 'It costs, but he's done it.'

'On the other hand,' Razmik said. 'You'd need a passport at the other end.'

'If your brother can take me out, he can bring me back. If I find there's no way of getting ashore at the other end, I'll stay on board and return. Coming back isn't exactly what I want most in this world, but it would have to do.'

'I think,' Razmik said slowly, 'it is not in our interests that you leave the country.'

'The icon must be delivered, the money collected. How do you expect me to do that from here?'

'That is your problem, and I have to tell you, my friend, that your life depends on it. We've been to plenty of trouble, got ourselves into a spot of bother with the militia, and for what? Five thousand dollars?' He shook his head. 'Not worth it. On the other hand, we stand to make a decent sum if what you say is true. So we see you, my friend, as our next meal ticket and we're going to hang on to it, eh?'

He had turned to the other men, who were nodding approval.

Baranov grinned uncertainly. 'You're the ones with the guns. I'll see what I can do.'

'Right,' Razmik said, 'the car will go back into town in an hour when there's enough traffic on the road not to arouse interest.' He turned to the man with the seafaring brother. 'Then you can take the other car to the intersection back on the ring motorway where there's a filling station with a long-distance automatic phone. Call Archangel and fix things up. The car will set out tonight and keep moving.'

Gathering vehicles and crews to explore the stretch of highway between Moscow and Zagorsk proved difficult.

'Not a high priority,' the CID colonel told Alyosha. 'We have more useful objectives than intervening in gang warfare. Anyway, the mafia is better at eliminating itself than we can ever be.'

'Multiple murder,' Alyosha said. 'That, and an important theft.'

'No one has told me the theft is important, and as for the killings, they've saved us a deal of trouble over the coming years.'

Alyosha shrugged. 'What can we spare – two, three cars with crews?'

The colonel had been in trouble with his superiors over some of the deployments he had sanctioned in recent weeks and was not in the mood to run risks. 'I can spare two cars,' he announced. 'You can have them until this time tomorrow and I want regular reports. From what I understand, you propose to search hundreds of square kilometres of forest on either side of the highway.' He shook his head. 'It's hopeless. These people will simply lie low for however long they think fit and filter back into the city when we're all busy on something else.'

'I wouldn't mind catching them,' Alyosha said. 'They're primitive killers. And Ponomarev at the Specials believes there's a connection with the disappearance of an American. He's getting flak from Foreign Affairs.'

'My heart bleeds for the Specials, and for the Americans, come to that.' The colonel was not known as a champion of interdepartmental co-operation.

'I suppose,' Alyosha said, 'there's no chance of calling up a military helicopter?' There was no hope in his voice.

'None at all,' the colonel said, waving him away.

Later, Alyosha gave instructions to his men. 'You will work your way north up the Yaroslavl Highway from the city limits, checking every track into the forest as you go. Wherever there's an isolated shack or house, you'll check it out, understood?'

The men nodded.

'You'll work fast, starting right away, and you'll radio back anything worth hearing. You're hunting a bunch of killers, so check your weapons and see you don't walk into an ambush.'

Mug shots of known Armenian gangsters had been passed round. One of the men asked, 'If we recognise any of these beauties, do we shoot first and ask polite questions later?'

'You shoot first. And if you kill an innocent citizen, you're in deep trouble.'

After the briefing, Alyosha called Ponomarev at the Specials and explained what he had arranged.

'Hopeless,' Ponomarev said.

'You couldn't have done better.'

'The times are not propitious for honest policemen. Our society isn't interested.'

'Did you get a tap on their phone?' Alyosha asked.

'It's in place, unless they've connected the wrong number.'

'Nothing yet from the listening desk?'

'Nothing. But I have foolish hopes.'

The time was shortly before 11 a.m.

Over at *Vperiod*, Lyubimov broke from typing his story to call Raya.

'Can we meet?'

'I'd love to. I've just heard we return to Yerevan in the morning.'

'That is outrageous.'

'I agree.'

'Unacceptable.'

'Yes.'

'We must do something about it.'

'What can we do?'

'Let's meet at the Georgia House in the Arbat at one. I'll reveal a plan I have over the macaroni cheese concoction they serve there.'

'It had better be a good plan,' she said.

'It's wonderful, you'll see.'

'Mmmm . . .' She bestowed her low, throaty laugh on him as she hung up.

He returned to his typewriter. He had taken the tale as far as his meeting in Taman with Darya Petriayeva in her slippers at the trim house with the pink bougainvillaea at the doorway.

This lady's husband, who appeared to be dying, sat silent in a corner throughout, ignoring our talk of theft and killings and wrongful arrest, his mind contemplating more eternal verities. The tea was scalding, the facts we were examining pathetic, dreadful. Was this some kind of microcosm of what is wrong with our country?

A few minutes after eleven the two cars set out from the house in the forest. Both stopped at the filling station on the clover-leaf intersection with the motorway circling the city. The call was made to the apartment in Tushino, the message given to the woman Masha and an appointment made for an hour later. The time was exactly 11.45. The messenger drove on towards the city, alert for police patrol cars, taking side roads where he could. His associate in the other car stayed behind, wrestling with the long-distance telephone service, waiting for the connection to Archangel. He had parked the car where it could not be seen from the highway.

Shortly after 12.15 the duty officer on the KGB listening desk called Ponomarev to tell him a call had been intercepted at 11.45. A meeting had been arranged, he said, between a woman answering to the name of Masha at the apartment and a male, unknown, calling in from a number which had not been traced. 'They'll meet,' he told Ponomarev, 'at the intersection of Mira Prospect and the Garden Ring on the northeast corner at 12.45. You'll be in time if you hurry.'

Ponomarev slammed the phone down without a word. As he dashed for the car pound he was heard muttering, 'Incompetent bastards . . . a bloody half-hour to get around to calling me . . .'

His driver blared his way through the heavy midday traffic, jumping lights and at one point steering his car onto the pavement in a brave attempt to circumvent a long line of vehicles caught in a bottleneck. By 12.45 they were within 200 yards of the Garden Ring, heading north on Sretenka at a crawl. A string of oaths was pouring out of Ponomarev while the driver, a phlegmatic North Russian, shook his head and pressed his thumb intermittently on the horn to no effect. At 12.50 they were at the intersection. On the northeast corner crowds were waiting for a green light to cross the broad avenue. Ponomarev leapt out of the car, gained the pavement and mingled with the crowd. He did not see the dark-haired woman in a floral dress crossing with the mass of shoppers and office workers and heading for the Metro. By then a Mercedes was speeding north on Mira Prospect. Contact had been made and a suitcase and shopping bag lay on the back seat.

'No problem,' the driver muttered to himself. Soon the car passed the cosmonaut monument and the exhibition grounds, continuing northward and crossing the clover leaf intersection as the other Mercedes pulled out onto the highway, contact with Archangel having been achieved.

29

Lyubimov made his way from the Metro, carried along by the throng of sightseers along the Arbat, past youths squatting before sad little collections of bric-a-brac, each with its display of discarded campaign medals and army caps and badges. Others sat behind trestle tables loaded with matrioshka dolls and delicately enamelled boxes. A small child, her school satchel on the ground by her feet, played a thin folk tune on a violin. From a barrow sweets were on offer. There was the inevitable queue for ice cream. At the Georgia House Raya was waiting and they descended to the restaurant in the basement with its Georgian folk version of art nouveau complete with chandeliers. They took their place in the queue for the solitary dish on the menu, and queued again for tea in tall glasses.

'No sugar,' they were told. 'We have honey.'

Dollops of clear honey were dropped into their glasses and they found a table.

Both were overcome by a new shyness, as if this were their first meeting and not, possibly, their last. They ate in silence for a while.

Raya spoke at last. 'You said on the telephone that you had an idea.'

Slava Lyubimov nodded. 'A brilliant idea. My best ever.'

'So?'

There was another silence.

'I am not too sure how to put it in such a way that you are bound to agree,' Lyubimov said.

'There is no way you can be sure I'll agree to something

I haven't heard, so why not try me?' She smiled and he took it as a sign of encouragement. Why was it so difficult to talk to women?

'In fact, it was two ideas.'

'That doubles the problem.'

He nodded again. 'My difficulty is, I don't know which one to put forward first.'

'Can they not somehow go together, in tandem?'

She was being helpful, gently taking over the dialogue, the more self-assured of the two. But wasn't the man supposed to be in command on such occasions? He must pull himself together.

'So,' he said, taking a gulp of the sweet tea, 'my questions are these. Will you come to bed with me tonight and will you come back from Yerevan very soon and marry me?'

He had no idea what answer to expect. Two negatives? At best a feminine equivocation of some kind, designed to demonstrate virtue and a seemly modesty? Even a slap in the face?

'I realise we haven't known each other for long, but it's how I feel, and it truly is a completely new feeling for me. Of course, you'll need time to consider the second half of my question. I quite understand that. But you're leaving tomorrow, and so the first half is, well, urgent, isn't it?' He knew he was babbling, trying to delay the moment when she would say no – even say it twice.

She was looking at him with her liquid brown eyes with their extraordinary depths – looking straight at him as if she had expected both questions and had even prepared her reply. Then she said, 'I would like to make love and perhaps we can arrange that this evening. As to marriage, it seems an interesting idea, but let's wait for tomorrow morning to decide. What do you say to that?'

'I thought you were going to say no,' he replied.

'Why did you think that?'

'Well, we've only known each other for, what, a few days in all.'

'But we've been through a sort of revolution together, and we are both experts on Lermontov. Doesn't that give us interests in common?' She laughed, throwing her head back a little. Again, the wonderful sinuous line of her neck told him he would never see anything more beautiful.

'That is exactly what I've been thinking,' he told her. 'And all right, I don't understand much about economics, but I'm a quick learner and you can teach me and that will make a third thing we'll have in common: despair over the country's economy.'

Two elderly ladies had settled at their table and were conversing volubly in Georgian. Lyubimov leaned forward, taking Raya's small face in his hands, and kissed her on the mouth. The ladies stopped abruptly, forks poised above their plates, staring.

'We are to get married,' Lyubimov told them suddenly. News of this quality was something to share.

'It has not really been decided yet,' Raya said, 'but it is altogether possible.'

'Good, good,' one of the ladies said, and plunged her fork back into her plate of macaroni. Her companion seemed to be taken aback by the kiss, or possibly by being made the confidante of two strangers. Then the discussion resumed in Georgian, and Raya and Lyubimov looked at each other and burst out laughing. This, Lyubimov thought, was clearly the great moment of one's life, celebrated over a glass of tea with honey, there being no sugar available in Moscow today. Honey, somehow, was better.

Dropping his voice, he said, 'Can I come to your room, then?'

She nodded. 'At eleven. I'm afraid I'll be working before that.'

She gave him her warmest smile. 'And you?'

'I'm writing up the story of the icon for the paper, and I seem to be involved in the Specials' manhunt as well.'

'I beg you to be careful.'

As they made their way out of the restaurant and up into

the heat of the street, he took her hand and held it until they reached the Metro, where they kissed and parted.

Back at *Vperiod* he picked up the story, banging it out on the Erica:

Enter a dubious American, one Victor Gordon, international art dealer with Moscow contacts. He arrives here on 10 August and books in at the Hotel Rossia – just another Western businessman trying to make a few dollars out of the mess we are in. We must assume that Gordon contacted our friend Peter Baranov, made an appointment and took a cab out to Baranov's dacha at Zaveti Ilyicha. At all events, the militia believe that is how things went, and as we shall see, so much the worse for the unfortunate cab driver, who was found later, dead in his own bathtub.

'How's it going?' Panov asked, looking up from a mess of notes on his desk.

'It's going well. Everything is going well.'

'And that Armenian beauty of yours?'

'Marvellous.'

'My Nina approves of her. I never heard her approve of another female before,' Panov grunted. 'Or a male, come to that.'

'Now shut up,' Lyubimov said. 'I've a dozen pages to write before this evening.'

'Those eyes,' Panov said, his big paws scrabbling among his papers, 'I never saw such eyes.'

'I have what I need,' Baranov told Razmik. Grigoriev's possessions were spread out on the table in the front room and Baranov was deep in an examination of an address book. 'There's an Anton Kurtz here, and from the notes it's pretty clear that he's our man.'

'You'll have to arrange for someone to pick up the icon at the port on the other side since we are not allowing you to leave with it,' Razmik said.

'We'll see about that,' Baranov said evasively. 'So when do we set out?'

'The car taking you north will set out tonight and run through the night. That should take you past Yaroslavl before daylight. It's some three hundred kilometres from here. After that there are no big centres for the rest of the way, just villages and small towns – a clear run. With no hold-ups it should get you into Archangel the day after tomorrow. The lads will share the driving so there'll be no stops.'

'Gas?'

'We'll have a couple of cans in the boot and the lads will know how to help themselves along the way.'

At eight they shared sausages and bread and drank mineral water. A half-litre bottle of vodka was passed round, giving each of them barely more than a mouthful.

The evening news bulletin from Moscow Radio had carried nothing on the shoot-out at the Restoration Works and no sign of official dismay at the theft of a precious icon.

The car was made ready, the petrol cans loaded, a plastic bag with the remains of the food and drink placed beside the icon, still wrapped in its blanket. Then they climbed into the car: the driver with Zaven, brother of the seaman, next to him, Baranov in the back. There had been embraces and the slapping of backs, and as the car manoeuvred in the narrow lane and headed back towards the highway, Razmik and those with him waved as if they were seeing friends off on vacation. At the highway the car turned right, heading north towards Zagorsk, Yaroslavl, and far beyond, Archangel.

It was on the way back to the office from the abortive expedition to the corner of Mira and the Garden Ring that Ponomarev had what he later called his only truly creative idea of the entire case. By two o'clock he had reached Lyubimov by phone at *Vperiod*.

'I seem to remember you told me you had an Armenian girl here in Moscow. Correct?'

'Correct, Major.'

'Is she good looking?'

'As a matter of fact, very, but . . .'

'Never mind but. Is she resourceful – a girl with guts who might be willing to help the hard-pressed militia?'

'Possibly.'

'And can you contact her and ask her to come to see me at my office right away?'

'I can try, but . . .'

'Please, no buts again. You can come yourself and you'll see what it's all about. It may even add to this story you are writing. I await both of you.' And Ponomarev rang off.

It was nearly five when Lyubimov and Raya were processed and finally waved through the guardpost at the Militia headquarters.

Ponomarev looked hard at Raya, said nothing. Then he turned to Lyubimov. 'Congratulations.'

Lyubimov grinned.

'Can someone tell me what this is about?' Raya asked.

'It's simple,' Ponomarev said. 'The citizens of Moscow need your help.'

'Perhaps you'd explain so that I can judge whether I am able to provide it.'

On Ponomarev's desk was a grey dossier with its contents spread out by its side and a few mug shots, full face and profile, of a dark young man with a sallow, immature face and a wary expression.

'I would like you to look at these,' Ponomarev said, 'and I will tell you what we in the militia want of you.' He handed over the photographs and Raya examined them. There was a look of distaste on her face.

'This is what I am asking,' Ponomarev said. Slowly, in a measured voice designed to make the venture seem as normal as possible, he outlined the plan that had occurred to him as he travelled back to the office, angry and frustrated, that noon. When he had finished there was a silence, broken by Lyubimov.

'It is a lot to ask.'

'I am well aware of that, but an Armenian girl will carry

more conviction than a Russian and I simply didn't have anyone – not at such short notice.'

'It's dangerous.'

Ponomarev shrugged. 'Our man will be nearby.'

'Even so.'

Raya had said nothing. She was smiling. 'Isn't it odd,' she said at last, 'the way men like to answer for a woman. After all, the major's proposition was addressed to me and there you both are, arguing its merits between you as if I had no mind of my own.'

'Sorry,' Lyubimov said.

'So what is your opinion?' Ponomarev asked.

'I'll do it.'

'You're sure – ' Lyubimov started.

She turned to him. 'I'm afraid I do have a mind of my own. It's something you'll have to adjust to over the years.' To Ponomarev she said, 'Let's go through the whole thing again, step by step, so that I've got it right.'

She listened attentively as Ponomarev elaborated his idea, asking sharp questions from time to time. When he had finished she said, 'Right, we might as well start now with the phone call.'

'It has to be as realistic as we can make it,' Ponomarev said. 'We'll need a bit of background noise such as you'd get in a crowded apartment, and you must speak in a hushed voice – urgent and a bit frightened. Are you any good as an actress?'

'I had a prize for declaiming poetry at school.'

'That'll do. Now we get a secretary in to provide background.'

A woman was summoned from a nearby office and told to take her place on the far side of the room and at a signal from Ponomarev to do the kind of shouting and cursing to be expected from any housewife who had to share a kitchen with half a dozen other families.

'Easy,' the woman said. 'It happens every evening of my life.'

Ponomarev turned to Raya. 'Ready?'

'Whenever you say.'

He dialled the apartment in Tushino and handed the phone to Raya. A woman's voice answered.

'Is that Masha?' Raya's voice was hushed. In the background the policewoman started her complaints to an imaginary neighbour.

'Who are you?'

'I'm Zaven's girl.'

'I never heard of you.'

'I made him promise not to talk about me but we've been together for quite a bit.'

'What do you want?'

'I can't talk from here. Can I come round to see you for a few minutes?'

The row in the kitchen was gathering pace, Ponomarev controlling it with the gestures of a bandmaster.

'What is it you want?'

'I can't talk. This place is full of people.'

There was a pause. Then, 'OK, come here if you must.'

'Thanks. I'll be there in half an hour. Zaven's told me where you are.'

'Brilliant, both of you!' Ponomarev had ceased conducting, a broad grin on his face. 'I've a car waiting downstairs, so now for the next act.'

'I'll come with you,' Lyubimov told Raya.

'No you won't,' Ponomarev said. 'We're taking no chances on someone recognising you.'

'I really don't need anyone to hold my hand,' Raya announced. 'As I said before, it's something you'll have to get used to over the years.' She gave him a knowing smile.

In the militia car on the run to Tushinskaya Street she chatted with the driver, who told her that with two children, a baby on the way, a two-roomed apartment with shared kitchen and bathroom, and a militiaman's pay, something in his life had to change.

'What will you do?'

'I'm going into business.'
'What business?'
'Retail.'
He didn't know what kind of retail business but he had a friend who knew about these things and had applied for a permit, which so far he hadn't got, and well, it would work out somehow.
'The free market, that's the point,' the driver said, waving a hand. 'We're told the future's the free market, not Communism, so I'm for the market, right?'
'I don't think it will be easy,' Raya said.
'Nothing's easy. Do you think this lousy job's easy, with clapped-out cars and no cash for a new pair of boots?'
He pulled up at the corner of Tushinskaya. 'It's the third block on the right,' he told Raya. 'You'll see a car with a driver at the wheel parked on the far side. He's our man and he knows about you, so you can call on him if there's a bit of trouble. I'll be here, waiting for you. Good luck!'
'Thanks,' Raya said. Then she got out of the car and set off along Tushinskaya, until she reached the apartment block Ponomarev had described. Ahead, on the far side of the road, she saw the militia car, the driver apparently asleep. It didn't seem much of a resource in the event of trouble. She turned into the courtyard and entered the first doorway on her left, took the lift to the fourth floor and rang the bell of Razmik's apartment. Almost at once the door was opened by Masha. She led Raya into the kitchen where Grigoriev had confronted Baranov a few days earlier, waved Raya to a chair and sat opposite her.
'As I said, Zaven never mentioned you.'
'I made him promise. I had trouble with my family. They don't approve.'
'I shouldn't wonder. How long have you known him?'
'About six months.'
'You know what he does?'
'More or less. He doesn't talk much, but when he says he'll see me, he always keeps his word. Only now he's

disappeared. We had an appointment last night, and I'm worried.'

'There's nothing to worry about – at least, not more than usual.'

'Have they arrested him?'

'No.'

'Where is he?'

'I'm not supposed to tell you.'

This would be the difficult part. Ponomarev had warned, 'Don't appear too eager: on the other hand, you're there to find out. Maybe you can weep a bit, it always helps.' Raya was surprised now to find that she was on the point of weeping – she who prided herself on having her emotions always under control. But this was not emotion: it was back to declaiming Pushkin and Lermontov at school – that sort of thing.

She searched in her bag for a handkerchief and dabbed at her eyes.

'He's not worth it,' Masha said. 'None of them are. They pay the bills and paw you about and that's about it. A beauty like you could do better any day of the week.'

'I love him,' Raya said, and despite the tears nearly laughed as she said it.

'There's no accounting,' Masha said.

'Please tell me, where is he and when will he be back?'

'Like I say, I'm not supposed to talk about it. I'm not even supposed to know, but one of the lads let on when I saw him this morning.'

There was a pause. Raya was afraid to insist, but was increasingly aware that women's solidarity appeared to be taking precedence over gang security in the mind of the woman opposite her.

'He's gone north with some of the others,' Masha said.

'North?'

'It's what I said.'

'To Leningrad? Why should they go there?'

'I never said Leningrad.'

'When will they be back?'

'I don't know that, but it's a long run and I'd put it at three or four days at least. But then, he might be up there for a while, I don't know.'

'Can I call him?'

Masha shook her head.

'You're being very sweet,' Raya said.

'You're daft about him, aren't you?'

Raya nodded and dabbed again at her eyes. 'You know how it is, I don't care for Russians, and then I meet someone from back home in Yerevan, and he's been kind and he makes me laugh . . .' She allowed her voice to trail off.

'You *are* in love,' Masha said. 'He's never struck me as particularly kind, but then I don't know him that well, do I?'

'Up north, you said.' Raya felt the objective slipping from her grasp. 'Where up north?'

The other woman's eyes narrowed and suddenly Raya sensed danger. Perhaps that was one question too far. Suddenly Masha said, 'When did you see him last?'

'Thursday evening,' Raya tried to make it sound positive.

'You sure?'

'Yes.' Positive again, but a touch of panic behind her voice now.

'Sure you're not mistaken?' The tone now was hard, aggressive.

'No, he came round to my place on Thursday, but why are you asking?'

'You have questions, I have questions. And I have one more. When did he shave off his moustache?'

Panic now. The mug shots had shown the pale face with a macho moustache, the edges dripping down below the line of the mouth. Was this question a trick? *Had* he shaved off his moustache? If so, when? How was this woman's mind working? Raya realised her answer could only be a gamble. She managed to force a smile onto her face.

'You're quite right to check on me like this. I *did* see him on Thursday and Zaven hasn't shaved his moustache off.'

A winning gambit or a loser? There was a moment of silence. What would happen if she'd got it wrong? Was there anyone else in the apartment? Would this woman who now seemed so menacing, attack her – and if so, how? They were at a table. Was there a drawer on the far side, and if so, did it contain kitchen knives? The table lay between her and the door of the kitchen. How to get out? Were these gangsters' women violent? The thought flashed into Raya's mind that she could tip the table up as she rose from her chair, and make a dash for the door. Real fear gripped her at last as the thought came: there may be a man in the apartment and Masha only had to call out . . .

It was as the terrifying thought struck her that Masha's hard little face broke into a smile.

'I had to check, darling. He's gone with some of the others to Archangel and don't ask me why because I don't know. And if you let on when he gets back I'll scratch your eyes out.'

Raya found when she got up from the table that her legs were unsteady, her hand trembling as she replaced her handkerchief in her bag.

'Thank you, and I swear I won't say a word. You've set my mind at rest. It was very kind.' And as they walked to the front door she added, 'Do you think he'll be in danger up there?'

'They're always in danger, I suppose, but as far as I can tell most of it was last night. You heard about the shooting?'

Raya nodded. At the door she turned and embraced the other woman. 'Thank you.'

'We girls must stick together, I suppose,' Masha said. 'A quiet life would be nice but what can you do when you've hitched up with a bunch of wild beasts?'

Down in the street the man at the wheel of the parked car seemed to have woken up. He signalled with a couple of fingers and Raya gave him a nod. Back in her car she was suddenly overcome with exhaustion and burst into tears.

'There, there,' the militia driver said. 'I don't know what it's all about but a good cry usually helps. It's what my wife tells me when things get heavy.'

Back at the Militia headquarters Ponomarev said: 'If we gave out medals for this sort of thing, you would have the one with the beautiful striped ribbon attached.' He turned to Lyubimov: 'Now take this wonderful young lady to the best dinner you can afford.' He came round his desk, took Raya in his arms and planted a kiss on either cheek. 'Beautiful,' he said to Lyubimov. 'You should do something about it. As for me, I need a decent map of the Archangel highway.'

30

General Gennadi Vorontsov had been a Deputy Defence Minister for precisely four days, brought from his post as Commander of Northern Air Defences by his old friend General Shaposhnikov to join the new team of Yeltsin supporters at the Defence Ministry. Shaposhnikov, now in charge at Defence, could reasonably claim to have smashed the previous week's coup almost single-handed by persuading his colleagues that nothing short of a bloodbath could win the day and that the armed forces would have no part of it. Now in charge, he had rapidly promoted like-minded men to surround him at the ministry. Installed in his new office, Vorontsov was still bathed in a glow of righteous democratic fervour – a decent man who had as yet no idea how to fill his day with democratic activity. Now he was being asked by an esteemed colleague to help out in a little matter of criminals to be apprehended on the road to Archangel. It seemed simple enough and had the added advantage of being a palpably worthy cause.

'Perhaps,' his ministerial colleague was saying on the telephone, 'you have a helicopter at your disposal which could be used in this connection. I understand the fugitives are armed and have a car which is faster than anything available to the militia. Ridiculous, but apparently true.'

'You say they are somewhere along the highway north of Vologda?'

'So I am told.'

'I daresay we could scramble a helicopter at our base at Konosha. That's a few kilometres off the highway, northwest of Vologda. There's no combat gunships there but we have several machines used for observation and shifting freight. They could mount a patrol along the highway and no doubt locate the vehicle. Tell the militia to call me with the details. I fancy my men will be glad of something to do.'

After talking to Ponomarev, General Vorontsov called the air base at Konosha and issued his instructions to the commander. An hour later a helicopter was airborne and flying north at 500 feet.

'It shouldn't be hard to spot,' the pilot told his navigator. 'There's virtually no cars down there, just a few trucks. Like as not, the car we're after will have a sun roof and that will reflect plenty of sunlight. It's something to watch for. And the famous highway north of Yaroslavl is nothing but a dirt road, so they can't be hitting much above eighty kilometres an hour.'

The going from Yaroslavl, through Tufanovo, Danilov and occasional straggling villages was slow, the suspension of the Merc coping as best it could with the ruts and potholes of the neglected roadway. The day was working itself up to achieve a sultry midday heat, replete with flies, dust and the unremitting glare of the endless North Russian plain. There was no talk in the car. Baranov dozed in the back seat, the two Armenians side by side in front. The news bulletin on the radio had contained nothing that interested them, and now it was piano music by Balakirev. Zaven, whose brother they were to meet in Archangel, turned the radio off.

'We could eat when we get to Vologda,' he told the driver. 'You can get a decent obed in the canteen of the Party Committee. They've this fantastic Finnish canned beer.'

'Since when have you been a paid-up Party member?' Baranov asked. 'And anyway, haven't they closed the Party down and sealed off its offices?'

'You don't need to hold a card,' Zaven said. 'I've eaten there before. It's who you know, isn't it?'

'Best not hang around,' the driver said. 'We've a bit of grub left. I'm for pushing on.'

Zaven shrugged. 'Please yourself, but the soup's good too.'

They were approaching Vologda, the golden domes of the white Spassky monastery coming into sight like distant jewels on the horizon.

'Watch it through the town,' Zaven said, 'in case they've contacted the militia. I know the place; I'll keep you off the main road for part of the way through. We cross the railway and a left turn takes you onto the last road westwards to Leningrad and Murmansk.' As they came into the town, past rows of log cabins and parched smallholdings, Zaven said, 'Did a job here not long ago. Guy in the Regional Party Committee put us onto it. Butter.'

'What about butter?' Baranov asked.

'You know Vologda's famous for its butter?'

'I knew that.'

'And that you can't get hold of the damn stuff any more?'

'I knew that too.'

'Well, this guy of ours has a brother in the local Soviet who issues the distribution permits, right, so he's hit on the idea of selling them to the highest bidder, right, and he's our pal, seeing that we know things about his little business arrangements with his brother he wishes we didn't know, which means we can get the permits at what I'd call a friendly price. So we run a truck up here, load it with this famous Vologda butter, run the stuff down to Moscow and get a very nice price for it in the private sector restaurants.'

'Neat,' the driver said.

'You'd be amazed what people will pay for a dab of Vologda butter on their bread. Admittedly, it's damn good butter.'

They were past the Leningrad turning, heading through the northern suburbs of the town and into the open countryside beyond. Now the road ran through a forest of birch, aspen and spruce. They overtook trucks from time to time, encountering no other cars and rarely seeing signs of life in the clearings along the roadside. Soon the driver pulled the car over onto a patch of waste ground and they ate the remains of their food and shared what was left of a bottle of water.

'Let's push on,' Baranov said. 'Sooner or later someone will guess where we're heading and signal ahead for the militia to put up a roadblock.'

'They've no way of knowing it's Archangel,' the driver said. 'When Razmik orders silence it's what he gets. I bet they think we're holed up somewhere in Moscow.'

Zaven said nothing.

At Velsk, built all in wood and now somnolent in the midday heat, they crossed a railway. Ahead was a hut set back from the road with an ancient petrol pump on a clearing before it. The driver pulled the Merc over and came to a halt by the pump, sounding his horn. A peasant woman appeared from the hut, shaking her head as she came. 'No petrol,' she was shouting at them as she approached the car.

'Come on, granny,' the driver shouted back. 'Of course you've got petrol. Is the pump here for decoration?'

She was still shaking her head. 'No supplies. We ran out.' She appraised the Mercedes. 'Nice car. Must have cost plenty.'

'Never mind the car, we want petrol. What's it worth to you to let us have something from your special stocks, eh?'

'Who's talking of special stocks? We haven't seen the tanker for six weeks. We're dry.'

Zaven had taken a wad of rouble bills from his pocket and now he was waving them at the woman. 'What's it worth to you, granny, to do us a favour, eh?'

The woman was eyeing the money, shrugging. 'I don't know, I'll go and talk to my man. Maybe he's got a can or two somewhere.'

'They've plenty of petrol,' Zaven said to Baranov. 'With this little comedy they get four times the official price, but being bloody fools they stack the roubles away under a mattress and don't understand that inflation is wiping it out faster than they get hold of it.'

Minutes later, their tank full, they were on their way.

The forest had thinned out, giving way to stretches of peat bog sprouting clumps of tall reeds. Here and there groves of alders and willows appeared, standing like oases along the horizon. This was the southernmost edge of the North Russian taiga, stretching for hundreds of miles up towards the country's northernmost limits. The thickly wooded land further south now gave way to floodplains supporting sparse stunted trees, standing like cripples about to lose their balance and fall. Gnats and flies were finding their way into the car, setting up a strident din and settling maddeningly on the faces and hands of the men.

'A godforsaken place,' Zaven said. 'There's fucking miles of this and it gets worse.'

Slowly they became aware of a sound which seemed to echo the buzz of the insects at a lower pitch. The sound grew steadily louder, imposing itself on their minds.

'What's that?' the driver asked.

'Sounds like a plane.'

'Could it be anything to do with us?'

'Never. Since when do they send planes after people like us?'

They drove on in silence.

'That's no plane,' Baranov said. 'I did my military service in the air force. It's a helicopter.' He turned to look through the back window of the car. 'I can see him. He's following the road, flying low.'

'Could be some survey or other,' Zaven said.

'I can see his markings,' Baranov said. 'Military.'

The helicopter was now flying directly above them, overtaking and returning in a tight circle to take another look at the moving car.

'It's us he's after,' Baranov said. 'What do we do?'

The helicopter had gained height, keeping pace with the car. Perhaps it was awaiting its orders by radio.

'If he lands on the road ahead of us we shoot our way through, right?' Zaven said.

'And what if he radios ahead for a roadblock to be set up somewhere? What the hell do we do then?'

'One thing's for sure,' Zaven said. 'If they get hold of us with that bloody icon thing in our possession it's evidence, right? Evidence of theft; murder, come to that. It ties us into the punch-up the other night. So I say we have to get rid of the bloody thing.'

'You're right,' the other man said.

Baranov, in the back of the car, found that he was able to think fast and with absolute clarity, and the foremost thought in his mind was that the icon must somehow be saved. An Andrei Roublev of superb quality – a version of the Old Testament Trinity, no less – it must not end its brief twentieth-century resurrection in some peat bog in the northern taiga. Nothing else, he decided, mattered, either for him or for these two primitives busy plotting their own survival.

The helicopter appeared content to keep an eye on them from a few hundred feet up, making no attempt to overtake them and land or to interfere in any other way. Maybe the pilot was enmeshed in red tape, unable to act because he couldn't get a clear order from his base.

But the orders had been clear enough.

'We could bring him to a halt by shooting at his tyres,' the pilot had radioed to base. 'Then I can land ahead of him and do the rest.'

'Sure he's your man?'

'Grey Merc with what looks like three men aboard. There aren't many like that around these parts.'

'OK, choose your moment. Keep in touch.'

To his navigator the pilot said, 'I'll come in low and fly alongside, then you'll open the door and take a pot shot at their tyres with the Kalash. Keep it low; we're not here to kill people.'

'Choose a break in the trees,' the navigator said. 'The forest is thinning out fast. I reckon we should let them run for another ten minutes.'

Their intentions were radioed back to the base at Konosha. 'Plan approved,' was signalled back to them.

'Our glorious Soviet Air Force, defender of the Soviet fatherland, is adding to its battle honours by hunting crooks on the road to Archangel,' someone commented. 'They should strike a medal.'

The countryside was changing, the Severnaya Dvina river now running alongside the road on their right, the unbroken forest giving way to isolated clumps of alder. They passed through the village of Kodima, a straggle of wooden huts, peasants tending smallholdings, two small children fussing at a gaggle of geese. A wooden church stood at the roadside, and the horizon was dotted with similar churches, sometimes standing alone on the plain, sometimes with huts huddled at their base – abandoned when the population shifted off the land, northwards to Archangel to find work in the sawmills. Beyond Kodima the marshland predominated, more insects found their way into the car, the heat intensified. Baranov had decided on a strategy.

'When the road runs through a wooded stretch again,' he said, 'make a quick stop, open the boot and I'll make a run for it with the icon. You'll wait for me: it'll only take a minute.'

'How will you get rid of it?'

'I'll break it up and shove the bits into the ground. It's fragile: you could break the thing across your knee. But it has to be in the woods, otherwise they'll see what we're doing from the helicopter.'

'Wouldn't it be better to chuck the thing in the river?' Zaven asked.

'Haven't you heard – wood floats.'

'Oh.'

'He's talking sense,' the driver said. He exchanged glances with Zaven and Baranov did not see him wink.

'The next town,' Zaven said, 'is Priluki. I reckon that's the danger spot for us. If they're going to radio ahead for a roadblock it's where they'll find farm carts and stuff to build some kind of barricade. After Priluki there's damn all till you get into Archangel.'

Ahead they could see trees.

'Looks likely,' Baranov said. 'Get ready to stop and release the boot's lock mechanism.' The helicopter had fallen back and was following the car at a distance of a few hundred metres. There were no other vehicles in sight. As the road entered the small wood the driver stamped hard on the brake, bringing the Mercedes to a halt in a cloud of dust. He had pressed the lock mechanism and Baranov leaped out, seized the icon from the boot and dashed for the trees. He was a few metres into the forest when he heard the sudden roar of the car's engine mingled with the throb of the helicopter's rotor blades.

'So we've lost the little bastard, evidence and all.' The driver was grinning, holding the big car steady on the uneven track, pushing her up to a hundred as if the extra speed was needed lest Baranov should run after them.

'Smart move,' Zaven said. 'Let's keep going.'

The helicopter pilot had caught a glimpse of the figure disappearing into the trees and was sending the information back to base.

'Keep after the car,' he was told. 'We're trying to telephone ahead of you to mount a roadblock.'

'Any luck?'

'None whatever, but the militia in Archangel have been alerted so they'll pick these characters up as they enter the town if we don't stop them sooner.'

'Hadn't I best return to base, then?'

There was silence while the matter was debated back in

Konosha. Then the pilot's radio announced: 'New orders. You will return at once. Mission concluded.'

'Glory at last,' the pilot told his navigator. 'Enemy sighted and pursued. Permission to engage enemy refused. Retreat ordered. A glorious but inconclusive battle.' He turned south, gaining height, and made for Konosha.

31

As Baranov stumbled through the trees, the icon still in its blanket under his arm, the sound of the car speeding along the highway left him indifferent. He was no longer thinking of escape. The objective which obsessed him now was to save the icon: to secrete it somewhere secure to which he could come back later and reactivate his plans for its future. If the car had waited for him he would not have returned to it anyway. Now these Armenian primitives had dealt themselves out of the game. He was once more a free agent, this time without his associates to look to, without Marchenko to pay off – free to organise the greatest art scam of the century, using his luck, his intelligence, and no one else's. It was, he told himself, his fate to be the guardian of Roublev's masterpiece.

A kind of exhilaration seized him as he plunged through the woods and emerged on the far side, the great plain lying before him in its shimmering summer haze, the horizon dotted with the strange wooden churches built by the Old Believers as they fled to the outer limits of the empire to escape the wrath of Peter the Great. Baranov reflected once again that it must have been these religious outcasts who had first brought the Roublev icon down to the southernmost edge of the empire, back in the sixteenth century. Now, in the twentieth, they were to give it sanctuary once more, this time up on the far northern taiga. The symmetry pleased him.

He saw himself as a kind of agent of history – the discoverer and now the ultimate protector of one of the great treasures of Russian religious art. In his mind this sacred duty alternated with the profane vision of undreamed-of wealth from smuggling the icon abroad, turning it into dollars, transforming the unique religious symbol into a commodity to be traded secretly in the art markets of the West. Baranov was able to think with stark clarity of both strands in the drama: he was unable to link and reconcile them.

Faintly he could hear the helicopter, flying slowly northwards along the highway. Unobserved, he could now advance across open ground, picking his way with care on the treacherous peat, giving way here and there to marshes and bog. There was a church which appeared to stand alone some two or three kilometres distant and he set off to inspect it. As he approached he saw that it was a typical wooden structure – a square nave with external galleries, surmounted by an octagon on which the tent roof supported in turn a drum and dome. The entire building had been assembled from carefully trimmed logs and planks, with wooden shingles clothing the dome. It stood on a plinth, with an external staircase, now in ruins, leaning against the front. The whole effect was one of decaying dignity, of what Baranov told himself was the kind of simple rural faith suitable for providing temporary sanctuary for Roublev's icon. 'I may not be a religious man,' he reflected, 'but I see their point. It moves the spirit.'

Walking on the heavy ground had exhausted him and he sat for a moment on a step at the church's porch to regain his breath. Then he tried the heavy door. To his surprise it swung back, squealing on its massive hinges – the only things not of wood in the entire fabric of the building. The interior was dark, illuminated now by the shaft of light from the open door. The rich, decaying smell of the place assailed him as he lifted the icon carefully, setting it down against a wall. Suddenly, he realised that he was walking not on wood but on stone. He knew that some of the northern wooden churches had been set on stone plinths and this must be one of them. It meant that there could be a cellar of some kind.

Methodically, he felt his way round the walls of the vestibule and then the nave, his eyes straining to detect a break in the paving stones, begging the builders of the place to have dug a crypt before getting to work with their axes.

It was near the west end that he found it: a large flagstone which sounded hollow as he stamped his foot on it. Then he saw that there had once been a ring with which to lift it, but the ring was no longer there. Beneath the stone there must be a hollow, possibly a hiding place which would be dry, secure, and undreamed of by anyone else.

It took him the best part of an hour to find a branch stout enough and suitably shaped to obtain the leverage needed to raise the stone. Once he had levered it up a few centimetres he was able to hold it in place with another piece of wood and rest for a while. He was beginning to feel faint from hunger and an immense weariness and it took every ounce of his strength to pull the heavy flagstone upwards and free of the hole it covered. His fear had been that the cavity, whatever it might be, would be damp; but lying on the ground on his stomach and thrusting his arm downwards he found he was touching a stone surface on which there was a layer of fine dust. It appeared that the space was shallow and that it extended beyond the square hole covered by the stone he had removed. It must have been a hiding place for the church's modest treasure back in the sixteenth century when this had been a place of worship for the Old Believers. Baranov felt that fate had somehow willed him to come here and had offered him an ideal hiding place for the icon. Almost reverently, he picked it up, still in its worn blanket from Taman far to the south, and laid it carefully below. Then, with a last expenditure of his remaining strength he shifted the stone back in place, stamping on it to make sure it was fitting snugly. It had been four hours since he had run from the car, and now the sun was hanging low in the sky, though this far north there would be no dark night, only a mysterious twilight.

He emerged from the church, pulling the door closed

behind him. Now he must make his way back to the road and hitch a lift northwards to Archangel. He had no clear idea of what his further plans might be, save that he must find a way of marking the spot where he had left the road, in order to find it later.

In the slowly fading light the landscape appeared different. The sounds were different, too. He fancied he heard an owl in the distance, and ahead of him a flight of bullfinches rose from the marshland. Swarms of gnats attacked furiously and soon he abandoned any hope of brushing them from his face and arms. His legs were weary beyond words and repeatedly he stopped to rest and to look back at the dome of the church, standing lonely in the desolate landscape with its secret treasure. He realised that he should have taken more careful measures to check his route from the road, since now he found himself stumbling across ground which was unfamiliar. The solid strips on which he was walking had become narrower, often ending in impassable bogs of water and loose mud. It was as if he were in a sand desert, disoriented, in danger of plunging into drifts where no foothold was possible. And he was utterly exhausted.

He had been following a ridge of firm ground for a time when he became aware that it was leading him not towards the road but on a line parallel to it. He moved down from the ridge towards his left, testing the ground as he went. It had become softer, more waterlogged, and soon it became impossible to tell firm ground from the patches of viscous mud, obscured by the vegetation on its surface. He had heard tales of travellers, lost in the featureless taiga, sucked down, drowned in the mud. A hopeless, numbing weariness possessed him, turning his limbs to lead, as he struggled on, now scarcely making any progress at all. And soon his feet were sinking ankle-deep in the mud as he failed increasingly to distinguish firmer ground on which to tread. And at last the time came when he lost one shoe, then the other, with the mixture of mud and water reaching at last above his ankles. He tried to extricate one foot, then the other, without success. And he felt himself sinking deeper. Desperately, seized with panic, he tried to retrace his steps onto firmer ground, but the mud held him. It was dawning on him that he would not – not ever – be able to extricate himself, that he was doomed to drown, to die, alone in the suffocating black mud. He realised that he was beginning to do what one was not supposed ever to do; he was struggling, and by so doing, sinking deeper. He had stumbled into a patch of ground where the oozing mud filled a hollow of some kind. And it was here that slowly, inexorably, he was sucked under, first to his waist, then to his armpits. That was when he started to shout, without hope since there was no soul to hear, and then to scream. Birds rose, frightened, from a nearby stretch of water. A hawk owl rose heavily from a clump of aspen, mystified by a sound the like of which it had never heard before.

When the black mud closed finally over his head, the birds settled again. Peter Baranov, bullyboy, art thief and true lover of painting, had given brief life to Andrei Roublev's third Trinity, had seized it from the resting place chosen for it by the Old Believers in their church in the south, to return it to them in their church in the far north of the Tsar's empire. An ultimate, truly artistic symmetry that would have appealed to him greatly.

32

'I'm trying to finish my piece on the icon story so far,' Lyubimov told Ponomarev on the telephone. 'We go to press tonight. Is there anything more you'd care to tell me?'

'Here at the Specials we don't normally talk to the press.'

'I know, Major, nevertheless . . .'

'We picked two of them up in Archangel.'

'Peter Baranov?'

'No, two Armenian thugs. No sign of your friend Baranov.'

'And the icon?'

'No sign of that either.'

'What do the Armenians say?'

'Nothing. Baranov? Never heard of him. The icon? What icon? All I can tell you is that an army helicopter pilot who trailed them along the highway to Archangel thinks he may have seen a third man leave the car somewhere along the way. He's not sure he saw anything, and if he did he doesn't remember where it was. And in any case, if there was such a third man it could have been another Armenian.'

'So the case stays open, Major?'

Ponomarev sighed. 'It stays open, thanks to your young friend from Yerevan.' There was a pause. 'None of my business, but I believe that from time to time fate throws something, someone truly worthwhile in our path. When that happens, only a fool fails to grab at what is offered. You, I like to think, are not a fool.'

'I asked her to marry me, Major.'

'And?'

'As a matter of fact, she called me after getting back to Yerevan. It seems that as a dutiful daughter she spoke first to her parents and they gave her their blessing. So that she has said yes.' Lyubimov tried to keep his voice steady, measured, and did not succeed.

'I am delighted for you,' Ponomarev said. 'Let me tell you, young man, that there is only one secret of a successful marriage.'

'What is that, Major?'

'If you're going to be late for dinner, call to tell her.'

Lyubimov laughed. 'Thank you for the advice.'

This story started in what Lermontov called the worst little town of all the seaside towns of Russia. Did it end on the taiga of the far north? Where is Peter Baranov? What of one Stepan Stepanovitch Marchenko, Chairman of the Regional Council for Religious Affairs in Krasnodar? He refuses to talk to the press. And the third version of Andrei Roublev's Old Testament Trinity – where is that? We have no idea. We can only promise our readers that we will return to all this if and when our militia uncovers the truth . . . if and when.

Lyubimov tore the last sheet from the Erica and read it through. He struck out the final *if and when.* It seemed to cast doubt on the dedication to his duties as an honest cop of his friend Major Ponomarev of the Specially Serious Crimes Squad.

'It's best as it is,' the Deputy Minister of Culture said to his old friend Professor Abramov. The professor was near to tears, holding the handset of his phone against his beard and searching for words to convey his distress.

'But Sergei Petrovitch, a Roublev, imagine it! I feel a sense of shame as a Russian and a lover of our heritage.'

'I tell you, it's best as it is. If it has gone to the West they'll never dare show it in public. If it hasn't, then maybe our militia will unearth it for you, though I must say I doubt that. No, no, some stones are best left unturned and this, my dear friend, is one of them.'

The Deputy Minister had other worries. Yeltsin's finance people had slashed the allocation of funds from the central budget to his ministry and he was struggling with the problem of how to keep the dancers dancing and the singers singing in the great theatres and opera houses of Moscow and the city that was now to be called St Petersburg. There was no room in his mind for an icon which had returned from the fifteenth century to plague them.

'You are nothing but a fool – a man incapable of providing properly for his family.'

Thus Stepan Marchenko's wife that evening down in Krasnodar. 'Where is this important new money you were supposed to have? We've bought stuff. We're in debt. And instead of money I hear talk of changes in the Soviet, of people losing their jobs after years of devoted service. Mark my words, you'll be next.'

Marchenko knew perfectly well that he would be next. So he said, 'You talk rubbish as usual. The new money will come. The Party will recover. Now leave me in peace.'